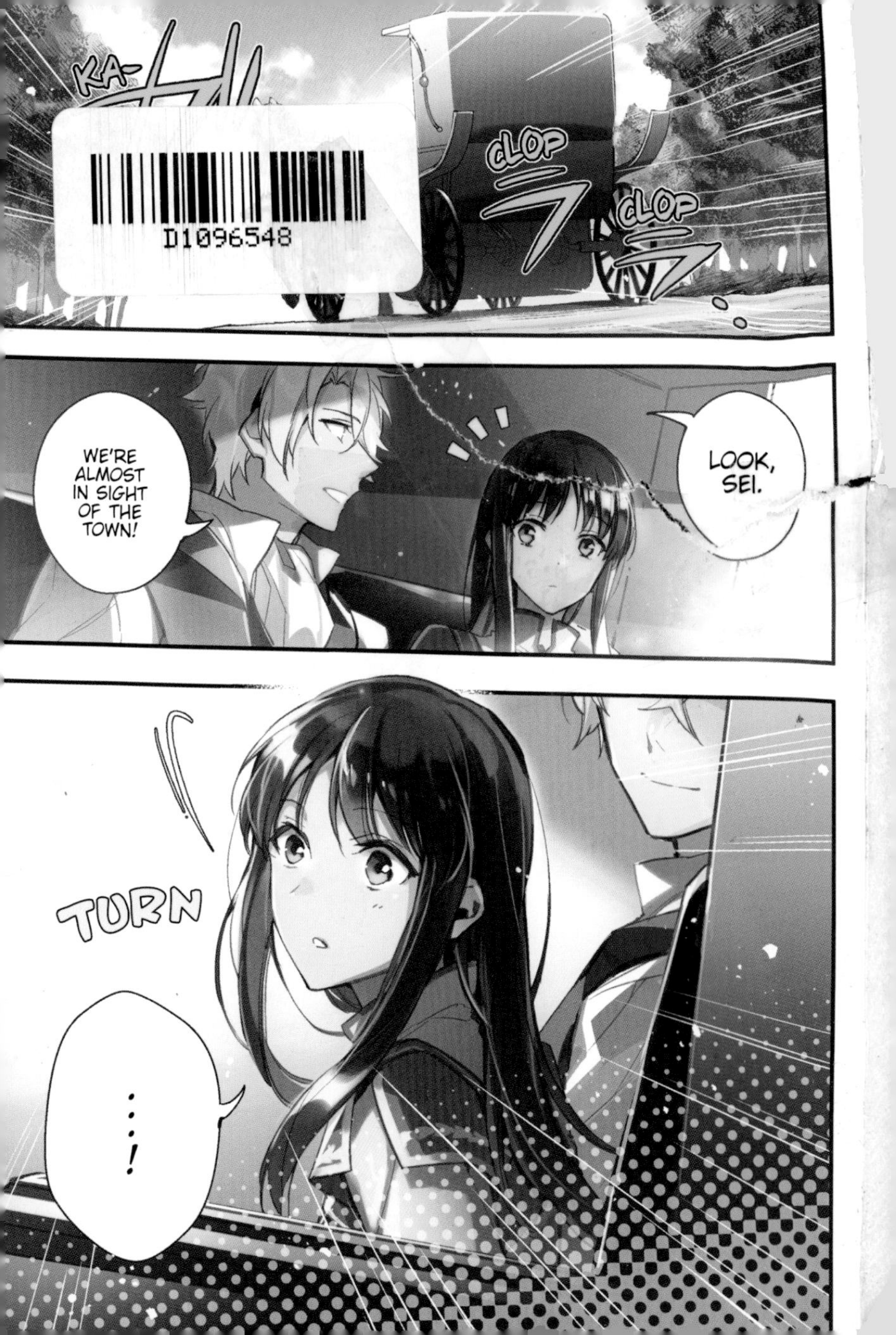
KA-
CLOP
CLOP
LOOK, SEI.
WE'RE ALMOST IN SIGHT OF THE TOWN!
TURN
...!

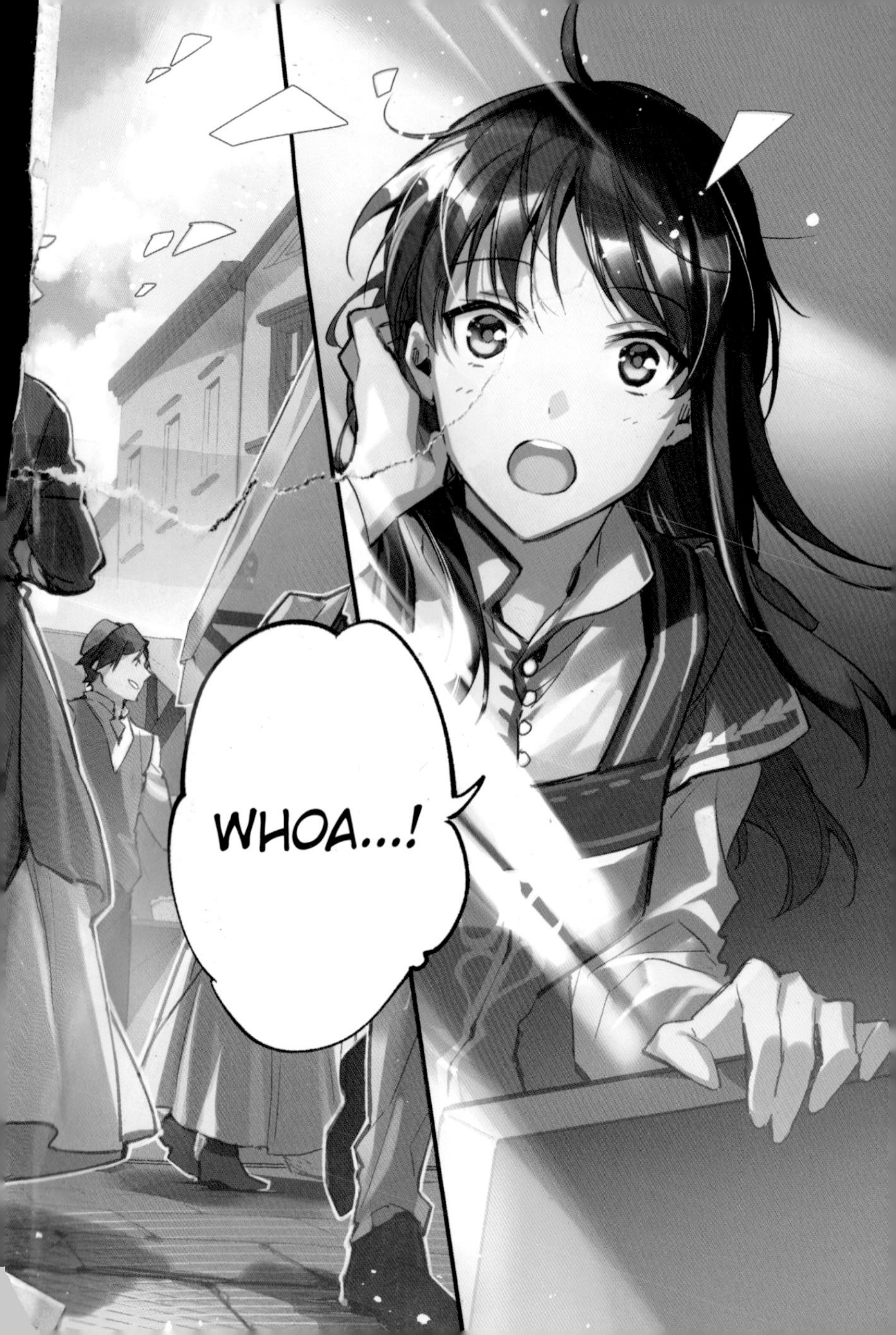
WHOA...!

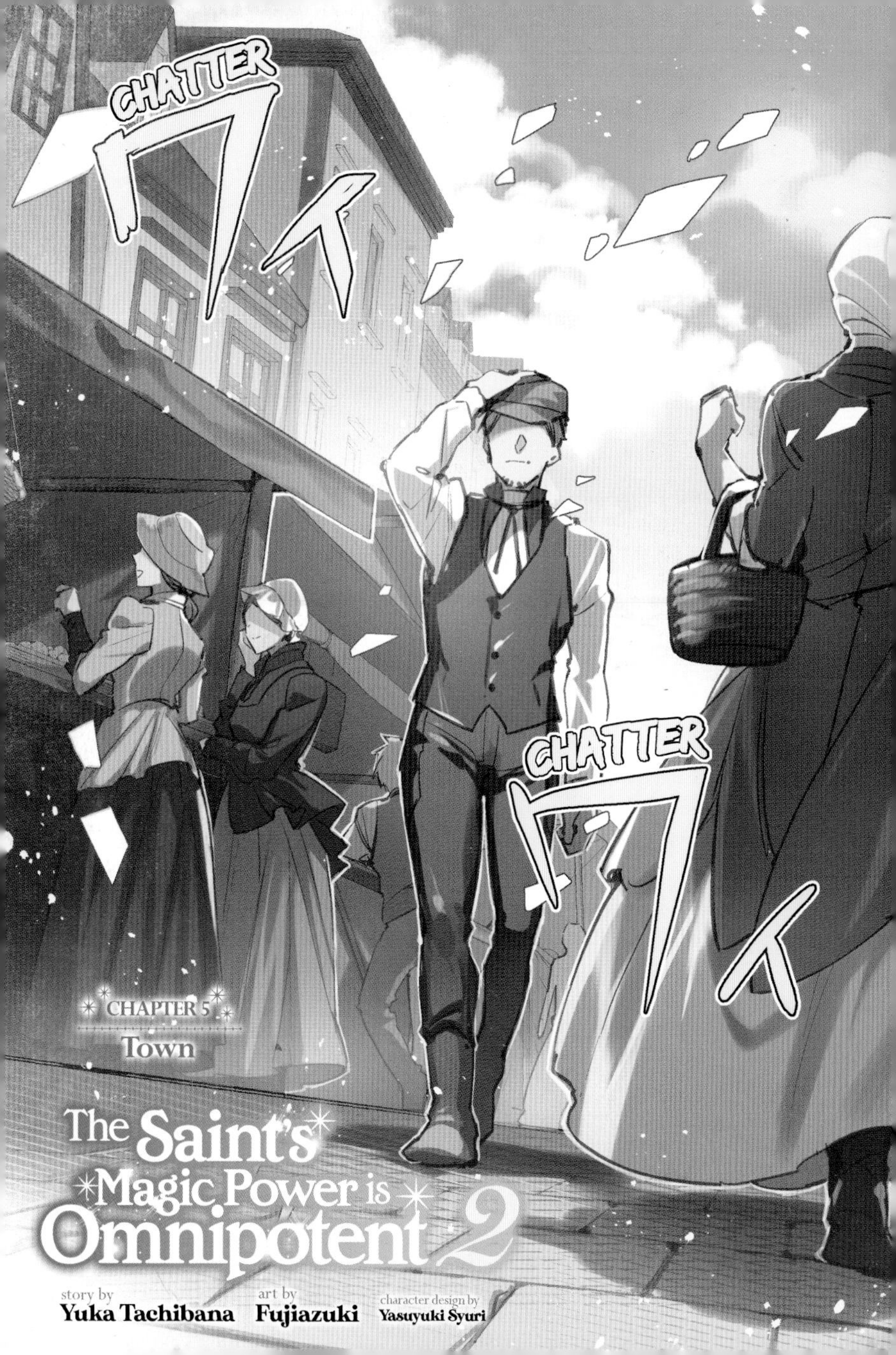
CHATTER
ワイ
CHATTER
ワイ
CHAPTER 5
Town
The Saint's Magic Power is Omnipotent 2
story by
Yuka Tachibana
art by
Fujiazuki
character design by
Yasuyuki Syuri

Contents

The **Saint's** Magic Power is **Omnipotent** *vol.2*

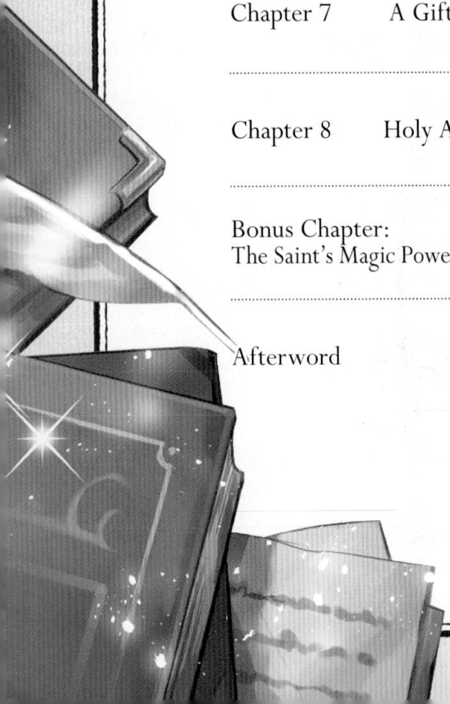

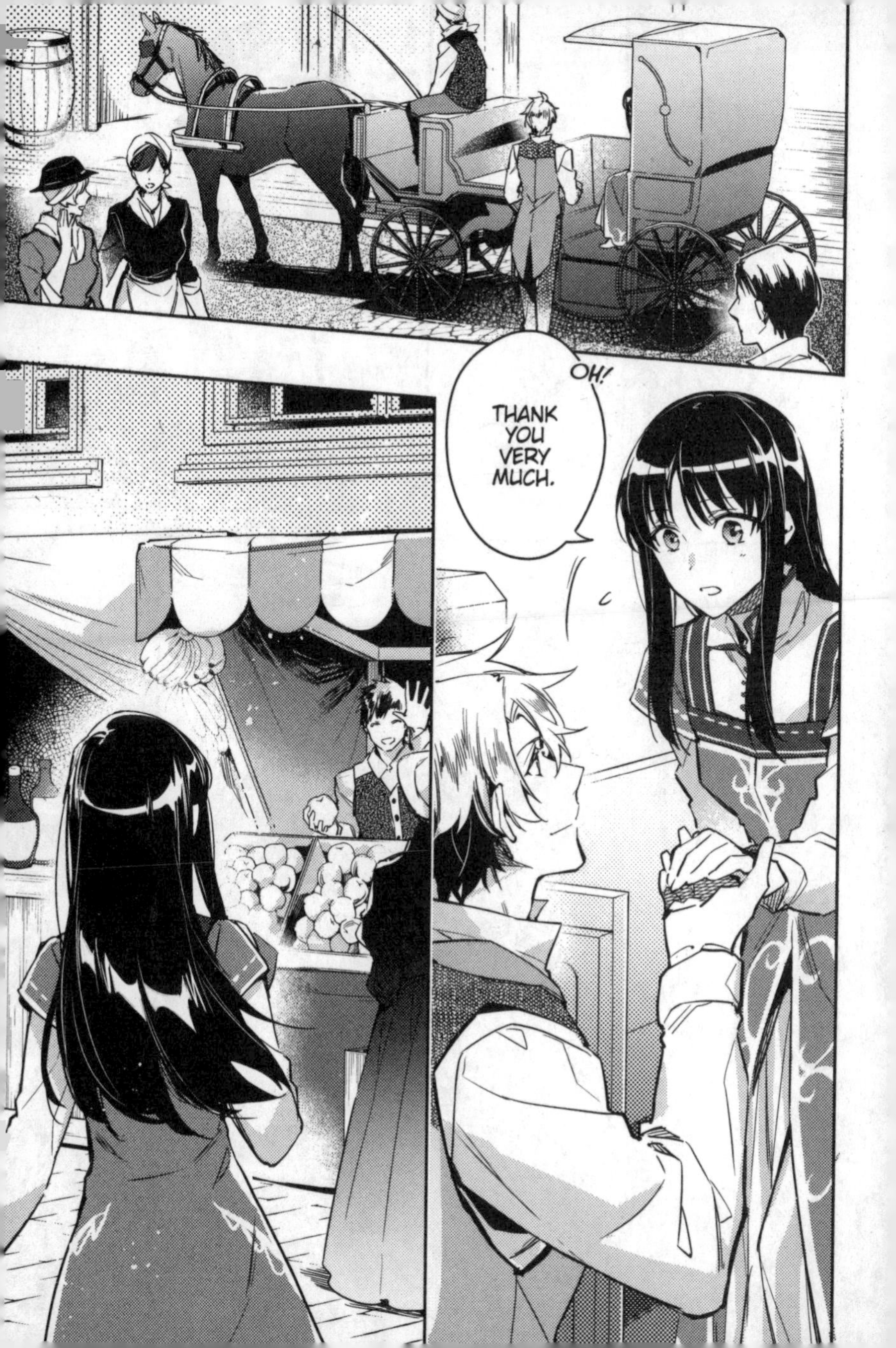
OH!
THANK YOU VERY MUCH.

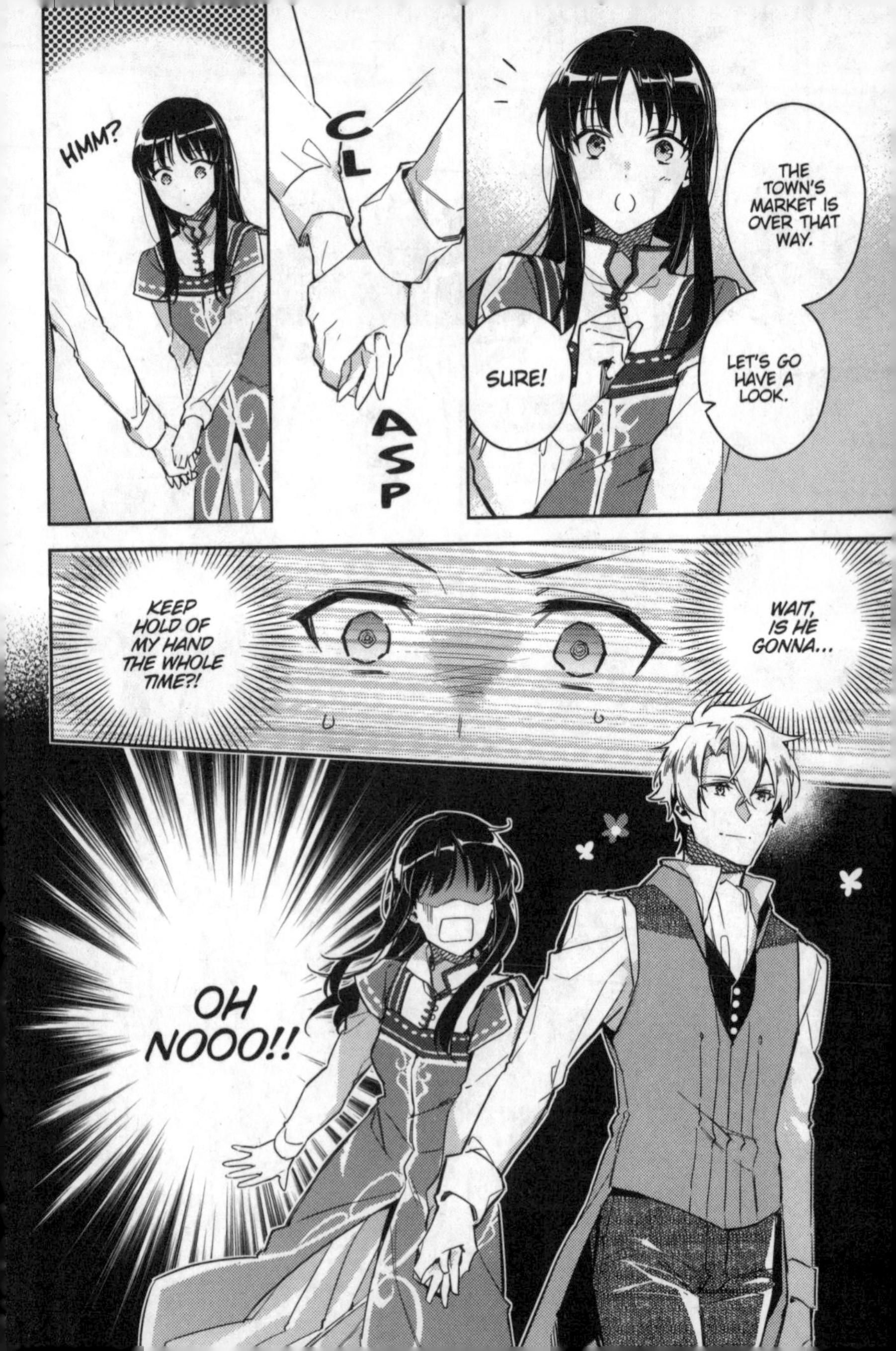
THE TOWN'S MARKET IS OVER THAT WAY.
LET'S GO HAVE A LOOK.
SURE!
CLASP
HMM?
WAIT, IS HE GONNA...
KEEP HOLD OF MY HAND THE WHOLE TIME?!
OH NOOO!!

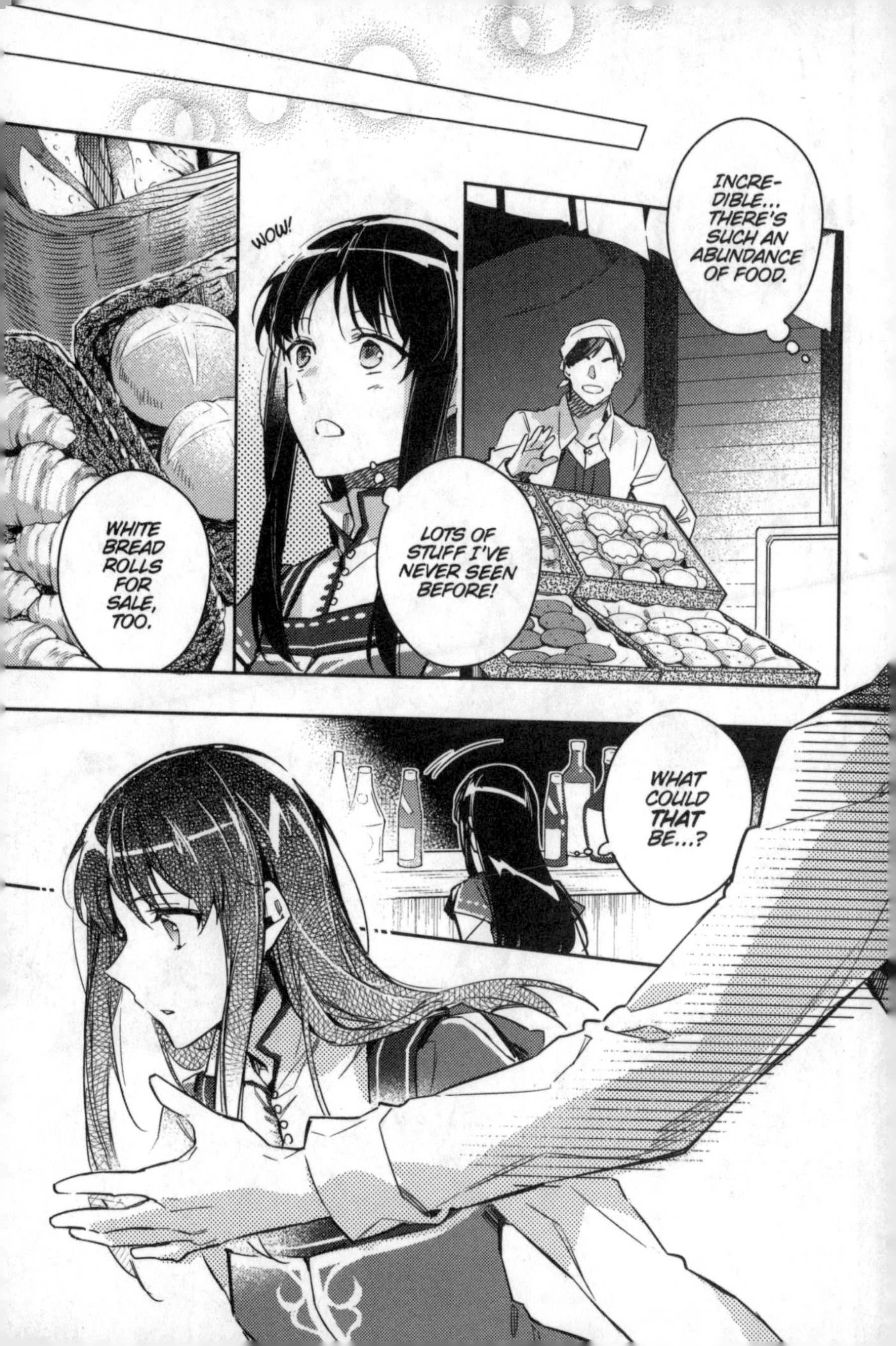
INCREDIBLE... THERE'S SUCH AN ABUNDANCE OF FOOD.
WOW!
LOTS OF STUFF I'VE NEVER SEEN BEFORE!
WHITE BREAD ROLLS FOR SALE, TOO.
WHAT COULD THAT BE...?

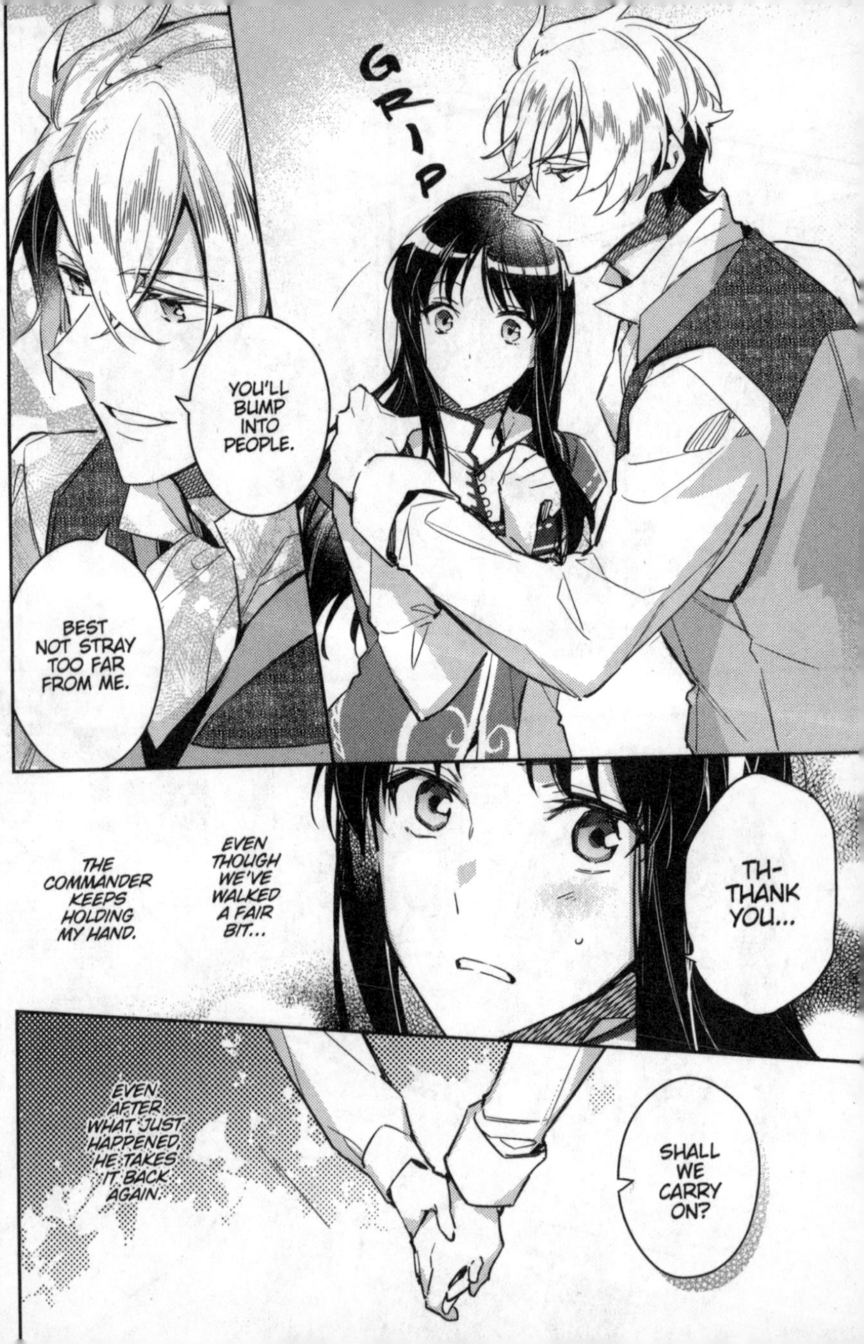
GRIP
YOU'LL BUMP INTO PEOPLE.
BEST NOT STRAY TOO FAR FROM ME.
TH- THANK YOU...
EVEN THOUGH WE'VE WALKED A FAIR BIT...
THE COMMANDER KEEPS HOLDING MY HAND.
SHALL WE CARRY ON?
EVEN AFTER WHAT JUST HAPPENED, HE TAKES IT BACK AGAIN.

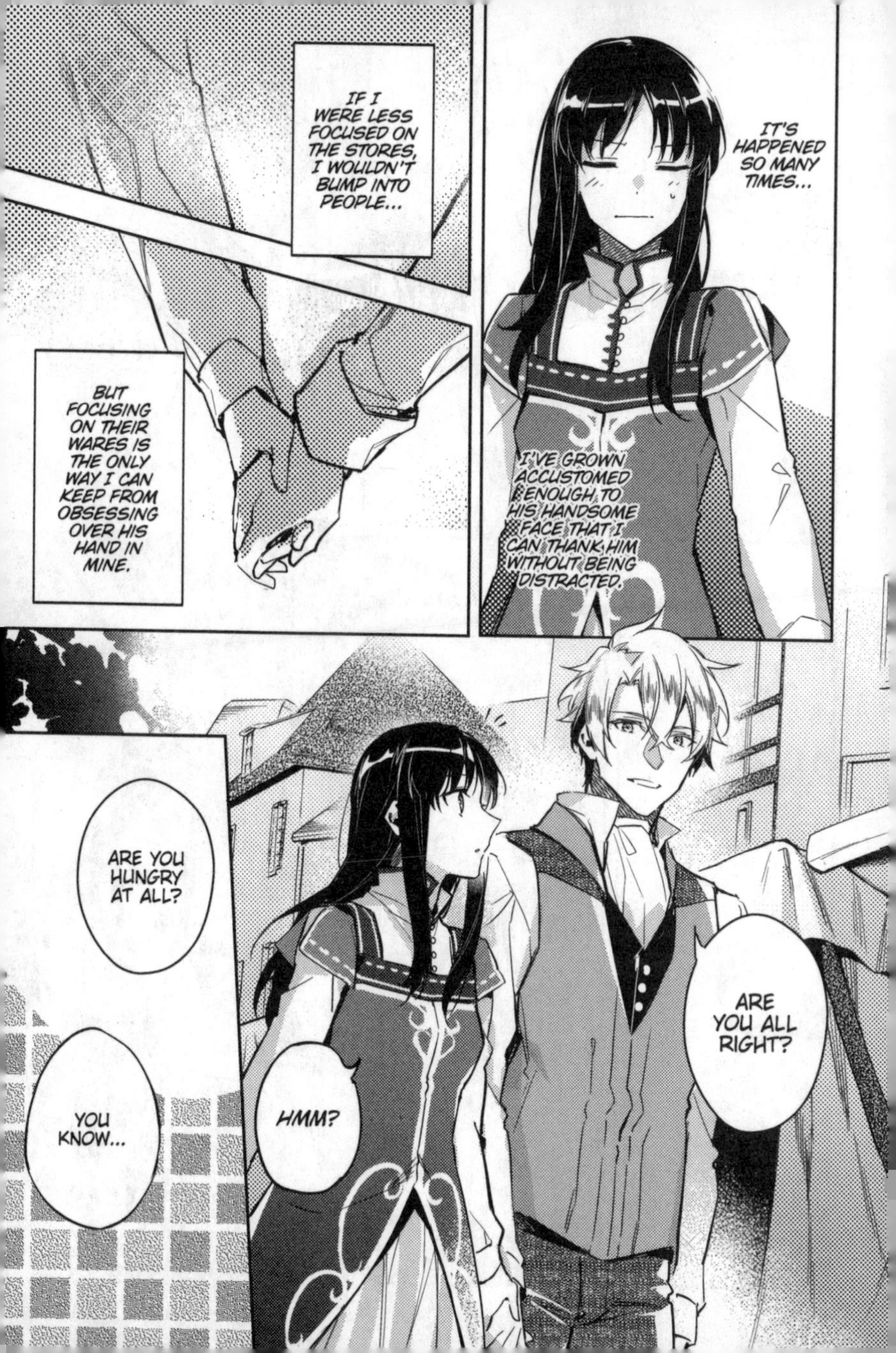
IT'S HAPPENED SO MANY TIMES...
I'VE GROWN ACCUSTOMED ENOUGH TO HIS HANDSOME FACE THAT I CAN THANK HIM WITHOUT BEING DISTRACTED.
IF I WERE LESS FOCUSED ON THE STORES, I WOULDN'T BUMP INTO PEOPLE...
BUT FOCUSING ON THEIR WARES IS THE ONLY WAY I CAN KEEP FROM OBSESSING OVER HIS HAND IN MINE.
ARE YOU ALL RIGHT?
HMM?
ARE YOU HUNGRY AT ALL?
YOU KNOW...

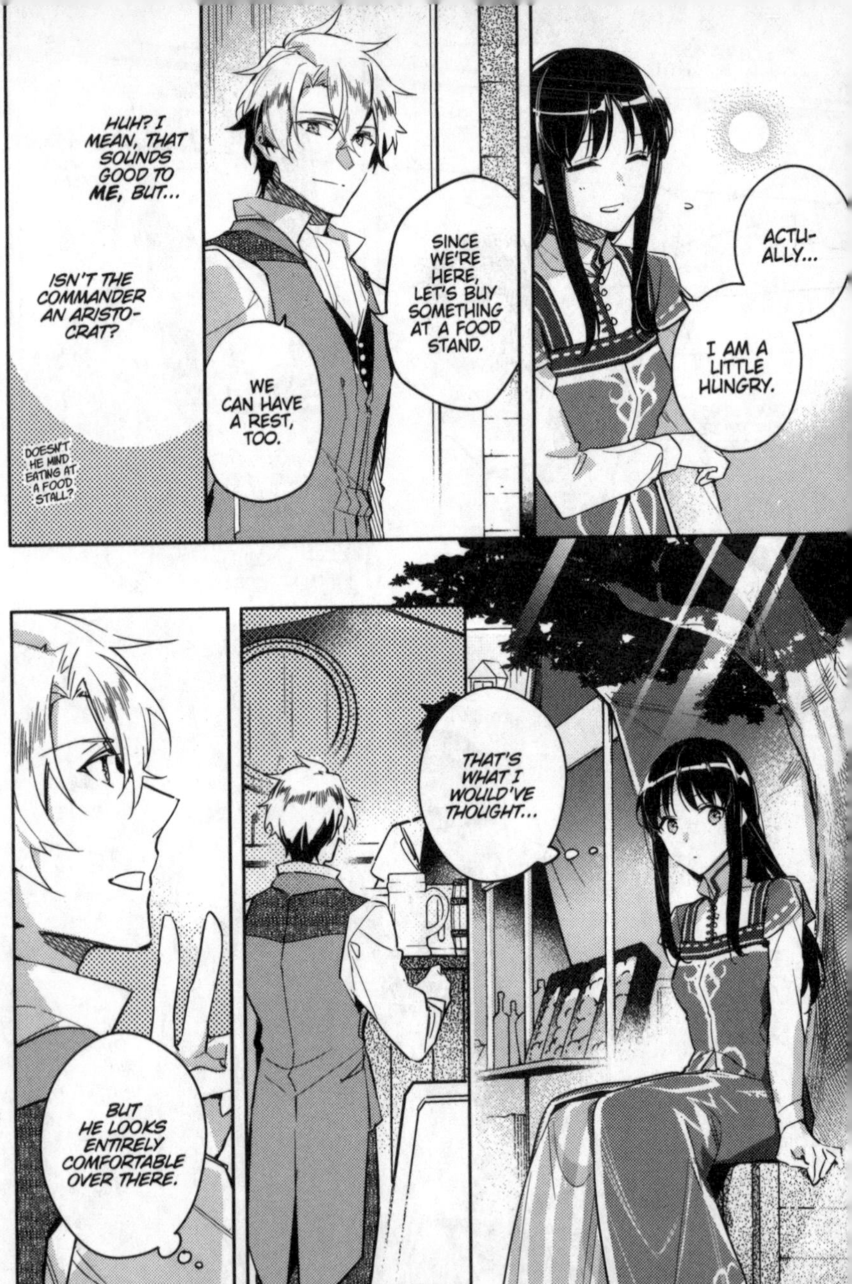
ACTU-ALLY...
I AM A LITTLE HUNGRY.
SINCE WE'RE HERE, LET'S BUY SOMETHING AT A FOOD STAND.
WE CAN HAVE A REST, TOO.
HUH? I MEAN, THAT SOUNDS GOOD TO ME, BUT...
ISN'T THE COMMANDER AN ARISTO-CRAT?
DOESN'T HE MIND EATING AT A FOOD STALL?
THAT'S WHAT I WOULD'VE THOUGHT...
BUT HE LOOKS ENTIRELY COMFORTABLE OVER THERE.

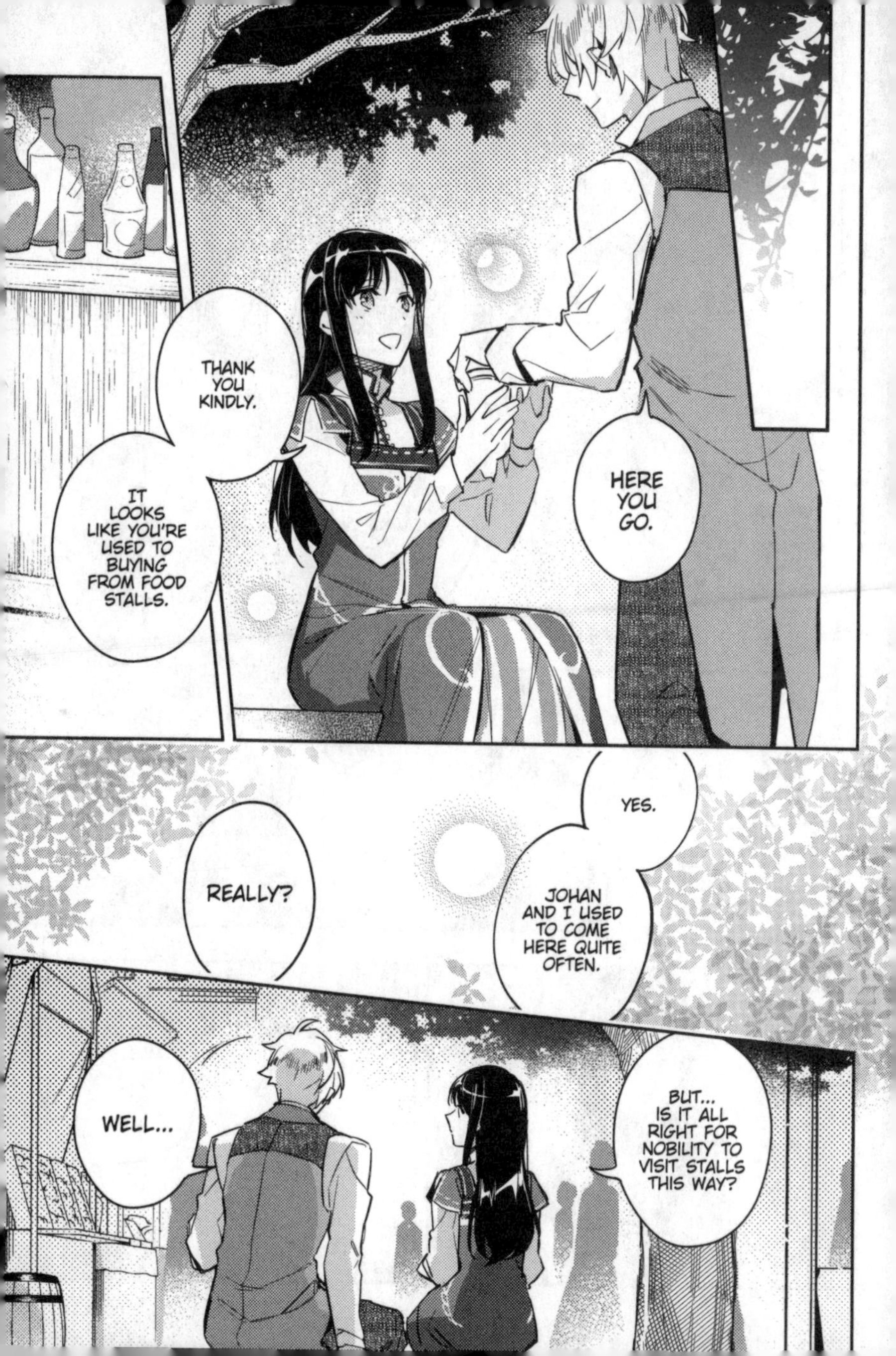
HERE YOU GO.
THANK YOU KINDLY.
IT LOOKS LIKE YOU'RE USED TO BUYING FROM FOOD STALLS.
YES.
JOHAN AND I USED TO COME HERE QUITE OFTEN.
REALLY?
BUT... IS IT ALL RIGHT FOR NOBILITY TO VISIT STALLS THIS WAY?
WELL...

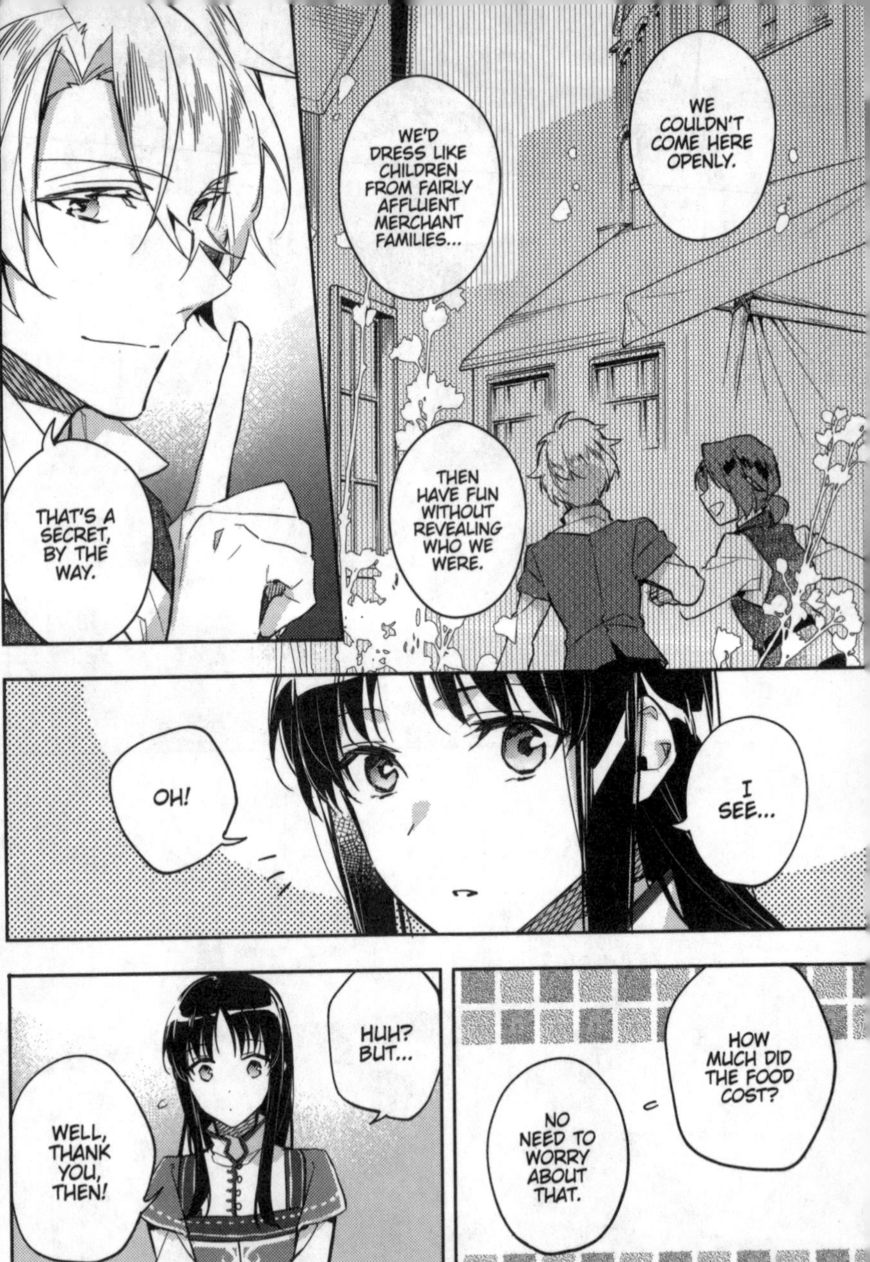
WE COULDN'T COME HERE OPENLY.
WE'D DRESS LIKE CHILDREN FROM FAIRLY AFFLUENT MERCHANT FAMILIES...
THEN HAVE FUN WITHOUT REVEALING WHO WE WERE.
THAT'S A SECRET, BY THE WAY.
I SEE...
OH!
HOW MUCH DID THE FOOD COST?
NO NEED TO WORRY ABOUT THAT.
HUH? BUT...
WELL, THANK YOU, THEN!

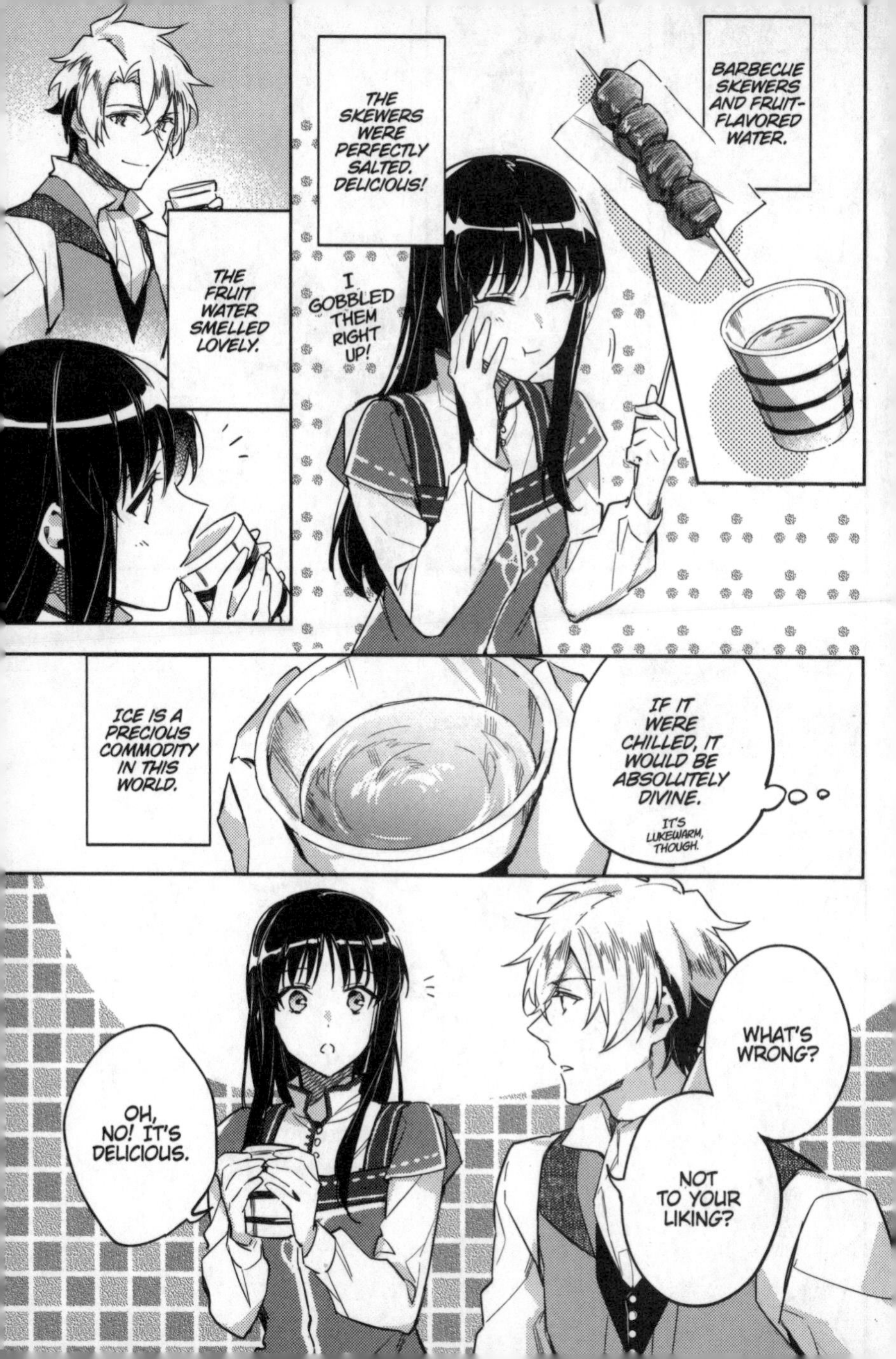

BARBECUE SKEWERS AND FRUIT-FLAVORED WATER.
THE SKEWERS WERE PERFECTLY SALTED. DELICIOUS!
I GOBBLED THEM RIGHT UP!
THE FRUIT WATER SMELLED LOVELY.
IF IT WERE CHILLED, IT WOULD BE ABSOLUTELY DIVINE.
IT'S LUKEWARM, THOUGH.
ICE IS A PRECIOUS COMMODITY IN THIS WORLD.
WHAT'S WRONG?
NOT TO YOUR LIKING?
OH, NO! IT'S DELICIOUS.

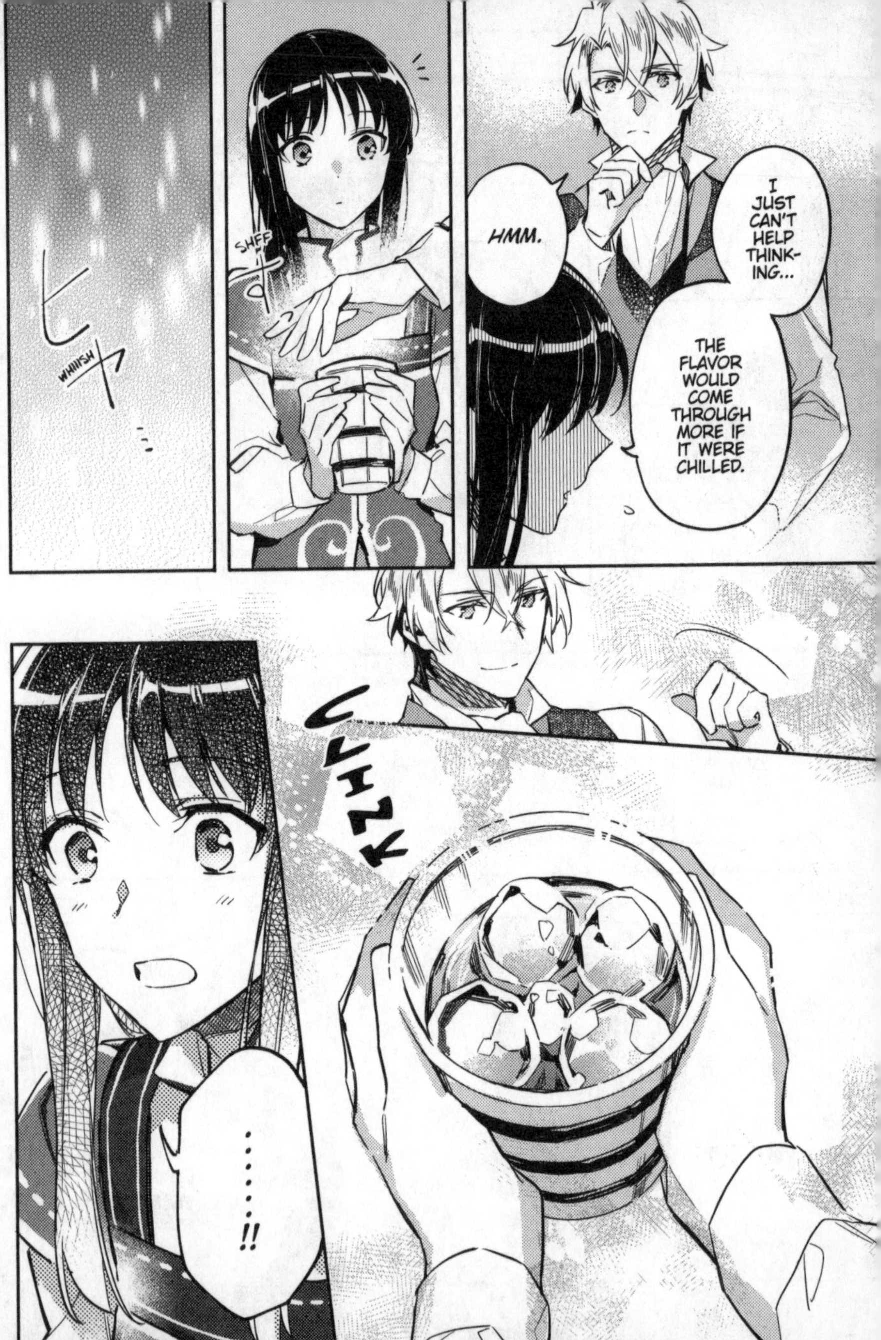

I JUST CAN'T HELP THINKING...
HMM.
THE FLAVOR WOULD COME THROUGH MORE IF IT WERE CHILLED.
SHFF
WHIIISH
CLINK
......!!

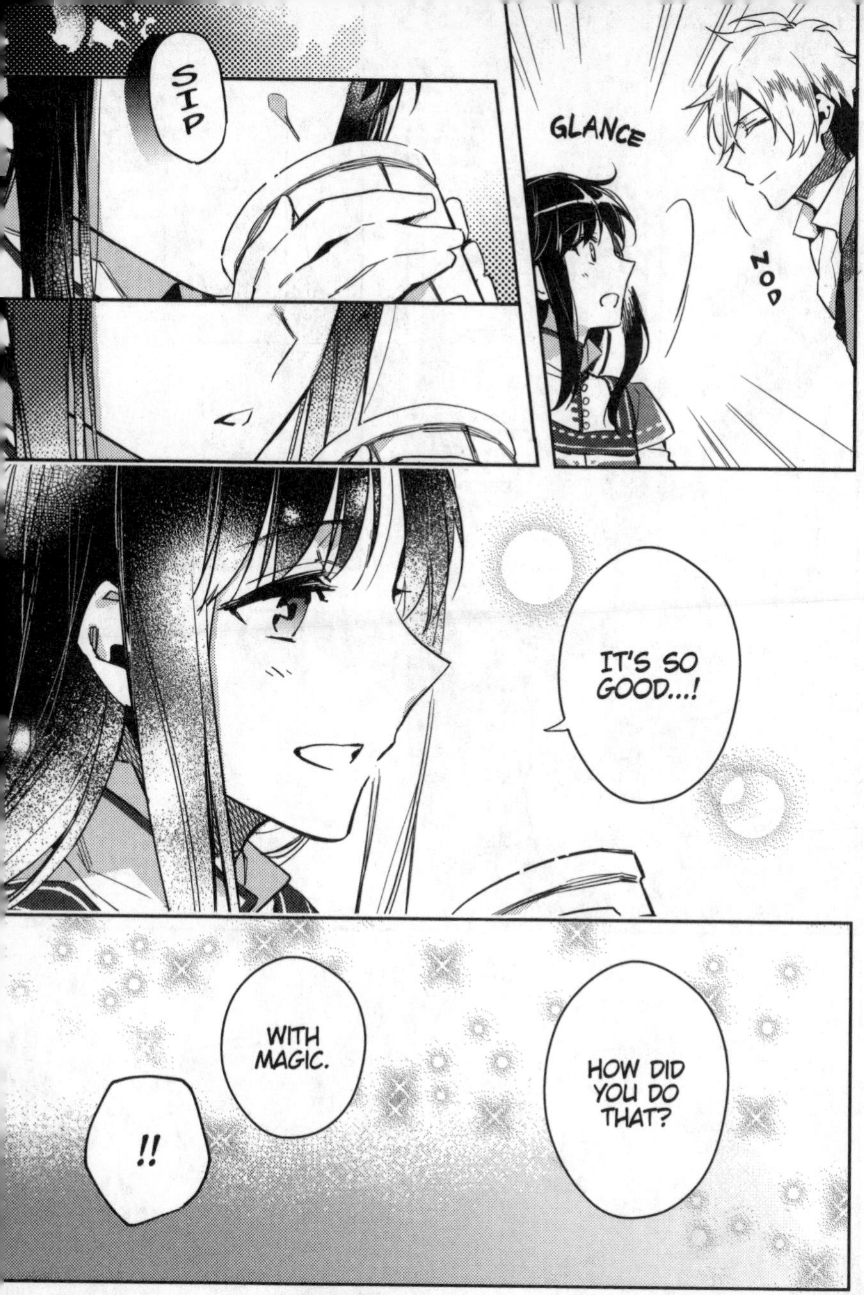
GLANCE
ZOD
SIP
IT'S SO GOOD...!
HOW DID YOU DO THAT?
WITH MAGIC.
!!

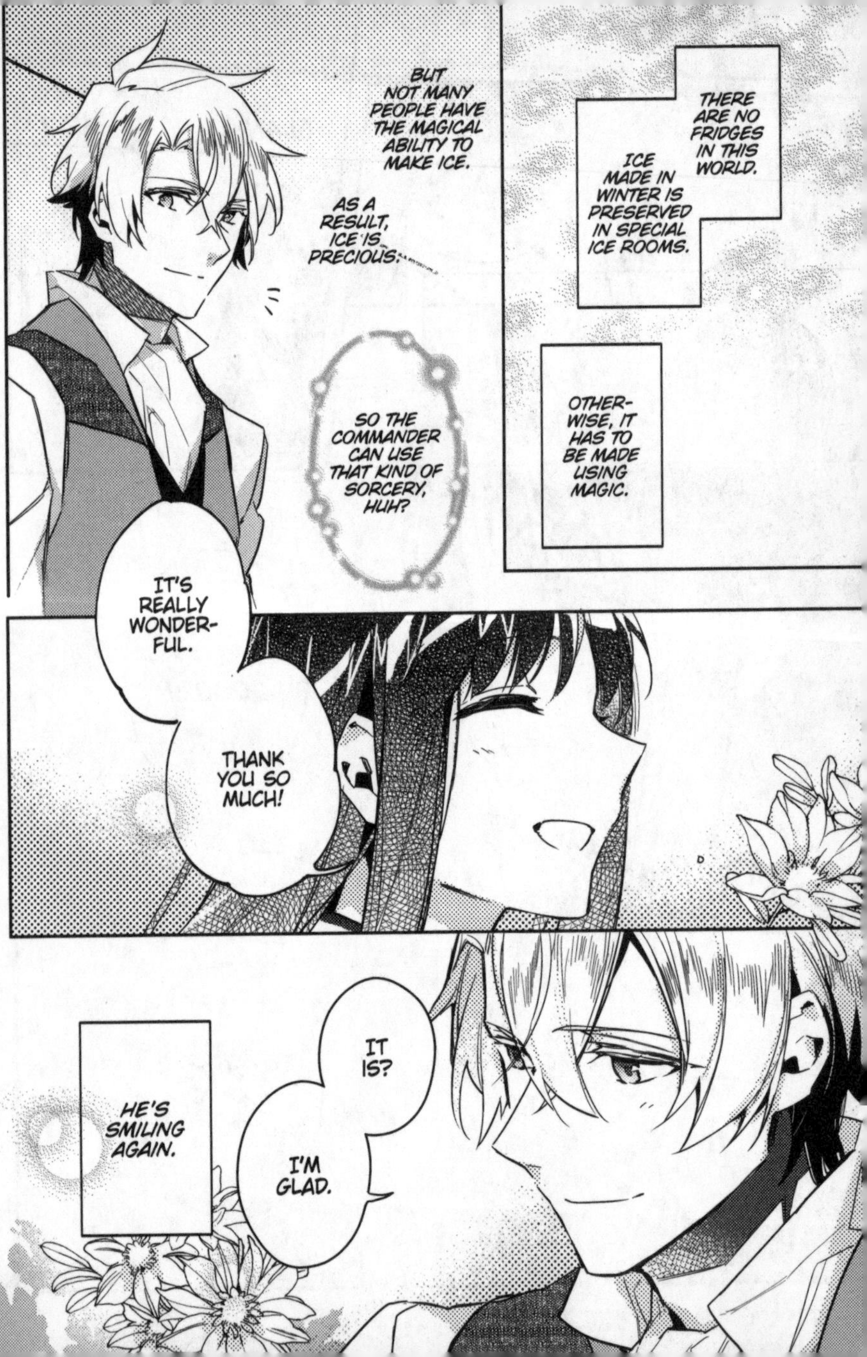
THERE ARE NO FRIDGES IN THIS WORLD.
ICE MADE IN WINTER IS PRESERVED IN SPECIAL ICE ROOMS.
OTHER-WISE, IT HAS TO BE MADE USING MAGIC.
BUT NOT MANY PEOPLE HAVE THE MAGICAL ABILITY TO MAKE ICE.
AS A RESULT, ICE IS PRECIOUS...
SO THE COMMANDER CAN USE THAT KIND OF SORCERY, HUH?
IT'S REALLY WONDER-FUL.
THANK YOU SO MUCH!
IT IS?
I'M GLAD.
HE'S SMILING AGAIN.

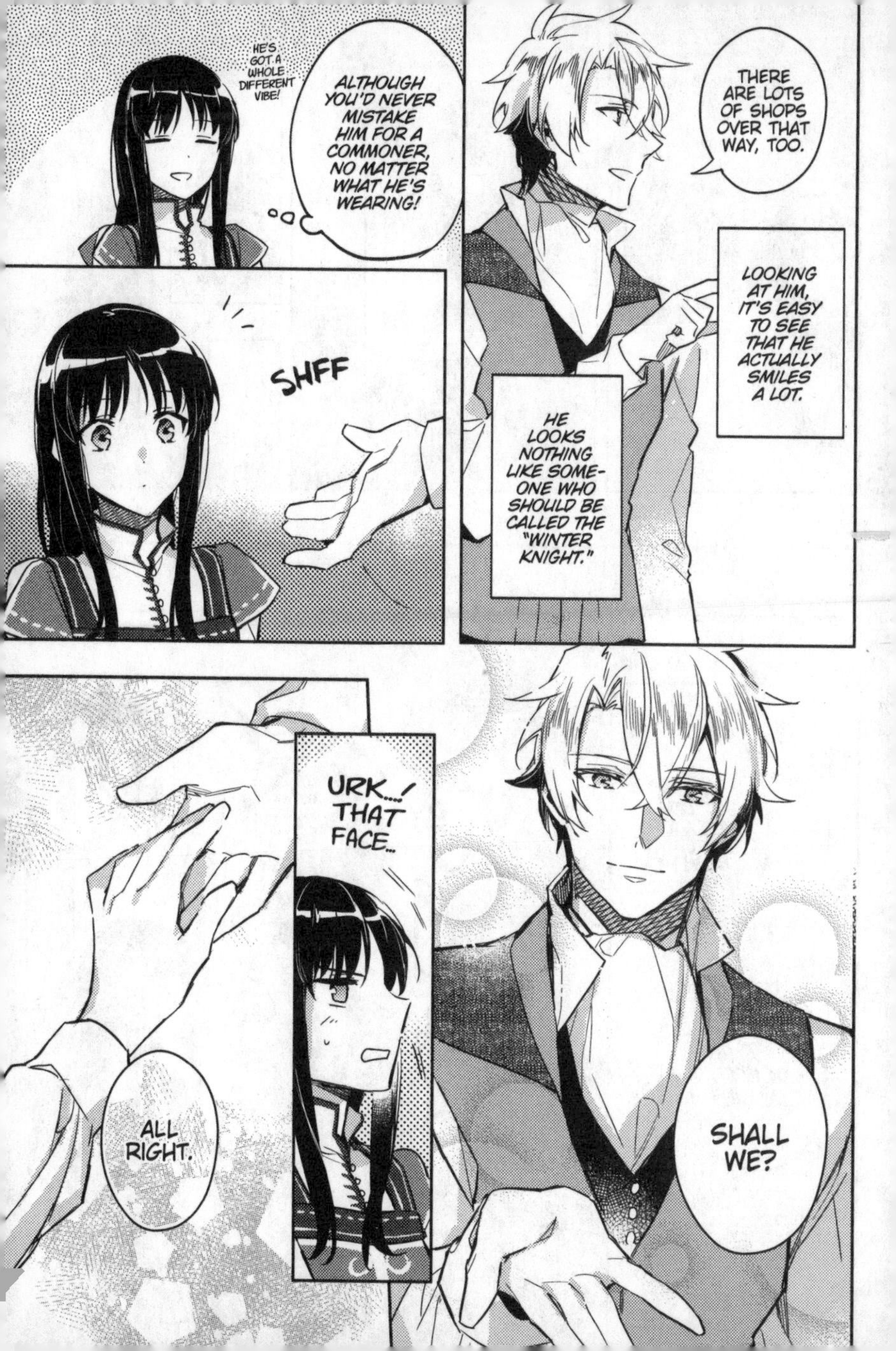
THERE ARE LOTS OF SHOPS OVER THAT WAY, TOO.
LOOKING AT HIM, IT'S EASY TO SEE THAT HE ACTUALLY SMILES A LOT.
HE LOOKS NOTHING LIKE SOME-ONE WHO SHOULD BE CALLED THE "WINTER KNIGHT."
ALTHOUGH YOU'D NEVER MISTAKE HIM FOR A COMMONER, NO MATTER WHAT HE'S WEARING!
HE'S GOT A WHOLE DIFFERENT VIBE!
SHFF
SHALL WE?
URK...! THAT FACE...
ALL RIGHT.

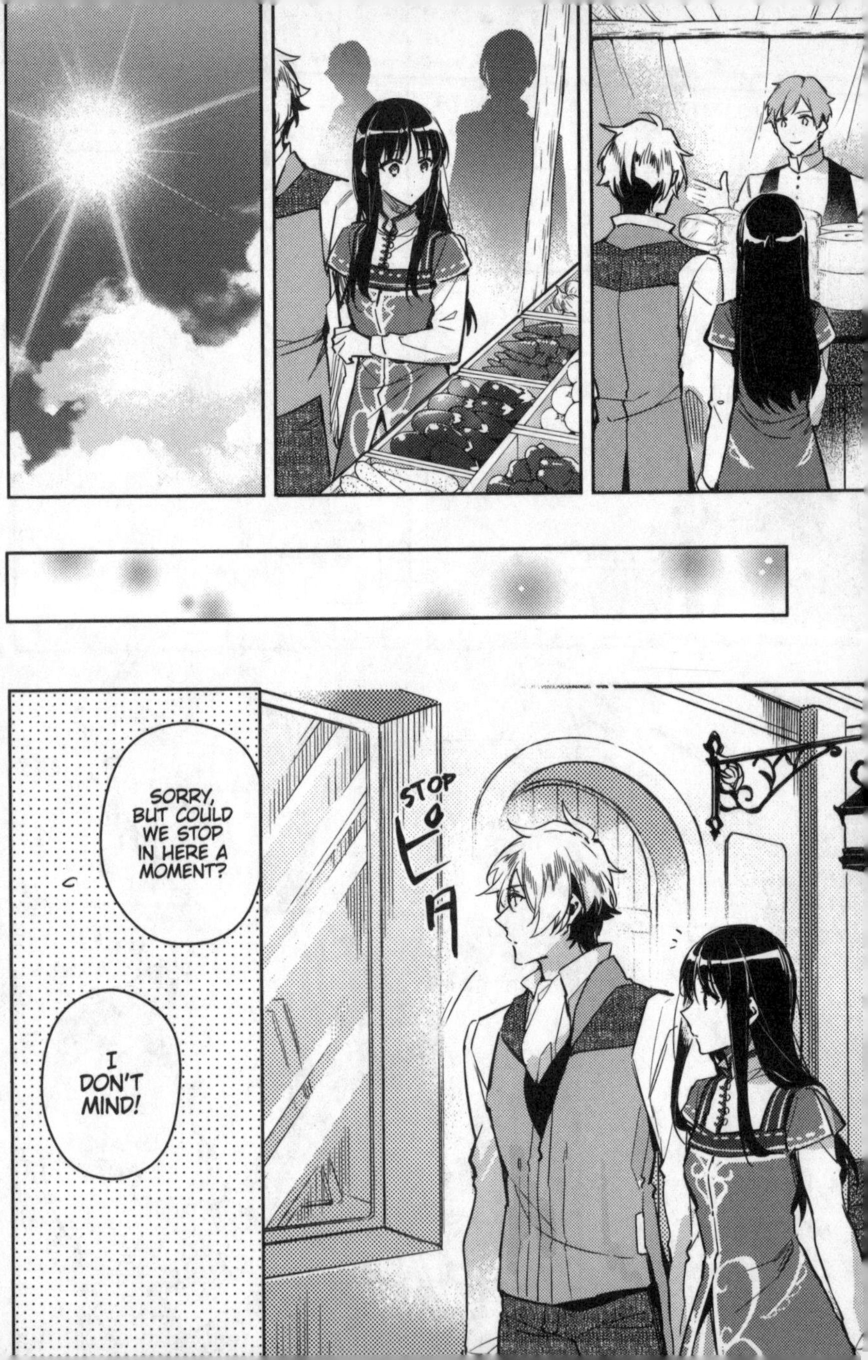
STOP
SORRY, BUT COULD WE STOP IN HERE A MOMENT?
I DON'T MIND!

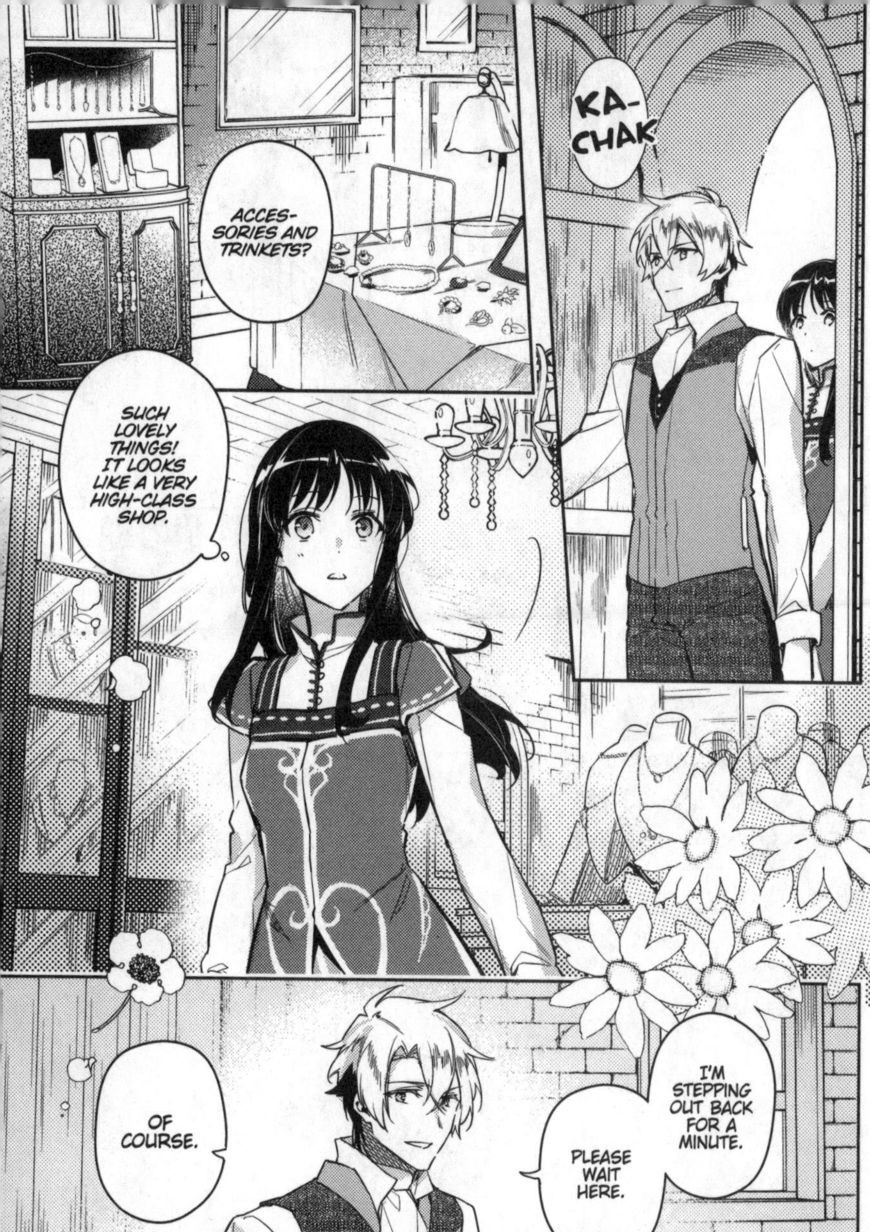
KA-CHAK
ACCES-SORIES AND TRINKETS?
SUCH LOVELY THINGS! IT LOOKS LIKE A VERY HIGH-CLASS SHOP.
I'M STEPPING OUT BACK FOR A MINUTE.
PLEASE WAIT HERE.
OF COURSE.

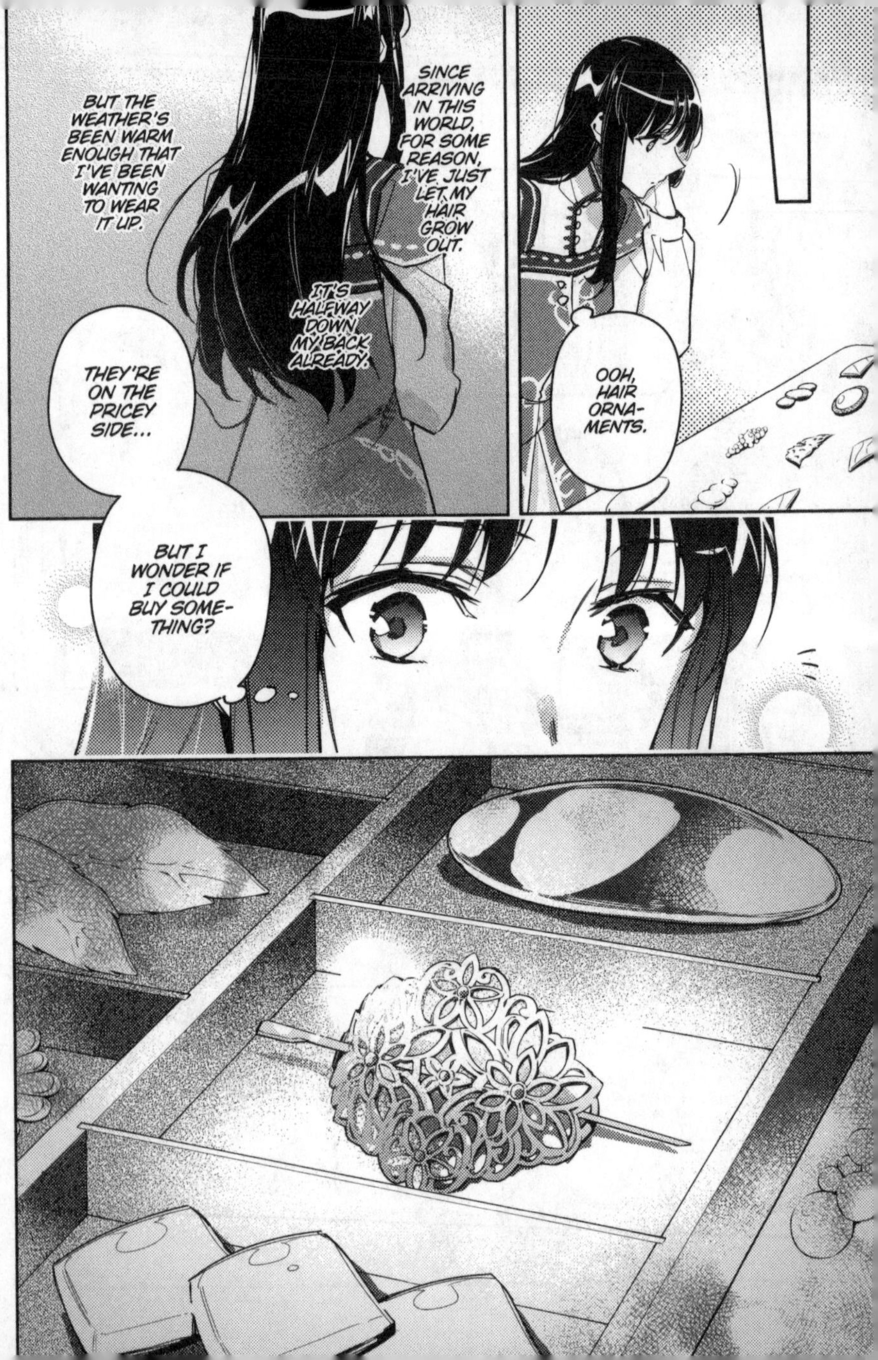
OOH, HAIR ORNA-MENTS.
SINCE ARRIVING IN THIS WORLD, FOR SOME REASON, I'VE JUST LET MY HAIR GROW OUT.
BUT THE WEATHER'S BEEN WARM ENOUGH THAT I'VE BEEN WANTING TO WEAR IT UP.
IT'S HALFWAY DOWN MY BACK ALREADY.
THEY'RE ON THE PRICEY SIDE...
BUT I WONDER IF I COULD BUY SOME-THING?

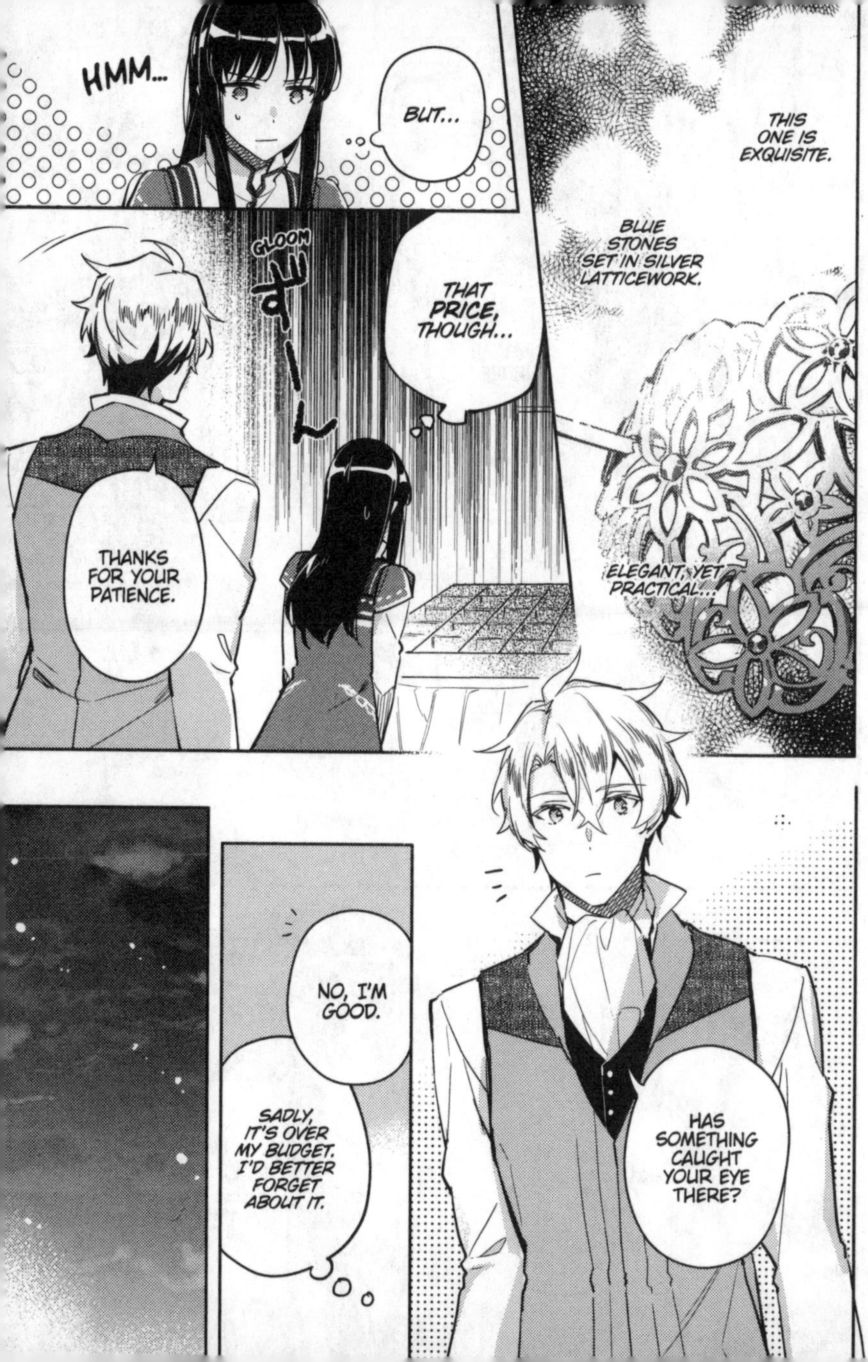
THIS ONE IS EXQUISITE.
BLUE STONES SET IN SILVER LATTICEWORK.
ELEGANT, YET PRACTICAL...
BUT...
HMM...
THAT PRICE, THOUGH...
GLOOM
THANKS FOR YOUR PATIENCE.
HAS SOMETHING CAUGHT YOUR EYE THERE?
NO, I'M GOOD.
SADLY, IT'S OVER MY BUDGET. I'D BETTER FORGET ABOUT IT.

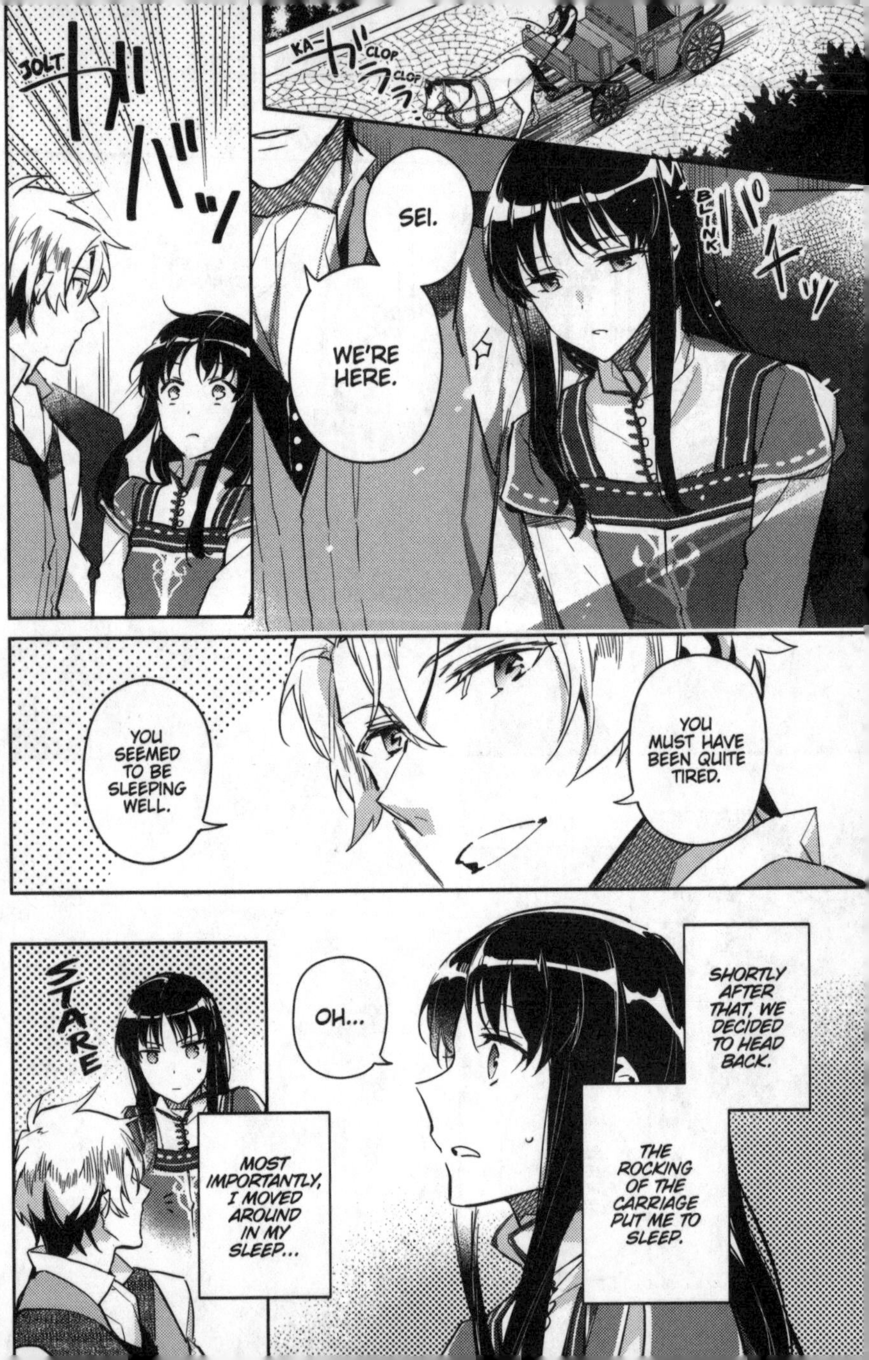
KA-
CLOP
CLOP
SEI.
WE'RE HERE.
BLINK
JOLT
YOU MUST HAVE BEEN QUITE TIRED.
YOU SEEMED TO BE SLEEPING WELL.
SHORTLY AFTER THAT, WE DECIDED TO HEAD BACK.
THE ROCKING OF THE CARRIAGE PUT ME TO SLEEP.
OH...
STARE
MOST IMPORTANTLY, I MOVED AROUND IN MY SLEEP...

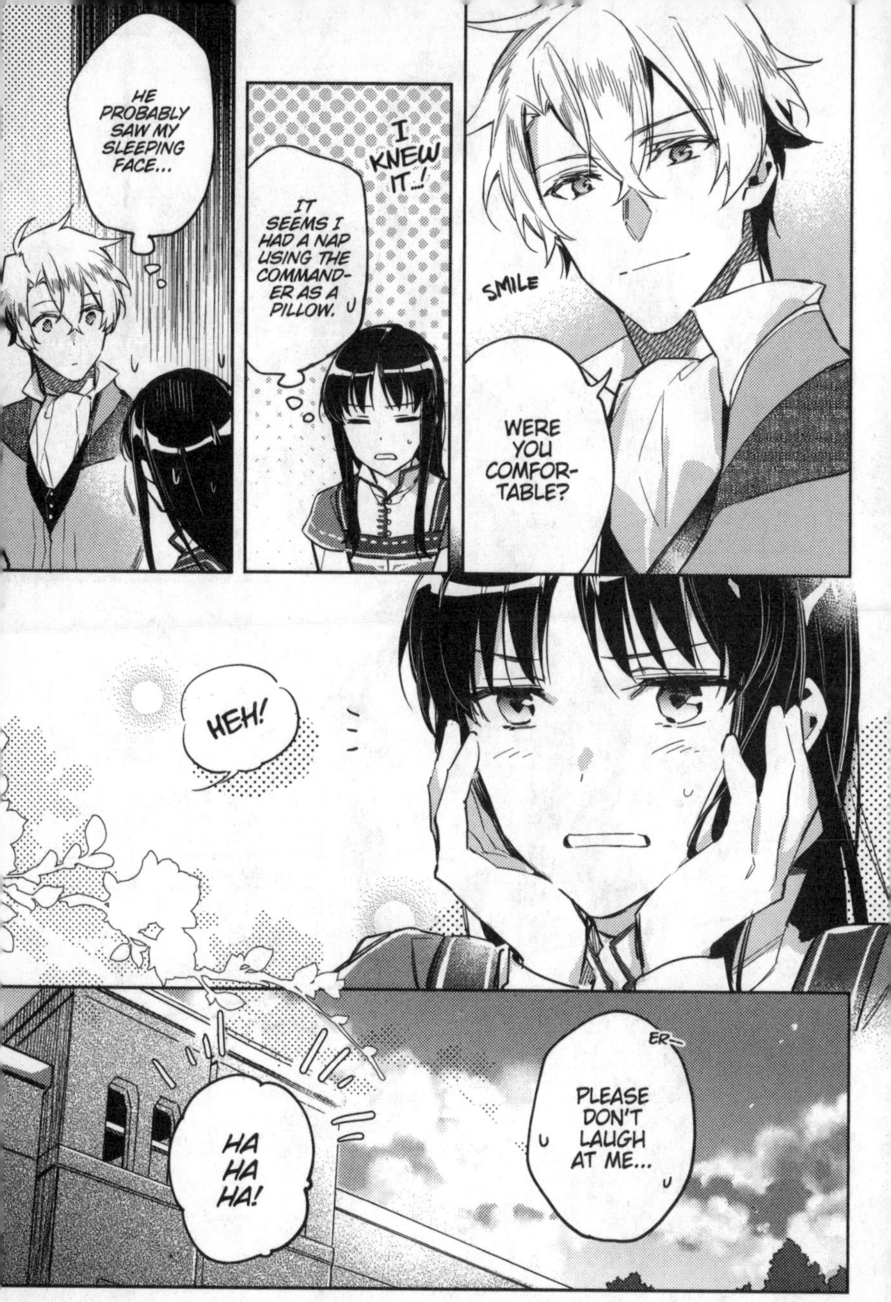
SMILE
WERE YOU COMFORTABLE?
I KNEW IT..!
IT SEEMS I HAD A NAP USING THE COMMANDER AS A PILLOW.
HE PROBABLY SAW MY SLEEPING FACE...
HEH!
ER—
PLEASE DON'T LAUGH AT ME...
HA HA HA!

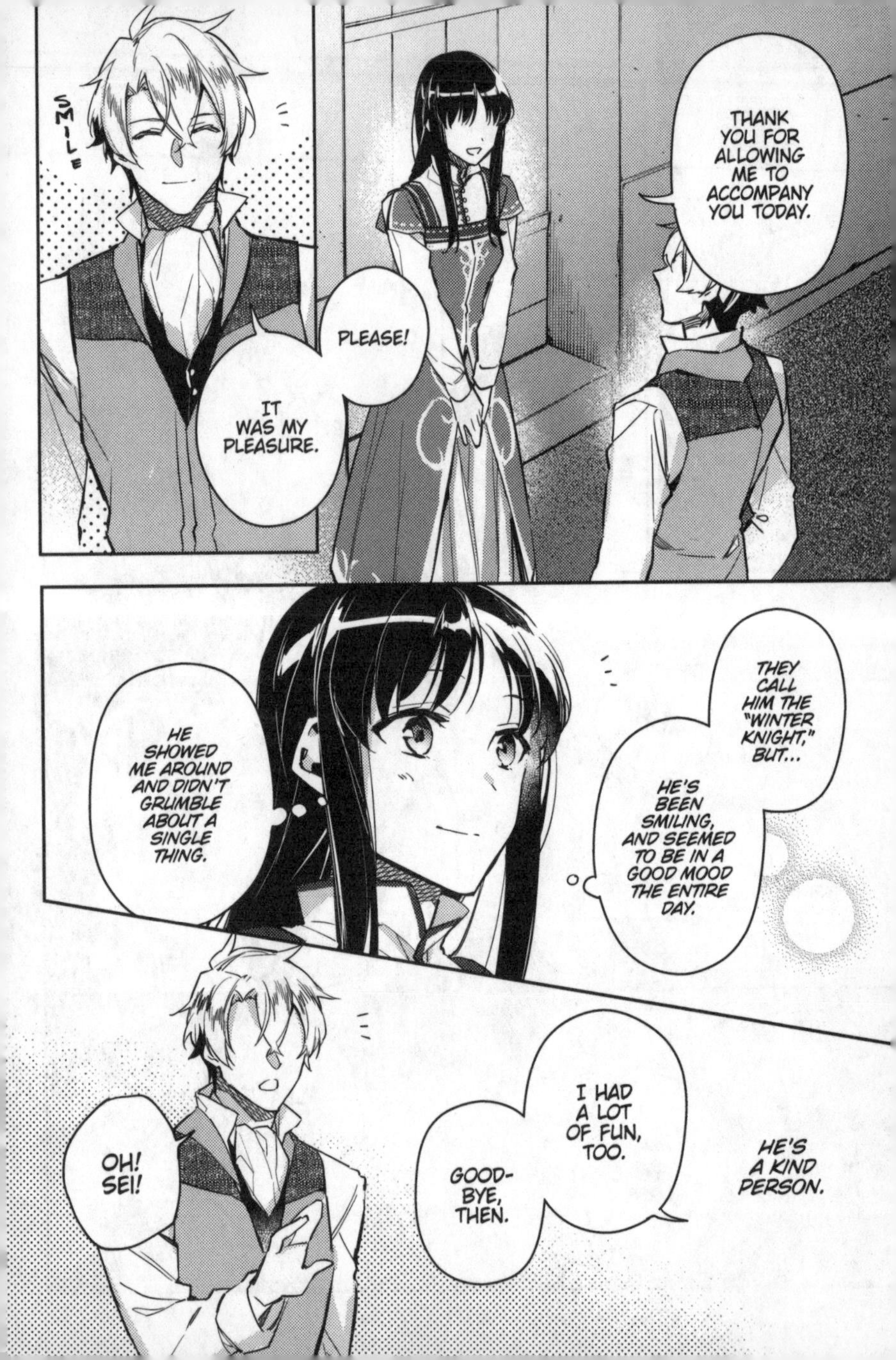
THANK YOU FOR ALLOWING ME TO ACCOMPANY YOU TODAY.
SMILE
PLEASE!
IT WAS MY PLEASURE.
THEY CALL HIM THE "WINTER KNIGHT," BUT...
HE'S BEEN SMILING, AND SEEMED TO BE IN A GOOD MOOD THE ENTIRE DAY.
HE SHOWED ME AROUND AND DIDN'T GRUMBLE ABOUT A SINGLE THING.
HE'S A KIND PERSON.
I HAD A LOT OF FUN, TOO.
GOOD-BYE, THEN.
OH! SEI!

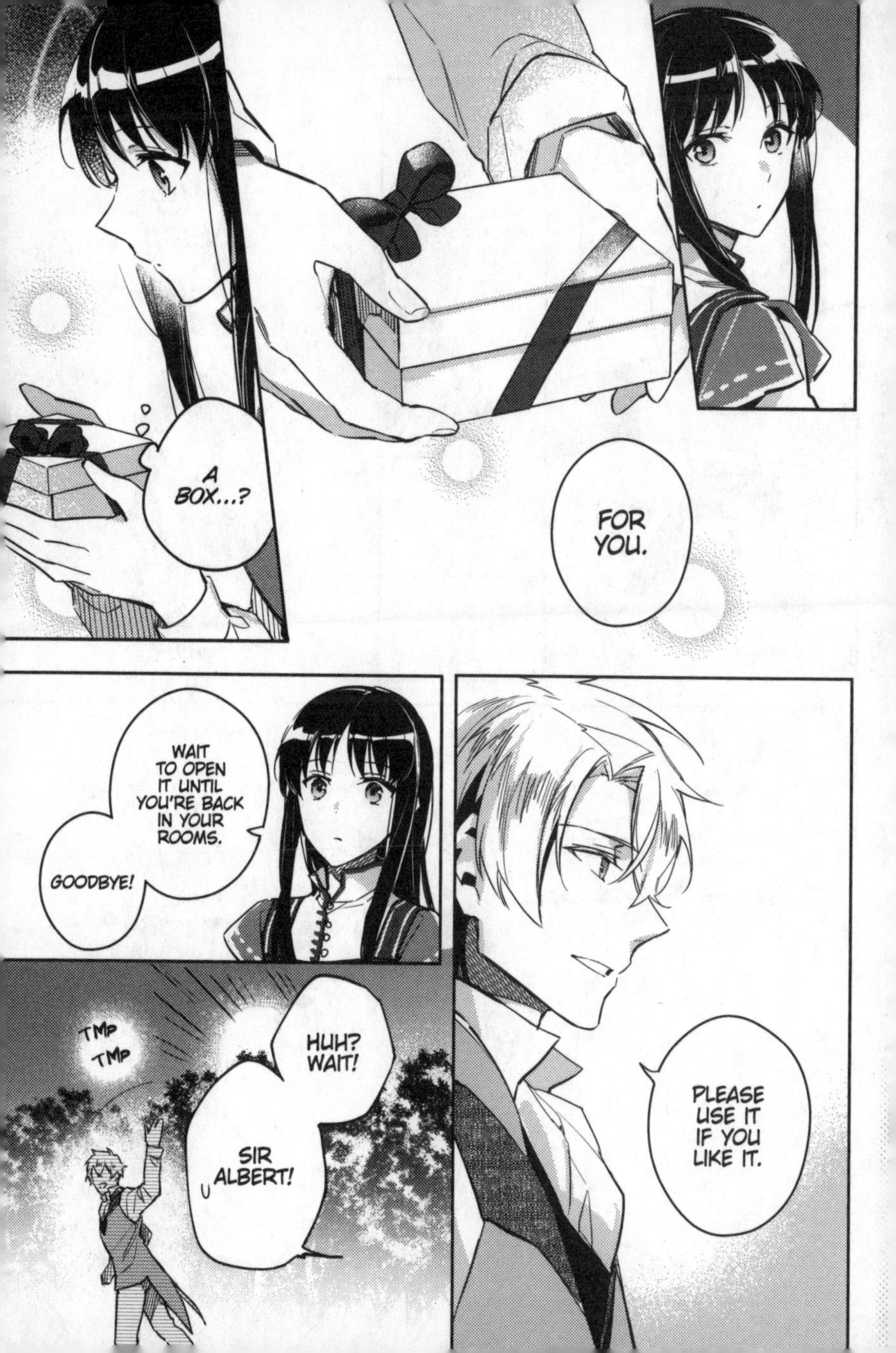
FOR YOU.
A BOX...?
PLEASE USE IT IF YOU LIKE IT.
WAIT TO OPEN IT UNTIL YOU'RE BACK IN YOUR ROOMS.
GOODBYE!
HUH? WAIT!
TMP TMP
SIR ALBERT!

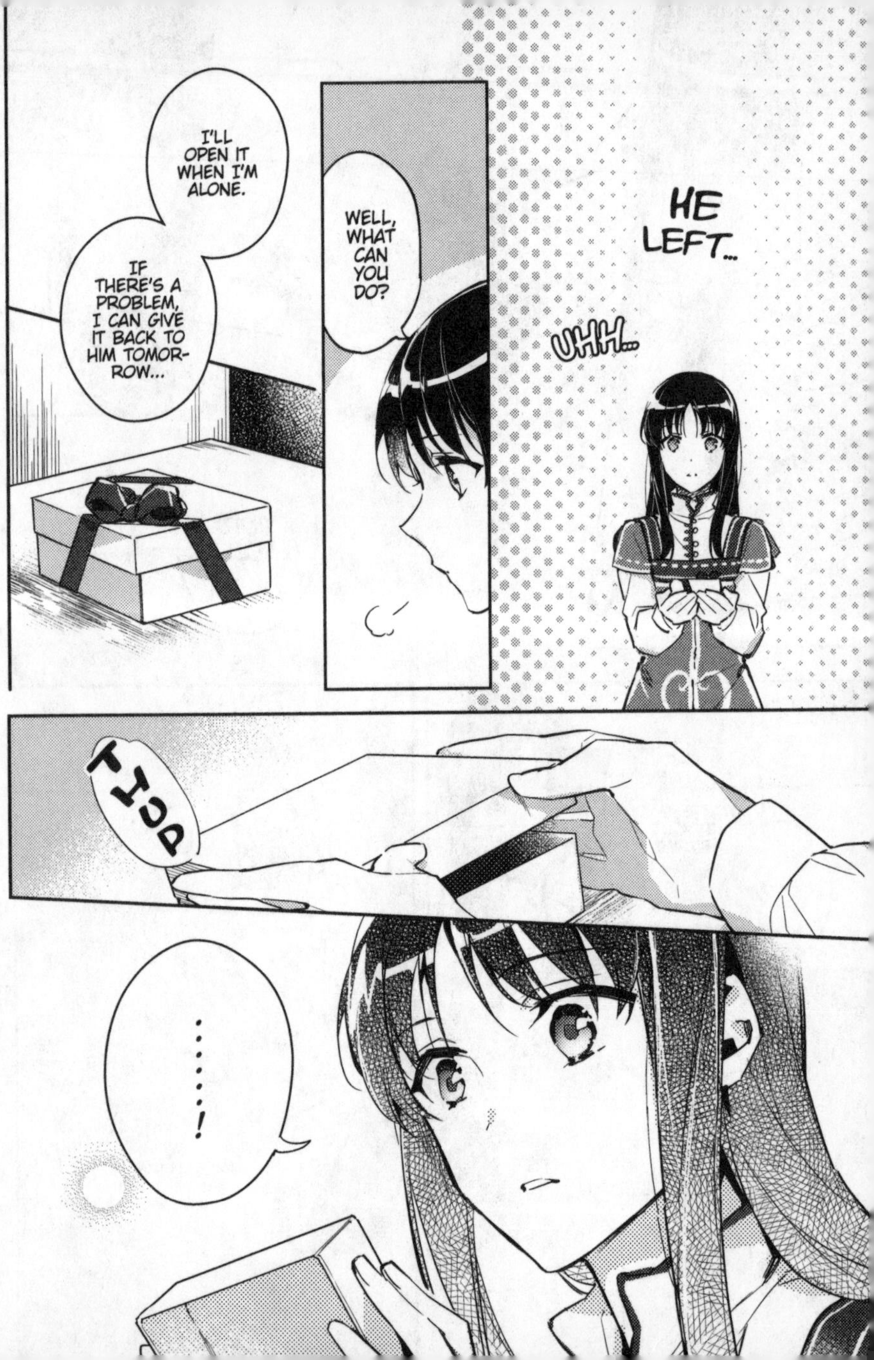
HE LEFT...
UHH...
WELL, WHAT CAN YOU DO?
I'LL OPEN IT WHEN I'M ALONE.
IF THERE'S A PROBLEM, I CAN GIVE IT BACK TO HIM TOMORROW...
PULL
......!

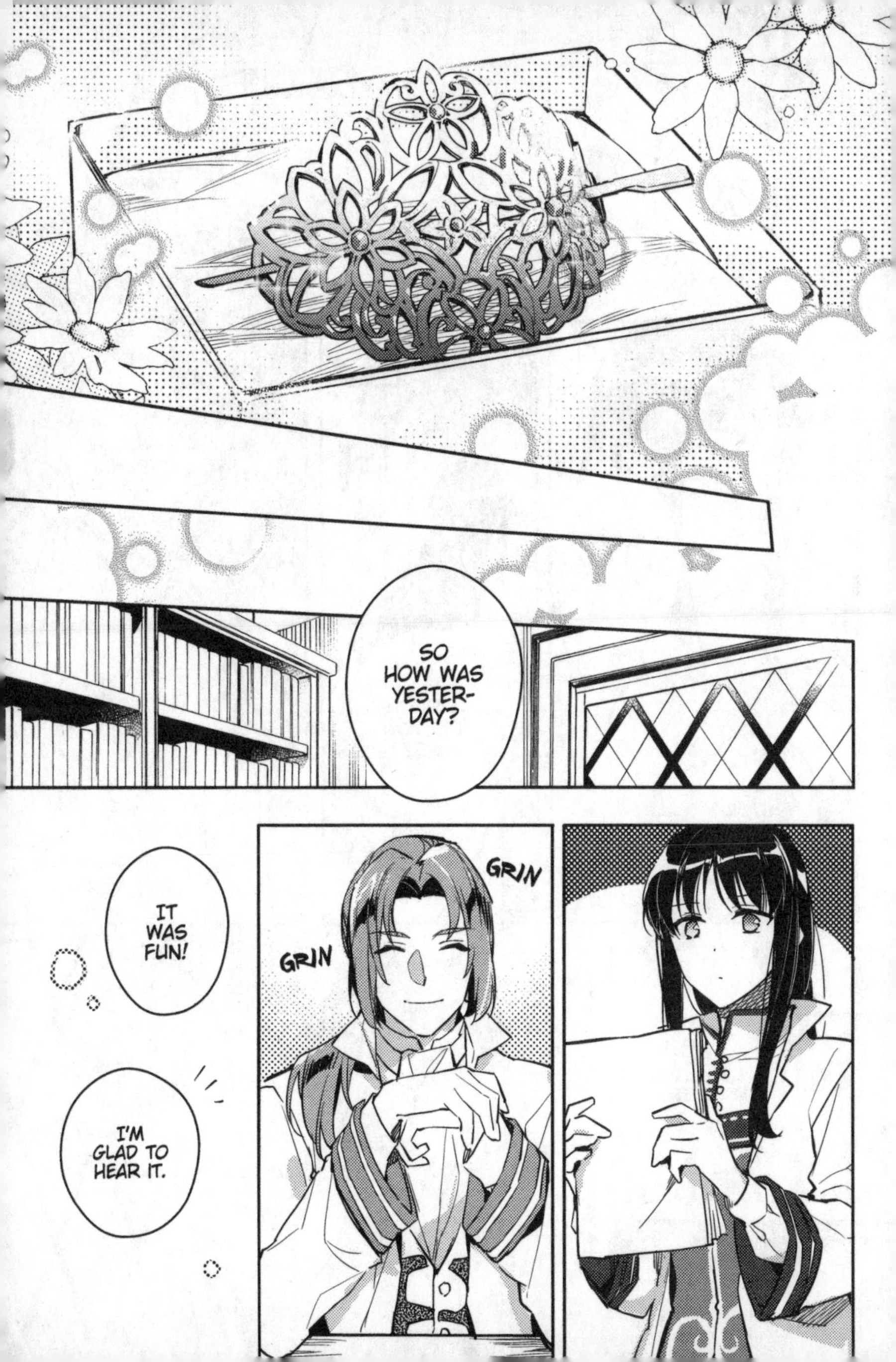
SO HOW WAS YESTER-DAY?
GRIN
GRIN
IT WAS FUN!
I'M GLAD TO HEAR IT.

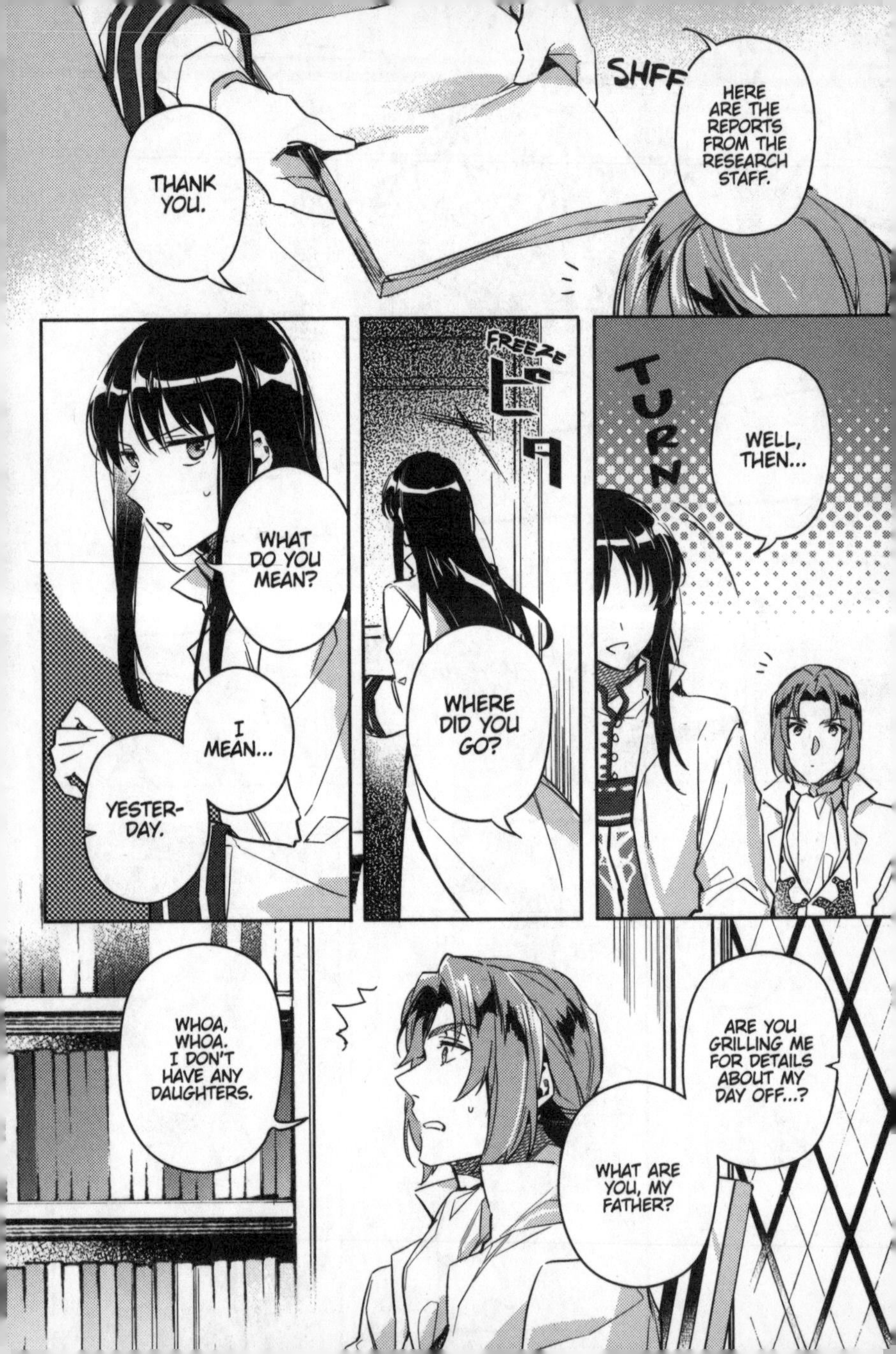
SHFF
HERE ARE THE REPORTS FROM THE RESEARCH STAFF.
THANK YOU.
TURN
WELL, THEN...
FREEZE
WHERE DID YOU GO?
WHAT DO YOU MEAN?
I MEAN... YESTER-DAY.
ARE YOU GRILLING ME FOR DETAILS ABOUT MY DAY OFF...?
WHAT ARE YOU, MY FATHER?
WHOA, WHOA. I DON'T HAVE ANY DAUGHTERS.

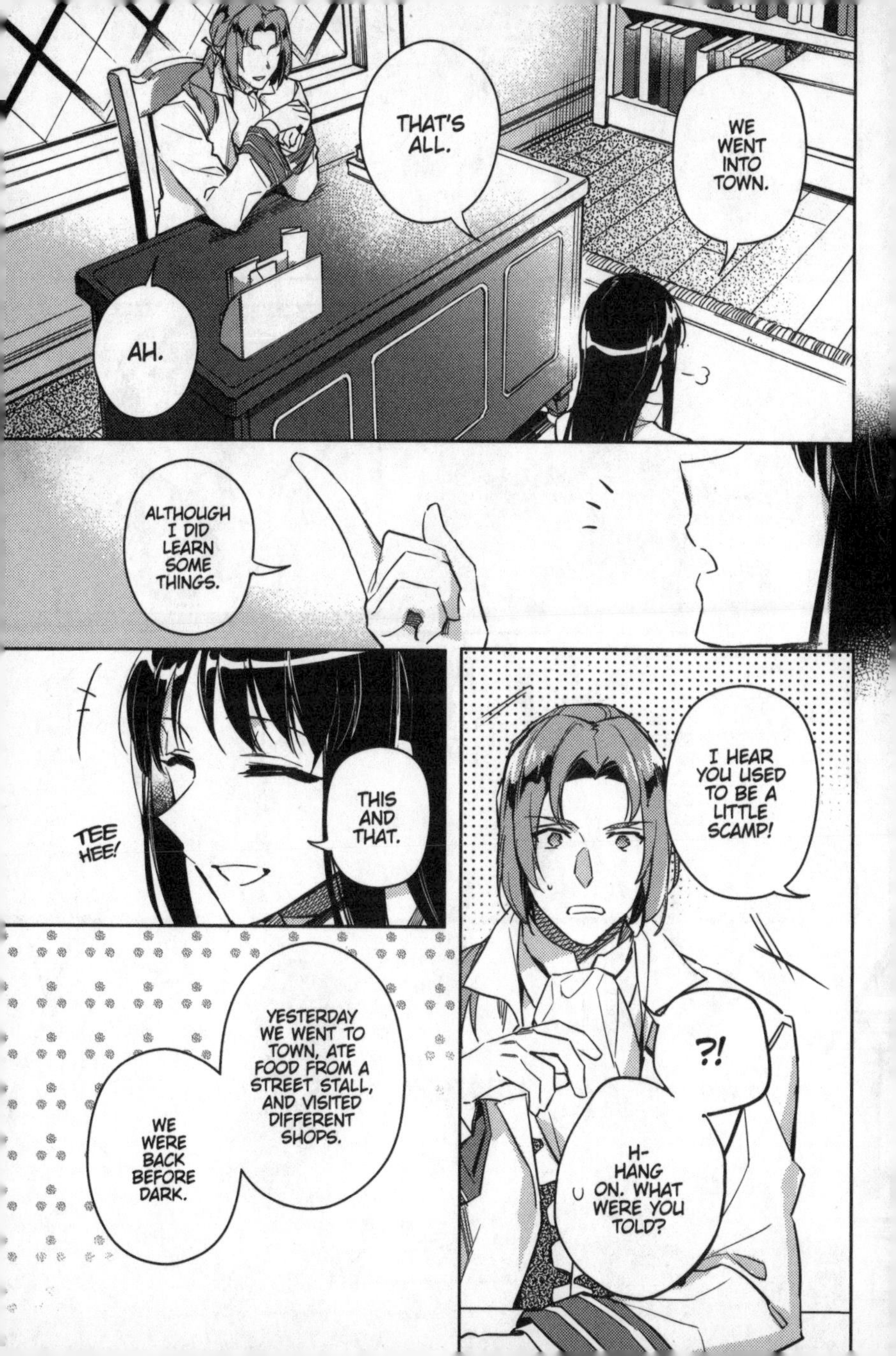
WE WENT INTO TOWN.
THAT'S ALL.
AH.
ALTHOUGH I DID LEARN SOME THINGS.
I HEAR YOU USED TO BE A LITTLE SCAMP!
?!
H-HANG ON. WHAT WERE YOU TOLD?
THIS AND THAT.
TEE HEE!
YESTERDAY WE WENT TO TOWN, ATE FOOD FROM A STREET STALL, AND VISITED DIFFERENT SHOPS.
WE WERE BACK BEFORE DARK.

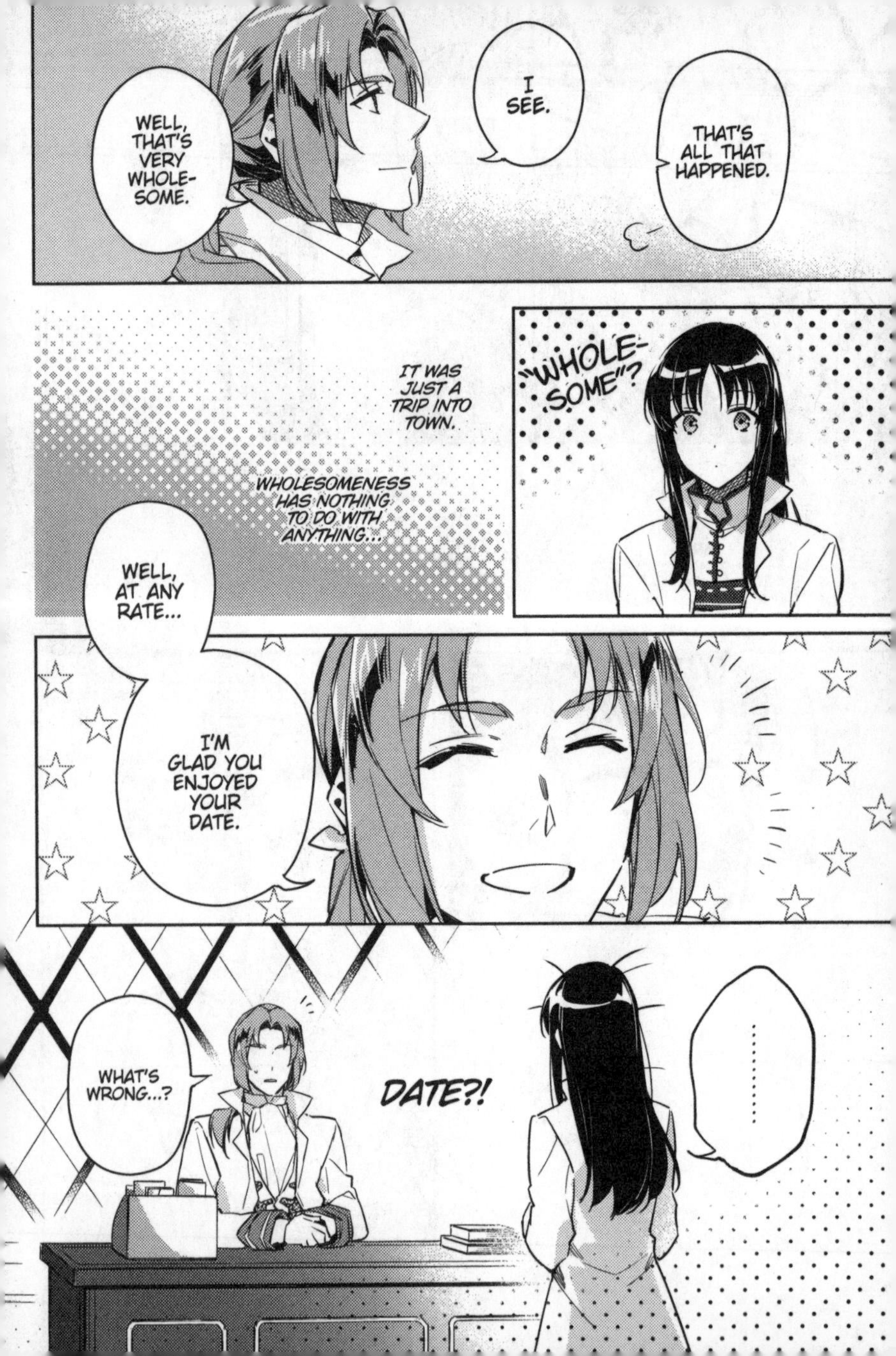
THAT'S ALL THAT HAPPENED.
I SEE.
WELL, THAT'S VERY WHOLE-SOME.
"WHOLE-SOME"?
IT WAS JUST A TRIP INTO TOWN.
WHOLESOMENESS HAS NOTHING TO DO WITH ANYTHING...
WELL, AT ANY RATE...
I'M GLAD YOU ENJOYED YOUR DATE.
......
DATE?!
WHAT'S WRONG...?

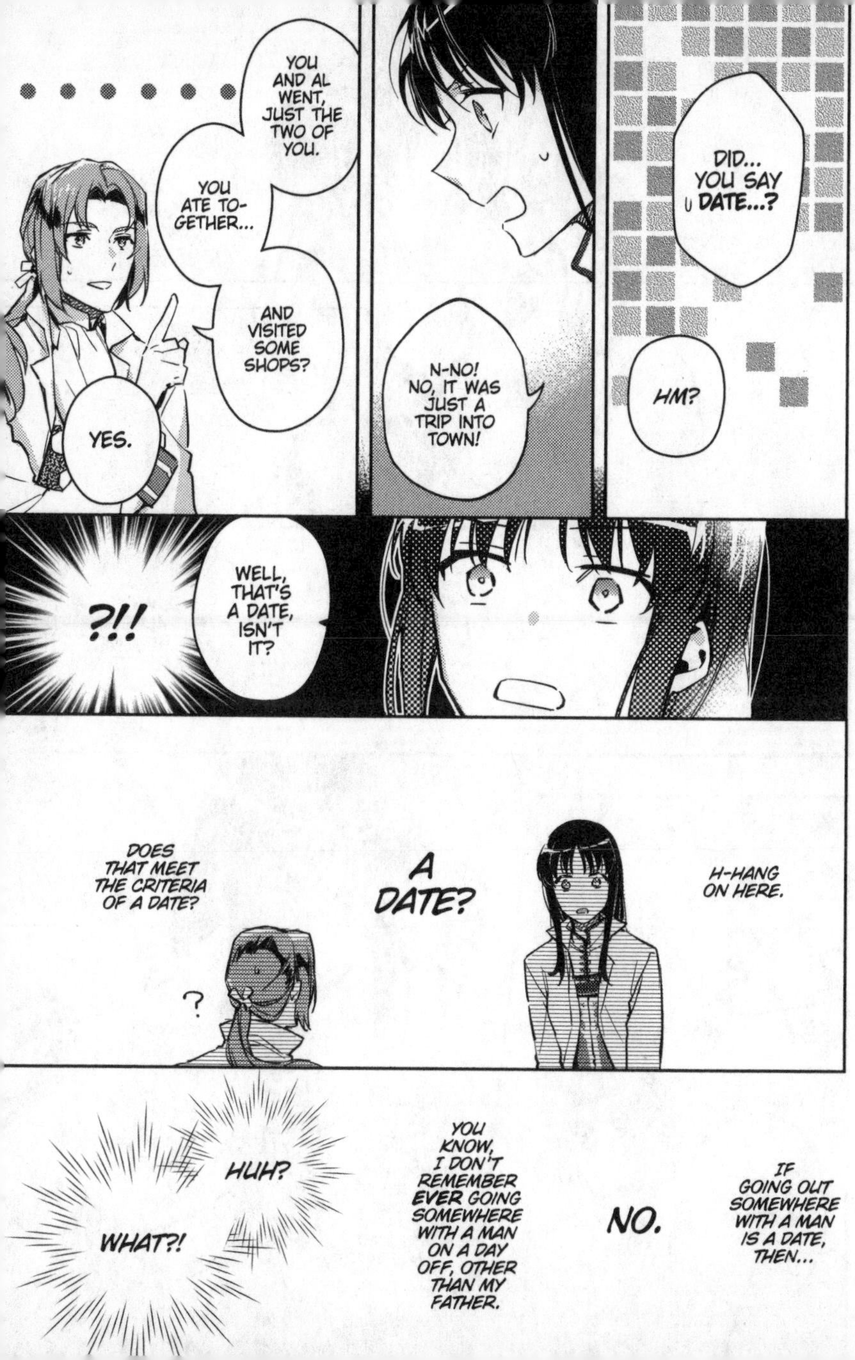
DID... YOU SAY DATE...?
HM?
N-NO! NO, IT WAS JUST A TRIP INTO TOWN!
YOU AND AL WENT, JUST THE TWO OF YOU.
YOU ATE TO-GETHER...
AND VISITED SOME SHOPS?
YES.
• • • • • •
WELL, THAT'S A DATE, ISN'T IT?
?!!
H-HANG ON HERE.
A DATE?
DOES THAT MEET THE CRITERIA OF A DATE?
?
IF GOING OUT SOMEWHERE WITH A MAN IS A DATE, THEN...
NO.
YOU KNOW, I DON'T REMEMBER EVER GOING SOMEWHERE WITH A MAN ON A DAY OFF, OTHER THAN MY FATHER.
HUH?
WHAT?!

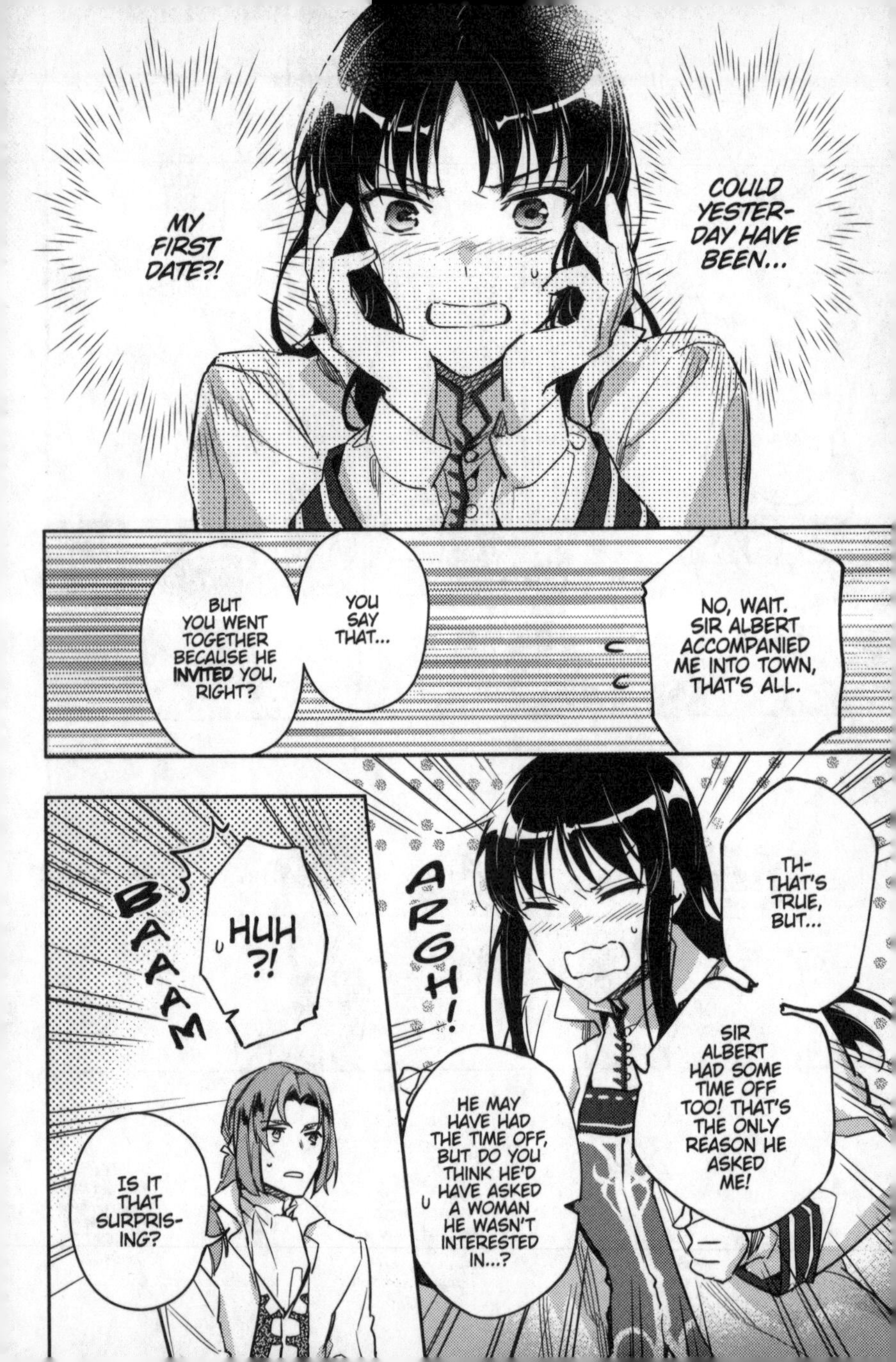
COULD YESTERDAY HAVE BEEN...
MY FIRST DATE?!
NO, WAIT. SIR ALBERT ACCOMPANIED ME INTO TOWN, THAT'S ALL.
YOU SAY THAT...
BUT YOU WENT TOGETHER BECAUSE HE INVITED YOU, RIGHT?
TH-THAT'S TRUE, BUT...
ARGH!
SIR ALBERT HAD SOME TIME OFF TOO! THAT'S THE ONLY REASON HE ASKED ME!
HE MAY HAVE HAD THE TIME OFF, BUT DO YOU THINK HE'D HAVE ASKED A WOMAN HE WASN'T INTERESTED IN...?
BAAAM
HUH?!
IS IT THAT SURPRISING?

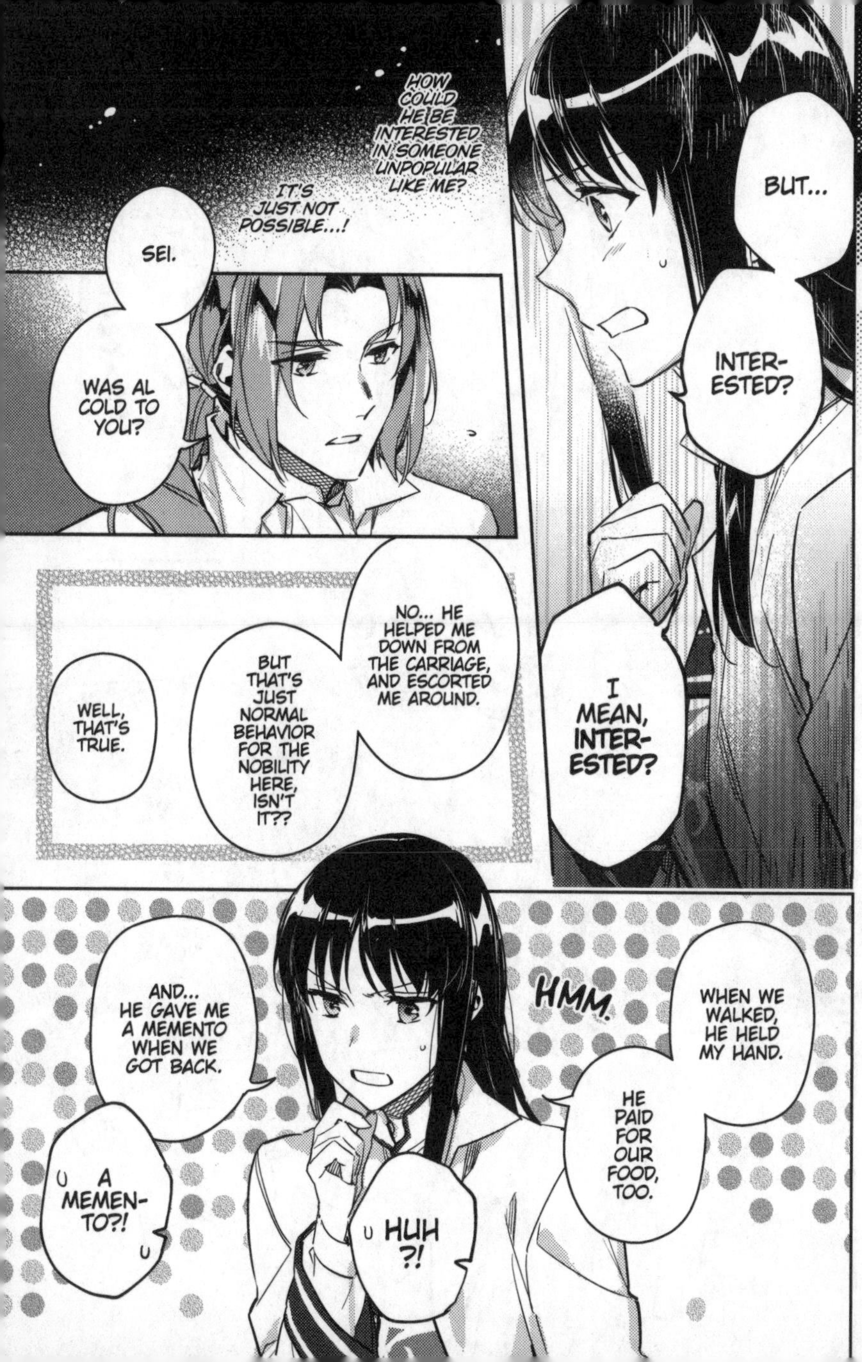

BUT...
INTERESTED?
I MEAN, INTERESTED?
HOW COULD HE BE INTERESTED IN SOMEONE UNPOPULAR LIKE ME?
IT'S JUST NOT POSSIBLE...!
SEI.
WAS AL COLD TO YOU?
NO... HE HELPED ME DOWN FROM THE CARRIAGE, AND ESCORTED ME AROUND.
BUT THAT'S JUST NORMAL BEHAVIOR FOR THE NOBILITY HERE, ISN'T IT??
WELL, THAT'S TRUE.
WHEN WE WALKED, HE HELD MY HAND.
HE PAID FOR OUR FOOD, TOO.
HMM.
AND... HE GAVE ME A MEMENTO WHEN WE GOT BACK.
HUH?!
A MEMENTO?!

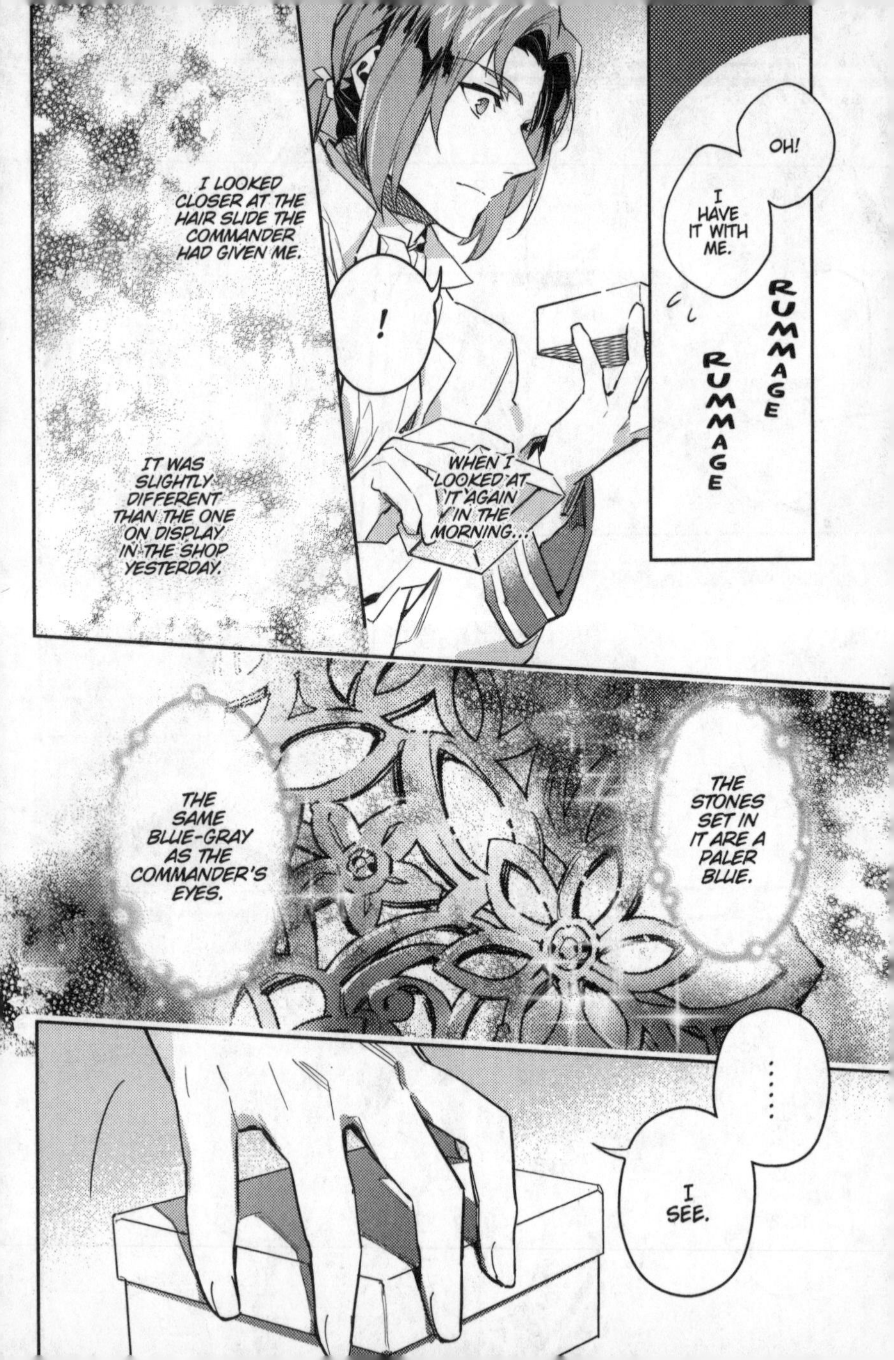
OH!
I HAVE IT WITH ME.
RUMMAGE
RUMMAGE
I LOOKED CLOSER AT THE HAIR SLIDE THE COMMANDER HAD GIVEN ME.
!
WHEN I LOOKED AT IT AGAIN IN THE MORNING...
IT WAS SLIGHTLY DIFFERENT THAN THE ONE ON DISPLAY IN THE SHOP YESTERDAY.
THE STONES SET IN IT ARE A PALER BLUE.
THE SAME BLUE-GRAY AS THE COMMANDER'S EYES.
......
I SEE.

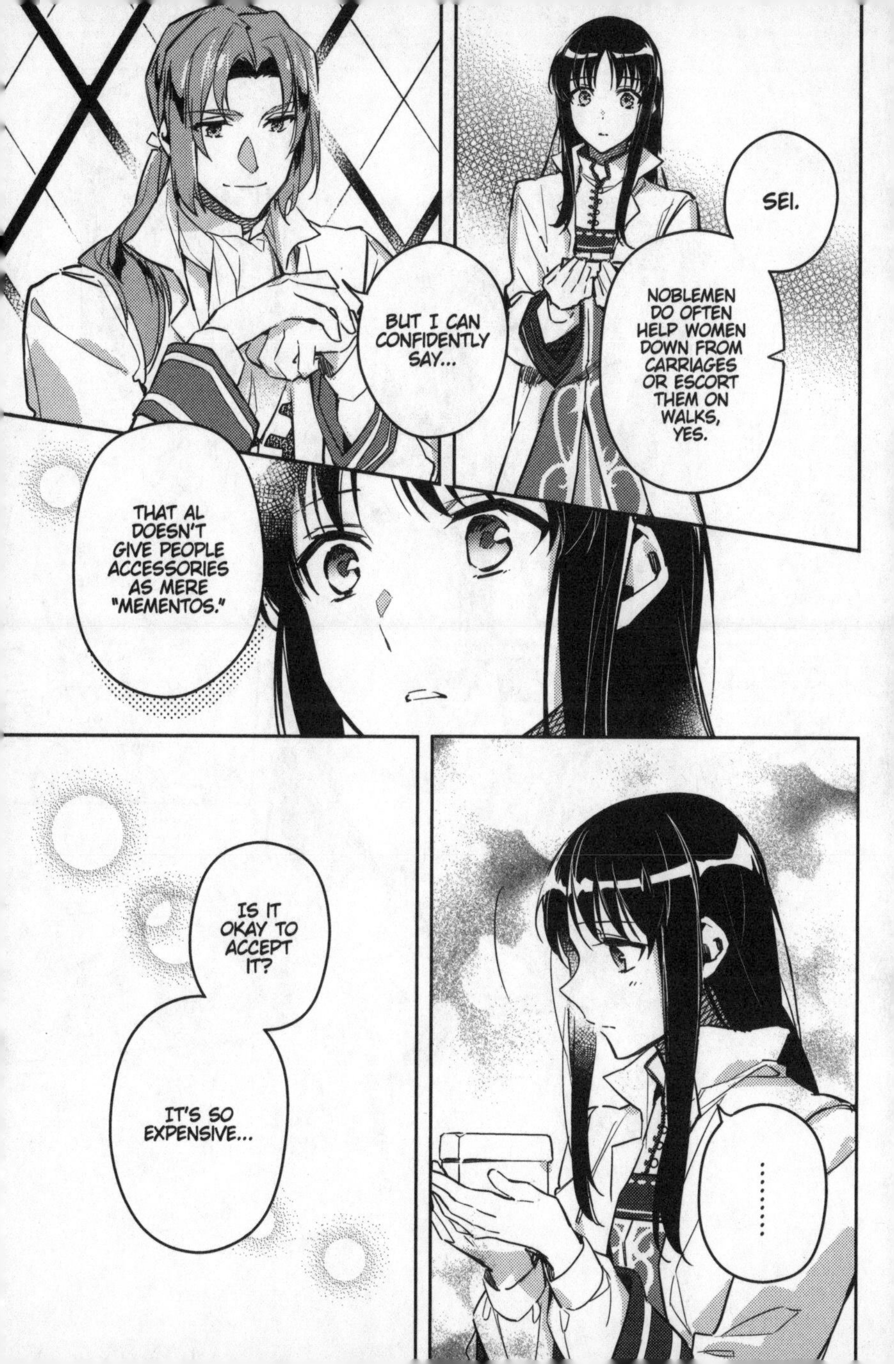
SEI.
NOBLEMEN DO OFTEN HELP WOMEN DOWN FROM CARRIAGES OR ESCORT THEM ON WALKS, YES.
BUT I CAN CONFIDENTLY SAY...
THAT AL DOESN'T GIVE PEOPLE ACCESSORIES AS MERE "MEMENTOS."
......
IS IT OKAY TO ACCEPT IT?
IT'S SO EXPENSIVE...

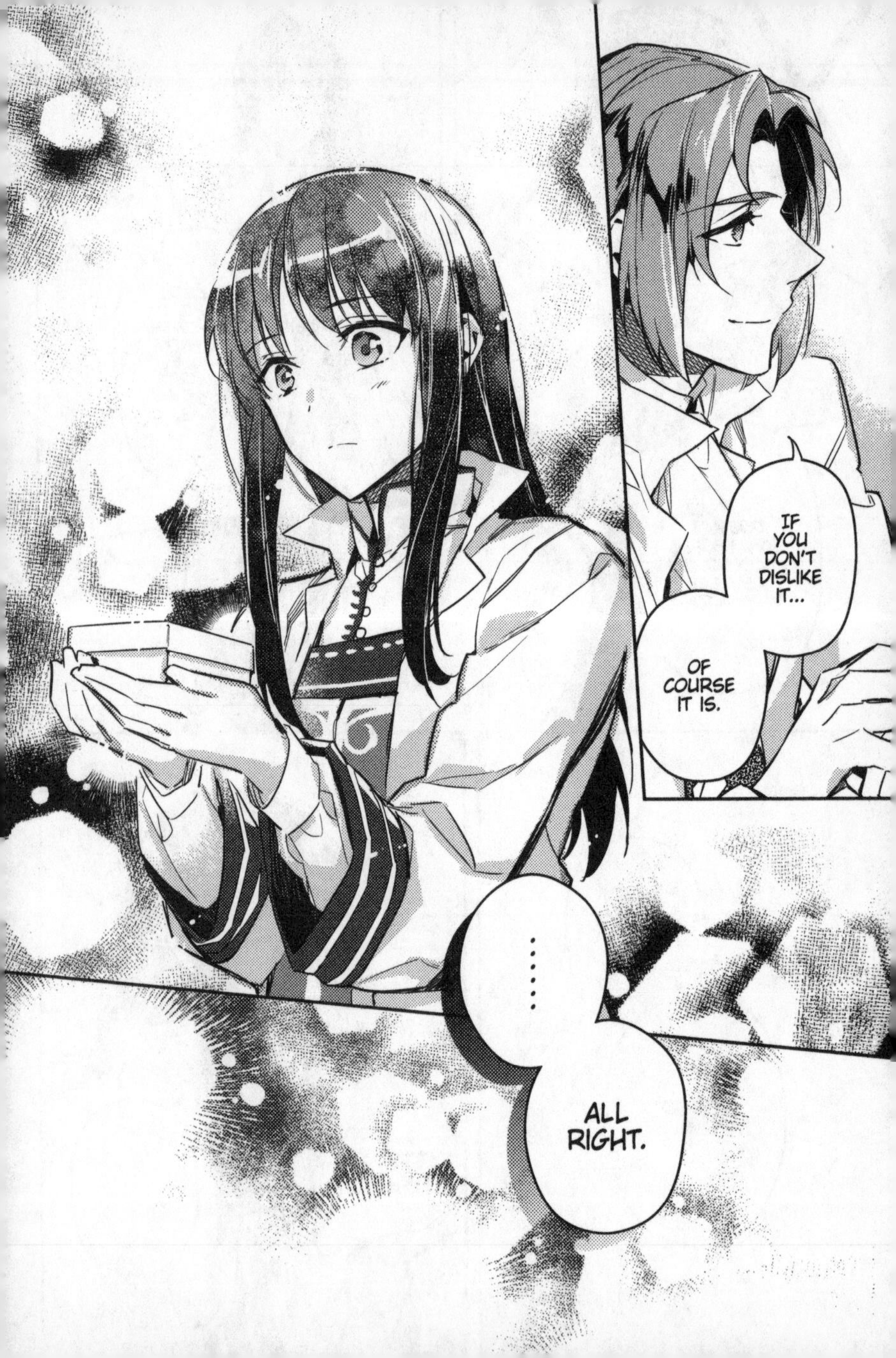
IF YOU DON'T DISLIKE IT...
OF COURSE IT IS.
......
ALL RIGHT.

The Saint's
Magic Power is
Omnipotent

The Saint's
Magic Power is
Omnipotent

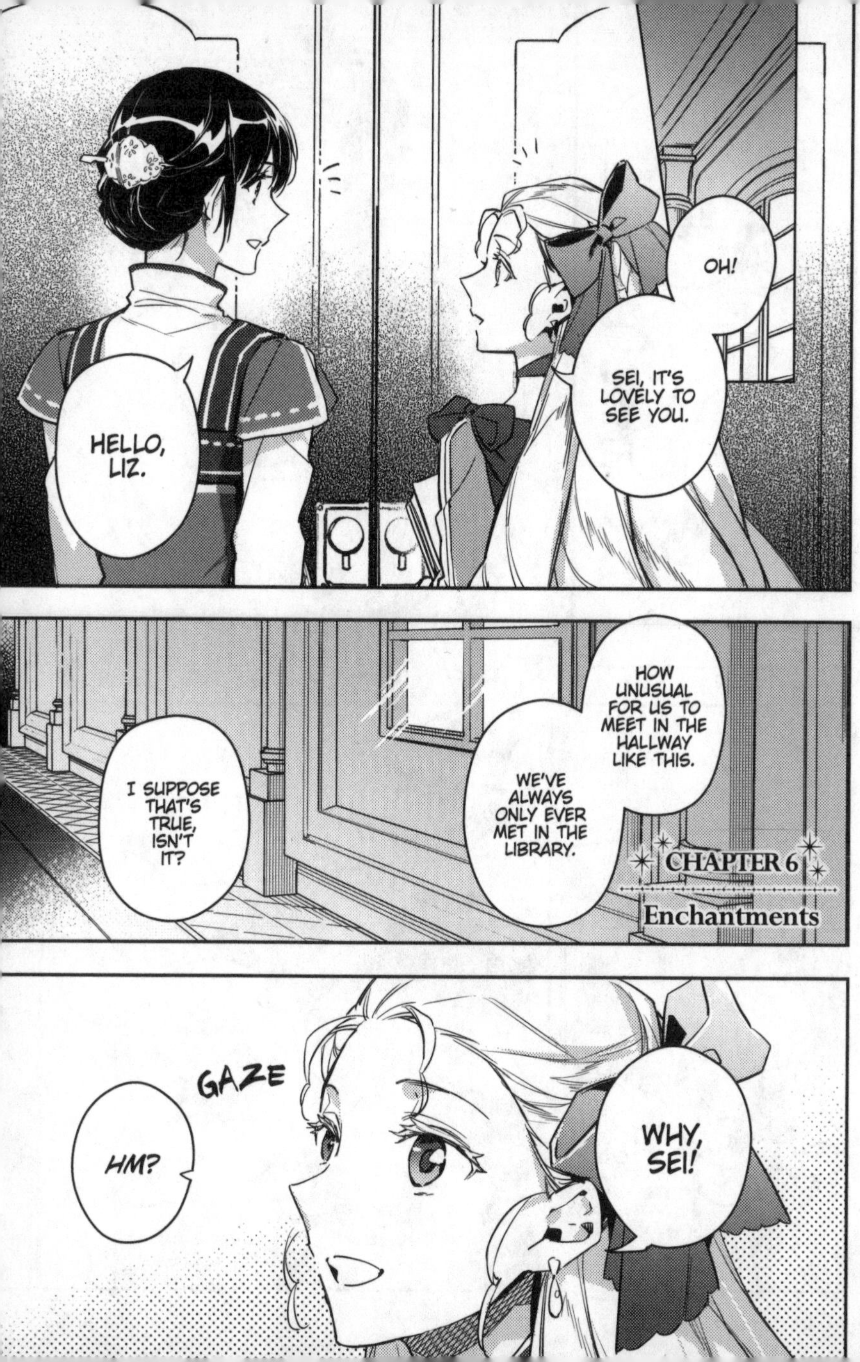
OH!
SEI, IT'S LOVELY TO SEE YOU.
HELLO, LIZ.
HOW UNUSUAL FOR US TO MEET IN THE HALLWAY LIKE THIS.
WE'VE ALWAYS ONLY EVER MET IN THE LIBRARY.
I SUPPOSE THAT'S TRUE, ISN'T IT?
CHAPTER 6
Enchantments
WHY, SEI!
GAZE
HM?

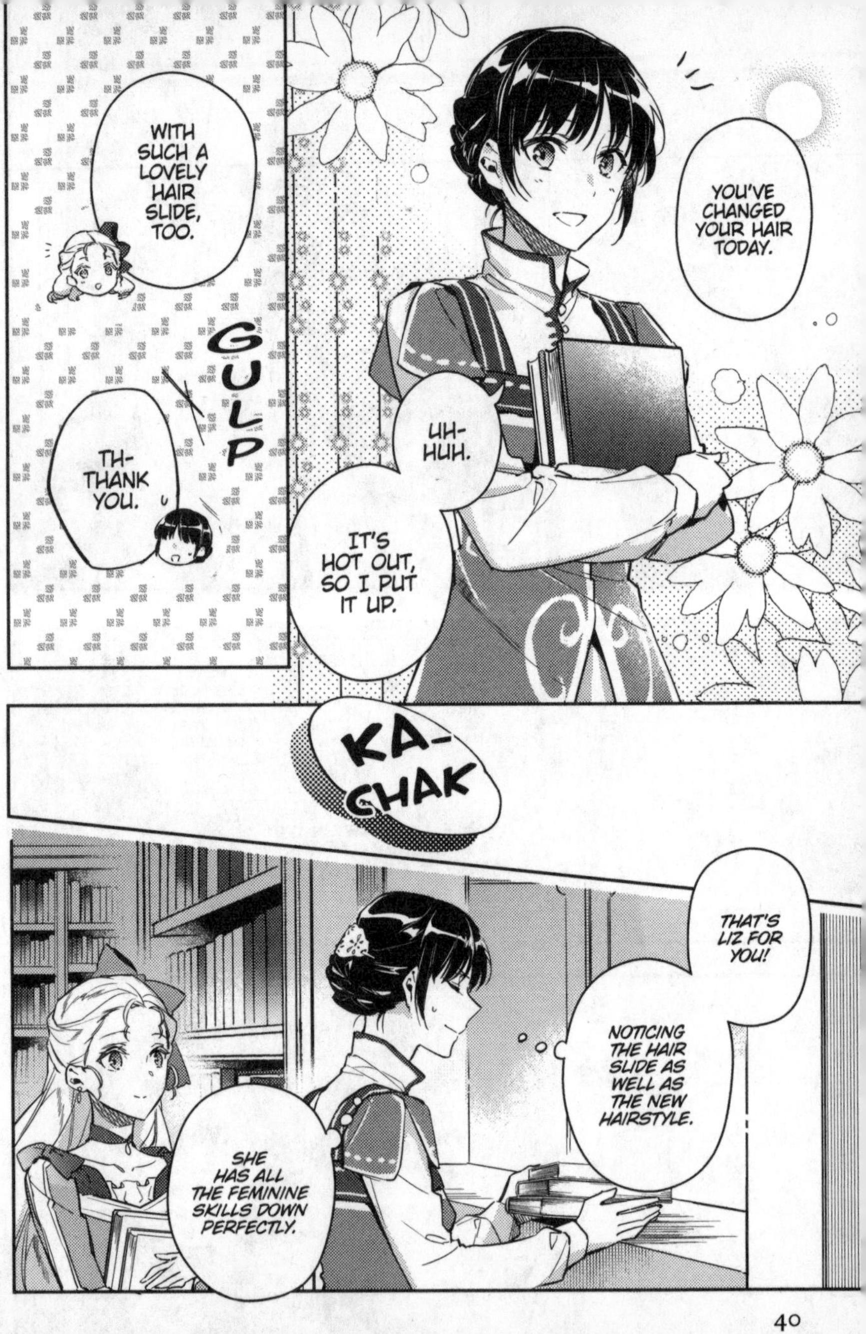
YOU'VE CHANGED YOUR HAIR TODAY.
UH-HUH.
IT'S HOT OUT, SO I PUT IT UP.
WITH SUCH A LOVELY HAIR SLIDE, TOO.
GULP
TH-THANK YOU.
KA-CHAK
THAT'S LIZ FOR YOU!
NOTICING THE HAIR SLIDE AS WELL AS THE NEW HAIRSTYLE.
SHE HAS ALL THE FEMININE SKILLS DOWN PERFECTLY.

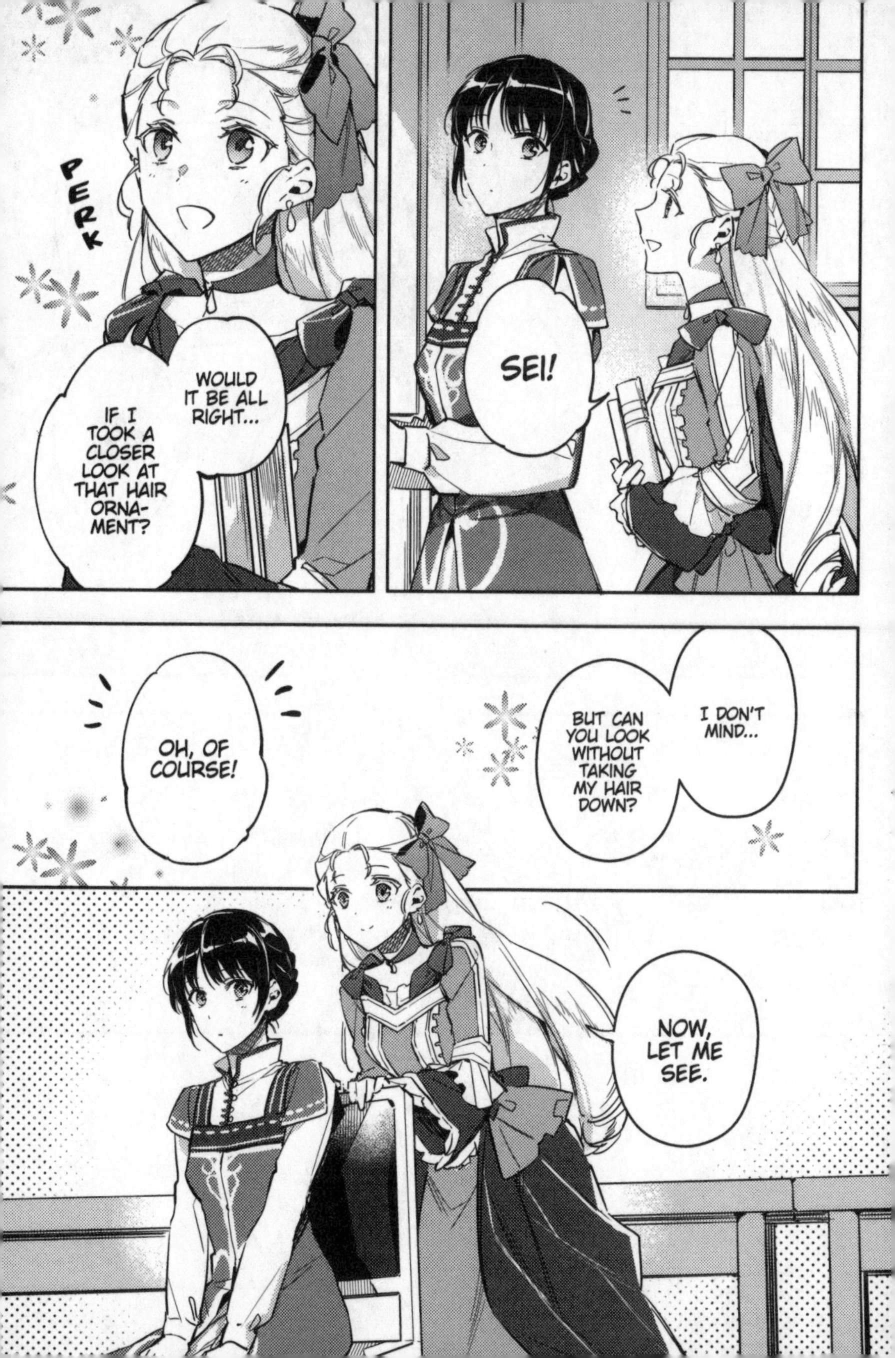
SEI!
PERK
WOULD IT BE ALL RIGHT...
IF I TOOK A CLOSER LOOK AT THAT HAIR ORNA-MENT?
I DON'T MIND...
BUT CAN YOU LOOK WITHOUT TAKING MY HAIR DOWN?
OH, OF COURSE!
NOW, LET ME SEE.

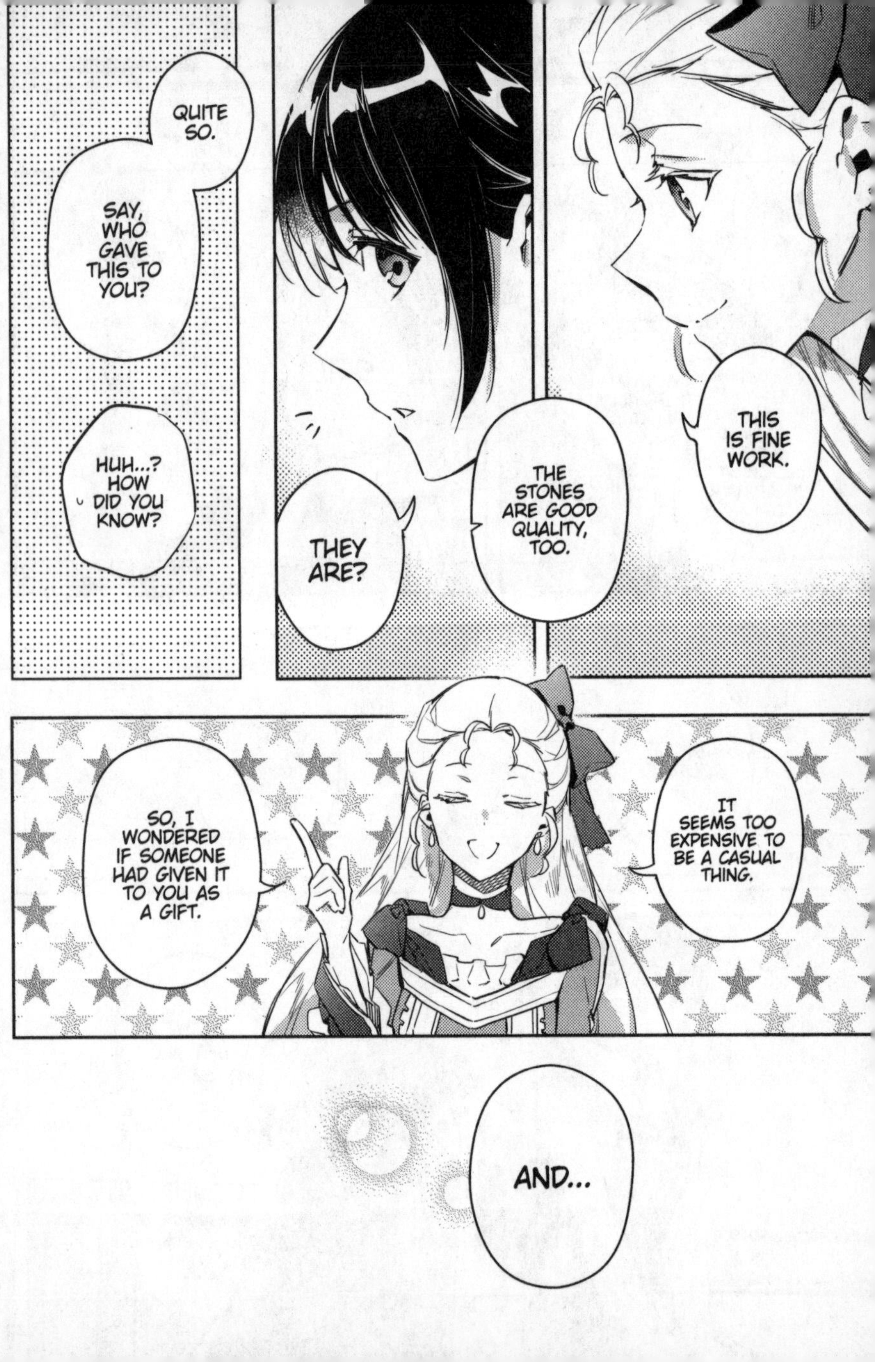
THIS IS FINE WORK.
THE STONES ARE GOOD QUALITY, TOO.
THEY ARE?
QUITE SO.
SAY, WHO GAVE THIS TO YOU?
HUH...? HOW DID YOU KNOW?
IT SEEMS TOO EXPENSIVE TO BE A CASUAL THING.
SO, I WONDERED IF SOMEONE HAD GIVEN IT TO YOU AS A GIFT.
AND...

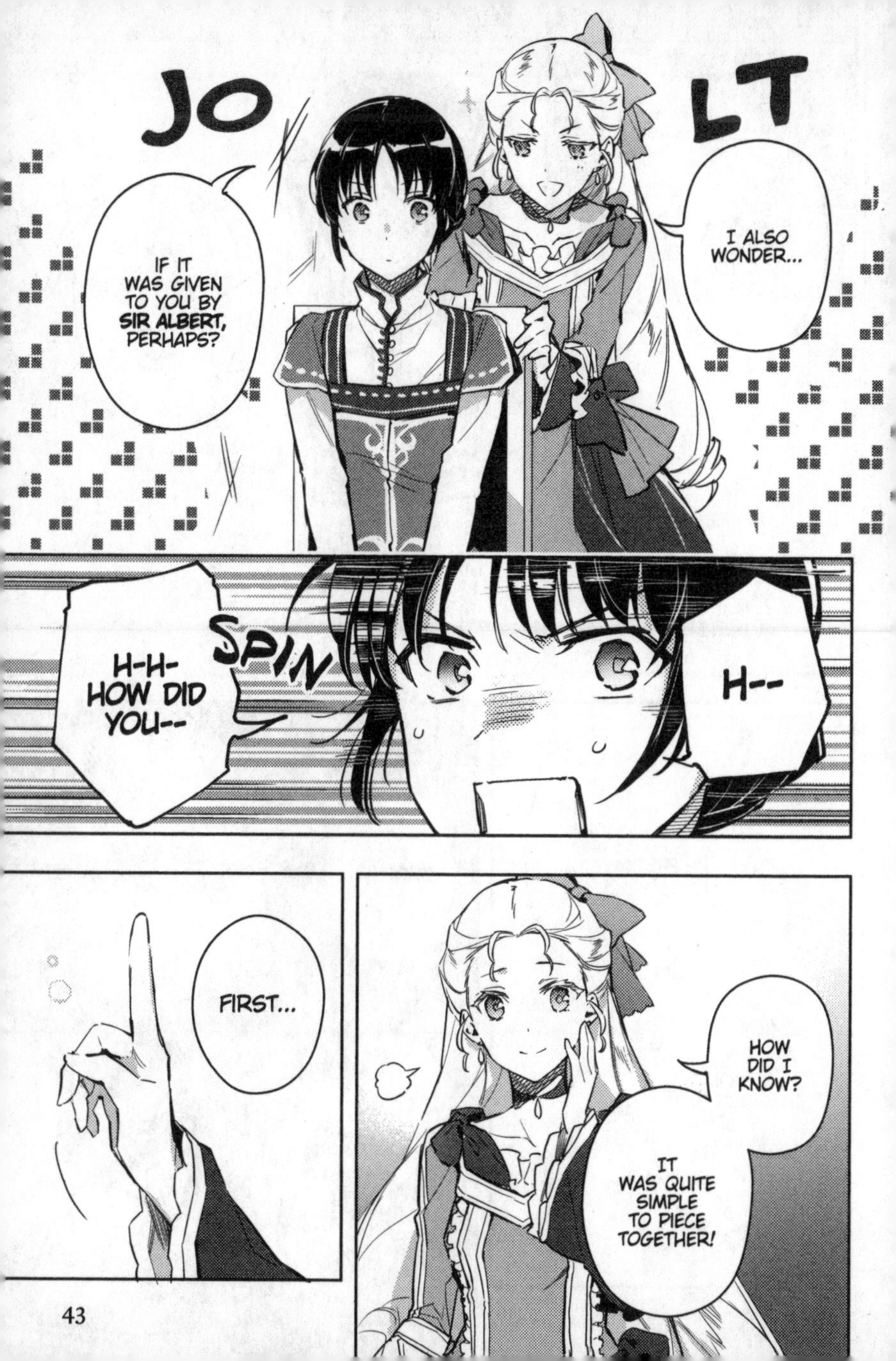
JOLT
I ALSO WONDER...
IF IT WAS GIVEN TO YOU BY SIR ALBERT, PERHAPS?
H--
SPIN
H-H-HOW DID YOU--
HOW DID I KNOW?
IT WAS QUITE SIMPLE TO PIECE TOGETHER!
FIRST...

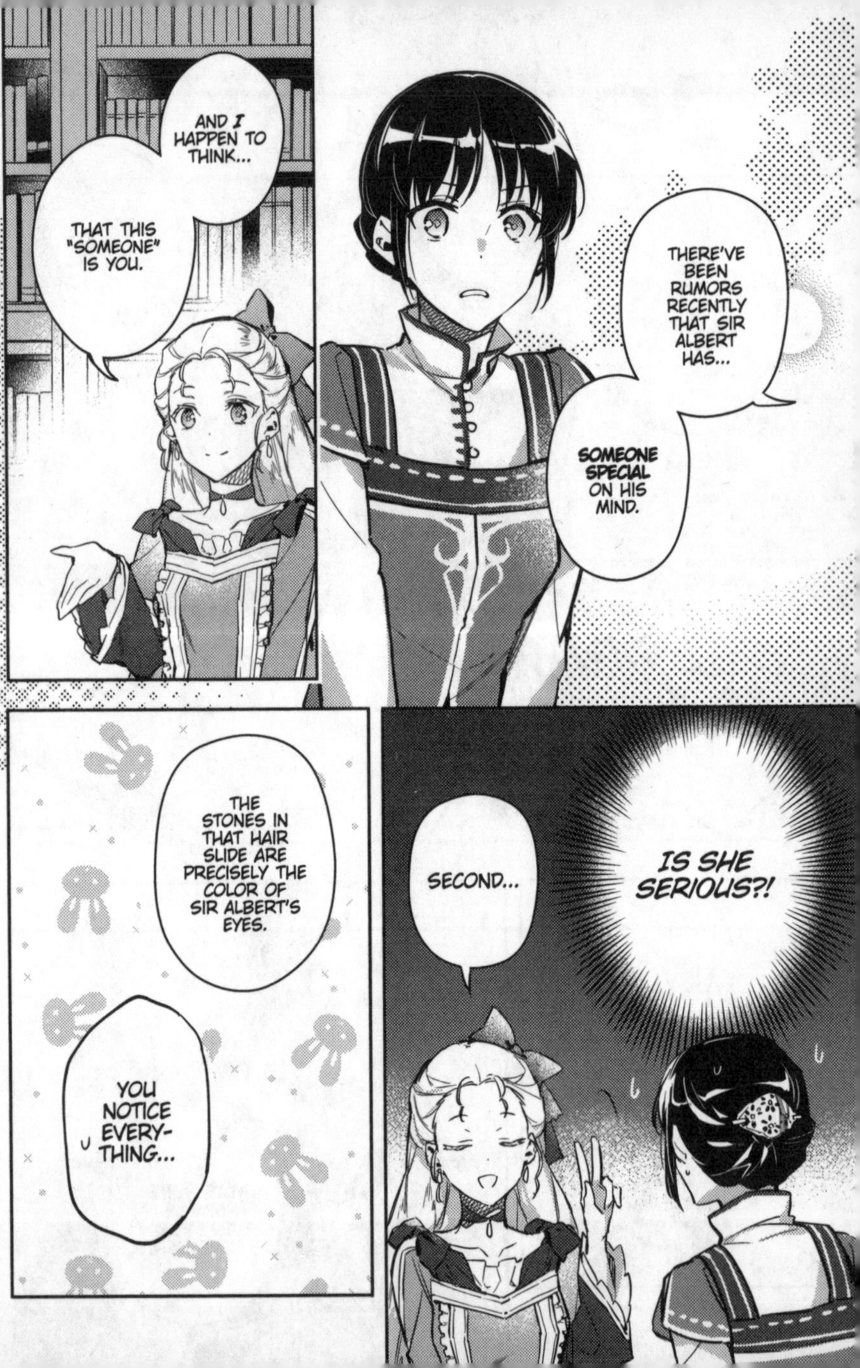
THERE'VE BEEN RUMORS RECENTLY THAT SIR ALBERT HAS...
SOMEONE SPECIAL ON HIS MIND.
AND I HAPPEN TO THINK...
THAT THIS "SOMEONE" IS YOU.
IS SHE SERIOUS?!
SECOND...
THE STONES IN THAT HAIR SLIDE ARE PRECISELY THE COLOR OF SIR ALBERT'S EYES.
YOU NOTICE EVERY-THING...

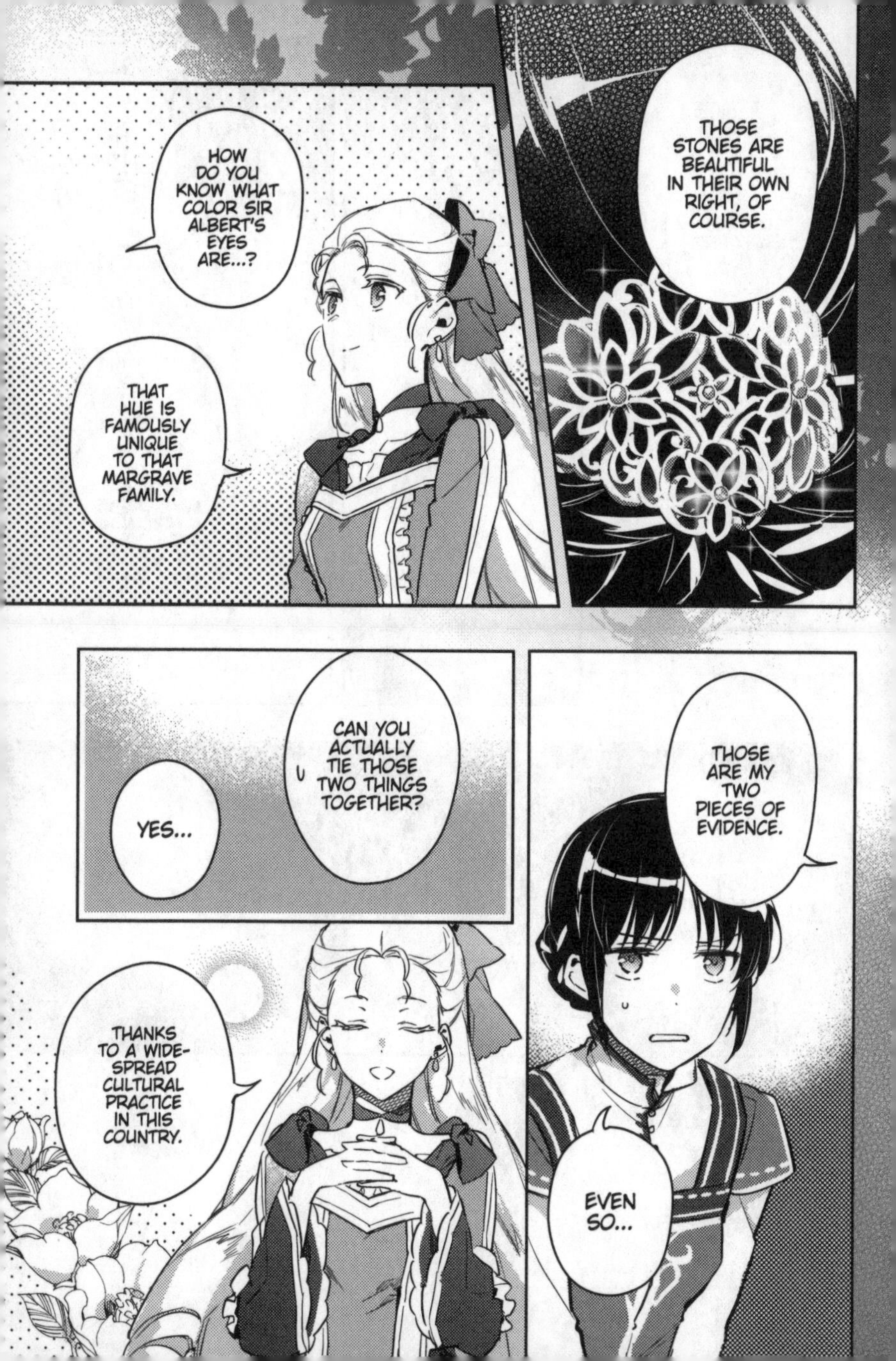
THOSE STONES ARE BEAUTIFUL IN THEIR OWN RIGHT, OF COURSE.
HOW DO YOU KNOW WHAT COLOR SIR ALBERT'S EYES ARE...?
THAT HUE IS FAMOUSLY UNIQUE TO THAT MARGRAVE FAMILY.
THOSE ARE MY TWO PIECES OF EVIDENCE.
EVEN SO...
CAN YOU ACTUALLY TIE THOSE TWO THINGS TOGETHER?
YES...
THANKS TO A WIDE-SPREAD CULTURAL PRACTICE IN THIS COUNTRY.

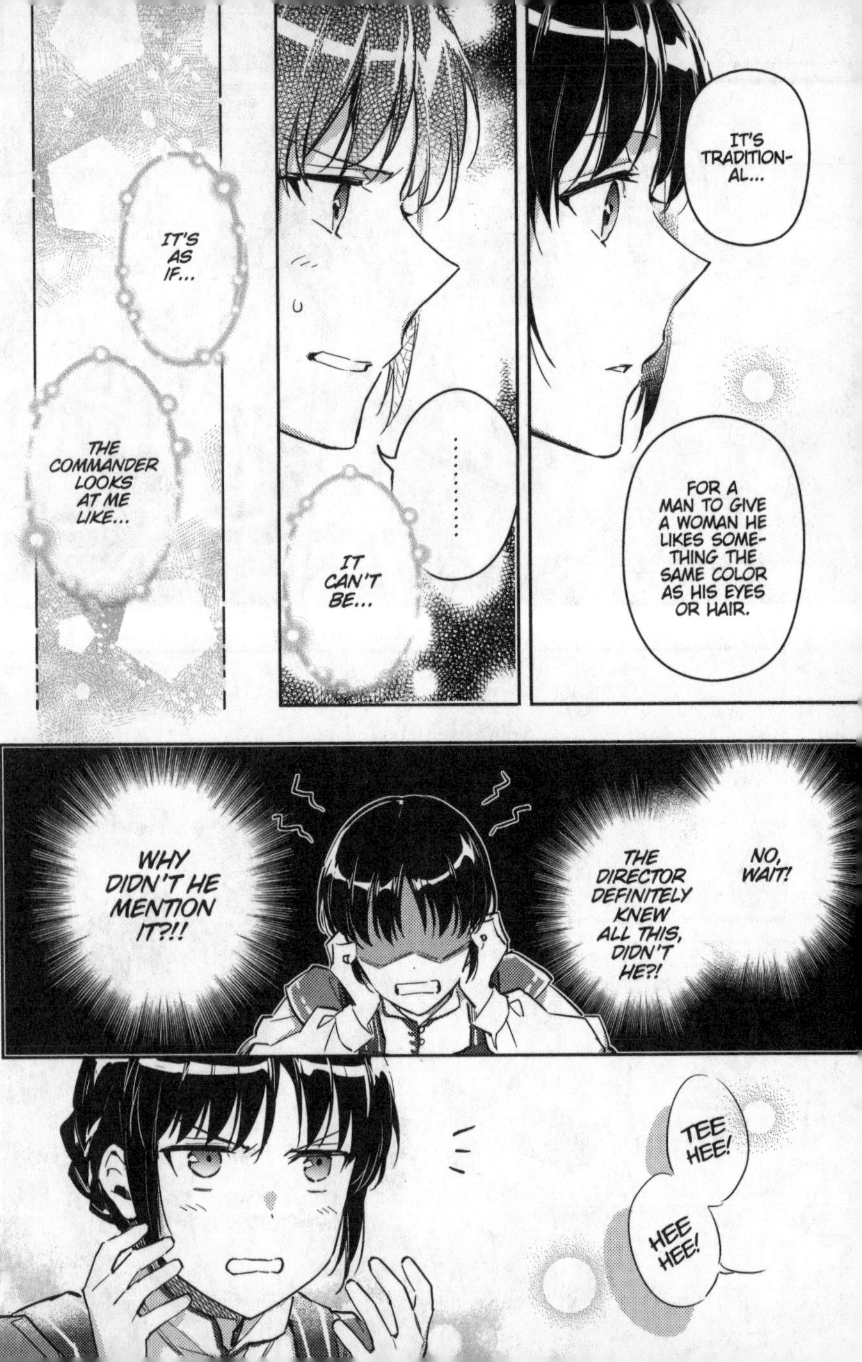
IT'S TRADITION-AL...
FOR A MAN TO GIVE A WOMAN HE LIKES SOME-THING THE SAME COLOR AS HIS EYES OR HAIR.
......
IT CAN'T BE...
IT'S AS IF...
THE COMMANDER LOOKS AT ME LIKE...
NO, WAIT!
THE DIRECTOR DEFINITELY KNEW ALL THIS, DIDN'T HE?!
WHY DIDN'T HE MENTION IT?!!
TEE HEE!
HEE HEE!

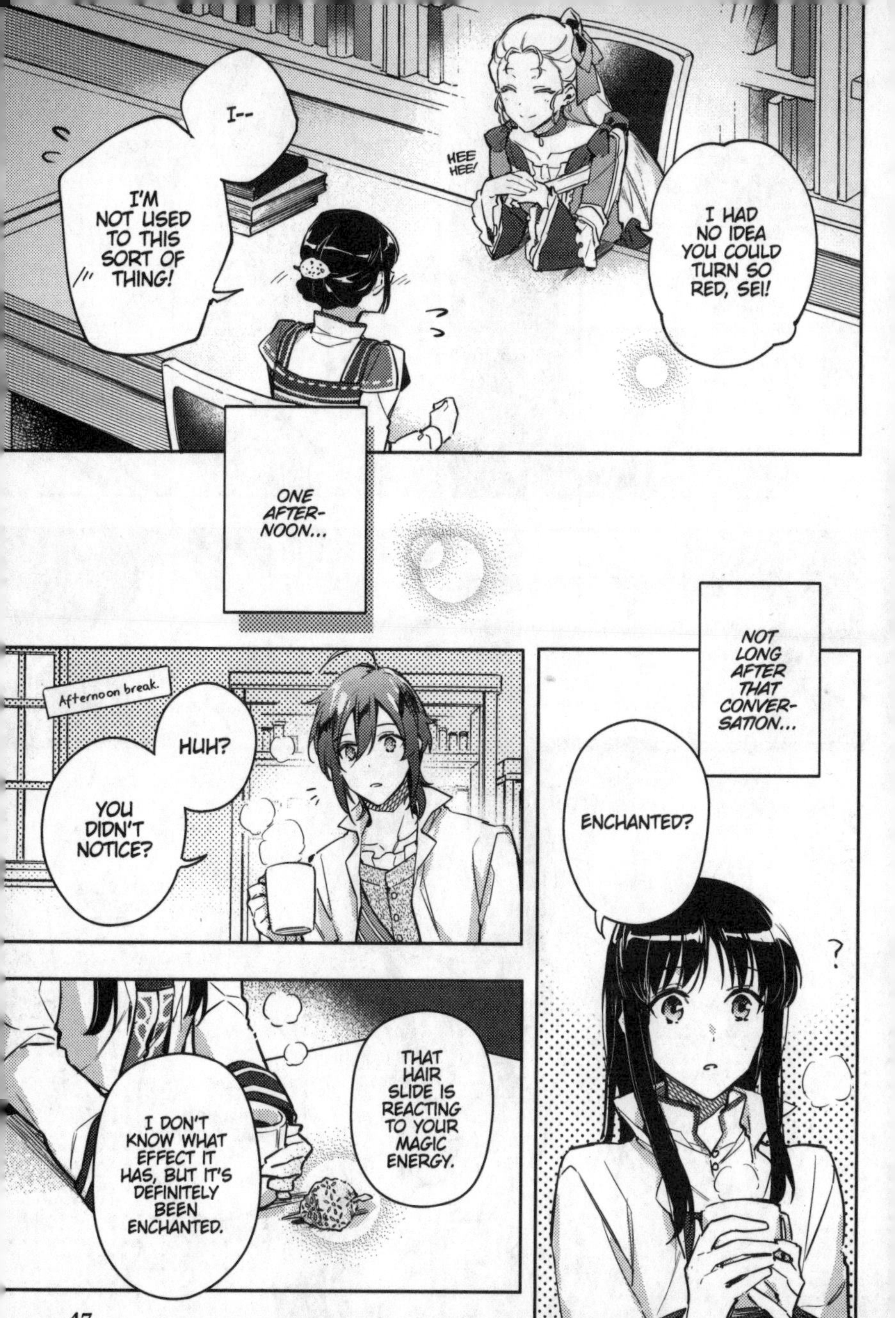
I HAD NO IDEA YOU COULD TURN SO RED, SEI!
HEE HEE!
I--
I'M NOT USED TO THIS SORT OF THING!
ONE AFTERNOON...
NOT LONG AFTER THAT CONVERSATION...
ENCHANTED?
?
Afternoon break.
HUH?
YOU DIDN'T NOTICE?
THAT HAIR SLIDE IS REACTING TO YOUR MAGIC ENERGY.
I DON'T KNOW WHAT EFFECT IT HAS, BUT IT'S DEFINITELY BEEN ENCHANTED.

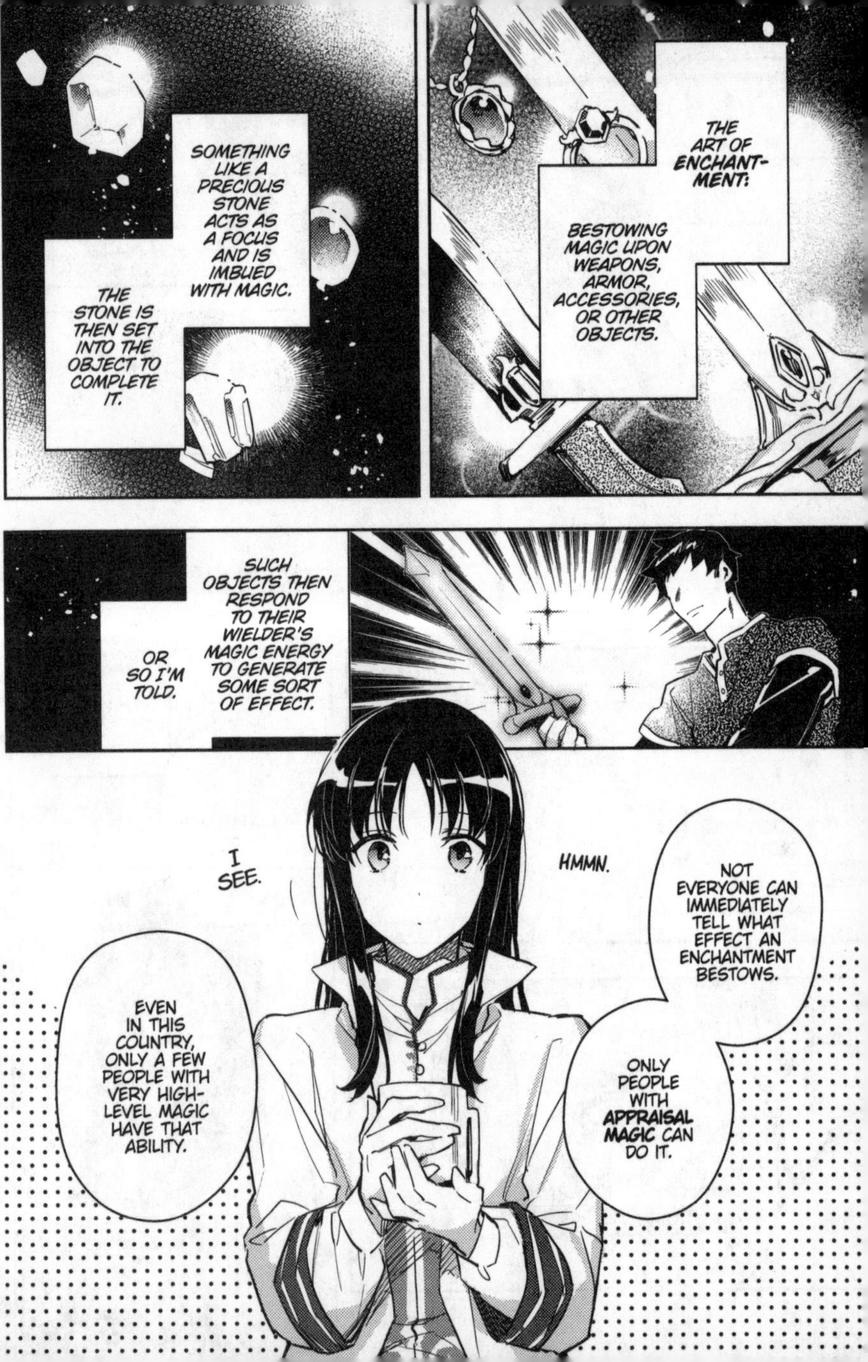

THE ART OF ENCHANTMENT:
BESTOWING MAGIC UPON WEAPONS, ARMOR, ACCESSORIES, OR OTHER OBJECTS.
SOMETHING LIKE A PRECIOUS STONE ACTS AS A FOCUS AND IS IMBUED WITH MAGIC.
THE STONE IS THEN SET INTO THE OBJECT TO COMPLETE IT.
SUCH OBJECTS THEN RESPOND TO THEIR WIELDER'S MAGIC ENERGY TO GENERATE SOME SORT OF EFFECT.
OR SO I'M TOLD.
NOT EVERYONE CAN IMMEDIATELY TELL WHAT EFFECT AN ENCHANTMENT BESTOWS.
HMMN.
I SEE.
ONLY PEOPLE WITH APPRAISAL MAGIC CAN DO IT.
EVEN IN THIS COUNTRY, ONLY A FEW PEOPLE WITH VERY HIGH-LEVEL MAGIC HAVE THAT ABILITY.

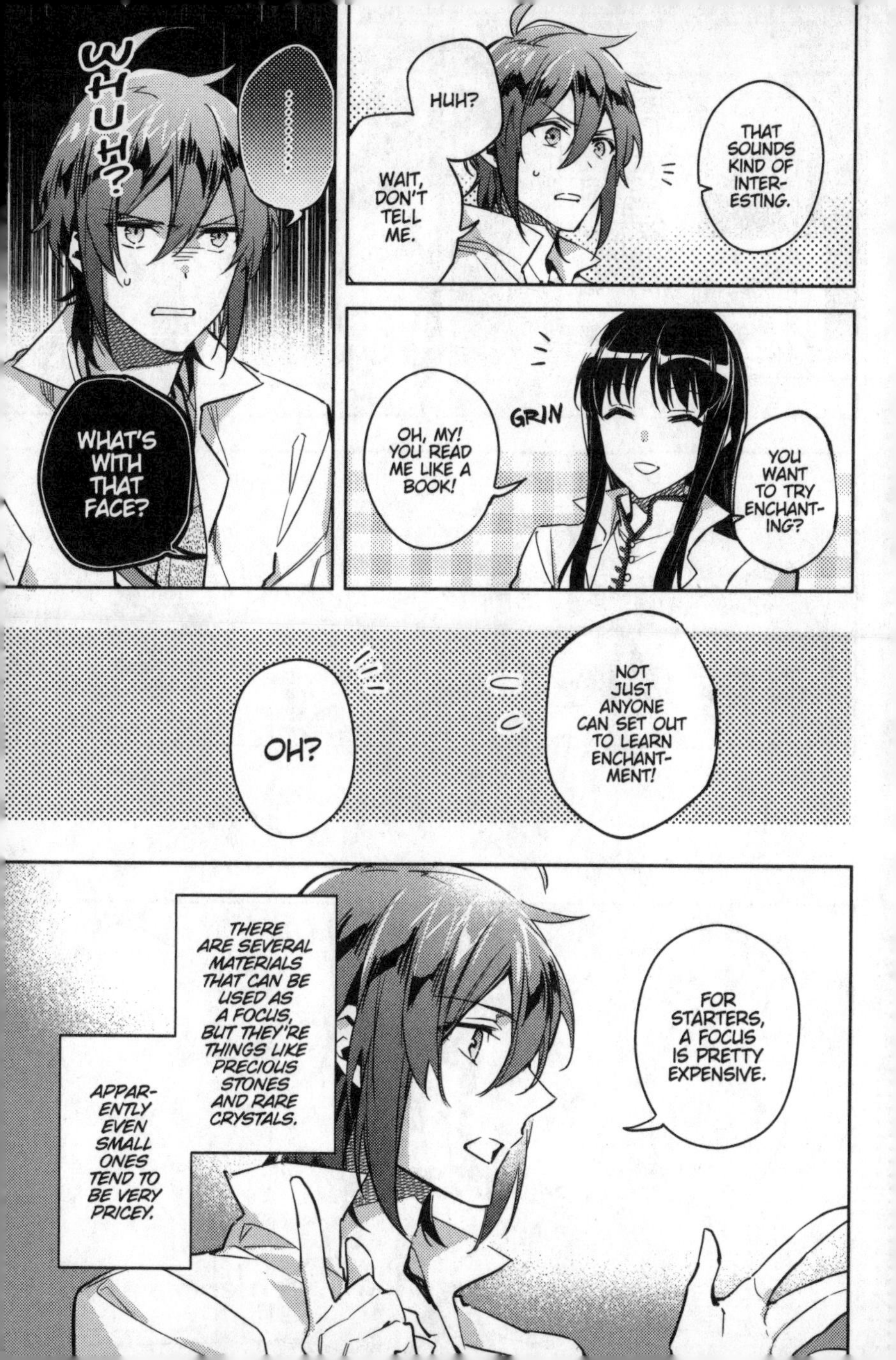
THAT SOUNDS KIND OF INTER-ESTING.
HUH?
WAIT, DON'T TELL ME.
YOU WANT TO TRY ENCHANT-ING?
GRIN
OH, MY! YOU READ ME LIKE A BOOK!
....
WHUH?
WHAT'S WITH THAT FACE?
NOT JUST ANYONE CAN SET OUT TO LEARN ENCHANT-MENT!
OH?
FOR STARTERS, A FOCUS IS PRETTY EXPENSIVE.
THERE ARE SEVERAL MATERIALS THAT CAN BE USED AS A FOCUS, BUT THEY'RE THINGS LIKE PRECIOUS STONES AND RARE CRYSTALS.
APPAR-ENTLY EVEN SMALL ONES TEND TO BE VERY PRICEY.

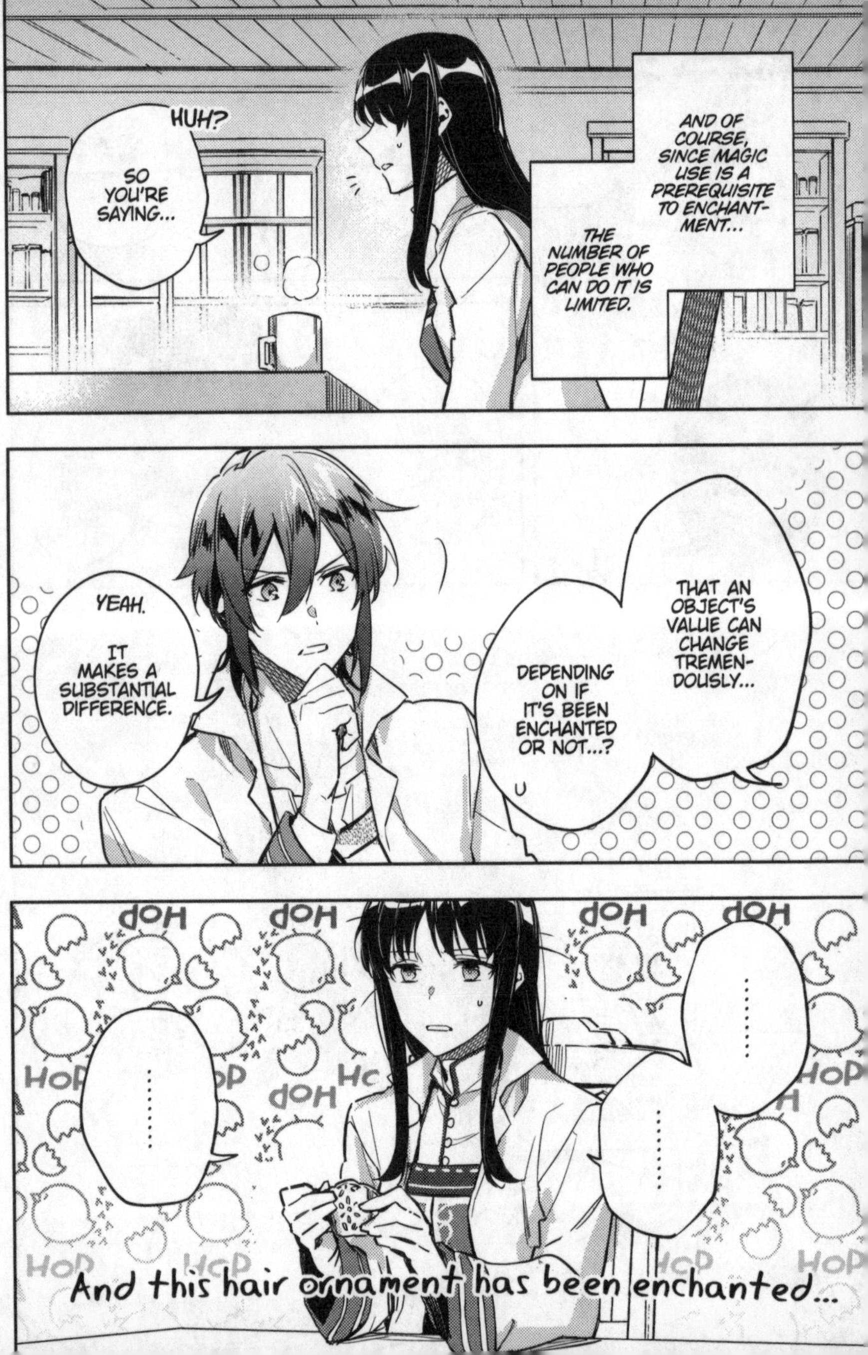
AND OF COURSE, SINCE MAGIC USE IS A PREREQUISITE TO ENCHANT-MENT...
THE NUMBER OF PEOPLE WHO CAN DO IT IS LIMITED.
HUH?
SO YOU'RE SAYING...
THAT AN OBJECT'S VALUE CAN CHANGE TREMEN-DOUSLY...
DEPENDING ON IF IT'S BEEN ENCHANTED OR NOT...?
YEAH.
IT MAKES A SUBSTANTIAL DIFFERENCE.
......
......
......
HOP HOP HOP HOP HOP HOP HOP HOP HOP HOP
And this hair ornament has been enchanted...

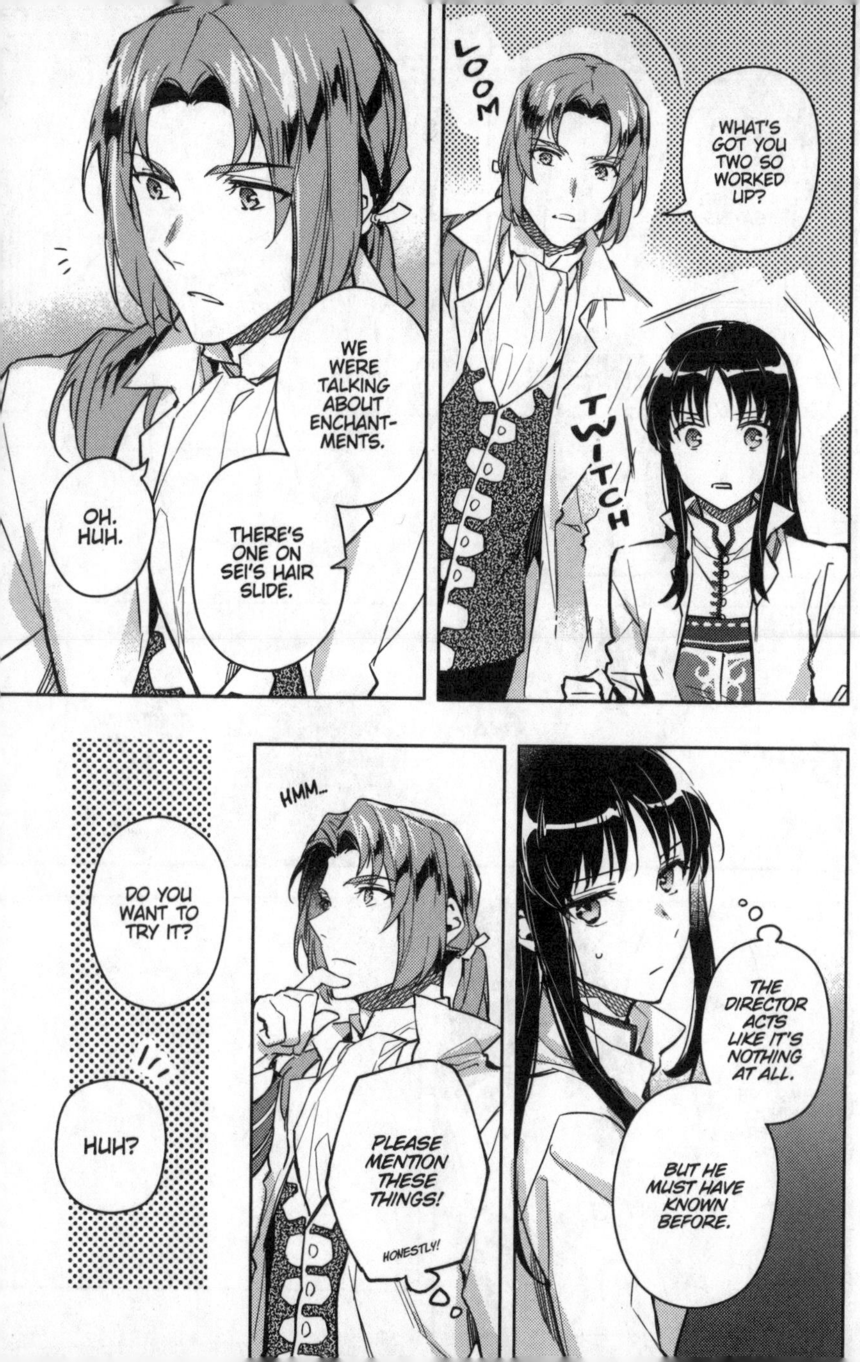
LOOM
WHAT'S GOT YOU TWO SO WORKED UP?
TWITCH
WE WERE TALKING ABOUT ENCHANT-MENTS.
THERE'S ONE ON SEI'S HAIR SLIDE.
OH. HUH.
THE DIRECTOR ACTS LIKE IT'S NOTHING AT ALL.
BUT HE MUST HAVE KNOWN BEFORE.
HMM...
PLEASE MENTION THESE THINGS!
HONESTLY!
DO YOU WANT TO TRY IT?
HUH?

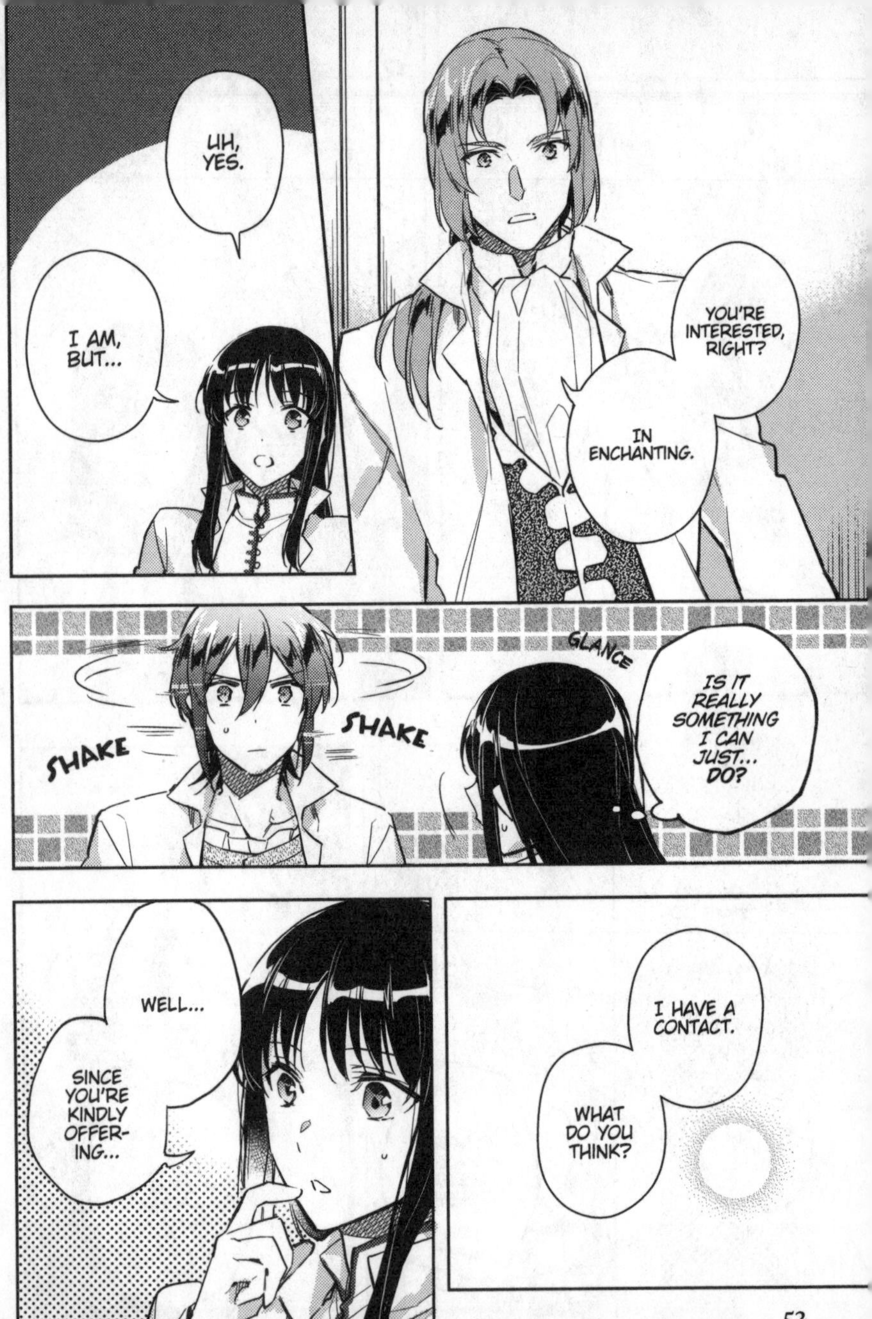
YOU'RE INTERESTED, RIGHT?
IN ENCHANTING.
UH, YES.
I AM, BUT...
GLANCE
IS IT REALLY SOMETHING I CAN JUST... DO?
SHAKE
SHAKE
I HAVE A CONTACT.
WHAT DO YOU THINK?
WELL...
SINCE YOU'RE KINDLY OFFER-ING...

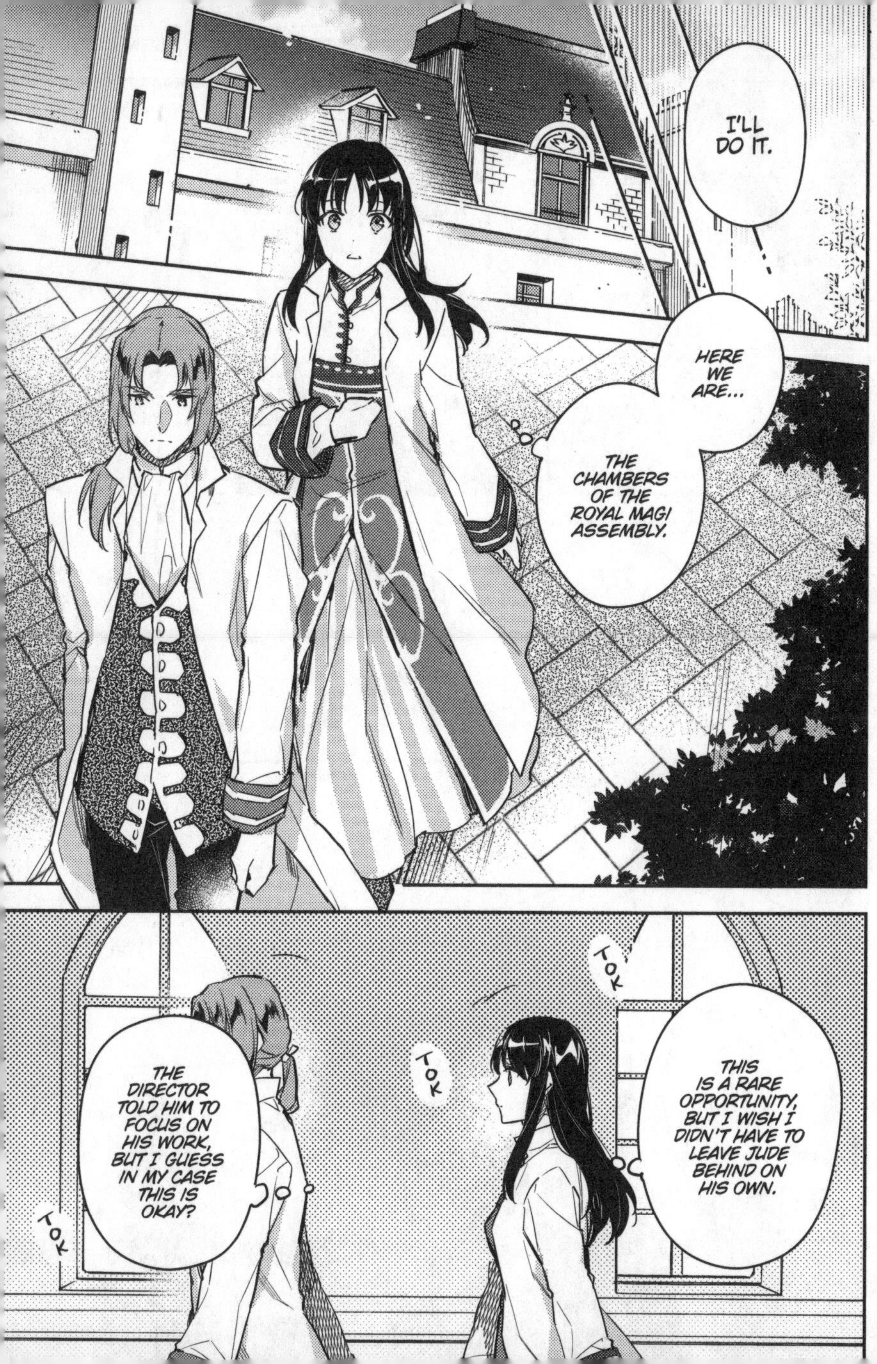
I'LL DO IT.
HERE WE ARE...
THE CHAMBERS OF THE ROYAL MAGI ASSEMBLY.
TOK
THIS IS A RARE OPPORTUNITY, BUT I WISH I DIDN'T HAVE TO LEAVE JUDE BEHIND ON HIS OWN.
TOK
THE DIRECTOR TOLD HIM TO FOCUS ON HIS WORK, BUT I GUESS IN MY CASE THIS IS OKAY?
TOK

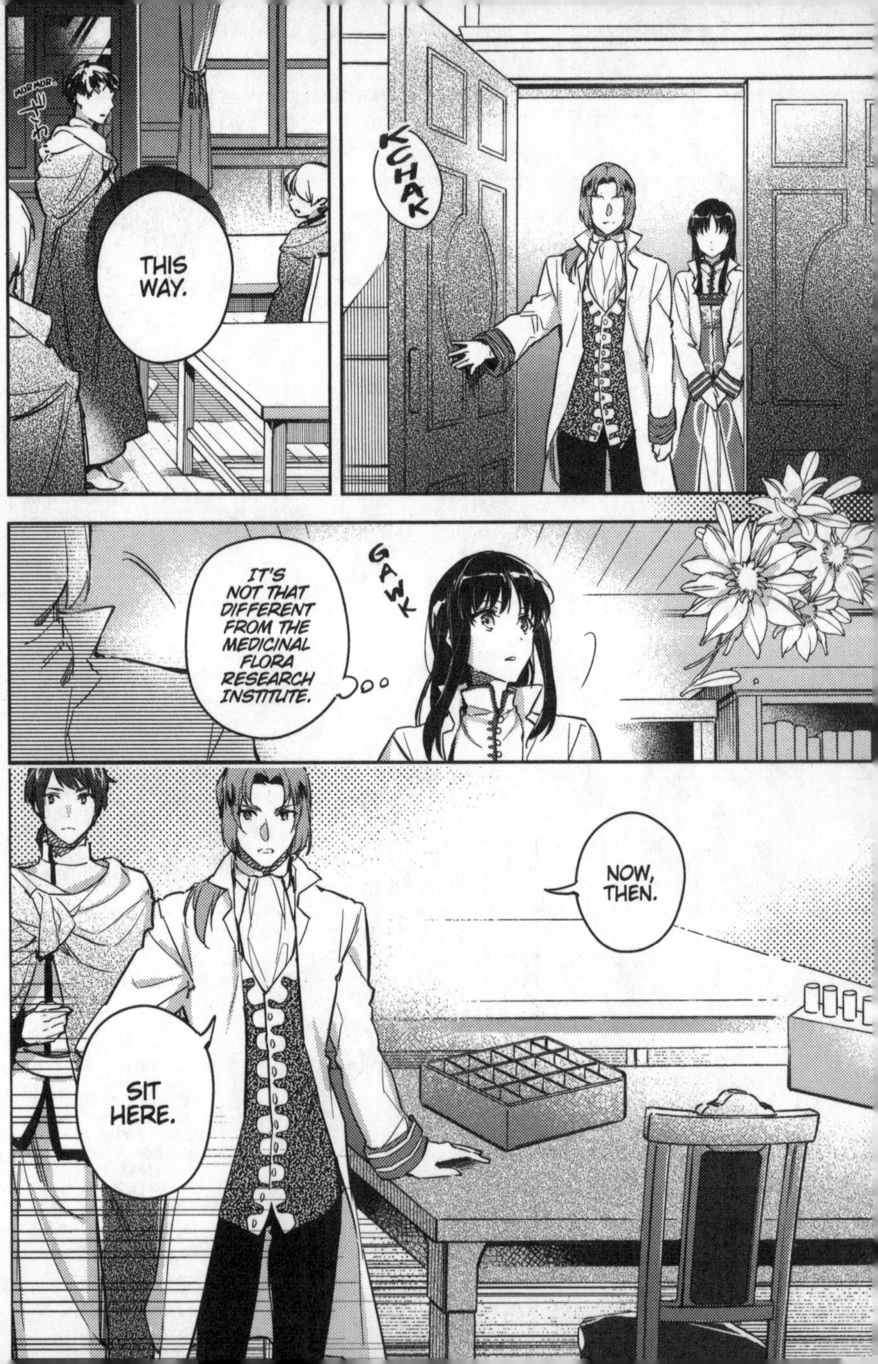
KCHAK
MURMUR
THIS WAY.
GAWK
IT'S NOT THAT DIFFERENT FROM THE MEDICINAL FLORA RESEARCH INSTITUTE.
NOW, THEN.
SIT HERE.

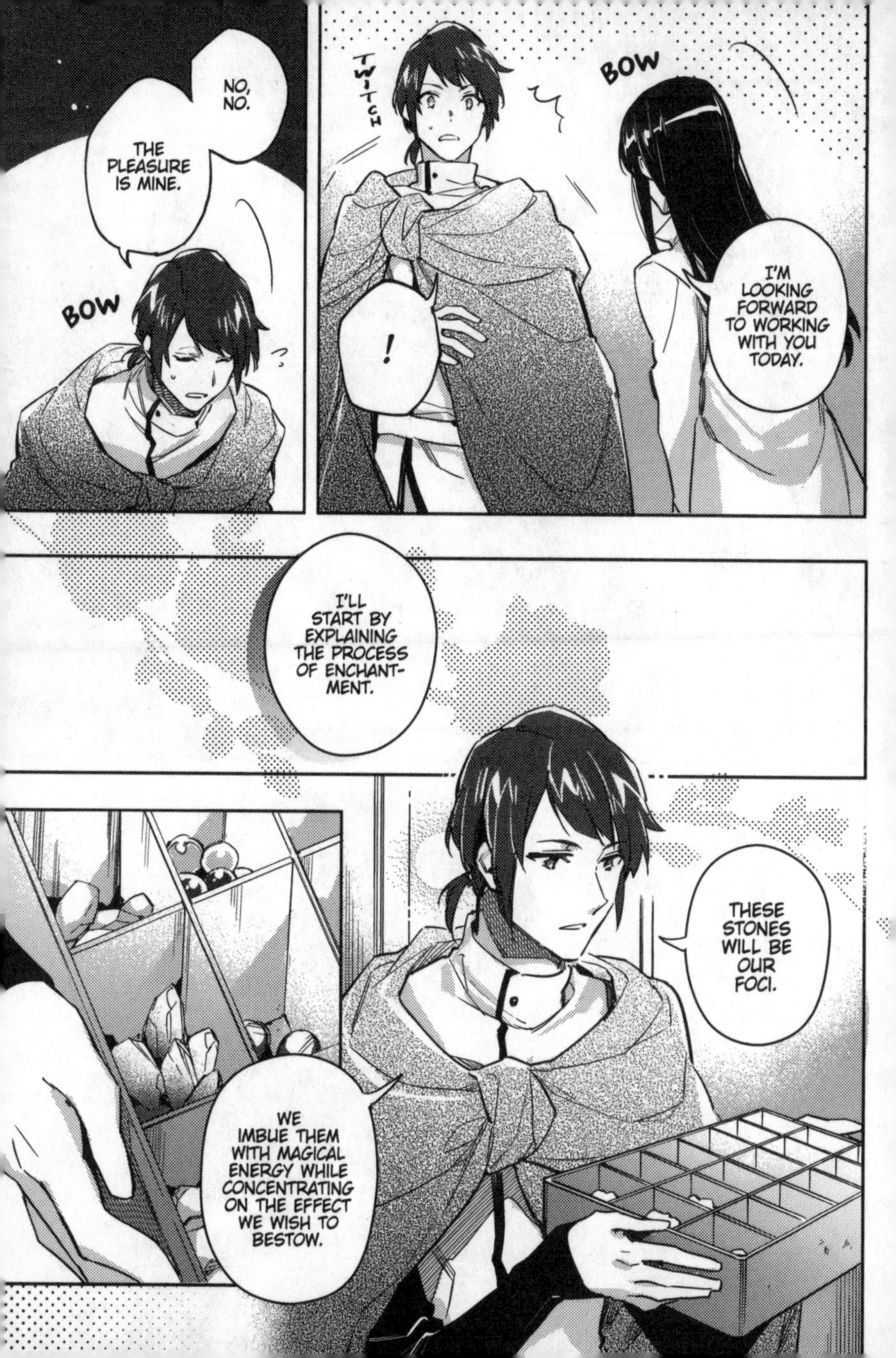
BOW
TWITCH
I'M LOOKING FORWARD TO WORKING WITH YOU TODAY.
!
NO, NO.
THE PLEASURE IS MINE.
BOW
I'LL START BY EXPLAINING THE PROCESS OF ENCHANT-MENT.
THESE STONES WILL BE OUR FOCI.
WE IMBUE THEM WITH MAGICAL ENERGY WHILE CONCENTRATING ON THE EFFECT WE WISH TO BESTOW.

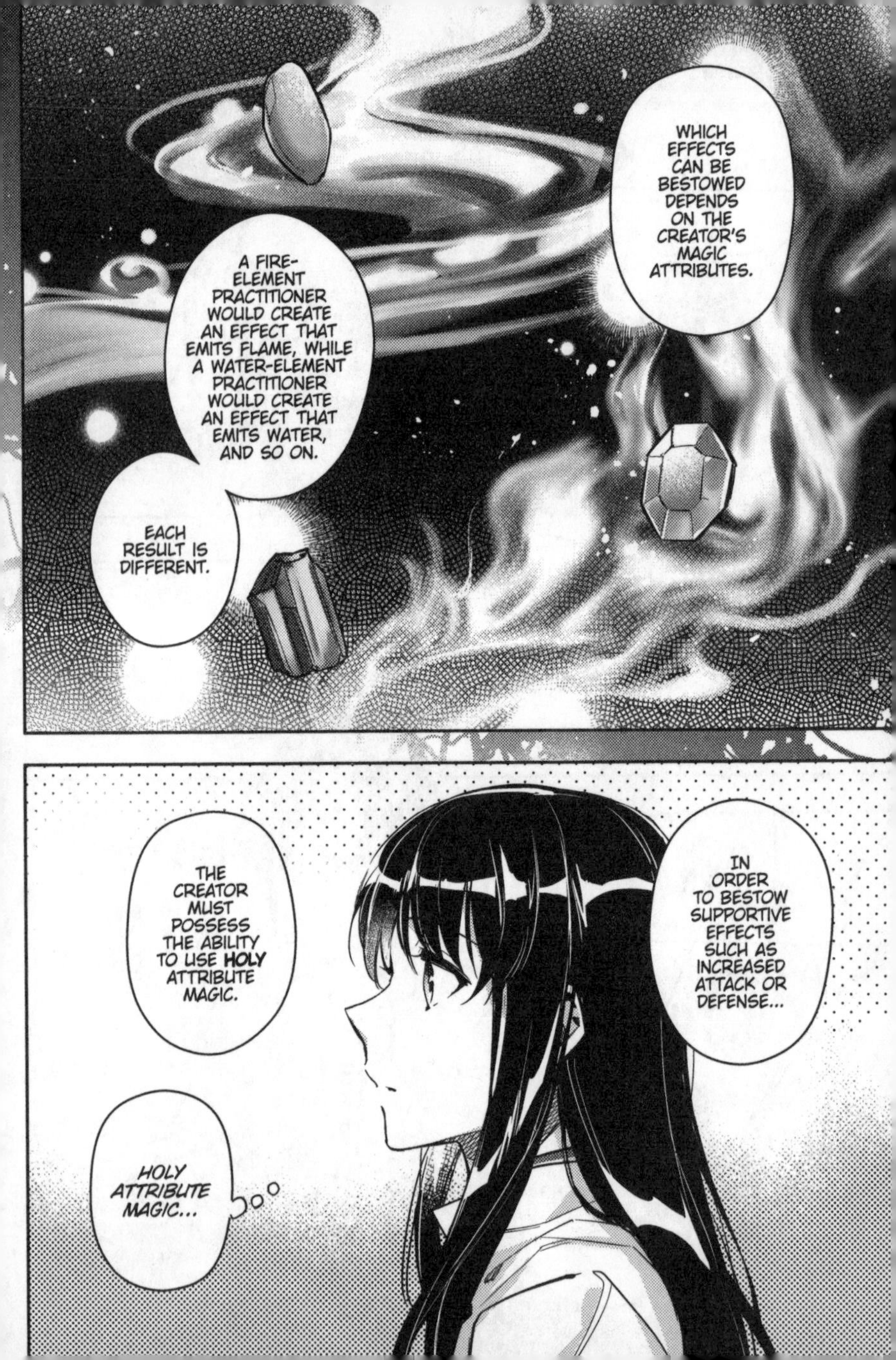
WHICH EFFECTS CAN BE BESTOWED DEPENDS ON THE CREATOR'S MAGIC ATTRIBUTES.
A FIRE-ELEMENT PRACTITIONER WOULD CREATE AN EFFECT THAT EMITS FLAME, WHILE A WATER-ELEMENT PRACTITIONER WOULD CREATE AN EFFECT THAT EMITS WATER, AND SO ON.
EACH RESULT IS DIFFERENT.
IN ORDER TO BESTOW SUPPORTIVE EFFECTS SUCH AS INCREASED ATTACK OR DEFENSE...
THE CREATOR MUST POSSESS THE ABILITY TO USE **HOLY** ATTRIBUTE MAGIC.
HOLY ATTRIBUTE MAGIC...

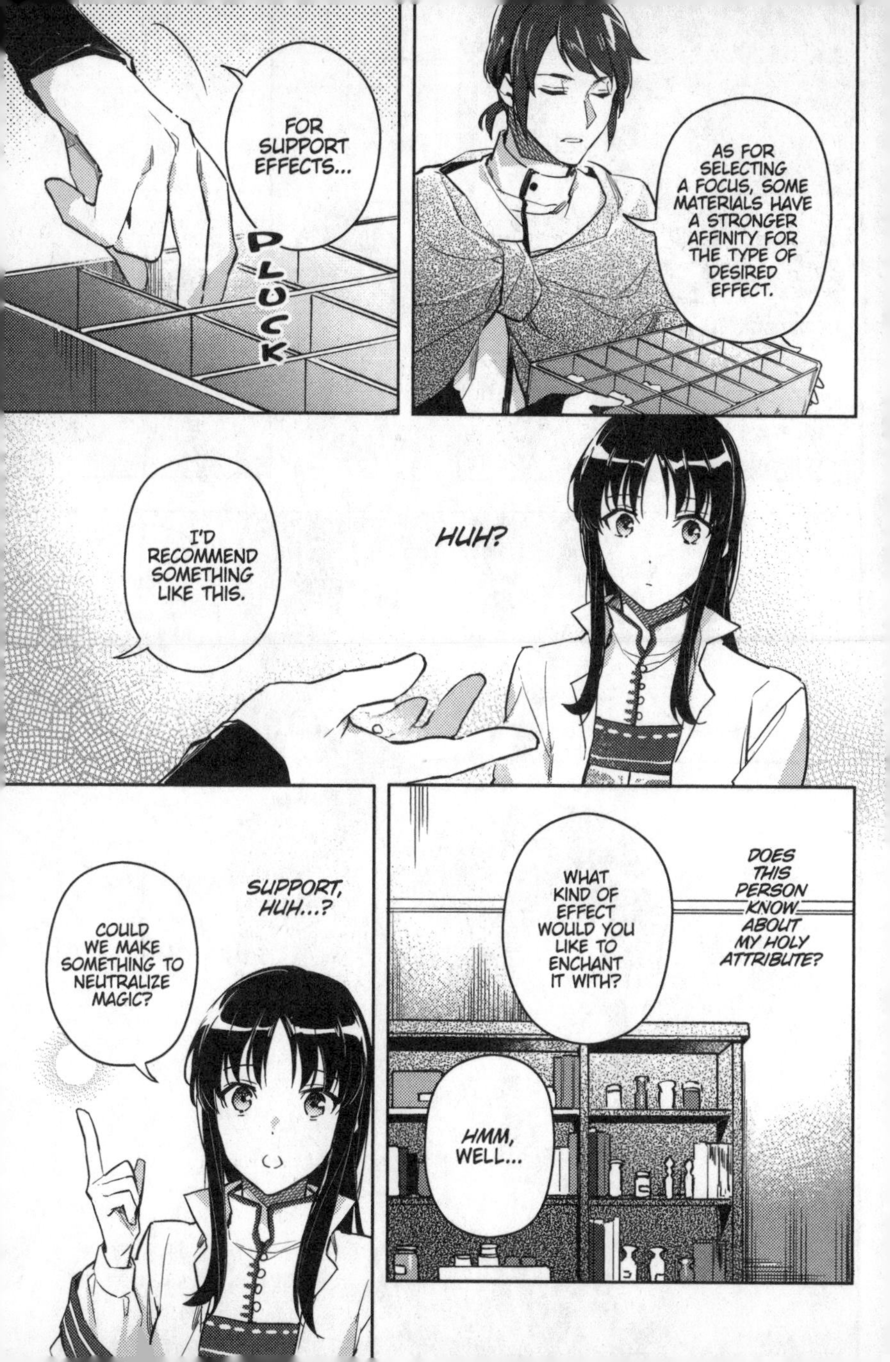
AS FOR SELECTING A FOCUS, SOME MATERIALS HAVE A STRONGER AFFINITY FOR THE TYPE OF DESIRED EFFECT.
FOR SUPPORT EFFECTS...
PLUCK
I'D RECOMMEND SOMETHING LIKE THIS.
HUH?
WHAT KIND OF EFFECT WOULD YOU LIKE TO ENCHANT IT WITH?
DOES THIS PERSON KNOW ABOUT MY HOLY ATTRIBUTE?
HMM, WELL...
SUPPORT, HUH...?
COULD WE MAKE SOMETHING TO NEUTRALIZE MAGIC?

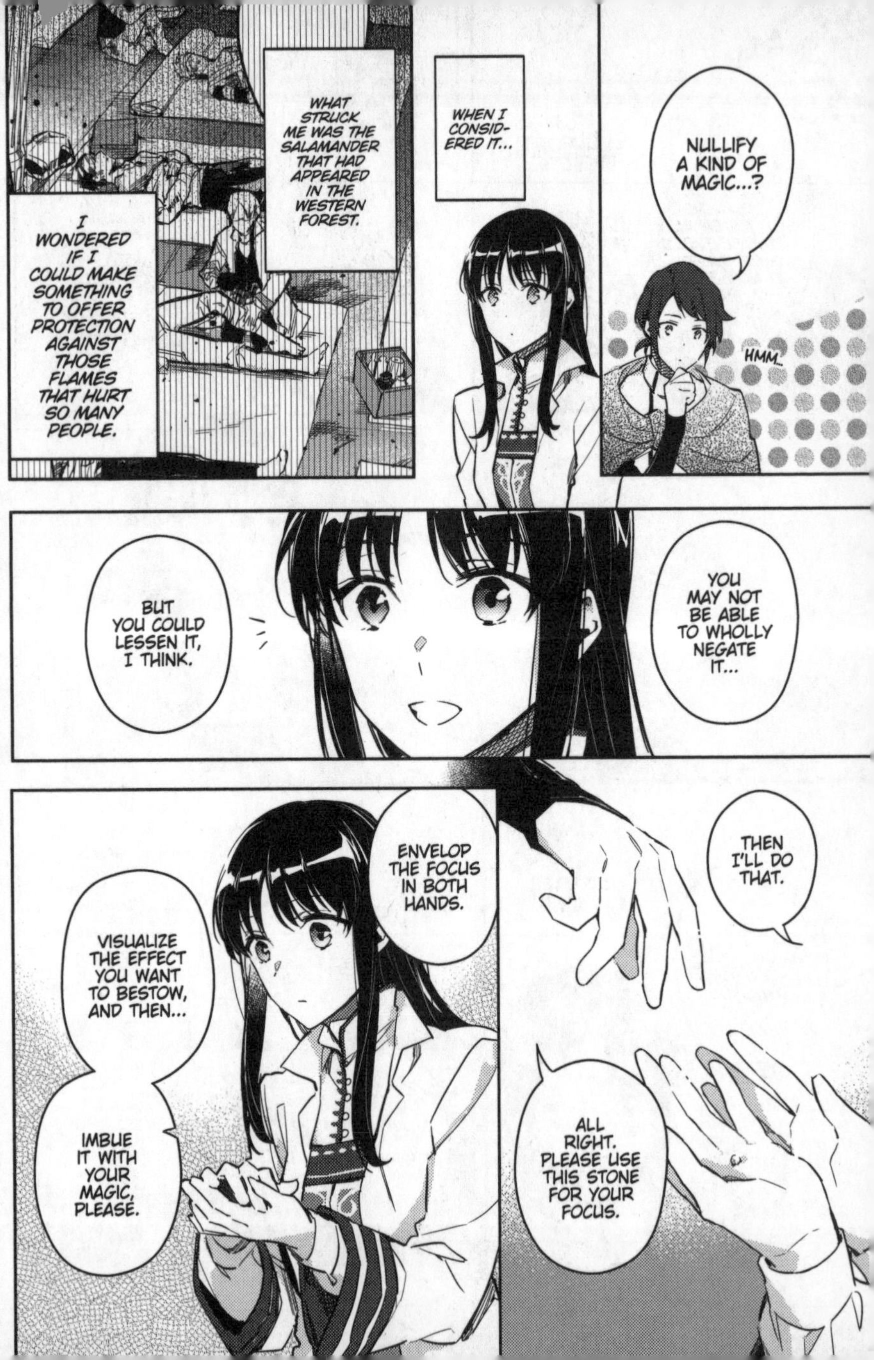
NULLIFY A KIND OF MAGIC...?
HMM...
WHEN I CONSIDERED IT...
WHAT STRUCK ME WAS THE SALAMANDER THAT HAD APPEARED IN THE WESTERN FOREST.
I WONDERED IF I COULD MAKE SOMETHING TO OFFER PROTECTION AGAINST THOSE FLAMES THAT HURT SO MANY PEOPLE.
YOU MAY NOT BE ABLE TO WHOLLY NEGATE IT...
BUT YOU COULD LESSEN IT, I THINK.
THEN I'LL DO THAT.
ALL RIGHT. PLEASE USE THIS STONE FOR YOUR FOCUS.
ENVELOP THE FOCUS IN BOTH HANDS.
VISUALIZE THE EFFECT YOU WANT TO BESTOW, AND THEN...
IMBUE IT WITH YOUR MAGIC, PLEASE.

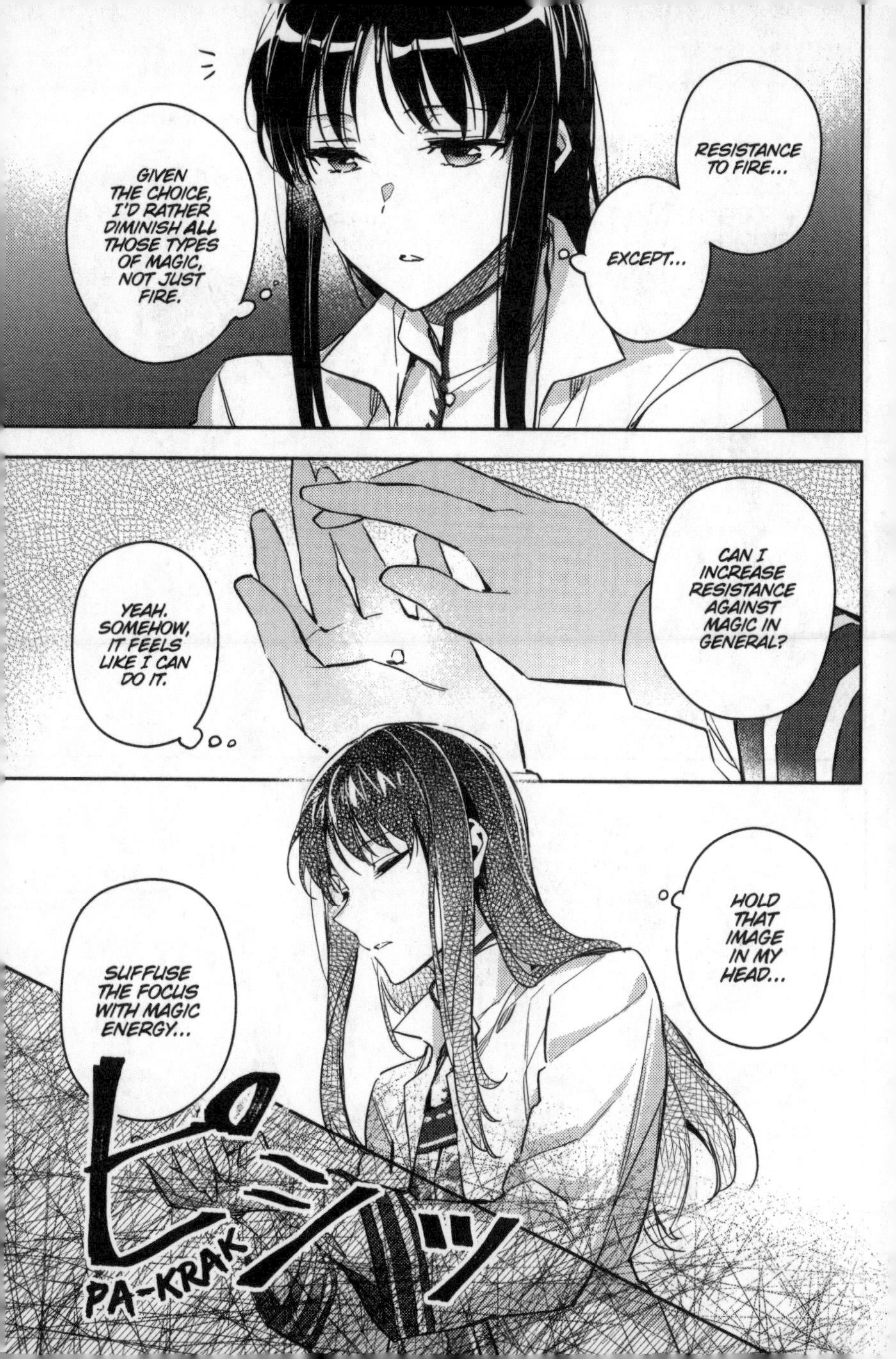
RESISTANCE TO FIRE...
EXCEPT...
GIVEN THE CHOICE, I'D RATHER DIMINISH ALL THOSE TYPES OF MAGIC, NOT JUST FIRE.
CAN I INCREASE RESISTANCE AGAINST MAGIC IN GENERAL?
YEAH. SOMEHOW, IT FEELS LIKE I CAN DO IT.
HOLD THAT IMAGE IN MY HEAD...
SUFFUSE THE FOCUS WITH MAGIC ENERGY...
PA-KRAK

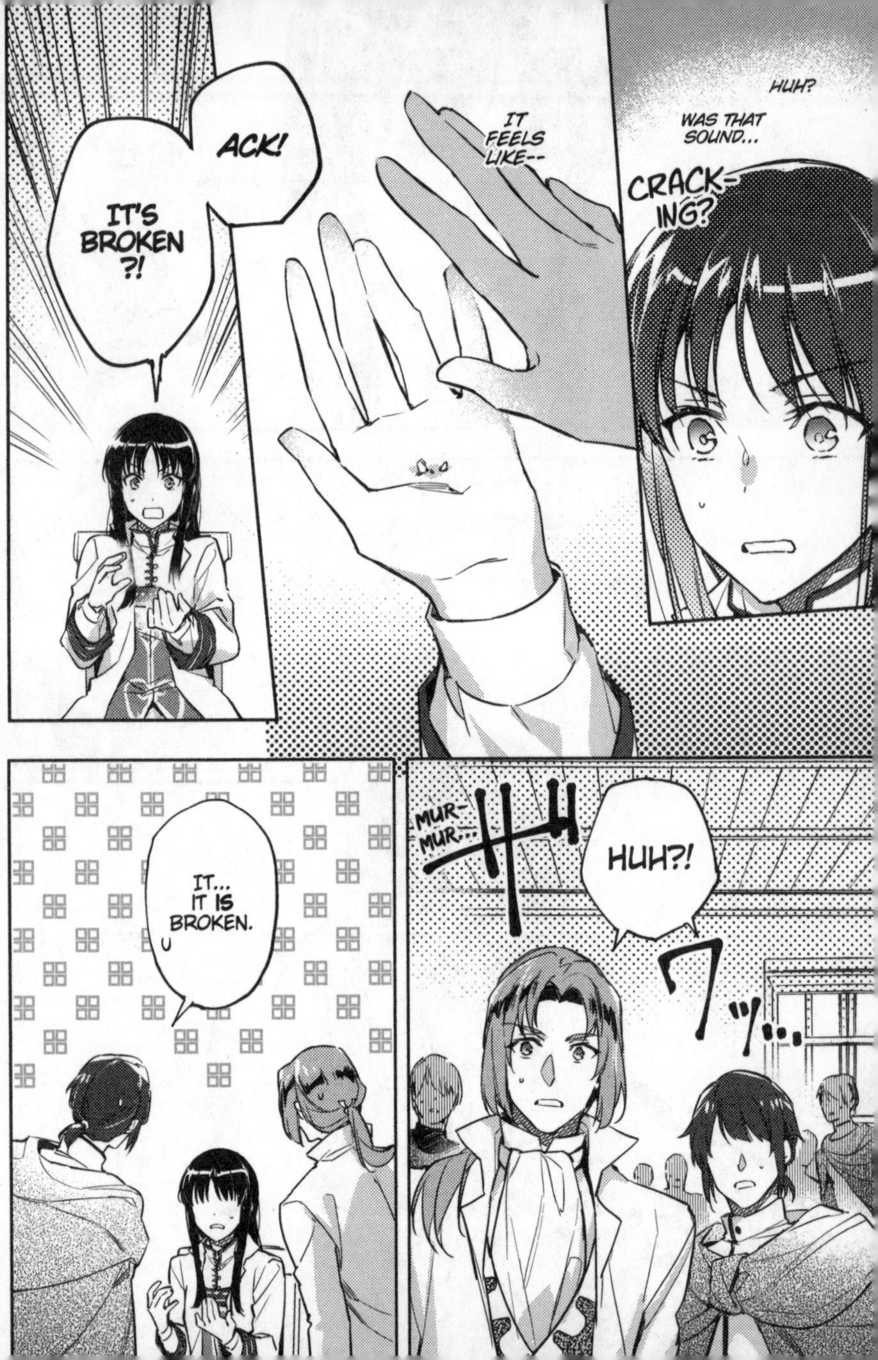
HUH?
WAS THAT SOUND...
CRACK-ING?
IT FEELS LIKE--
ACK!
IT'S BROKEN ?!
HUH?!
MUR-MUR...
IT... IT IS BROKEN.

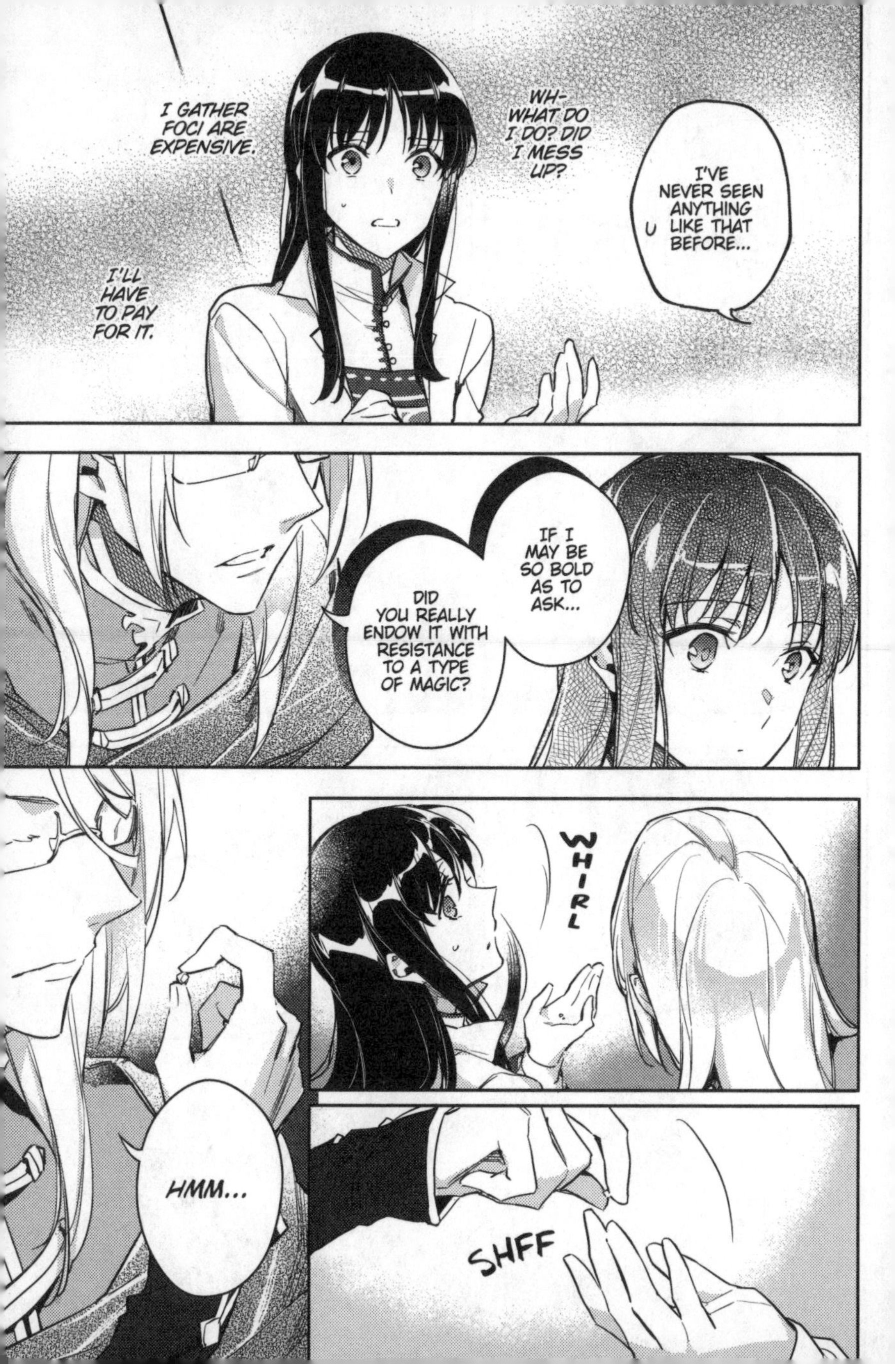
I'VE NEVER SEEN ANYTHING LIKE THAT BEFORE...
WH- WHAT DO I DO? DID I MESS UP?
I GATHER FOCI ARE EXPENSIVE.
I'LL HAVE TO PAY FOR IT.
IF I MAY BE SO BOLD AS TO ASK...
DID YOU REALLY ENDOW IT WITH RESISTANCE TO A TYPE OF MAGIC?
WHIRL
SHFF
HMM...

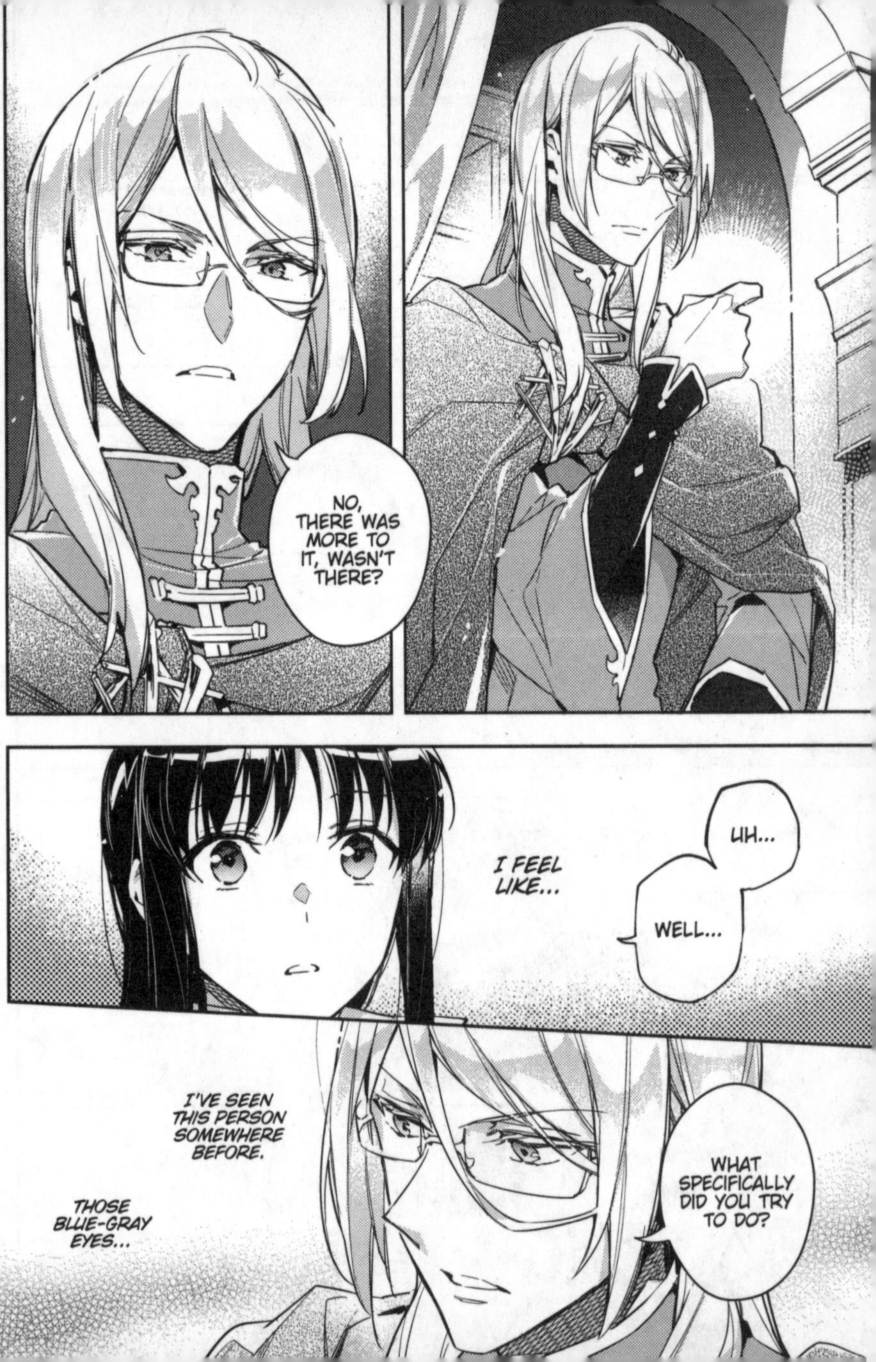
NO, THERE WAS MORE TO IT, WASN'T THERE?
UH...
WELL...
I FEEL LIKE...
WHAT SPECIFICALLY DID YOU TRY TO DO?
I'VE SEEN THIS PERSON SOMEWHERE BEFORE.
THOSE BLUE-GRAY EYES...

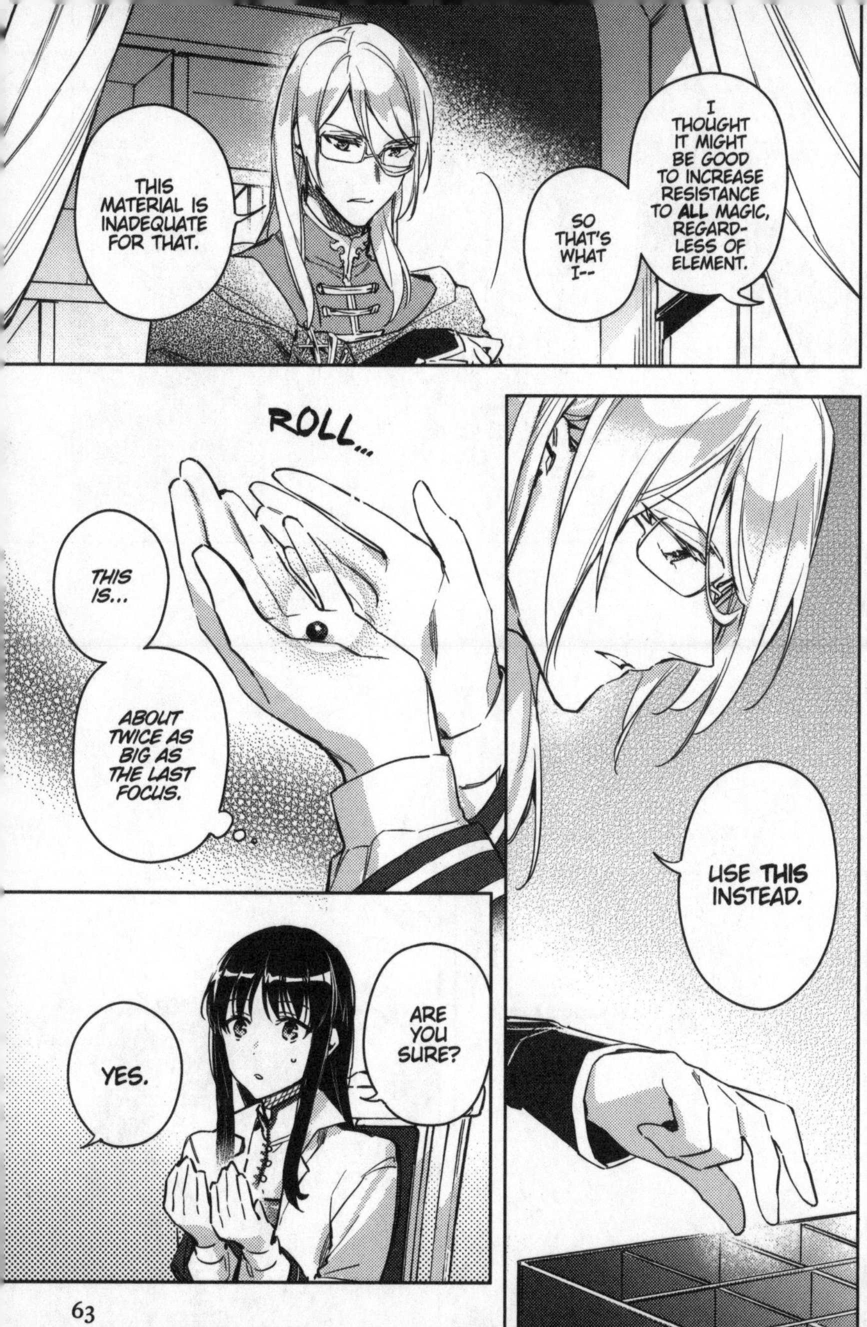
I THOUGHT IT MIGHT BE GOOD TO INCREASE RESISTANCE TO ALL MAGIC, REGARDLESS OF ELEMENT.
SO THAT'S WHAT I--
THIS MATERIAL IS INADEQUATE FOR THAT.
USE THIS INSTEAD.
ROLL...
THIS IS...
ABOUT TWICE AS BIG AS THE LAST FOCUS.
ARE YOU SURE?
YES.

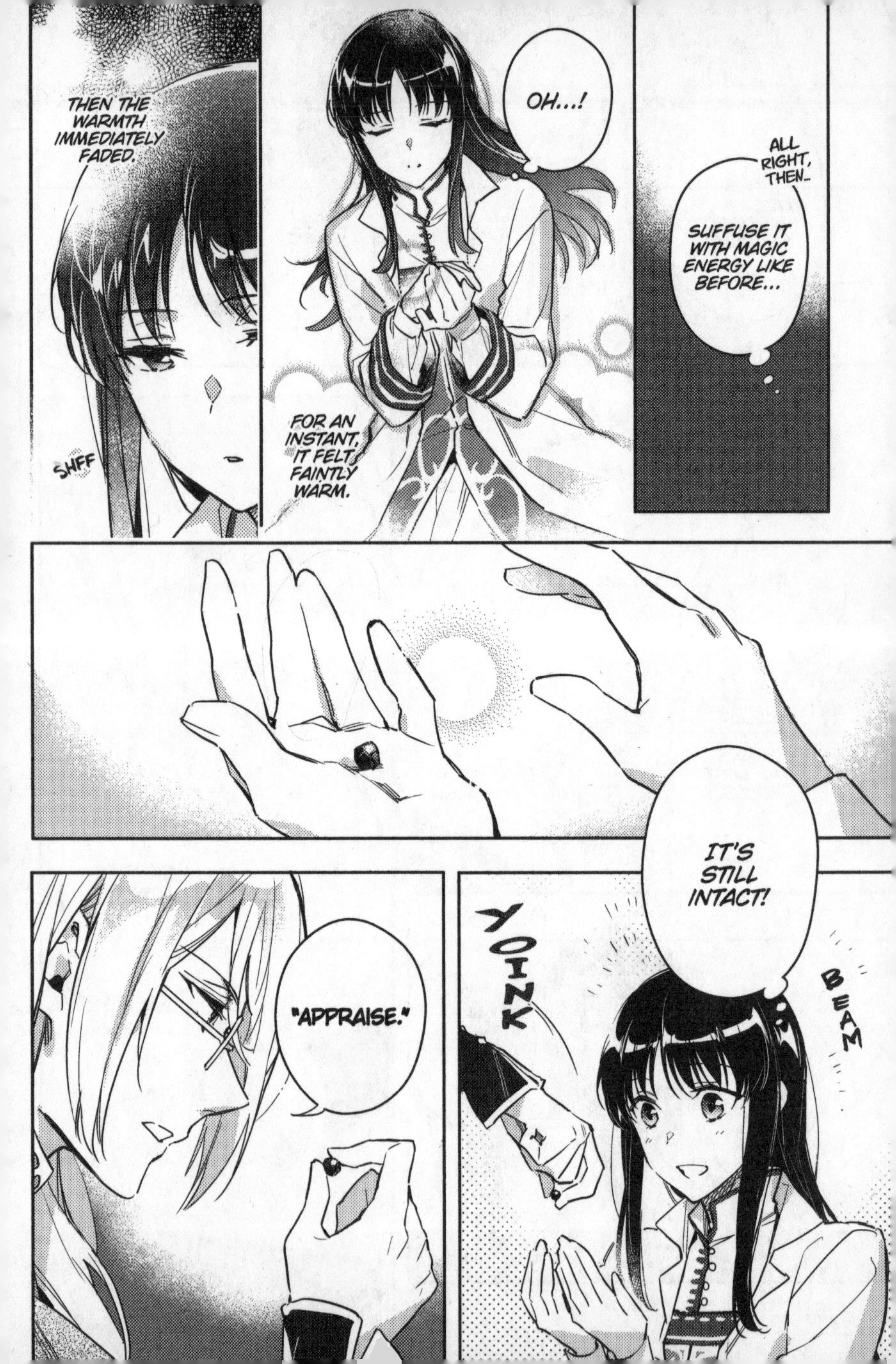

ALL RIGHT, THEN..
SUFFUSE IT WITH MAGIC ENERGY LIKE BEFORE...
OH...!
FOR AN INSTANT, IT FELT FAINTLY WARM.
THEN THE WARMTH IMMEDIATELY FADED.
SHFF
IT'S STILL INTACT!
BEAM
YOINK
"APPRAISE."

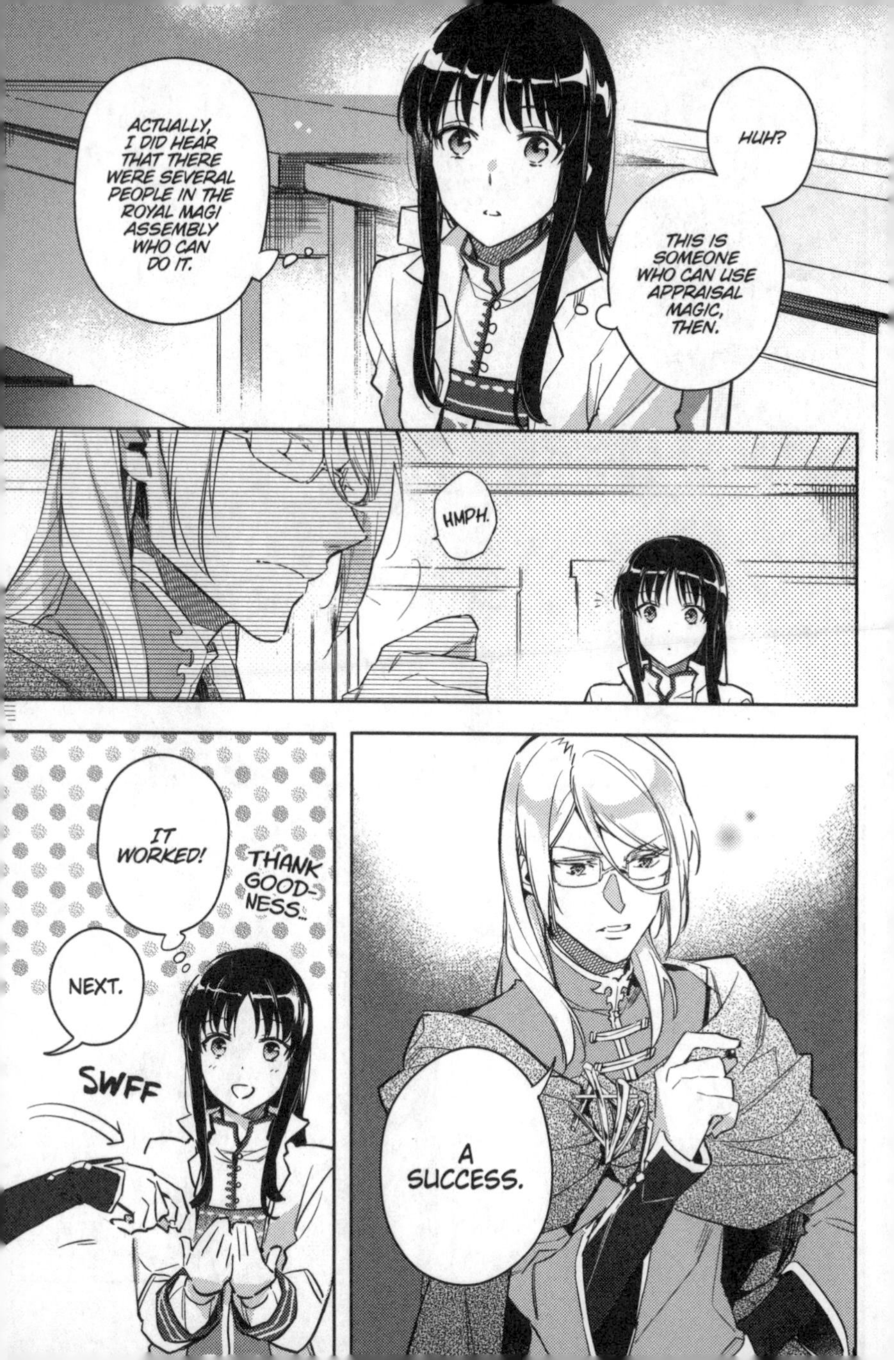
HUH?
THIS IS SOMEONE WHO CAN USE APPRAISAL MAGIC, THEN.
ACTUALLY, I DID HEAR THAT THERE WERE SEVERAL PEOPLE IN THE ROYAL MAGI ASSEMBLY WHO CAN DO IT.
HMPH.
A SUCCESS.
IT WORKED!
THANK GOODNESS...
NEXT.
SWFF

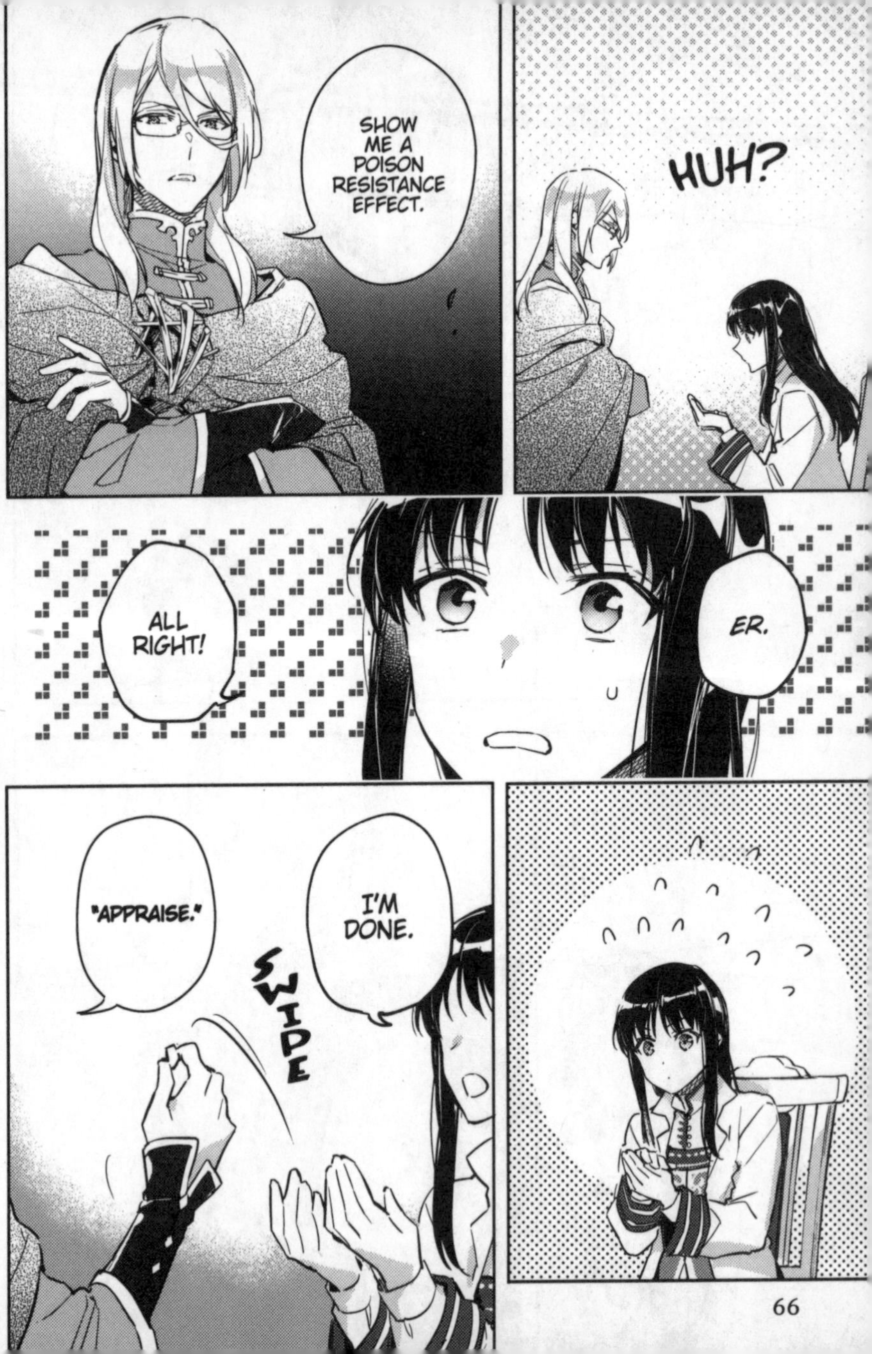
HUH?
SHOW ME A POISON RESISTANCE EFFECT.
ER.
ALL RIGHT!
I'M DONE.
SWIPE
"APPRAISE."

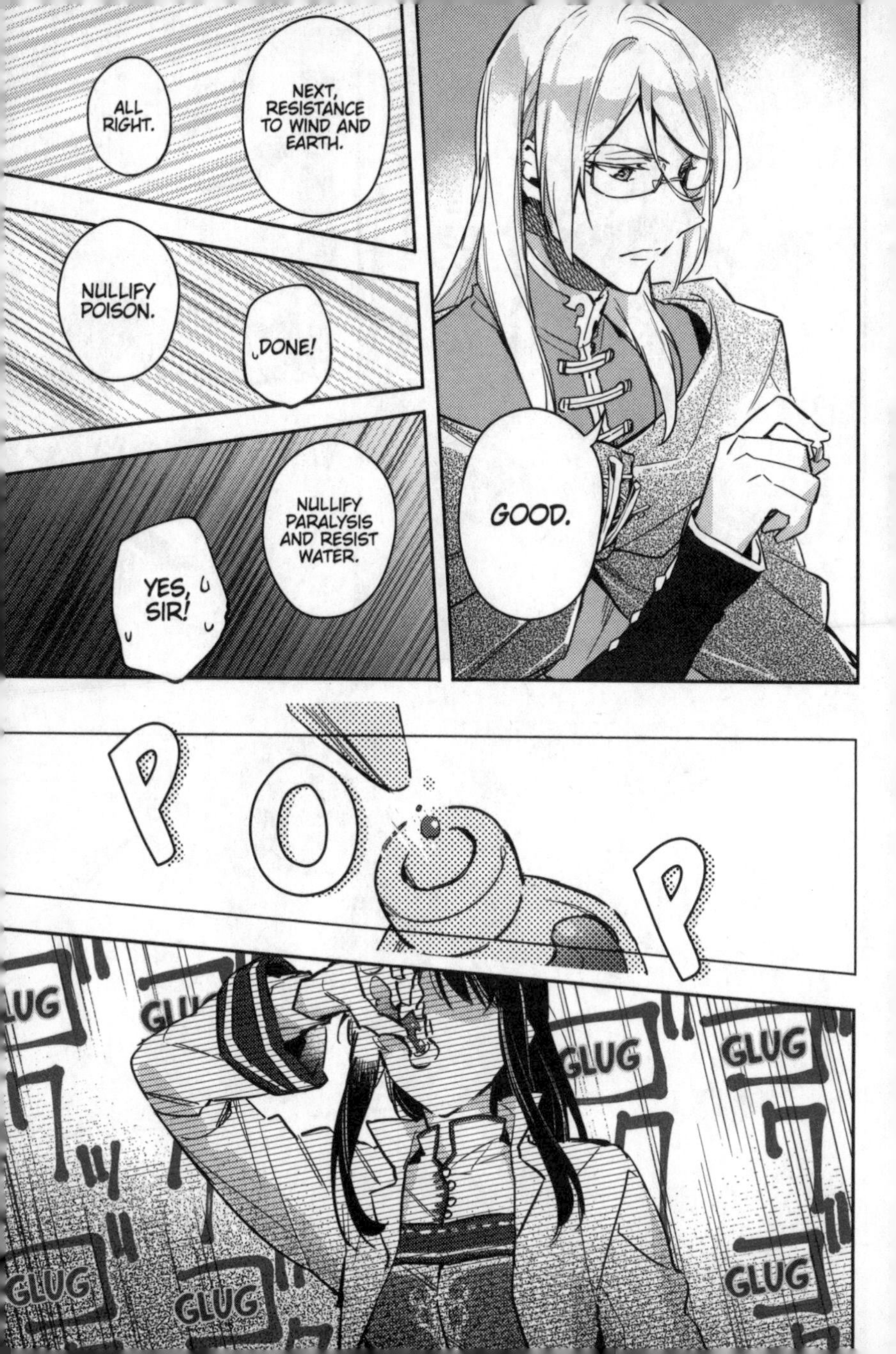
GOOD.
NEXT, RESISTANCE TO WIND AND EARTH.
ALL RIGHT.
NULLIFY POISON.
DONE!
NULLIFY PARALYSIS AND RESIST WATER.
YES, SIR!
POP
GLUG
GLUG
GLUG
GLUG
GLUG
GLUG
GLUG
GLUG

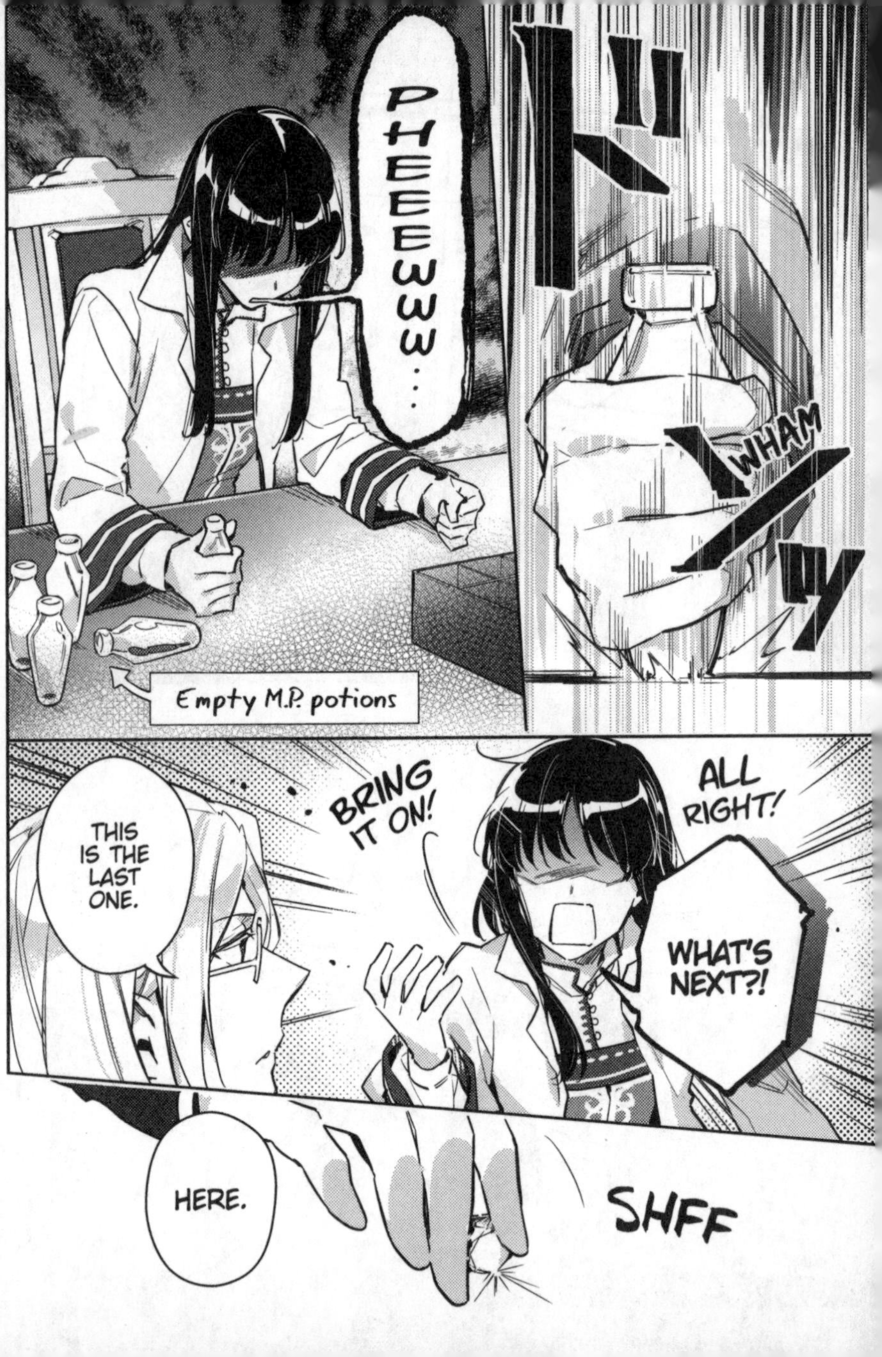
WHAM
PHEEEWWW...
Empty M.P. potions
ALL RIGHT!
WHAT'S NEXT?!
BRING IT ON!
THIS IS THE LAST ONE.
SHFF
HERE.

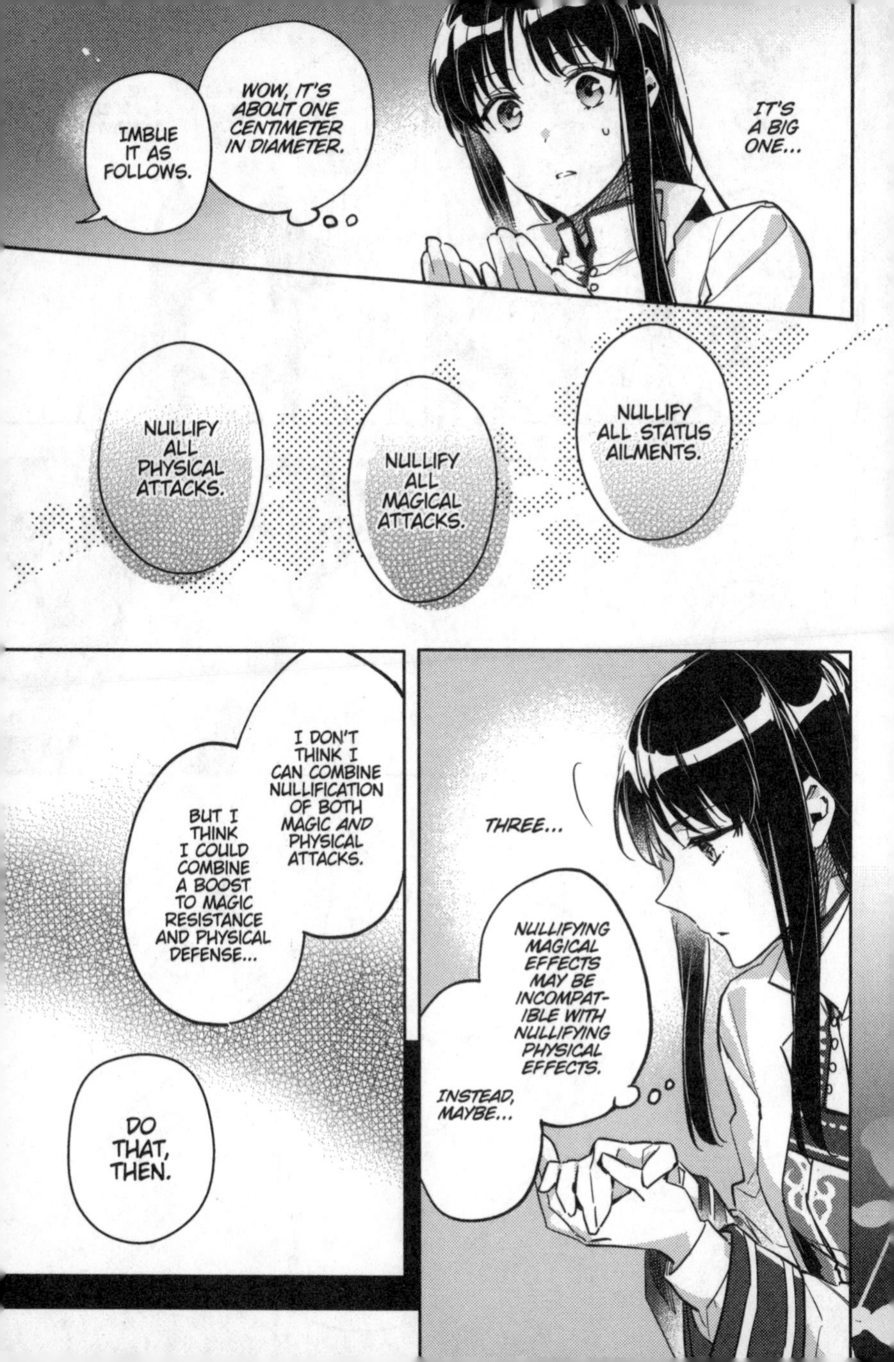
IT'S A BIG ONE...
WOW, IT'S ABOUT ONE CENTIMETER IN DIAMETER.
IMBUE IT AS FOLLOWS.
NULLIFY ALL STATUS AILMENTS.
NULLIFY ALL MAGICAL ATTACKS.
NULLIFY ALL PHYSICAL ATTACKS.
THREE...
NULLIFYING MAGICAL EFFECTS MAY BE INCOMPATIBLE WITH NULLIFYING PHYSICAL EFFECTS.
INSTEAD, MAYBE...
I DON'T THINK I CAN COMBINE NULLIFICATION OF BOTH MAGIC AND PHYSICAL ATTACKS.
BUT I THINK I COULD COMBINE A BOOST TO MAGIC RESISTANCE AND PHYSICAL DEFENSE...
DO THAT, THEN.

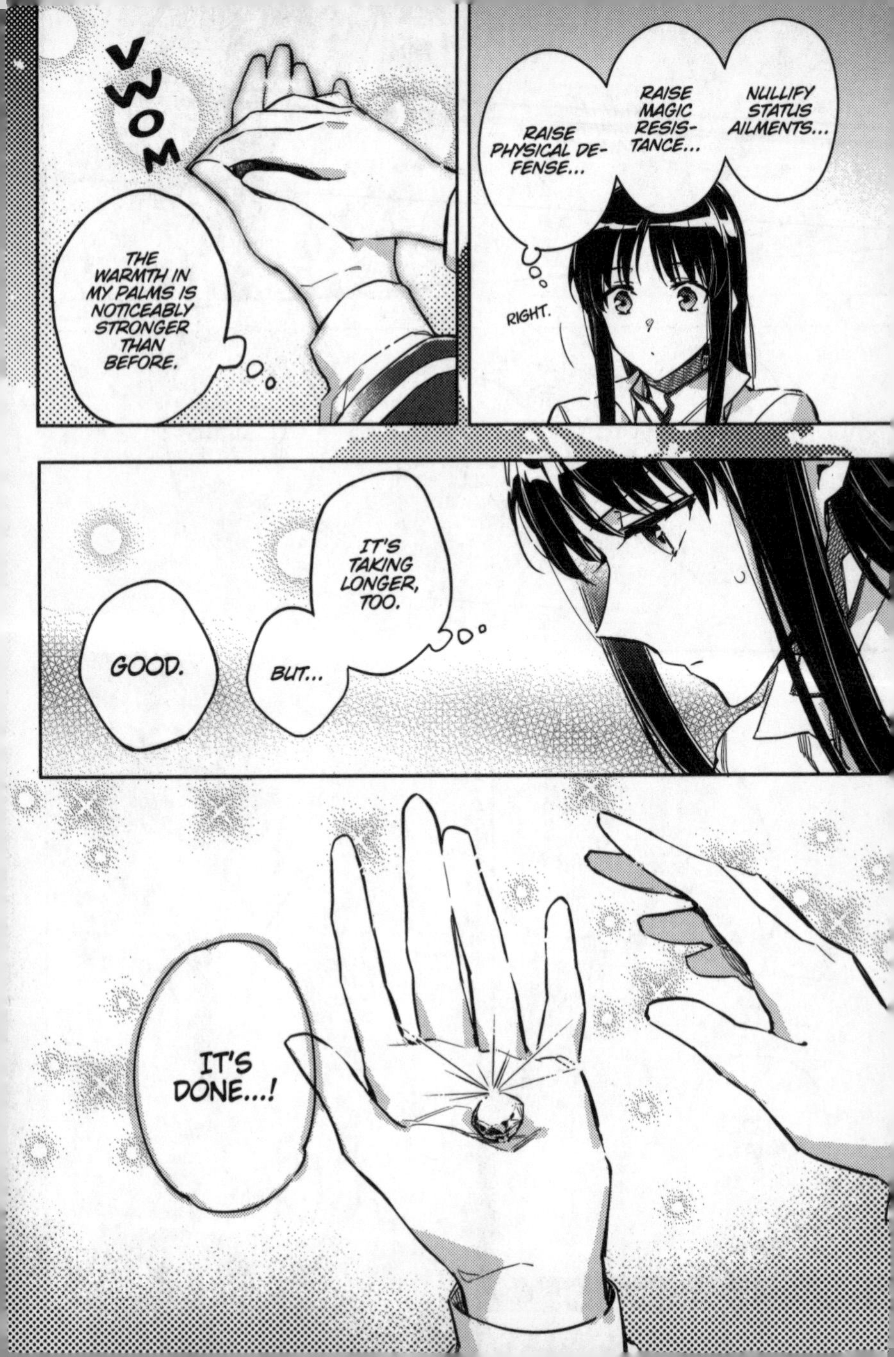
RAISE PHYSICAL DE-FENSE...
RAISE MAGIC RESIS-TANCE...
NULLIFY STATUS AILMENTS...
RIGHT.
VWOM
THE WARMTH IN MY PALMS IS NOTICEABLY STRONGER THAN BEFORE.
IT'S TAKING LONGER, TOO.
BUT...
GOOD.
IT'S DONE...!

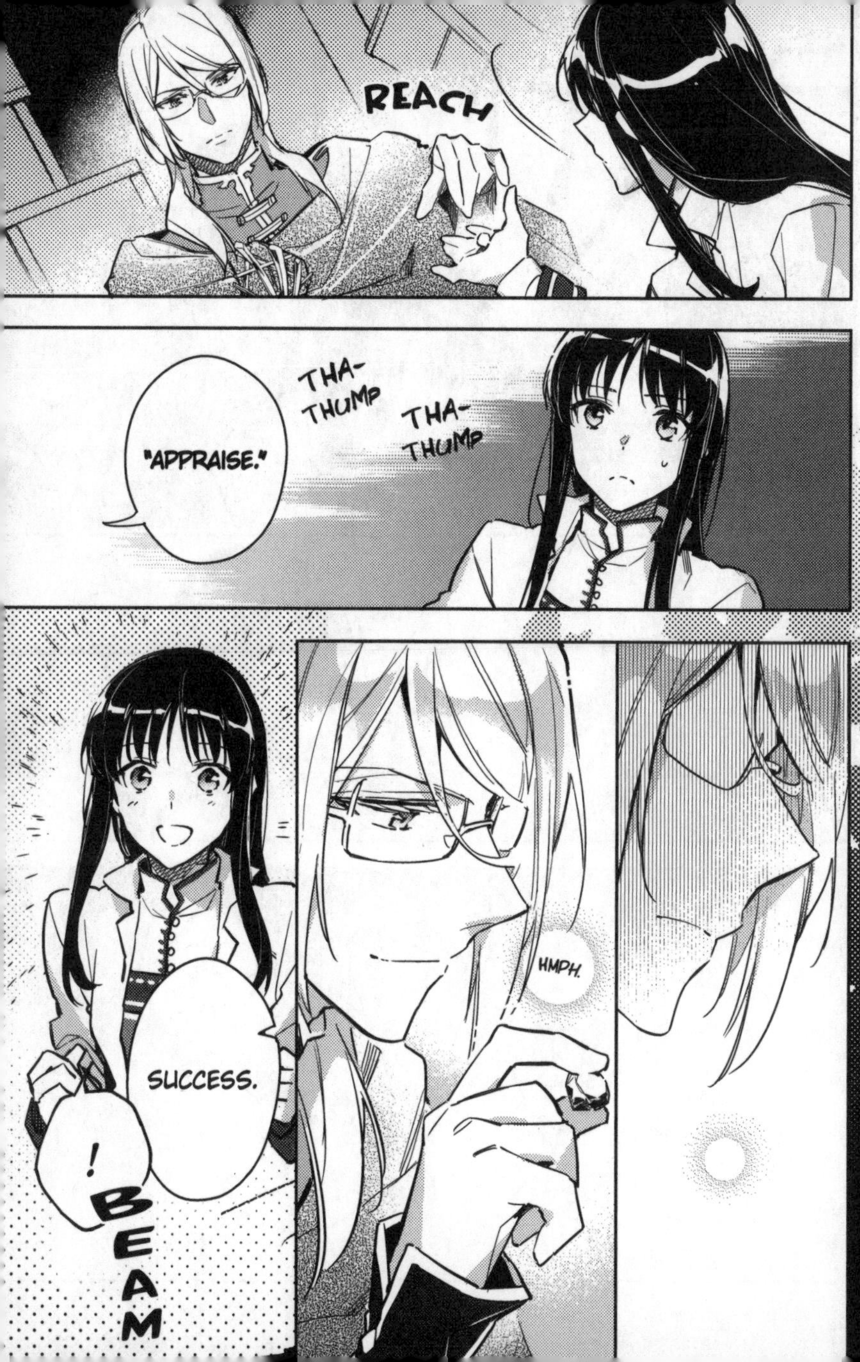
REACH
THA-THUMP
THA-THUMP
"APPRAISE."
HMPH.
SUCCESS.
!
BEAM

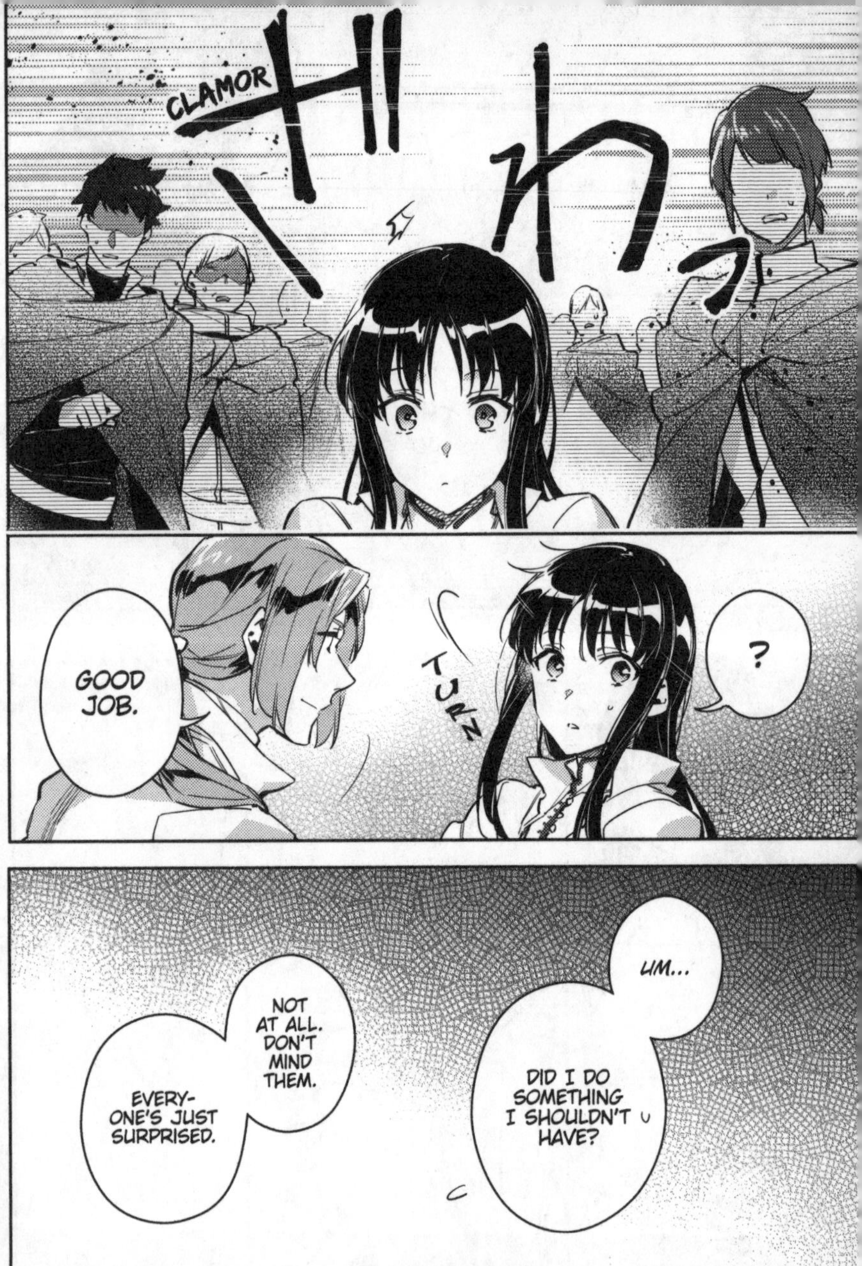
CLAMOR
?
TURN
GOOD JOB.
UM...
DID I DO SOMETHING I SHOULDN'T HAVE?
NOT AT ALL. DON'T MIND THEM.
EVERY-ONE'S JUST SURPRISED.

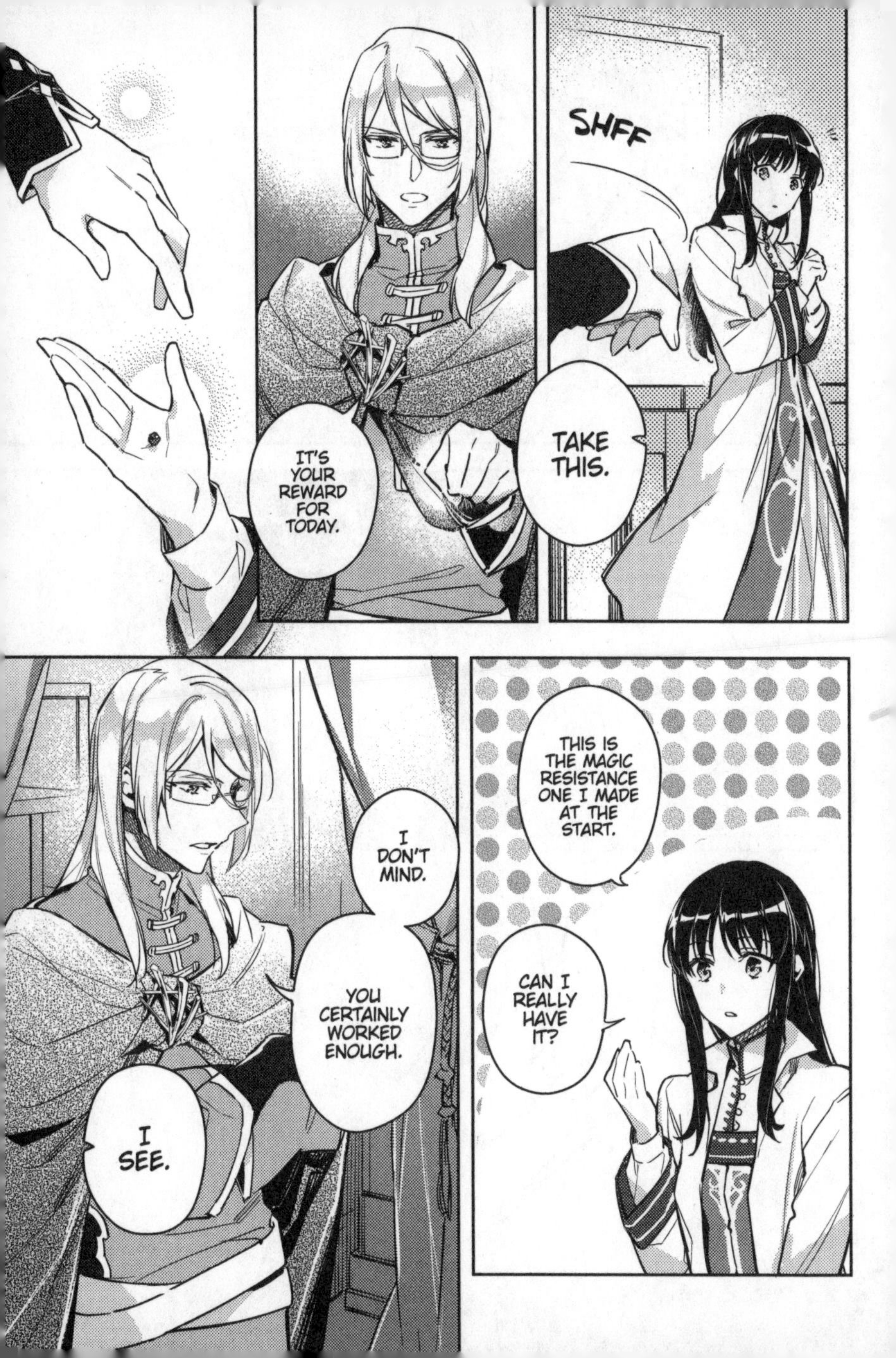
SHFF
TAKE THIS.
IT'S YOUR REWARD FOR TODAY.
THIS IS THE MAGIC RESISTANCE ONE I MADE AT THE START.
CAN I REALLY HAVE IT?
I DON'T MIND.
YOU CERTAINLY WORKED ENOUGH.
I SEE.

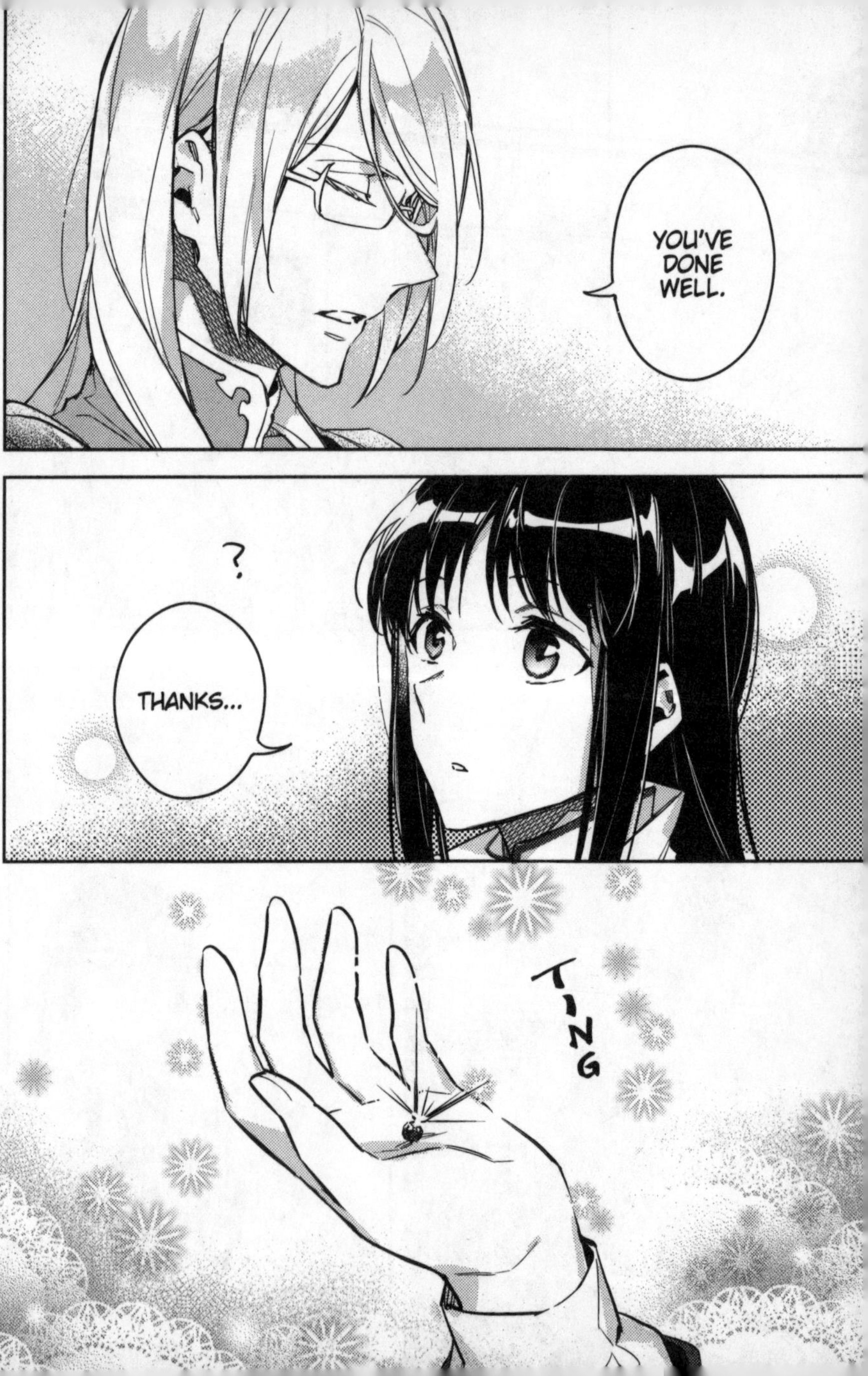
YOU'VE DONE WELL.
?
THANKS...
TING

The **Saint's** *Magic Power is* **Omnipotent**

The Saint's
Magic Power is
Omnipotent

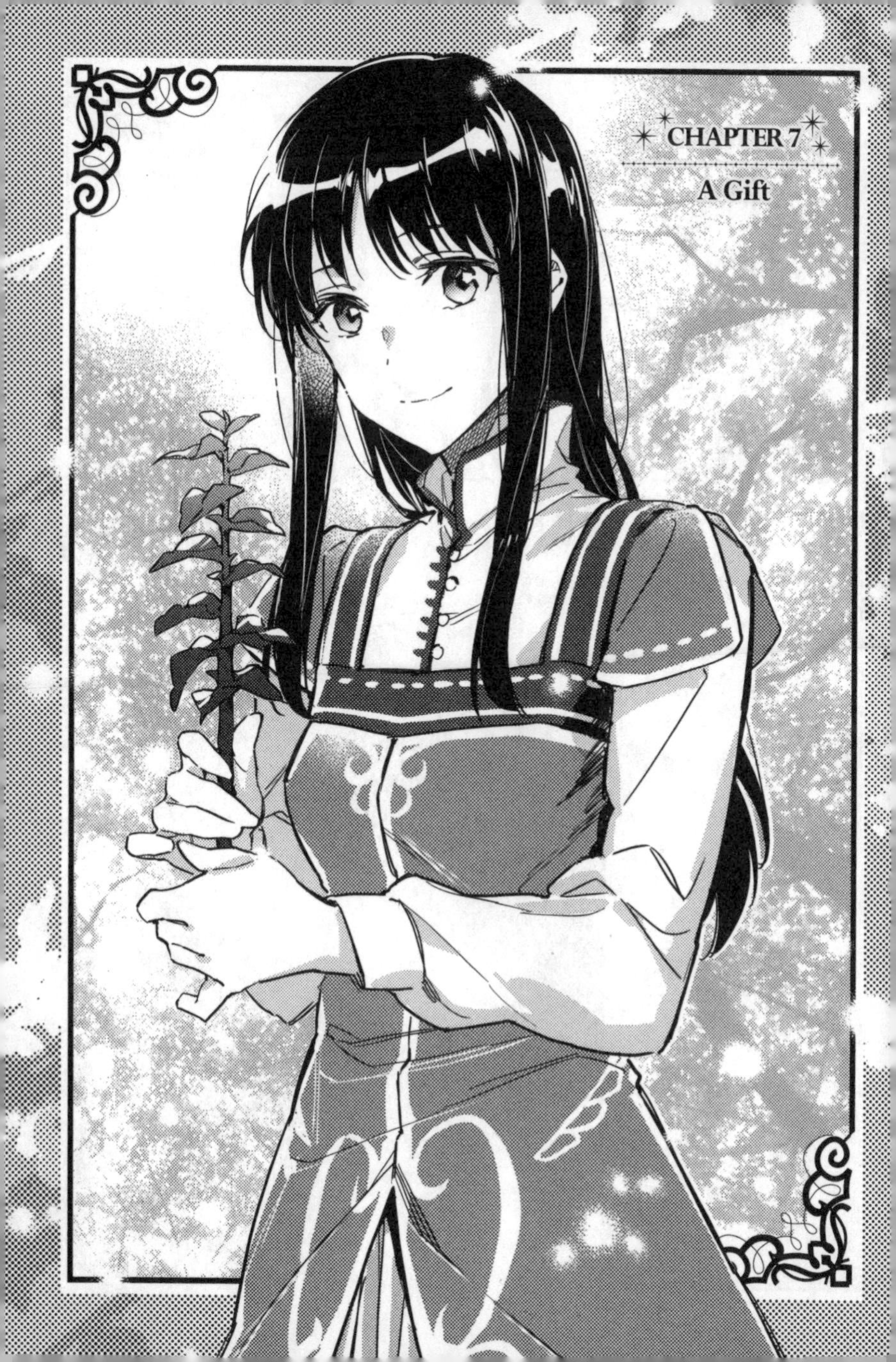
CHAPTER 7
A Gift

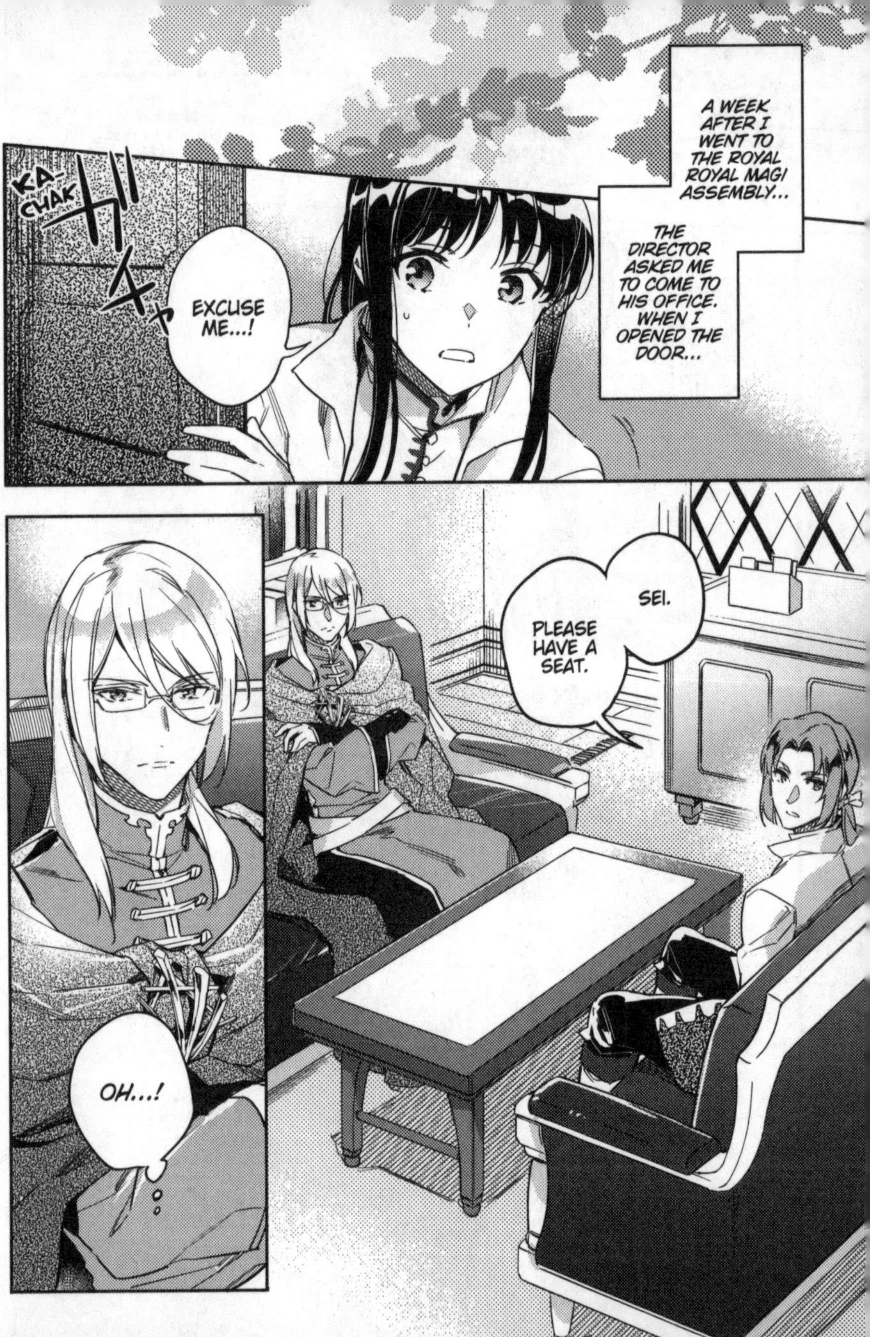
A WEEK AFTER I WENT TO THE ROYAL ROYAL MAGI ASSEMBLY...
THE DIRECTOR ASKED ME TO COME TO HIS OFFICE. WHEN I OPENED THE DOOR...
KA-CHAK
EXCUSE ME...!
SEI.
PLEASE HAVE A SEAT.
OH...!

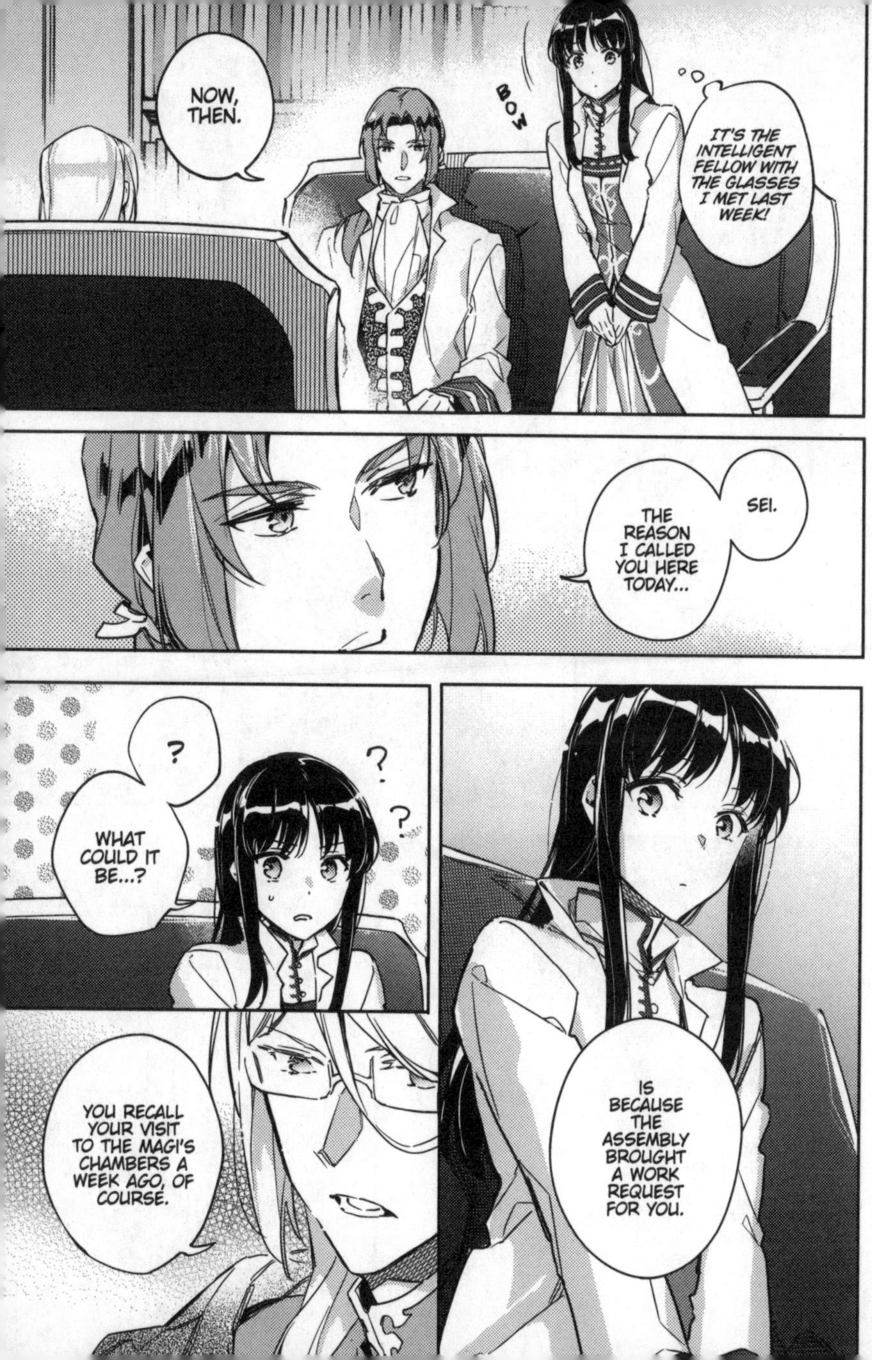
IT'S THE INTELLIGENT FELLOW WITH THE GLASSES I MET LAST WEEK!
BOW
NOW, THEN.
SEI.
THE REASON I CALLED YOU HERE TODAY...
IS BECAUSE THE ASSEMBLY BROUGHT A WORK REQUEST FOR YOU.
?
?
?
WHAT COULD IT BE...?
YOU RECALL YOUR VISIT TO THE MAGI'S CHAMBERS A WEEK AGO, OF COURSE.

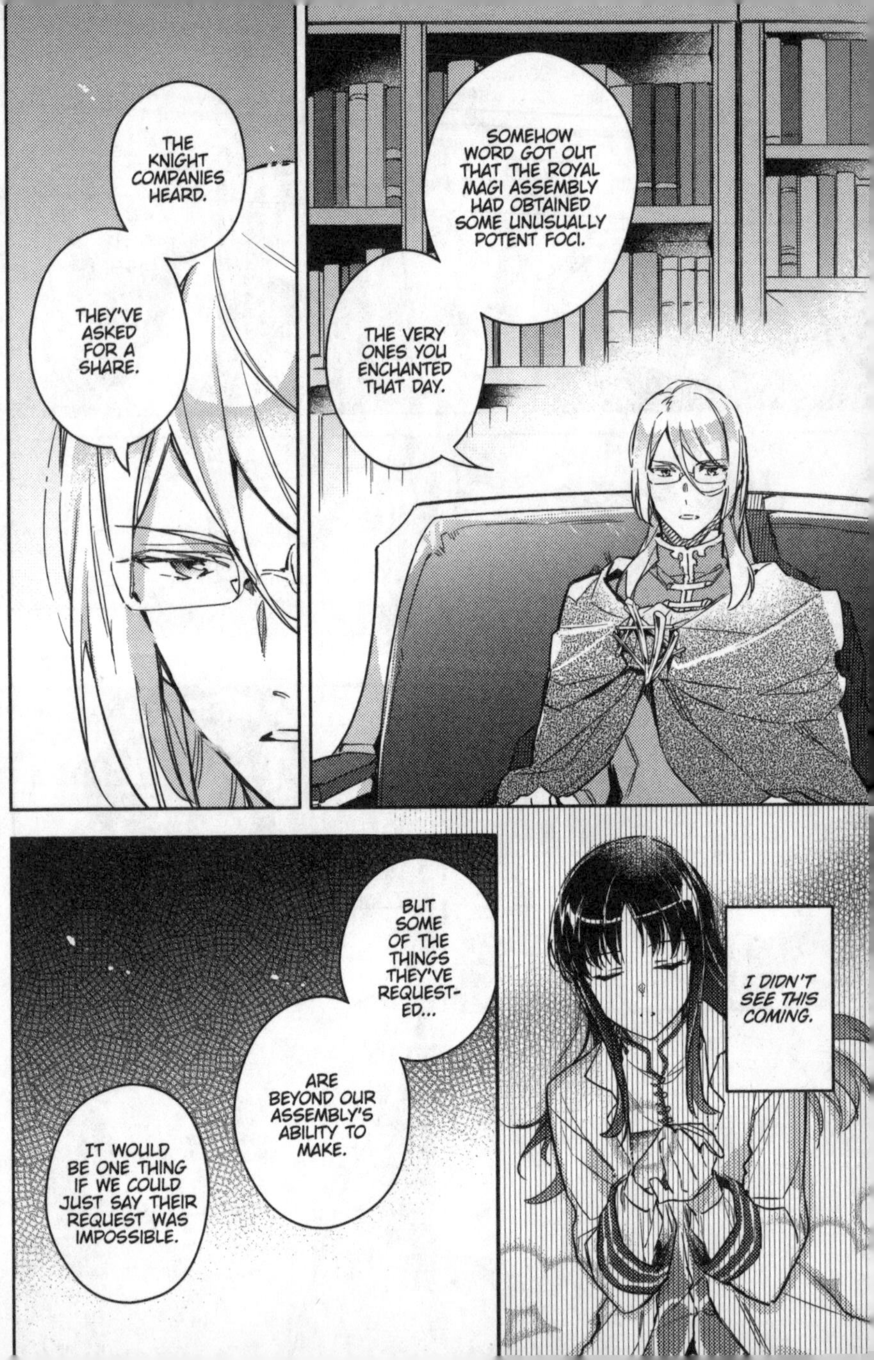
SOMEHOW WORD GOT OUT THAT THE ROYAL MAGI ASSEMBLY HAD OBTAINED SOME UNUSUALLY POTENT FOCI.
THE VERY ONES YOU ENCHANTED THAT DAY.
THE KNIGHT COMPANIES HEARD.
THEY'VE ASKED FOR A SHARE.
I DIDN'T SEE THIS COMING.
BUT SOME OF THE THINGS THEY'VE REQUEST-ED...
ARE BEYOND OUR ASSEMBLY'S ABILITY TO MAKE.
IT WOULD BE ONE THING IF WE COULD JUST SAY THEIR REQUEST WAS IMPOSSIBLE.

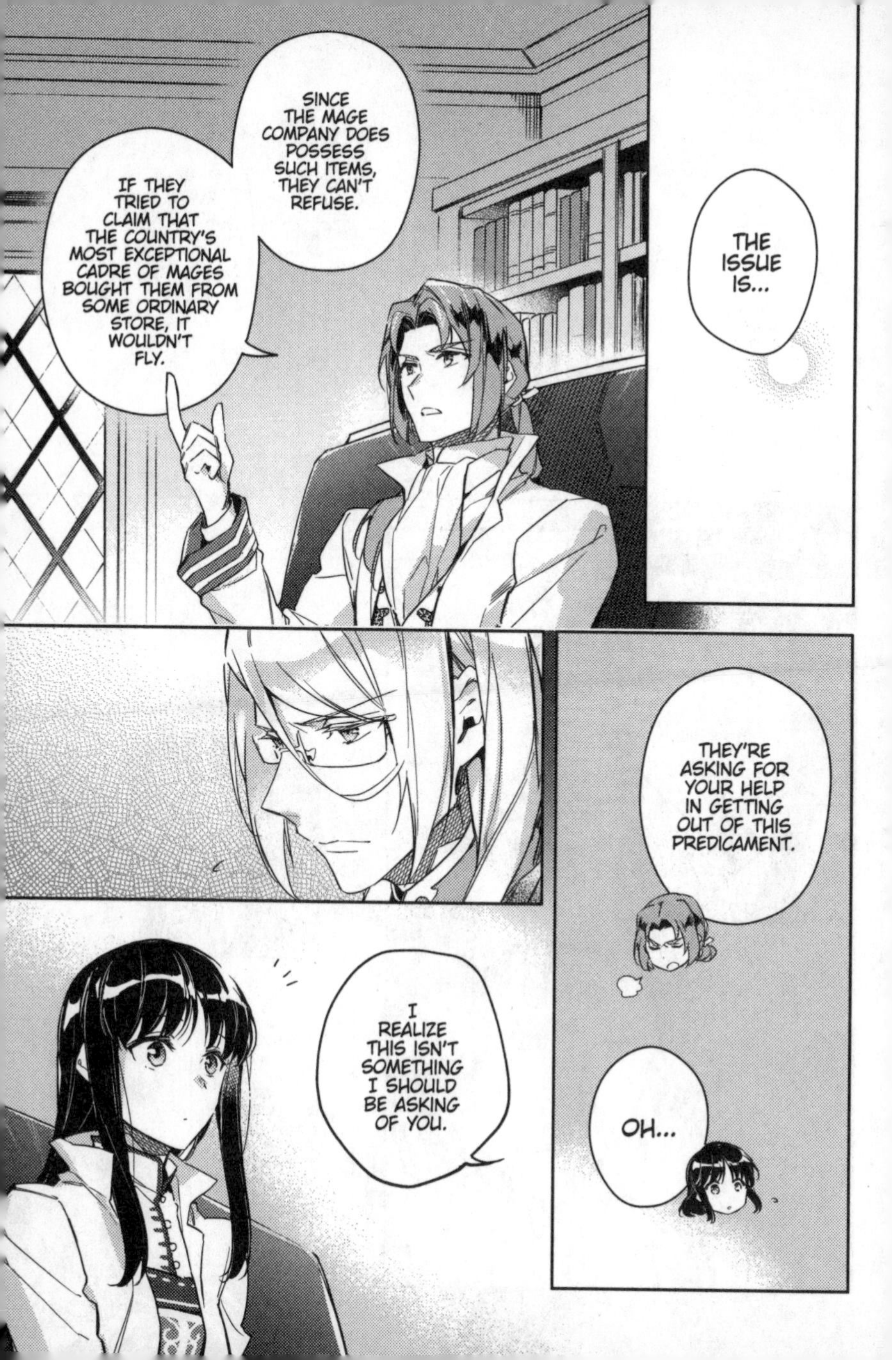
THE ISSUE IS...
SINCE THE MAGE COMPANY DOES POSSESS SUCH ITEMS, THEY CAN'T REFUSE.
IF THEY TRIED TO CLAIM THAT THE COUNTRY'S MOST EXCEPTIONAL CADRE OF MAGES BOUGHT THEM FROM SOME ORDINARY STORE, IT WOULDN'T FLY.
THEY'RE ASKING FOR YOUR HELP IN GETTING OUT OF THIS PREDICAMENT.
OH...
I REALIZE THIS ISN'T SOMETHING I SHOULD BE ASKING OF YOU.

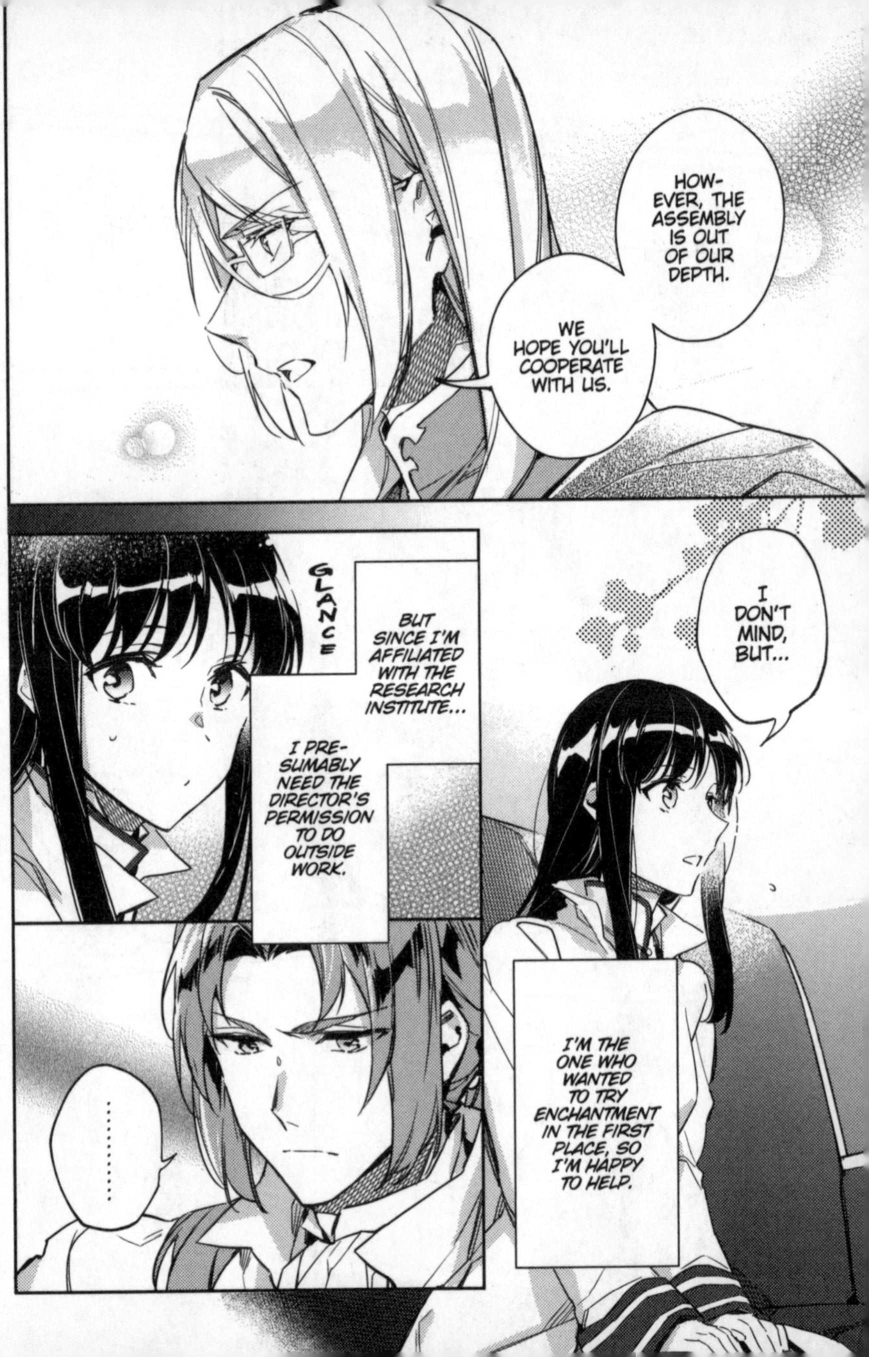
HOW-EVER, THE ASSEMBLY IS OUT OF OUR DEPTH.
WE HOPE YOU'LL COOPERATE WITH US.
I DON'T MIND, BUT...
GLANCE
BUT SINCE I'M AFFILIATED WITH THE RESEARCH INSTITUTE...
I PRESUMABLY NEED THE DIRECTOR'S PERMISSION TO DO OUTSIDE WORK.
......
I'M THE ONE WHO WANTED TO TRY ENCHANTMENT IN THE FIRST PLACE, SO I'M HAPPY TO HELP.

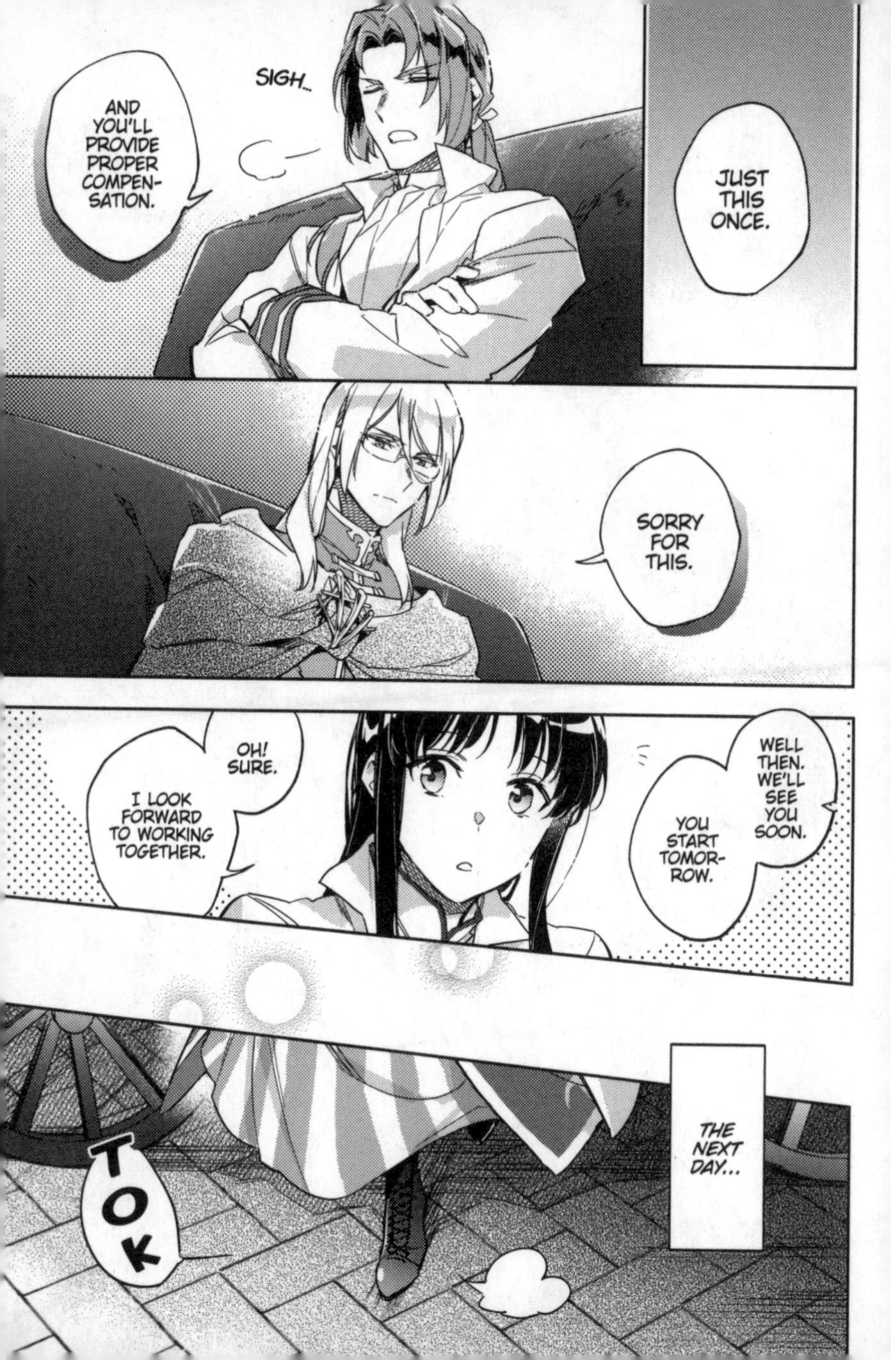
JUST THIS ONCE.
SIGH..
AND YOU'LL PROVIDE PROPER COMPENSATION.
SORRY FOR THIS.
WELL THEN. WE'LL SEE YOU SOON.
YOU START TOMORROW.
OH! SURE.
I LOOK FORWARD TO WORKING TOGETHER.
THE NEXT DAY...
TOK

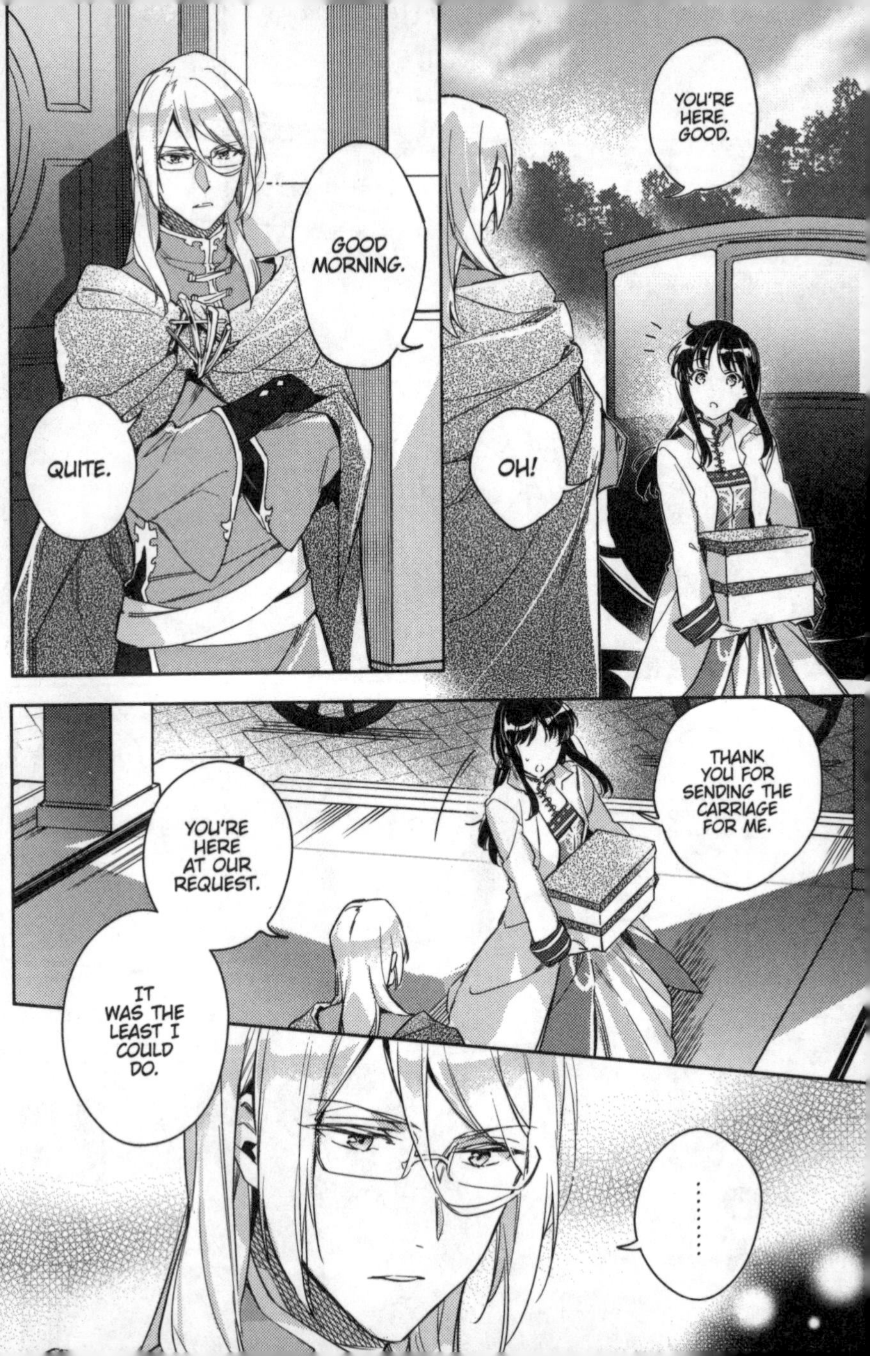
YOU'RE HERE. GOOD.
OH!
GOOD MORNING.
QUITE.
THANK YOU FOR SENDING THE CARRIAGE FOR ME.
YOU'RE HERE AT OUR REQUEST.
IT WAS THE LEAST I COULD DO.
......

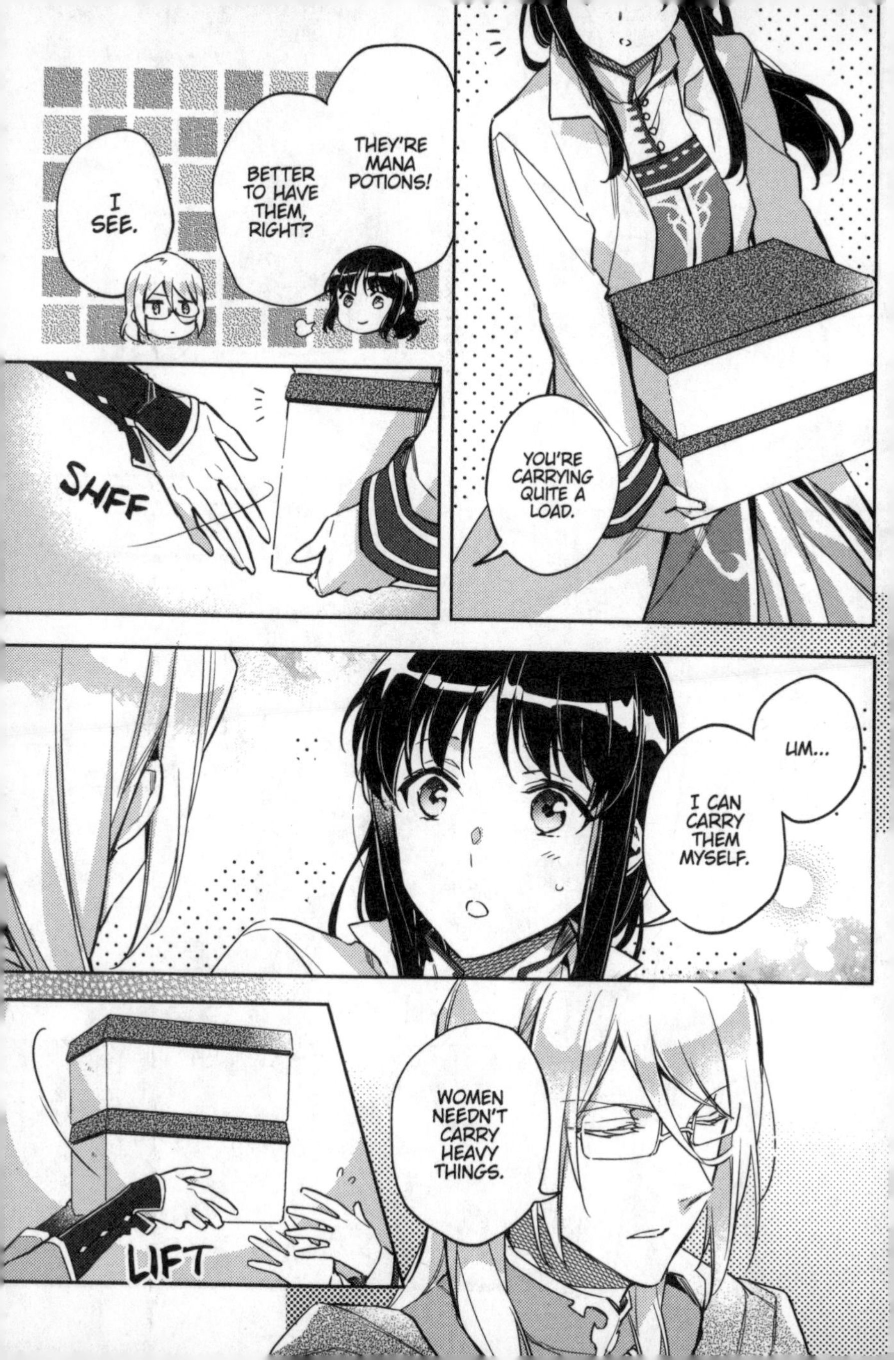
YOU'RE CARRYING QUITE A LOAD.
THEY'RE MANA POTIONS!
BETTER TO HAVE THEM, RIGHT?
I SEE.
SHFF
UM...
I CAN CARRY THEM MYSELF.
WOMEN NEEDN'T CARRY HEAVY THINGS.
LIFT

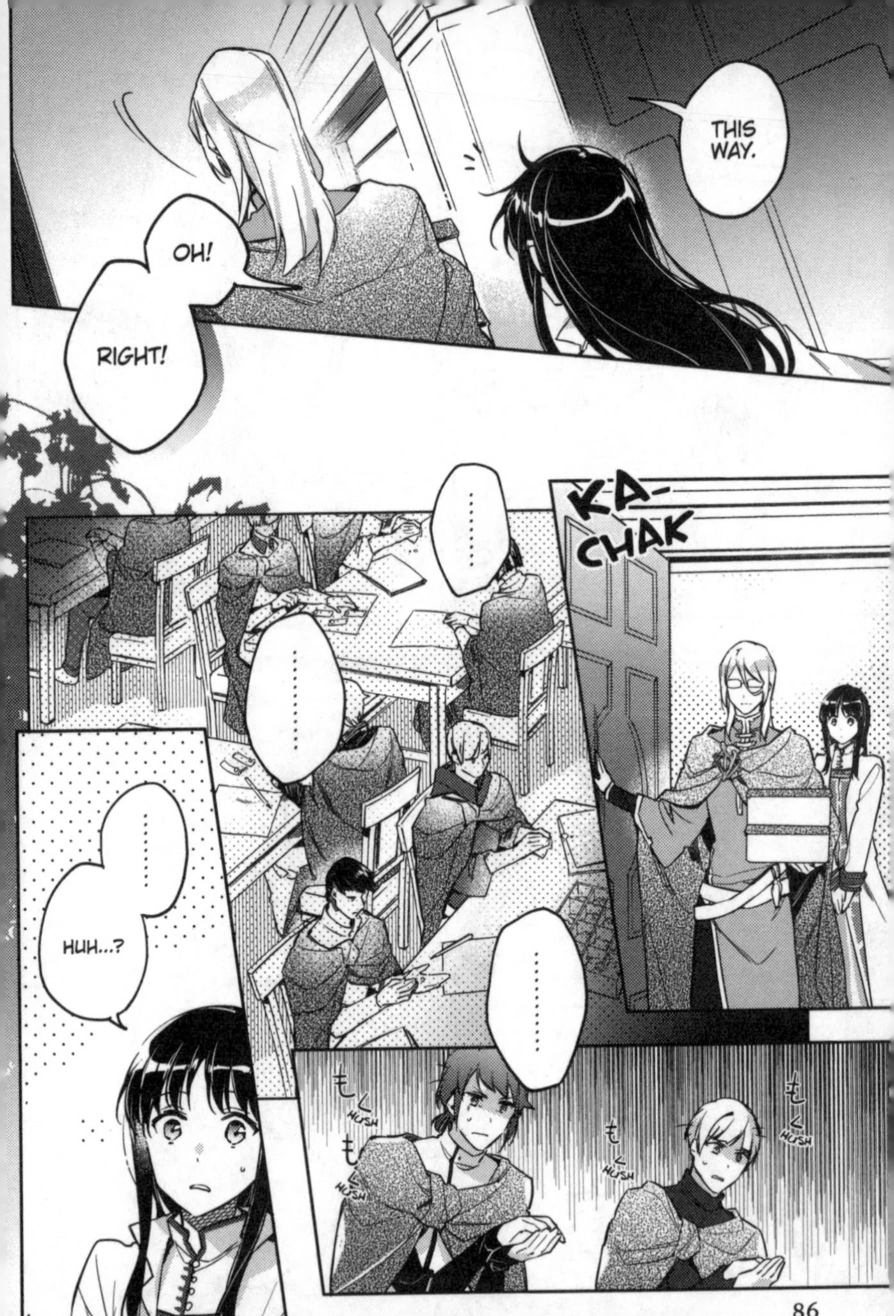
THIS WAY.
OH!
RIGHT!
KA-CHAK
......
......
......
もぐ HUSH
もぐ HUSH
もぐ HUSH
もぐ HUSH
......
HUH...?

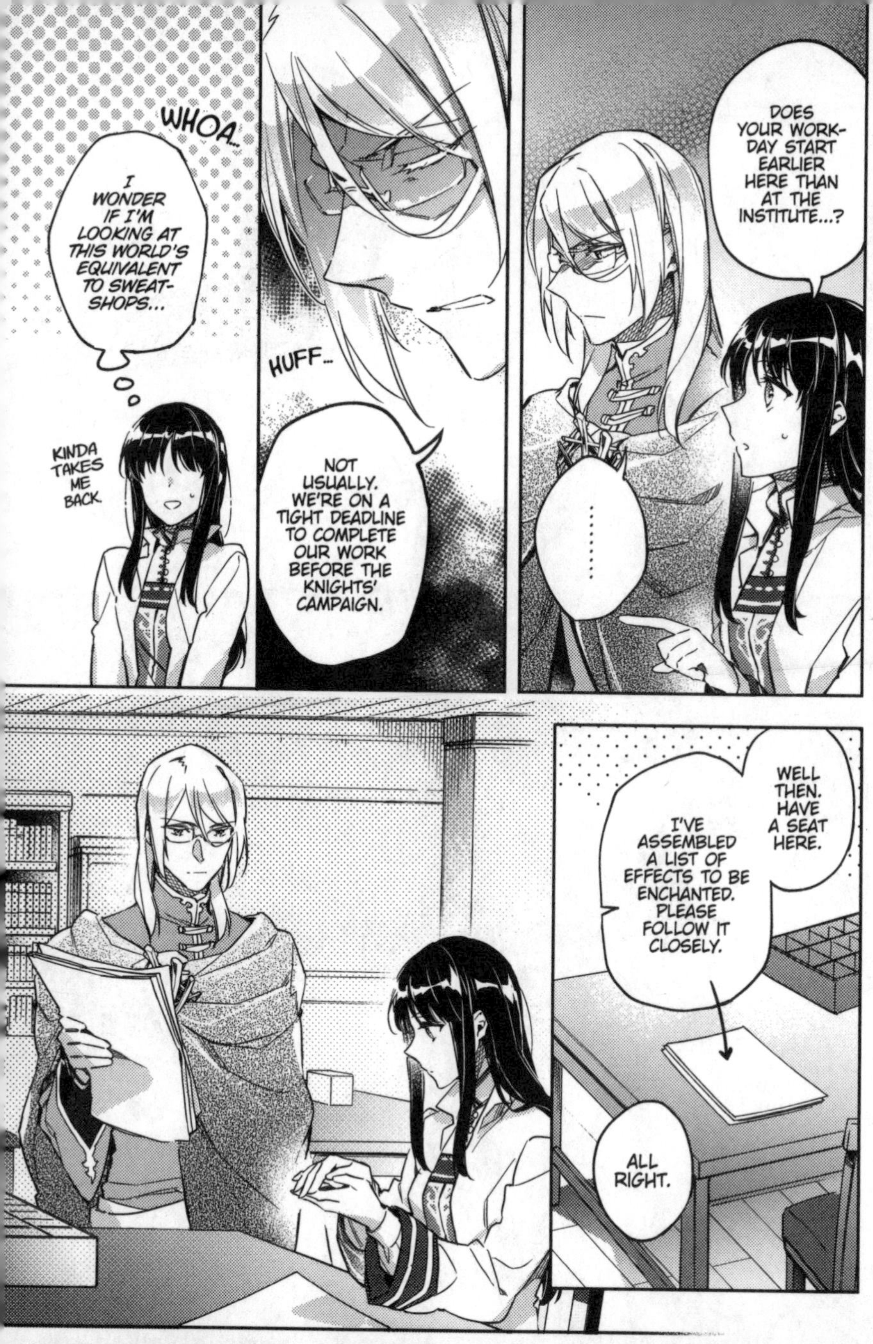
DOES YOUR WORK-DAY START EARLIER HERE THAN AT THE INSTITUTE...?
......
HUFF...
NOT USUALLY. WE'RE ON A TIGHT DEADLINE TO COMPLETE OUR WORK BEFORE THE KNIGHTS' CAMPAIGN.
WHOA...
I WONDER IF I'M LOOKING AT THIS WORLD'S EQUIVALENT TO SWEAT-SHOPS...
KINDA TAKES ME BACK.
WELL THEN. HAVE A SEAT HERE.
I'VE ASSEMBLED A LIST OF EFFECTS TO BE ENCHANTED. PLEASE FOLLOW IT CLOSELY.
ALL RIGHT.

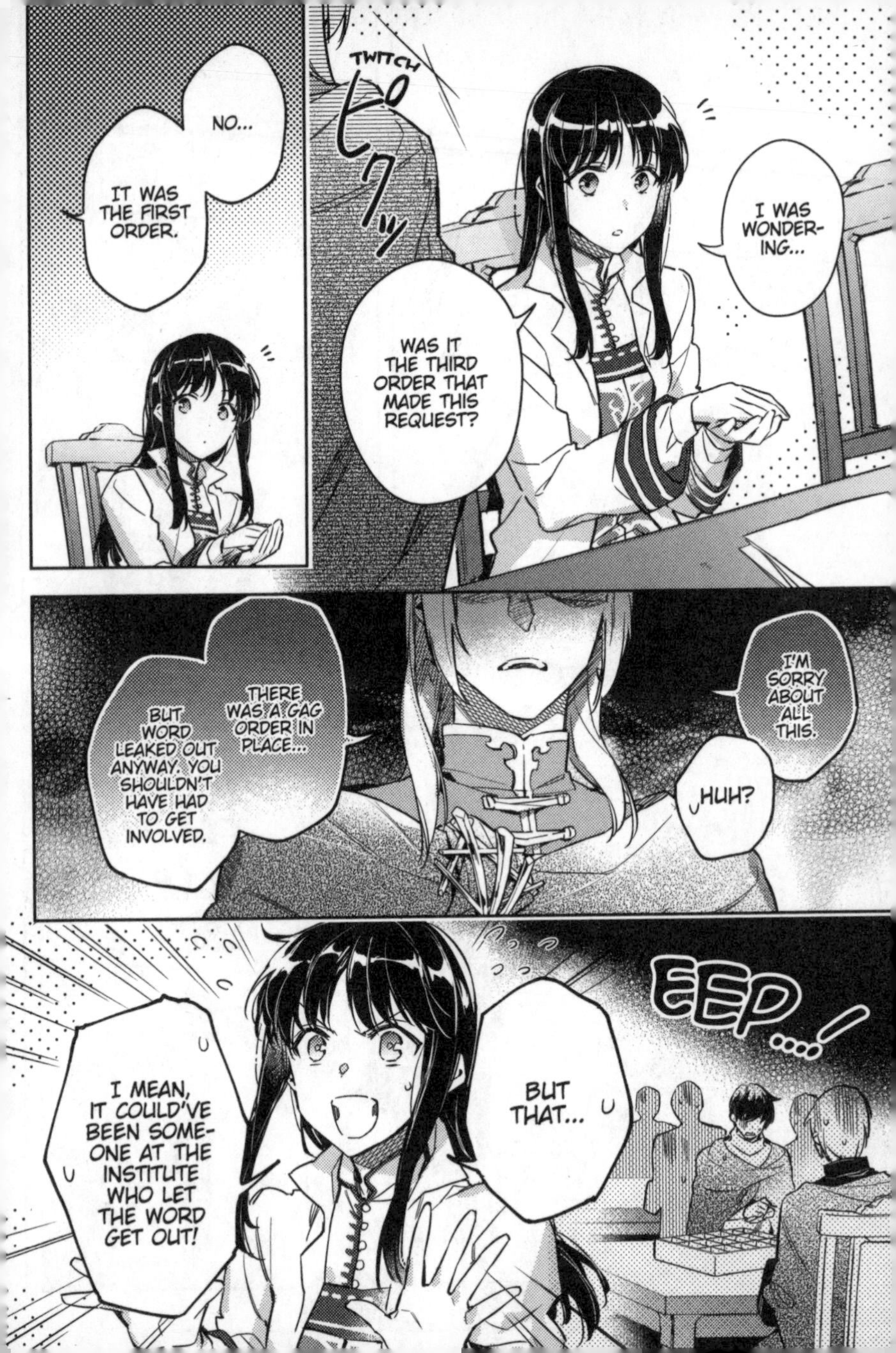
I WAS WONDERING...
WAS IT THE THIRD ORDER THAT MADE THIS REQUEST?
TWITCH
NO...
IT WAS THE FIRST ORDER.
I'M SORRY ABOUT ALL THIS.
HUH?
THERE WAS A GAG ORDER IN PLACE...
BUT WORD LEAKED OUT ANYWAY. YOU SHOULDN'T HAVE HAD TO GET INVOLVED.
EEP...!
BUT THAT...
I MEAN, IT COULD'VE BEEN SOMEONE AT THE INSTITUTE WHO LET THE WORD GET OUT!

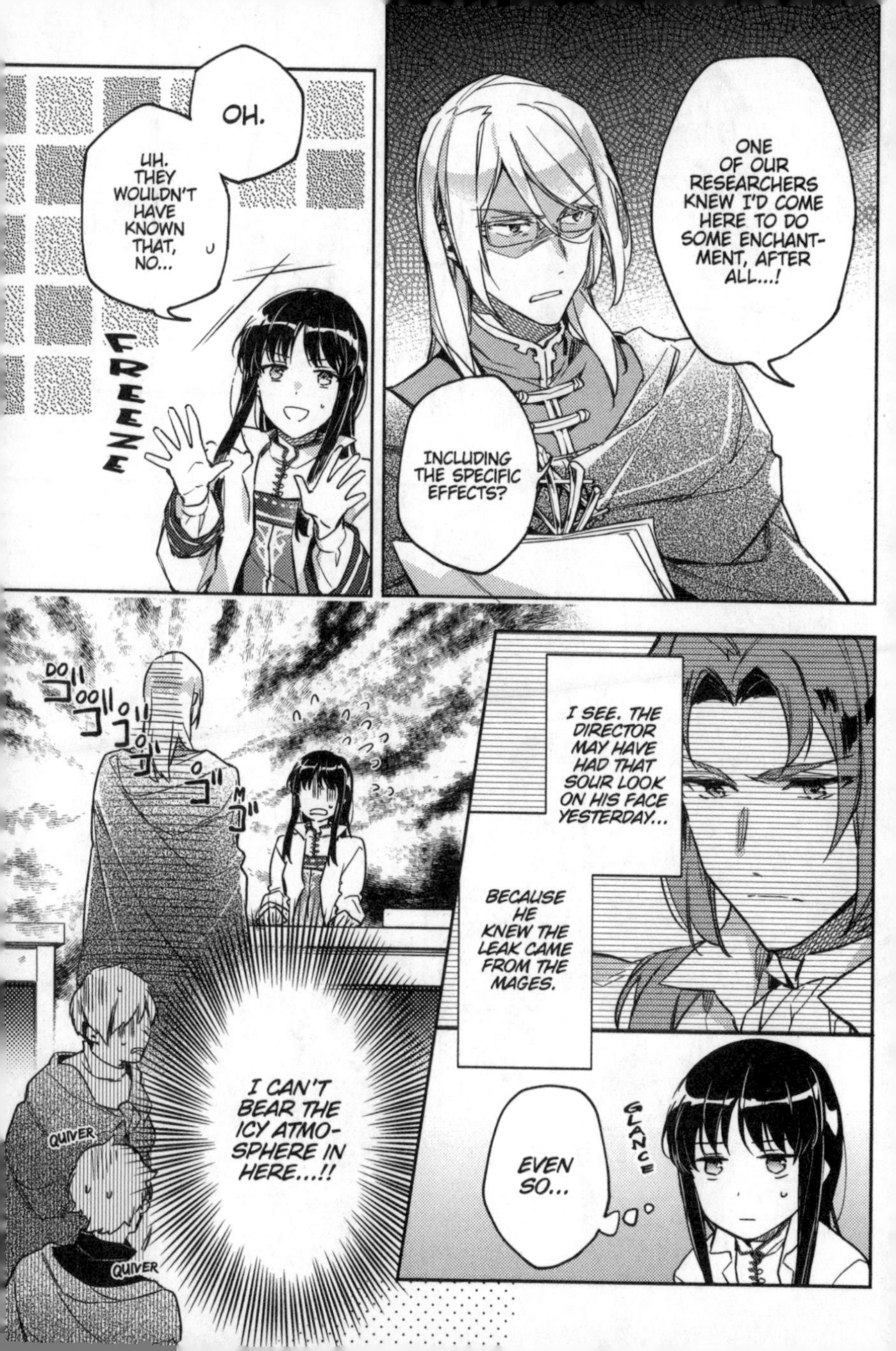
ONE OF OUR RESEARCHERS KNEW I'D COME HERE TO DO SOME ENCHANT-MENT, AFTER ALL...!
INCLUDING THE SPECIFIC EFFECTS?
OH.
UH. THEY WOULDN'T HAVE KNOWN THAT, NO...
FREEZE
I SEE. THE DIRECTOR MAY HAVE HAD THAT SOUR LOOK ON HIS FACE YESTERDAY...
BECAUSE HE KNEW THE LEAK CAME FROM THE MAGES.
GLANCE
EVEN SO...
DOOOOM
I CAN'T BEAR THE ICY ATMO-SPHERE IN HERE...!!
QUIVER
QUIVER

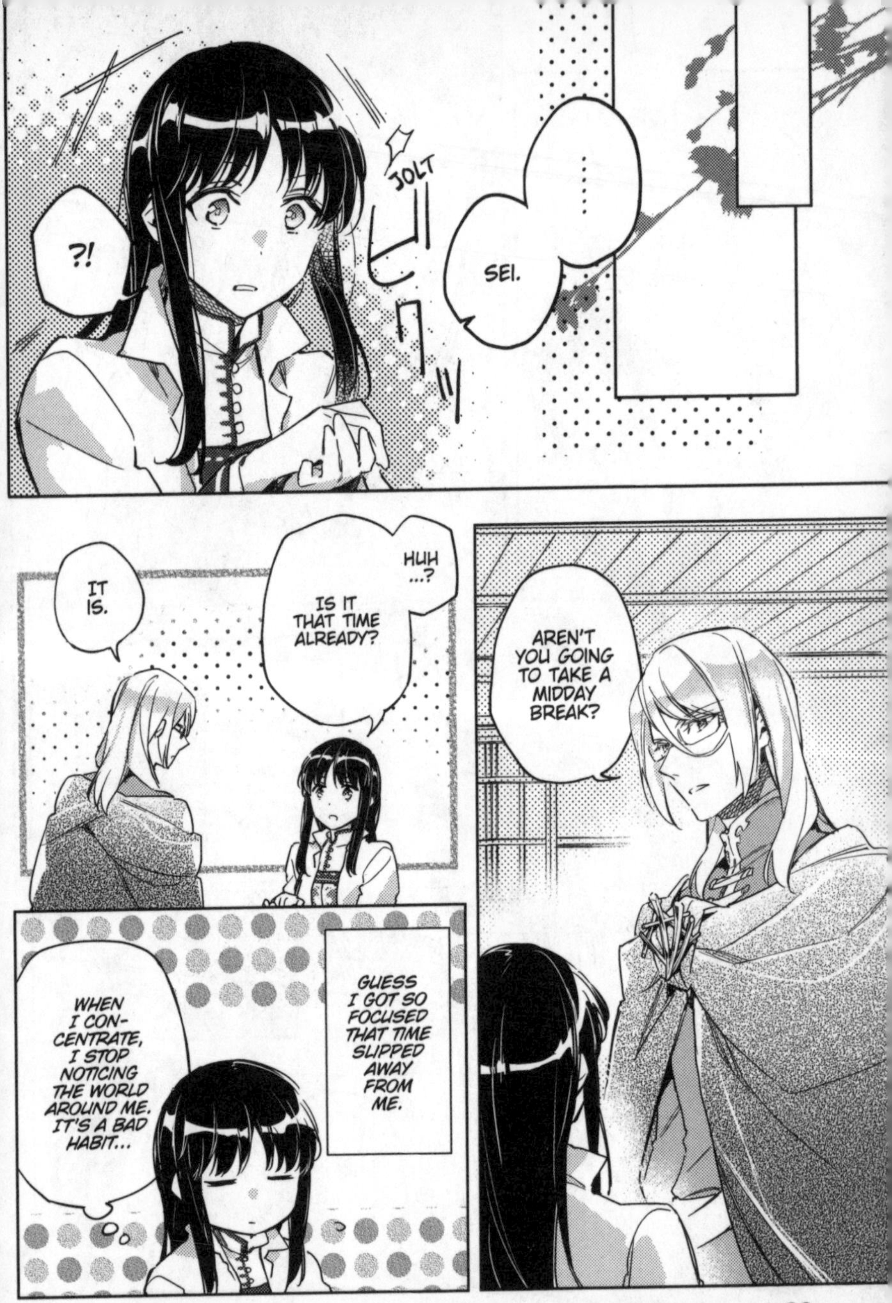
...
SEI.
JOLT
?!
AREN'T YOU GOING TO TAKE A MIDDAY BREAK?
HUH ...?
IS IT THAT TIME ALREADY?
IT IS.
GUESS I GOT SO FOCUSED THAT TIME SLIPPED AWAY FROM ME.
WHEN I CON-CENTRATE, I STOP NOTICING THE WORLD AROUND ME. IT'S A BAD HABIT...

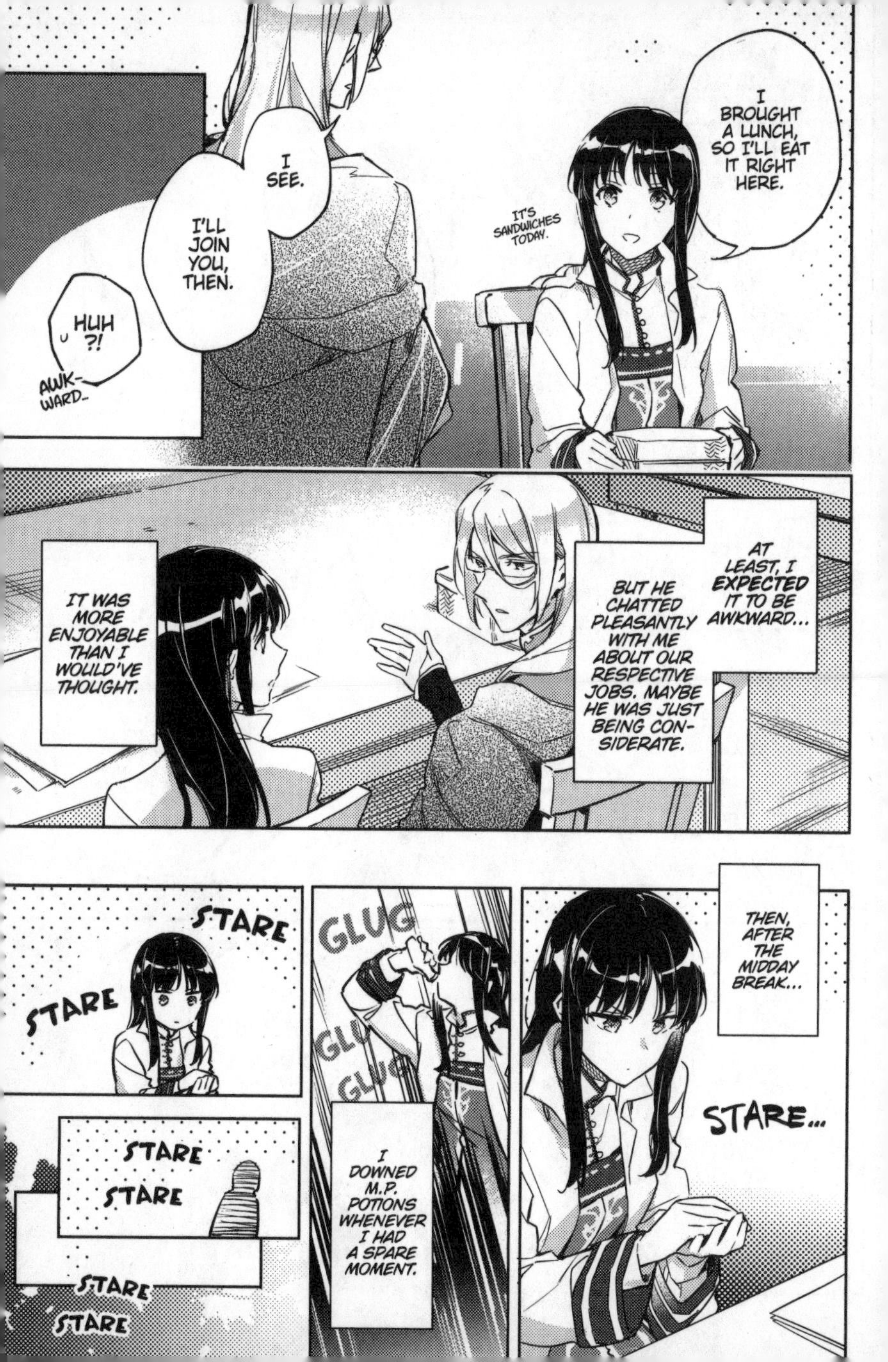
I BROUGHT A LUNCH, SO I'LL EAT IT RIGHT HERE.
IT'S SANDWICHES TODAY.
I SEE.
I'LL JOIN YOU, THEN.
HUH?!
AWK-WARD...
AT LEAST, I EXPECTED IT TO BE AWKWARD...
BUT HE CHATTED PLEASANTLY WITH ME ABOUT OUR RESPECTIVE JOBS. MAYBE HE WAS JUST BEING CON-SIDERATE.
IT WAS MORE ENJOYABLE THAN I WOULD'VE THOUGHT.
THEN, AFTER THE MIDDAY BREAK...
STARE...
GLUG
GLUG
GLUG
I DOWNED M.P. POTIONS WHENEVER I HAD A SPARE MOMENT.
STARE
STARE
STARE
STARE
STARE
STARE

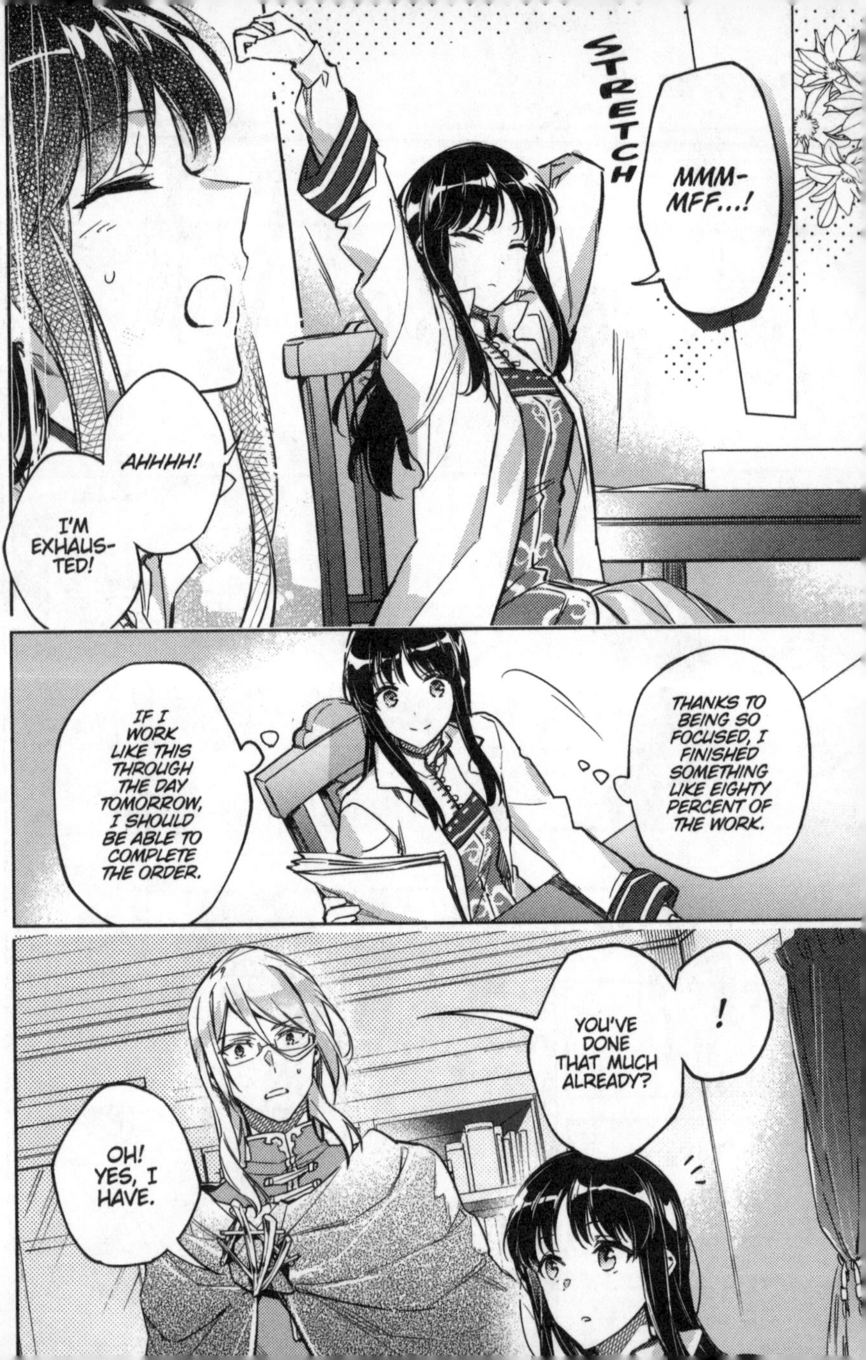
STRETCH
MMM-MFF...!
AHHHH!
I'M EXHAUS-TED!
THANKS TO BEING SO FOCUSED, I FINISHED SOMETHING LIKE EIGHTY PERCENT OF THE WORK.
IF I WORK LIKE THIS THROUGH THE DAY TOMORROW, I SHOULD BE ABLE TO COMPLETE THE ORDER.
YOU'VE DONE THAT MUCH ALREADY?
!
OH! YES, I HAVE.

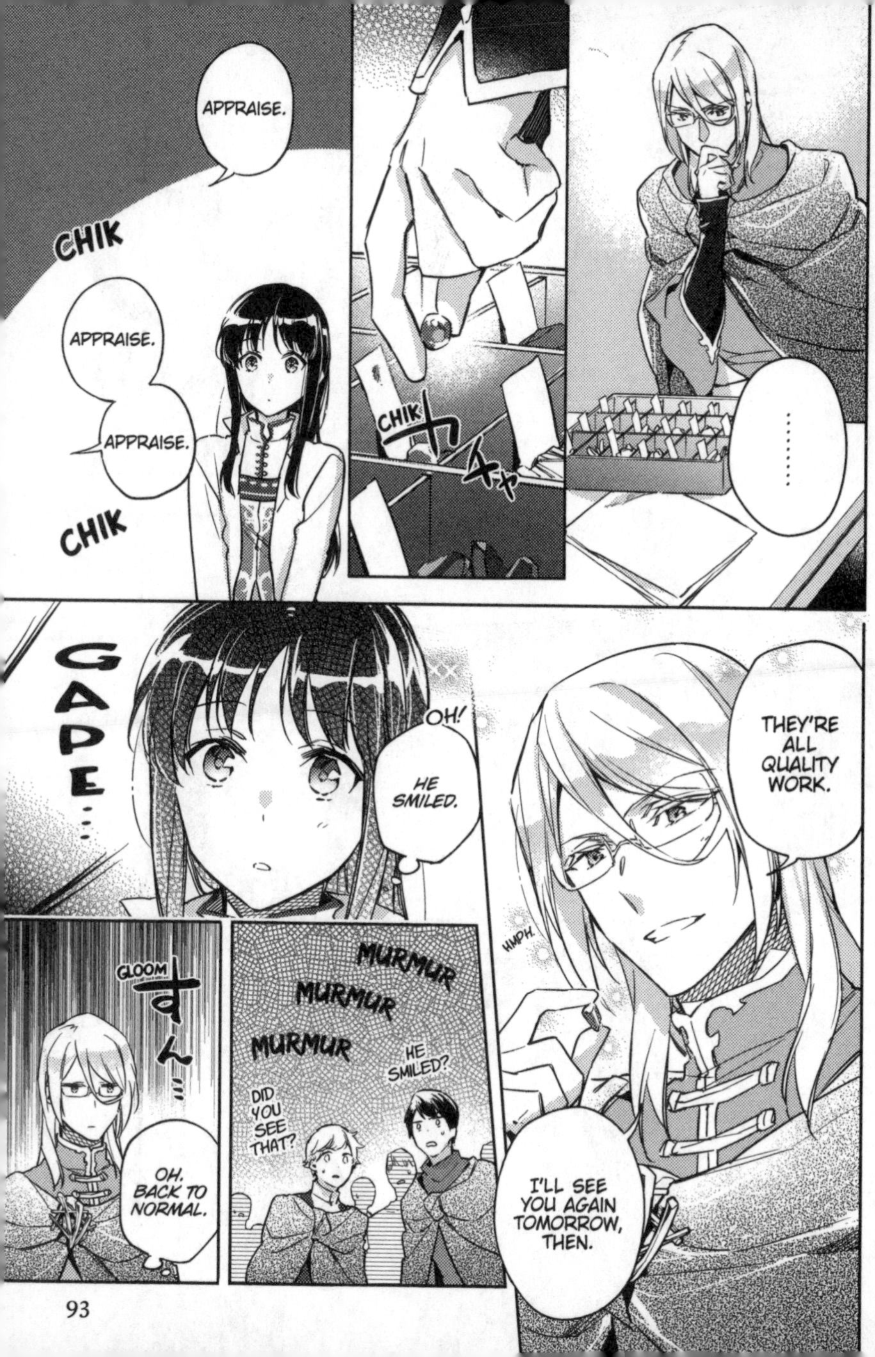
......
CHIK
APPRAISE.
CHIK
APPRAISE.
APPRAISE.
CHIK
THEY'RE ALL QUALITY WORK.
HMPH.
I'LL SEE YOU AGAIN TOMORROW, THEN.
GAPE...
OH!
HE SMILED.
MURMUR
MURMUR
MURMUR
HE SMILED?
DID YOU SEE THAT?
GLOOM
OH. BACK TO NORMAL.

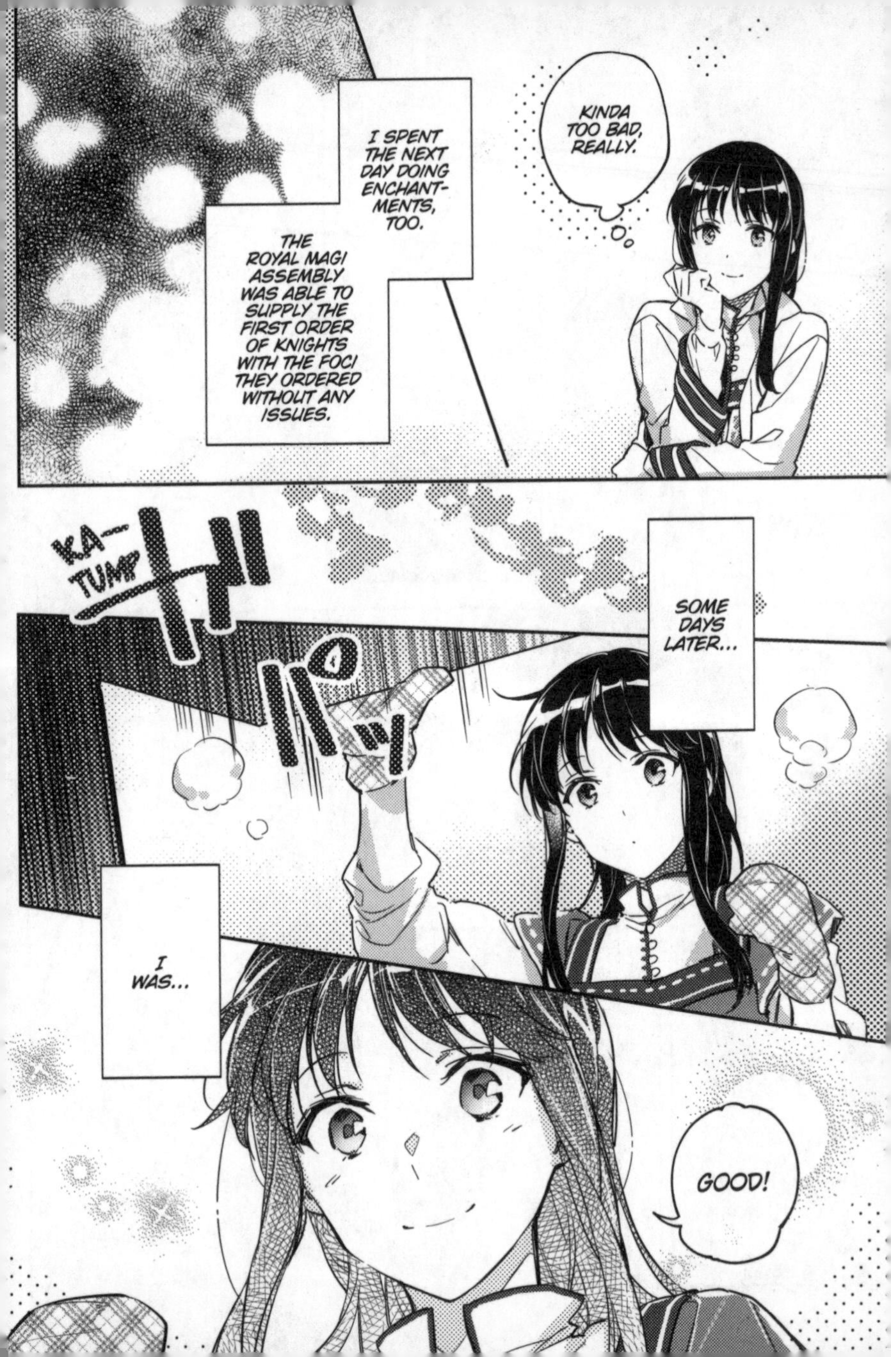
KINDA TOO BAD, REALLY.
I SPENT THE NEXT DAY DOING ENCHANTMENTS, TOO.
THE ROYAL MAGI ASSEMBLY WAS ABLE TO SUPPLY THE FIRST ORDER OF KNIGHTS WITH THE FOCI THEY ORDERED WITHOUT ANY ISSUES.
SOME DAYS LATER...
KA-TUMP
I WAS...
GOOD!

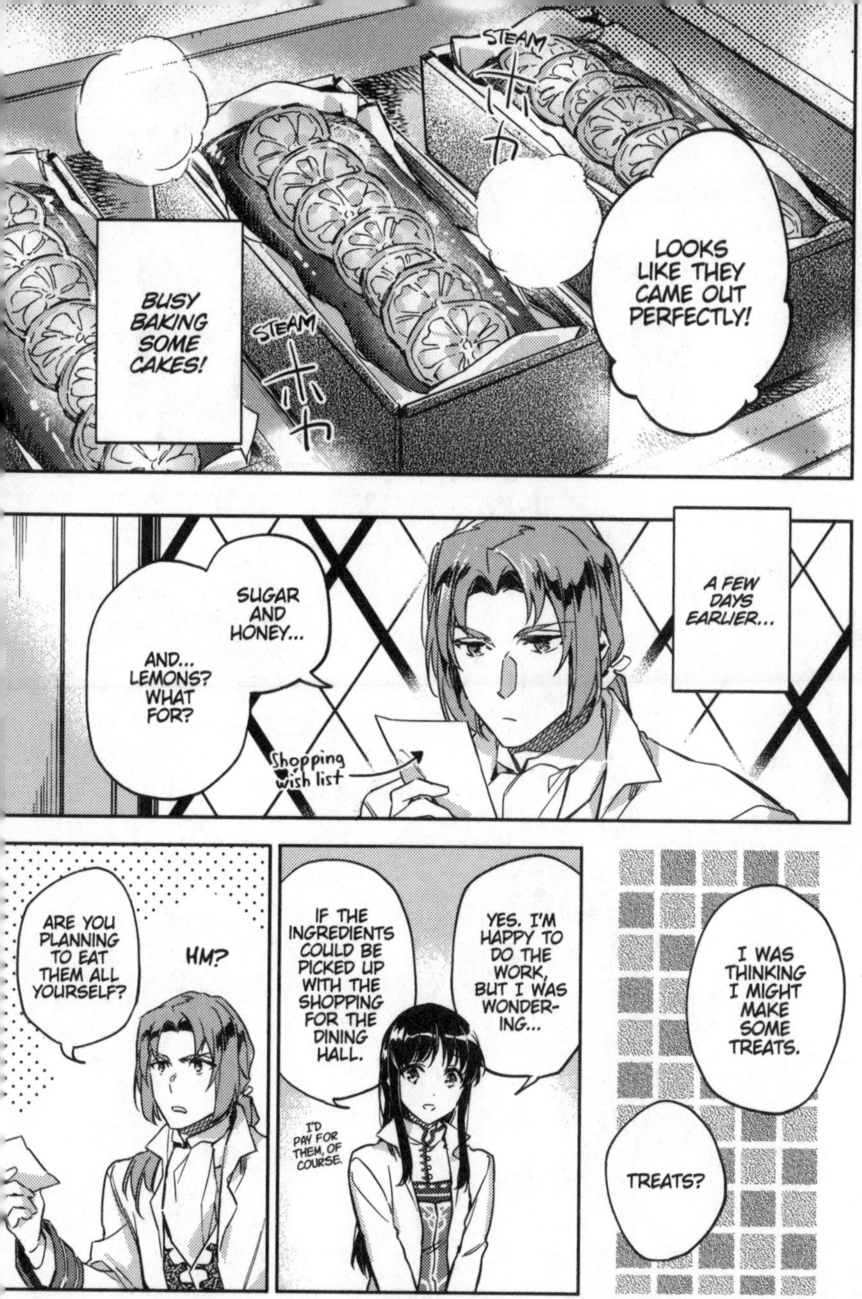
STEAM
LOOKS LIKE THEY CAME OUT PERFECTLY!
STEAM
BUSY BAKING SOME CAKES!
A FEW DAYS EARLIER...
SUGAR AND HONEY...
AND... LEMONS? WHAT FOR?
Shopping wish list
I WAS THINKING I MIGHT MAKE SOME TREATS.
TREATS?
YES. I'M HAPPY TO DO THE WORK, BUT I WAS WONDER-ING...
IF THE INGREDIENTS COULD BE PICKED UP WITH THE SHOPPING FOR THE DINING HALL.
I'D PAY FOR THEM, OF COURSE.
HM?
ARE YOU PLANNING TO EAT THEM ALL YOURSELF?

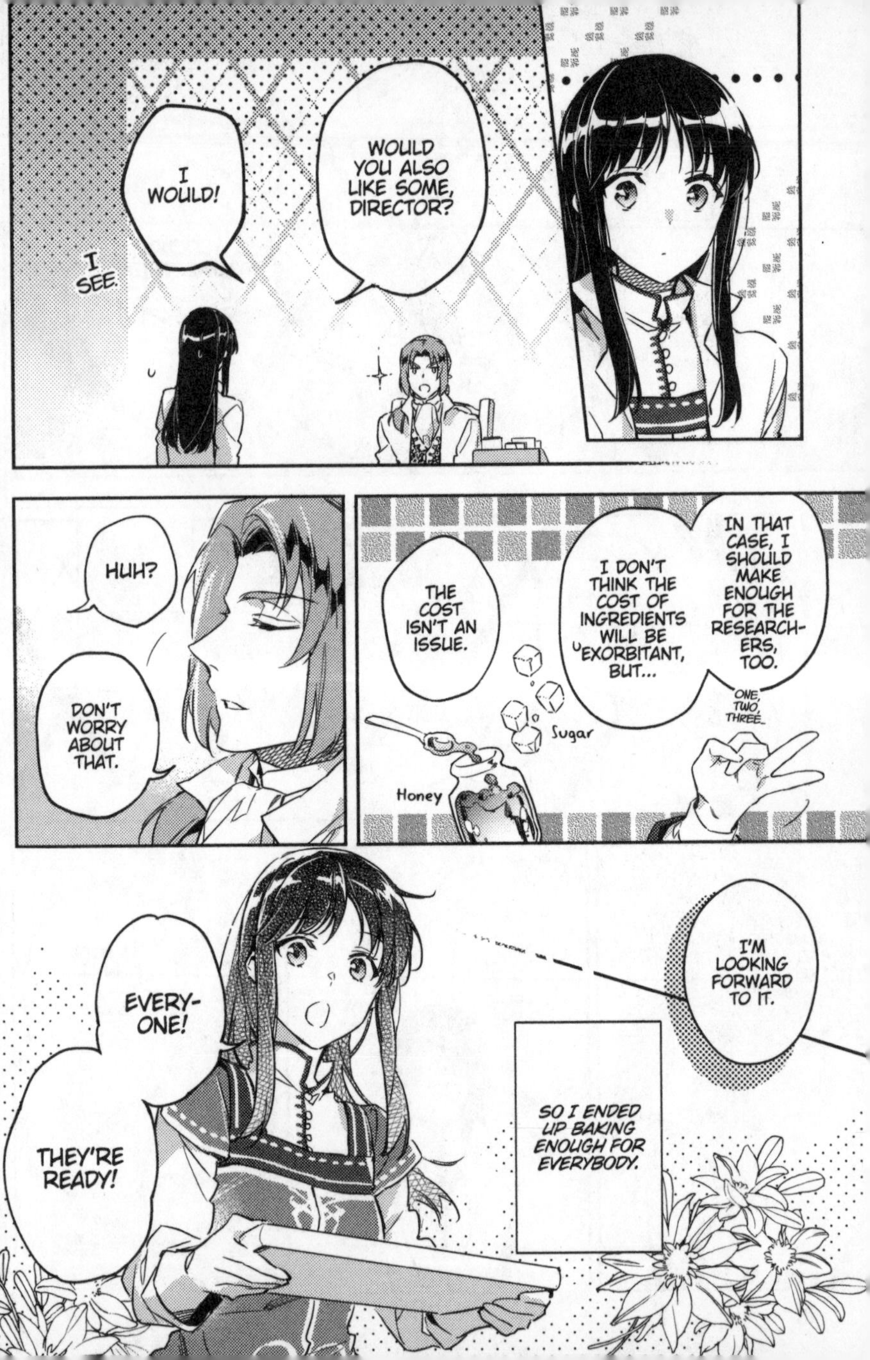
WOULD YOU ALSO LIKE SOME, DIRECTOR?
I WOULD!
I SEE.
IN THAT CASE, I SHOULD MAKE ENOUGH FOR THE RESEARCHERS, TOO.
ONE, TWO, THREE_
I DON'T THINK THE COST OF INGREDIENTS WILL BE EXORBITANT, BUT...
Sugar
Honey
THE COST ISN'T AN ISSUE.
HUH?
DON'T WORRY ABOUT THAT.
I'M LOOKING FORWARD TO IT.
SO I ENDED UP BAKING ENOUGH FOR EVERYBODY.
EVERY-ONE!
THEY'RE READY!

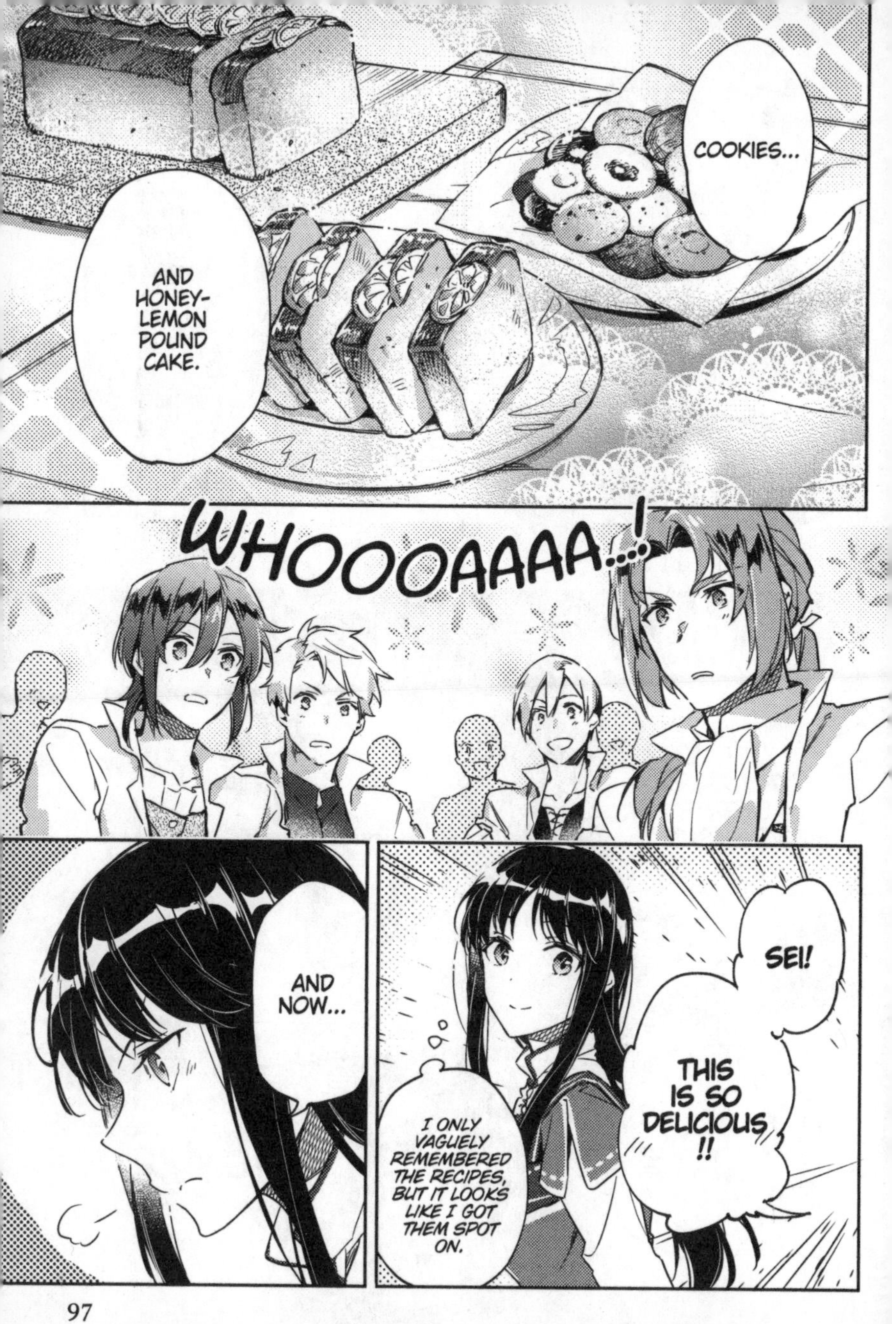
COOKIES...
AND HONEY-LEMON POUND CAKE.
WHOOOAAAA...!
SEI!
THIS IS SO DELICIOUS!!
I ONLY VAGUELY REMEMBERED THE RECIPES, BUT IT LOOKS LIKE I GOT THEM SPOT ON.
AND NOW...

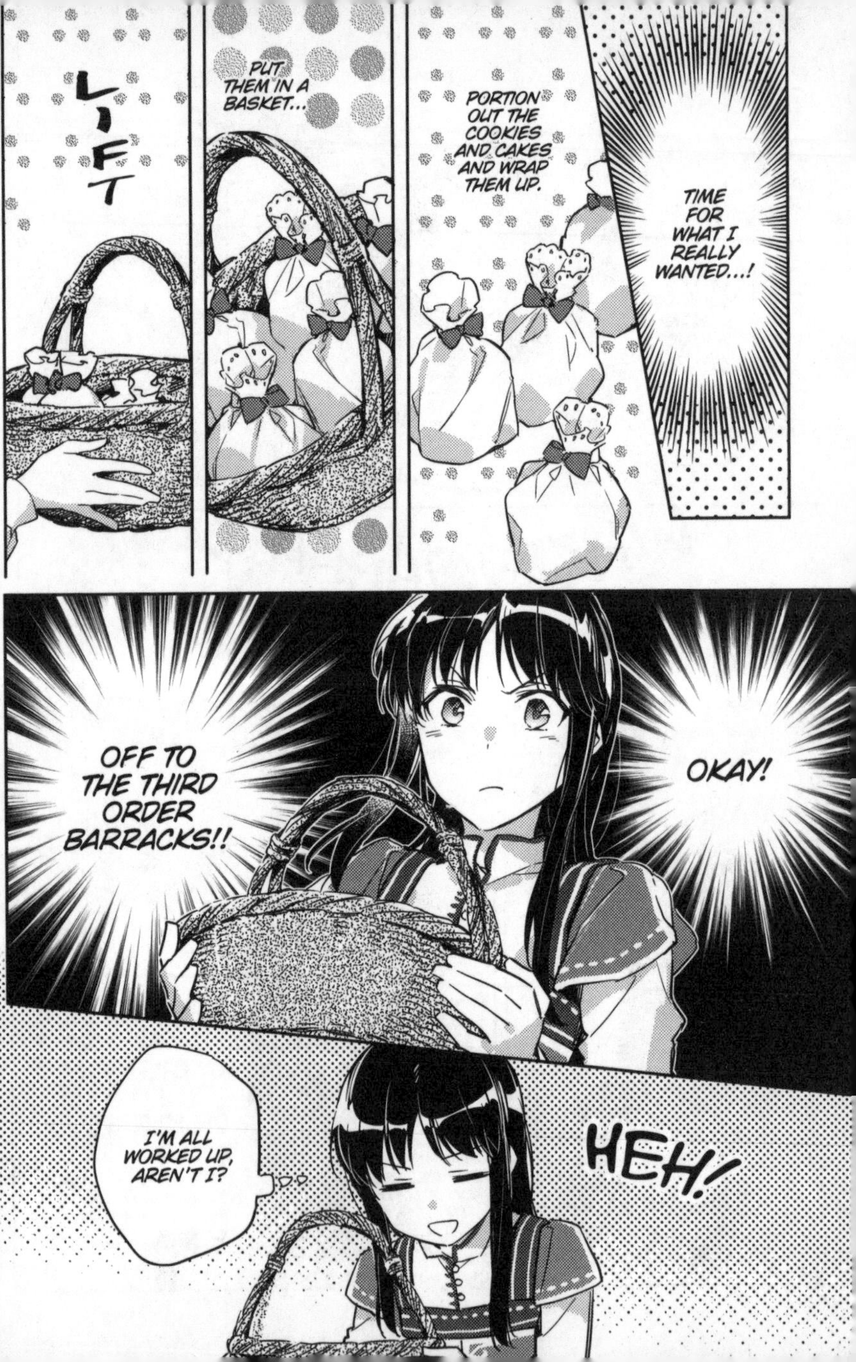
TIME FOR WHAT I REALLY WANTED...!
PORTION OUT THE COOKIES AND CAKES AND WRAP THEM UP.
PUT THEM IN A BASKET...
LIFT
OKAY!
OFF TO THE THIRD ORDER BARRACKS!!
HEH!
I'M ALL WORKED UP, AREN'T I?

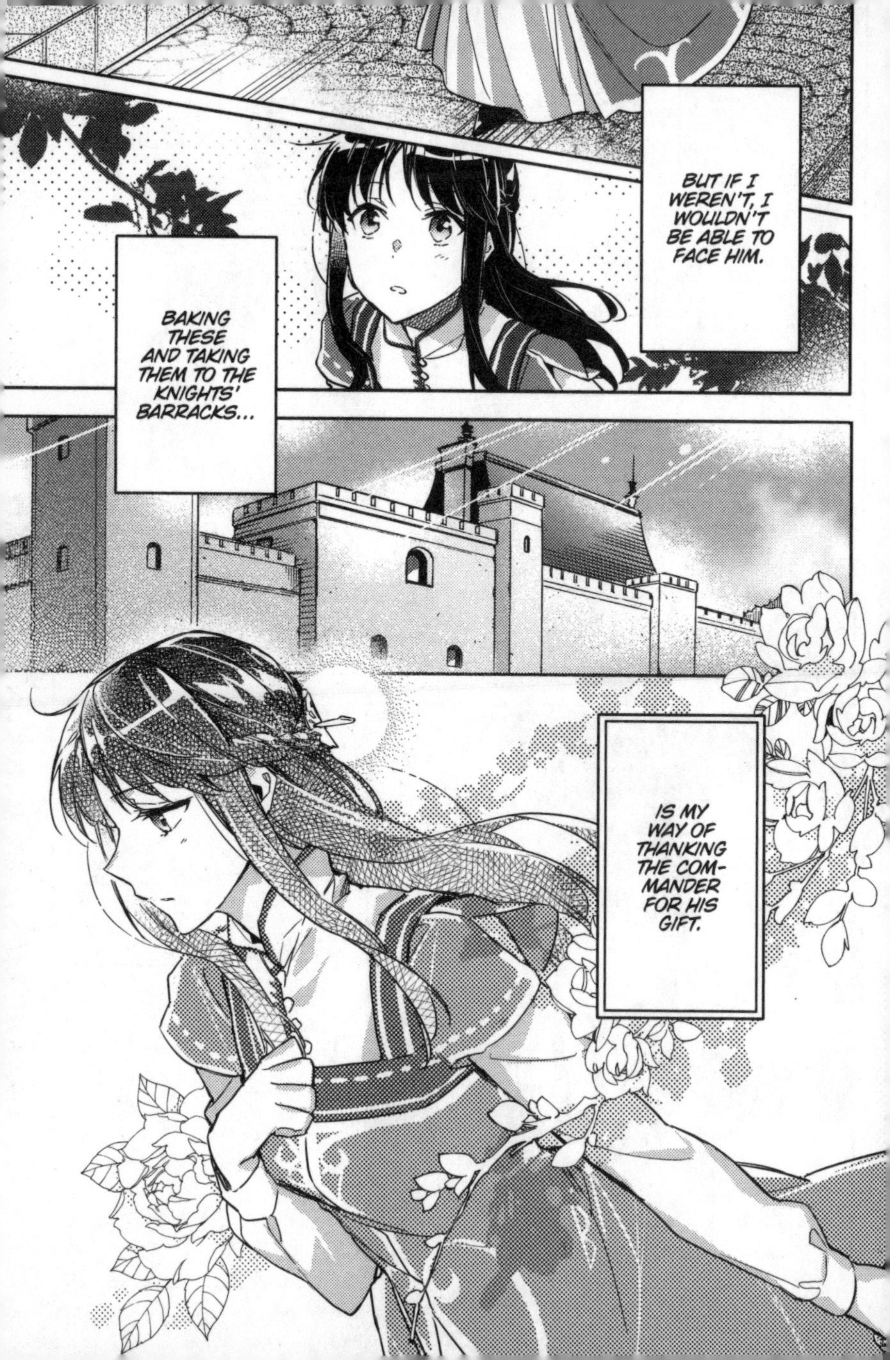
BUT IF I WEREN'T, I WOULDN'T BE ABLE TO FACE HIM.
BAKING THESE AND TAKING THEM TO THE KNIGHTS' BARRACKS...
IS MY WAY OF THANKING THE COMMANDER FOR HIS GIFT.

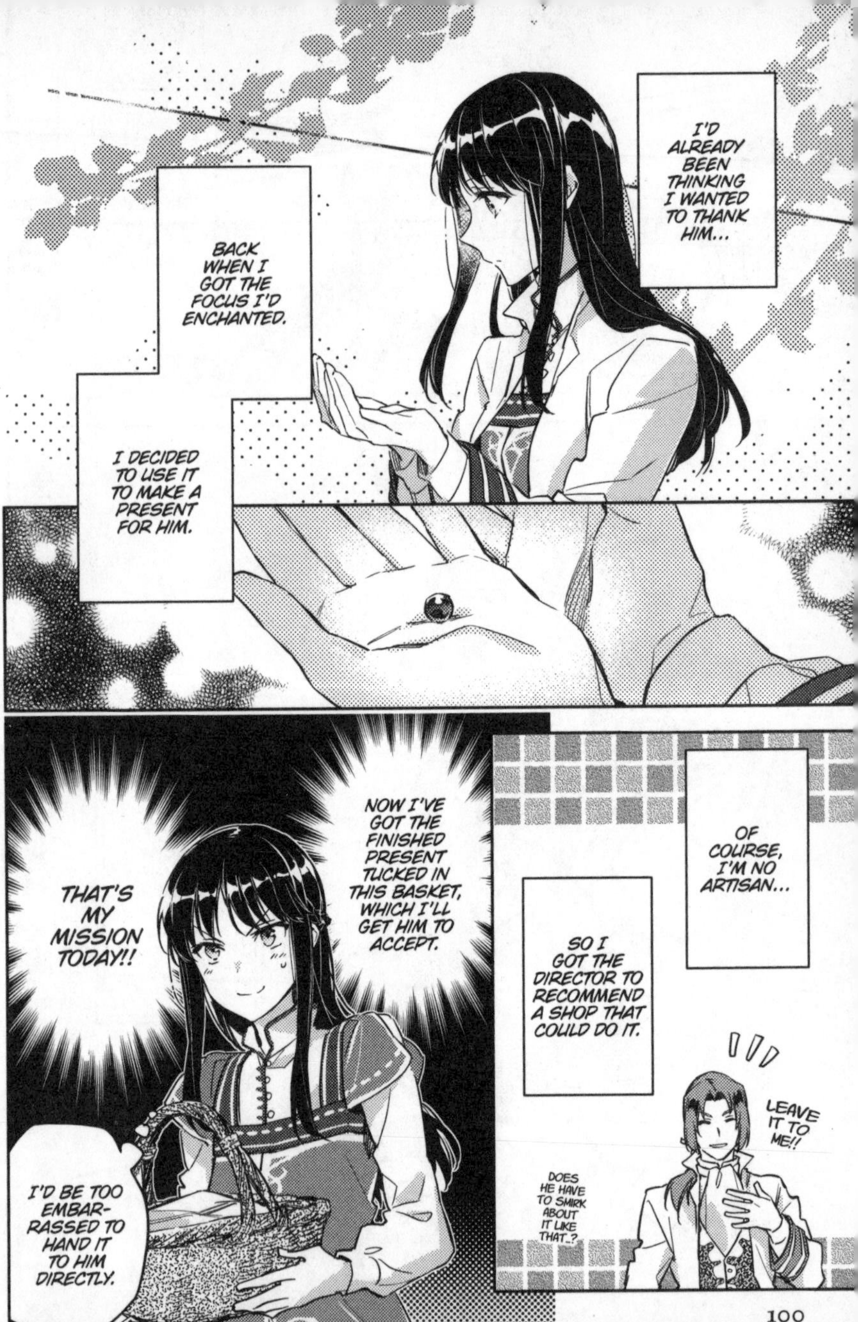
I'D ALREADY BEEN THINKING I WANTED TO THANK HIM...
BACK WHEN I GOT THE FOCUS I'D ENCHANTED.
I DECIDED TO USE IT TO MAKE A PRESENT FOR HIM.
OF COURSE, I'M NO ARTISAN...
SO I GOT THE DIRECTOR TO RECOMMEND A SHOP THAT COULD DO IT.
LEAVE IT TO ME!!
DOES HE HAVE TO SMIRK ABOUT IT LIKE THAT..?
NOW I'VE GOT THE FINISHED PRESENT TUCKED IN THIS BASKET, WHICH I'LL GET HIM TO ACCEPT.
THAT'S MY MISSION TODAY!!
I'D BE TOO EMBAR-RASSED TO HAND IT TO HIM DIRECTLY.

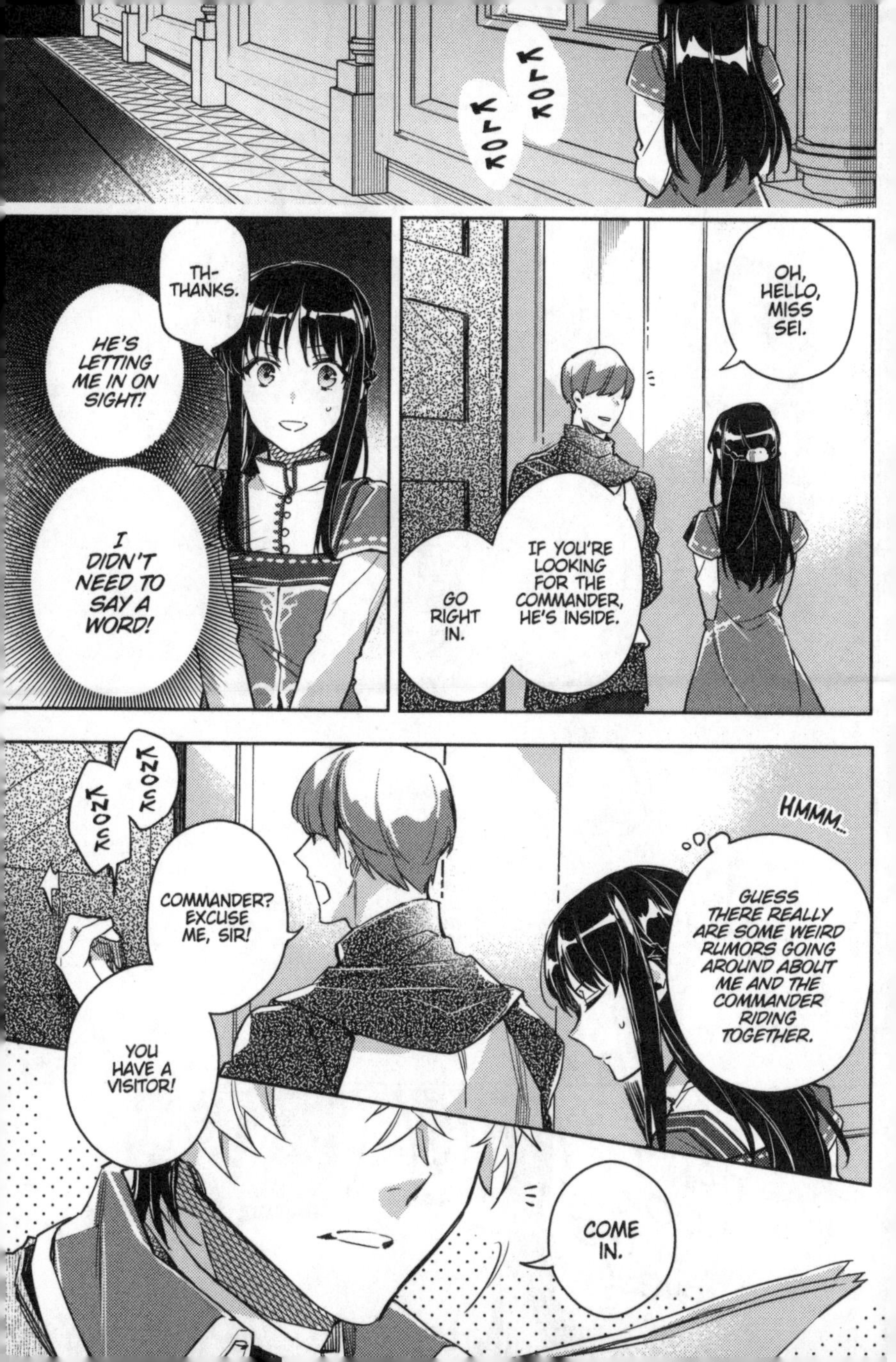
KLOK
KLOK
OH, HELLO, MISS SEI.
IF YOU'RE LOOKING FOR THE COMMANDER, HE'S INSIDE.
GO RIGHT IN.
TH- THANKS.
HE'S LETTING ME IN ON SIGHT!
I DIDN'T NEED TO SAY A WORD!
HMMM...
GUESS THERE REALLY ARE SOME WEIRD RUMORS GOING AROUND ABOUT ME AND THE COMMANDER RIDING TOGETHER.
KNOCK
KNOCK
COMMANDER? EXCUSE ME, SIR!
YOU HAVE A VISITOR!
COME IN.

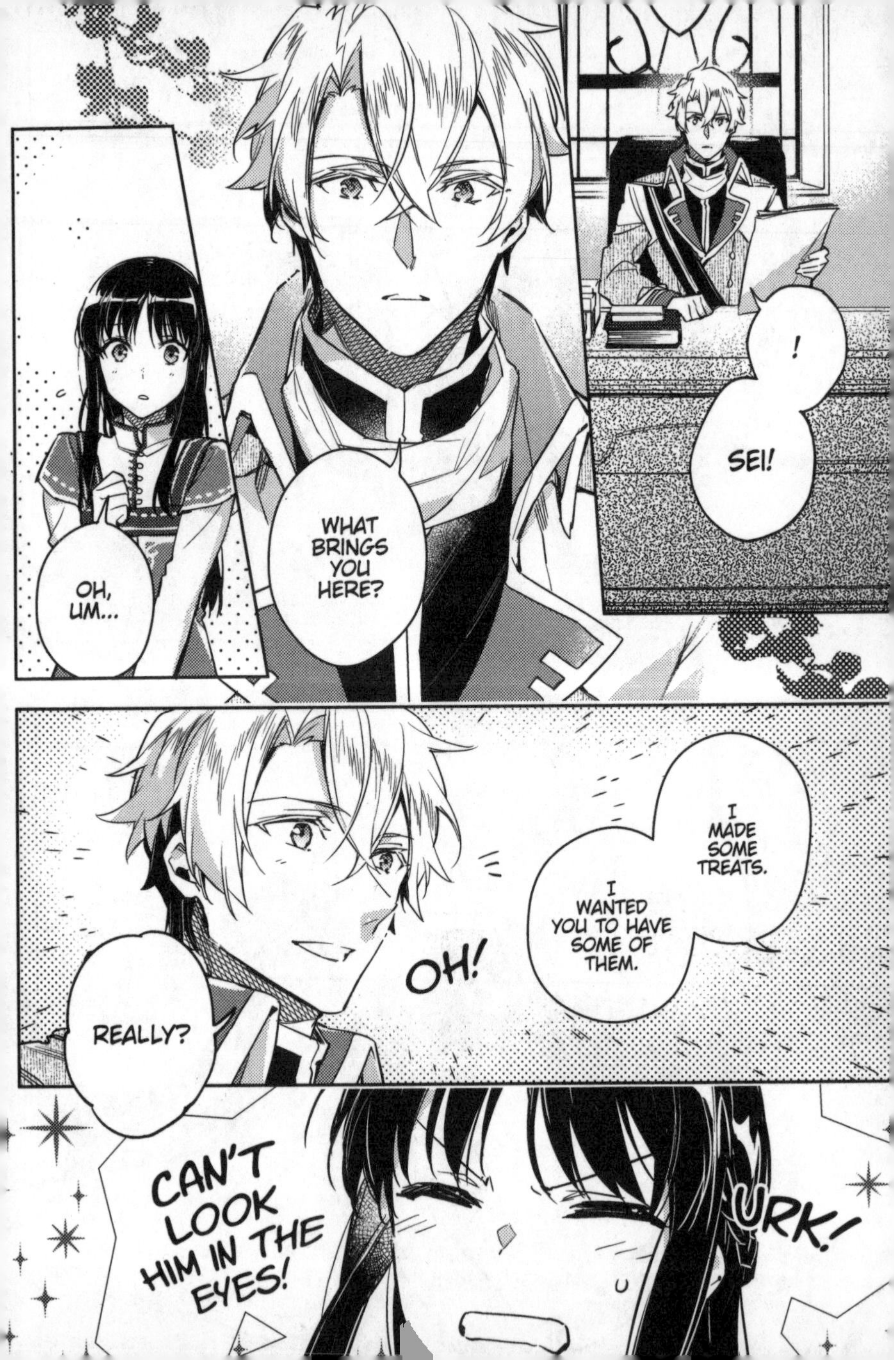
!
SEI!
WHAT BRINGS YOU HERE?
OH, UM...
I MADE SOME TREATS.
I WANTED YOU TO HAVE SOME OF THEM.
OH!
REALLY?
URK!
CAN'T LOOK HIM IN THE EYES!

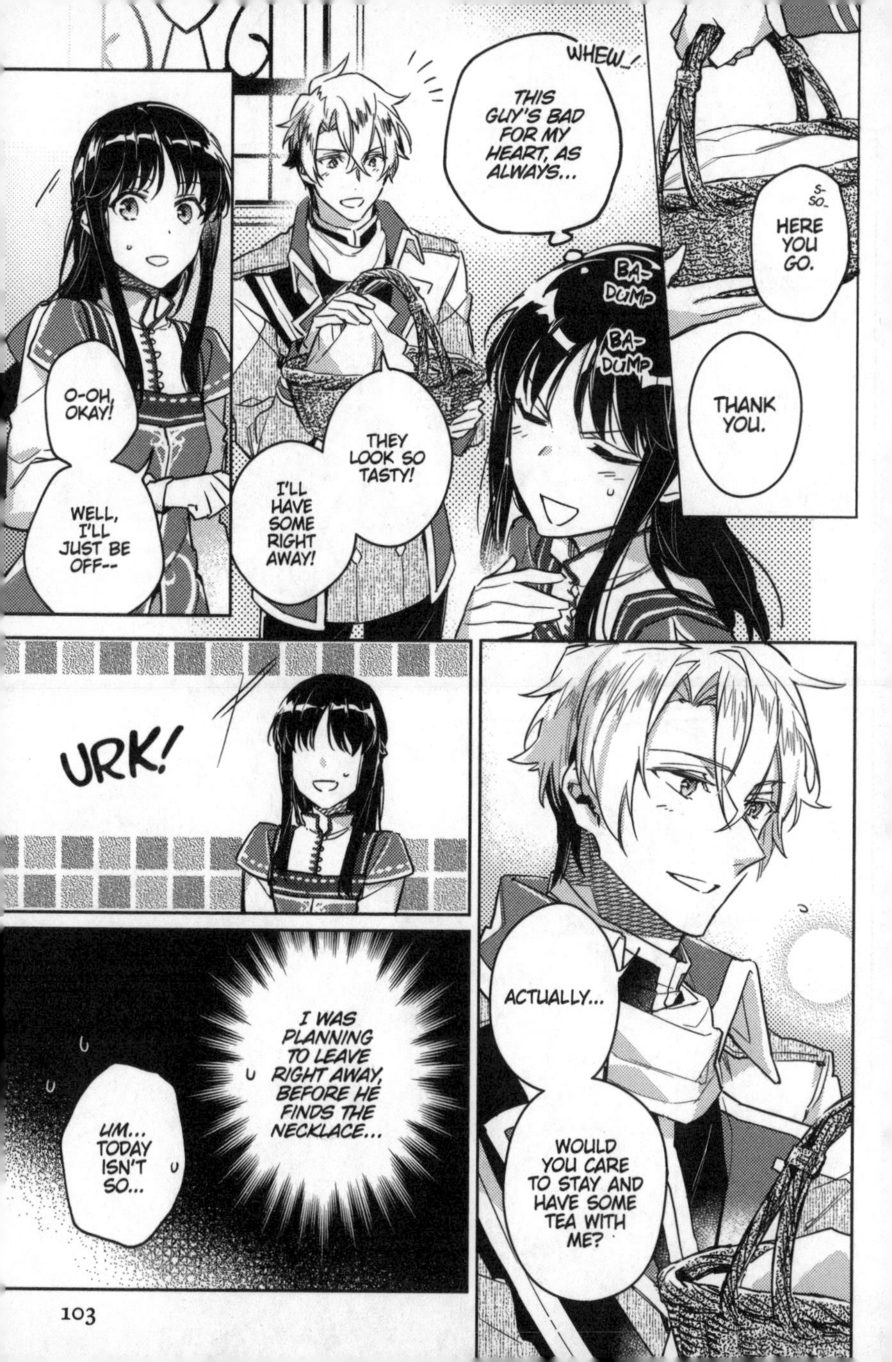

S-SO... HERE YOU GO.
THANK YOU.
WHEW...!
THIS GUY'S BAD FOR MY HEART, AS ALWAYS...
BA-DUMP
BA-DUMP
THEY LOOK SO TASTY!
I'LL HAVE SOME RIGHT AWAY!
O-OH, OKAY!
WELL, I'LL JUST BE OFF--
ACTUALLY...
WOULD YOU CARE TO STAY AND HAVE SOME TEA WITH ME?
URK!
I WAS PLANNING TO LEAVE RIGHT AWAY, BEFORE HE FINDS THE NECKLACE...
UM... TODAY ISN'T SO...

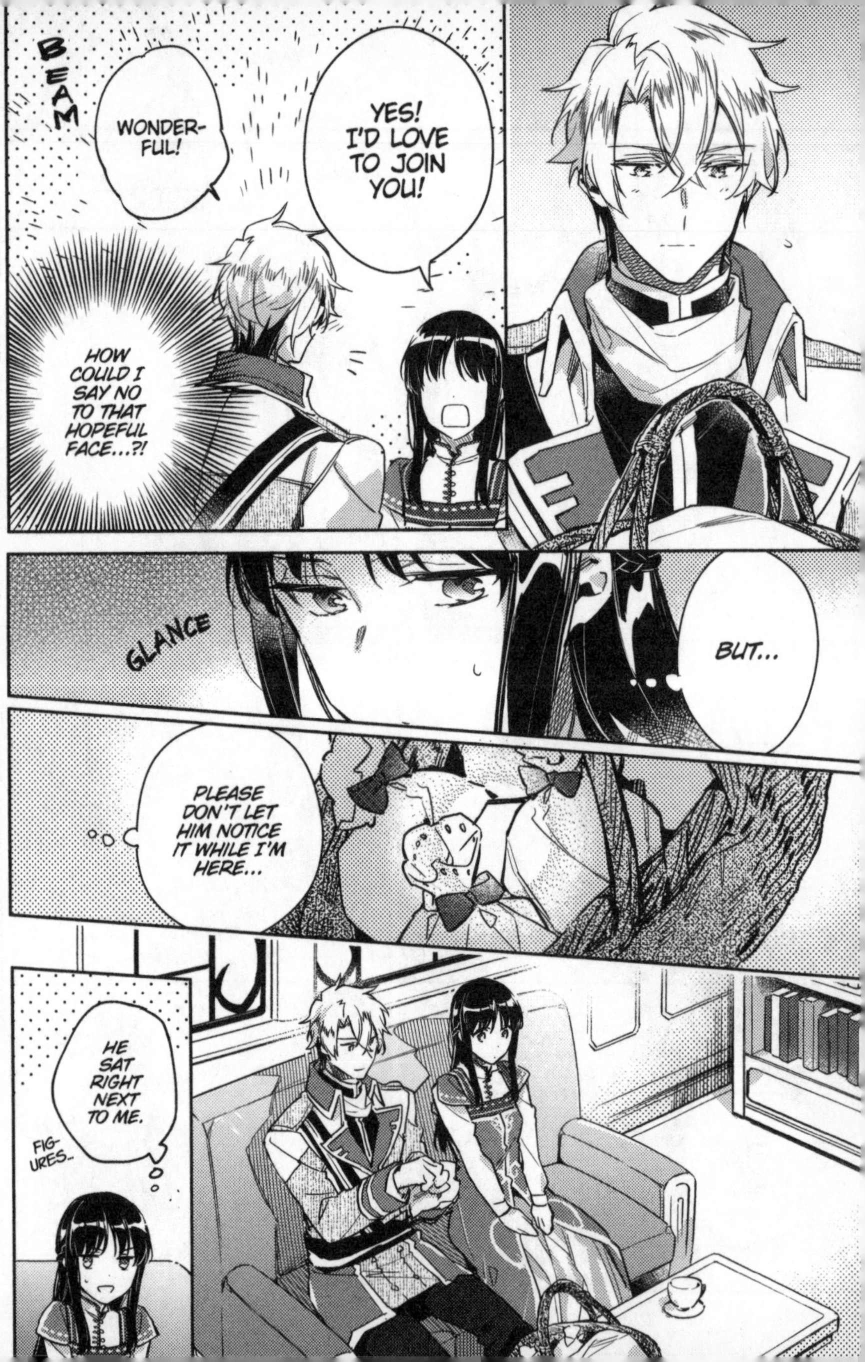
YES! I'D LOVE TO JOIN YOU!
WONDERFUL!
BEAM
HOW COULD I SAY NO TO THAT HOPEFUL FACE...?!
BUT...
GLANCE
PLEASE DON'T LET HIM NOTICE IT WHILE I'M HERE...
HE SAT RIGHT NEXT TO ME.
FIG-URES..

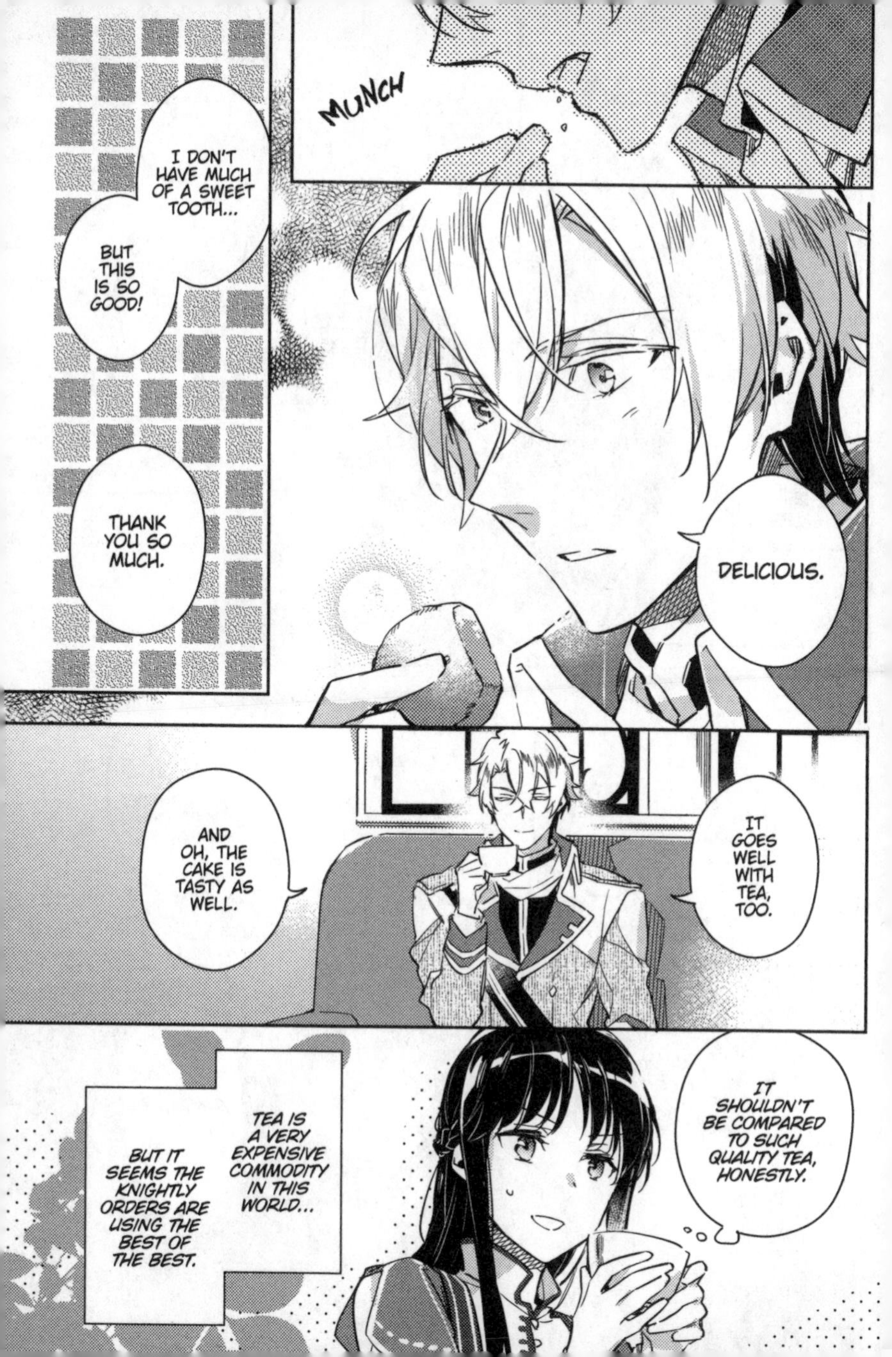
MUNCH
DELICIOUS.
I DON'T HAVE MUCH OF A SWEET TOOTH...
BUT THIS IS SO GOOD!
THANK YOU SO MUCH.
IT GOES WELL WITH TEA, TOO.
AND OH, THE CAKE IS TASTY AS WELL.
IT SHOULDN'T BE COMPARED TO SUCH QUALITY TEA, HONESTLY.
TEA IS A VERY EXPENSIVE COMMODITY IN THIS WORLD...
BUT IT SEEMS THE KNIGHTLY ORDERS ARE USING THE BEST OF THE BEST.

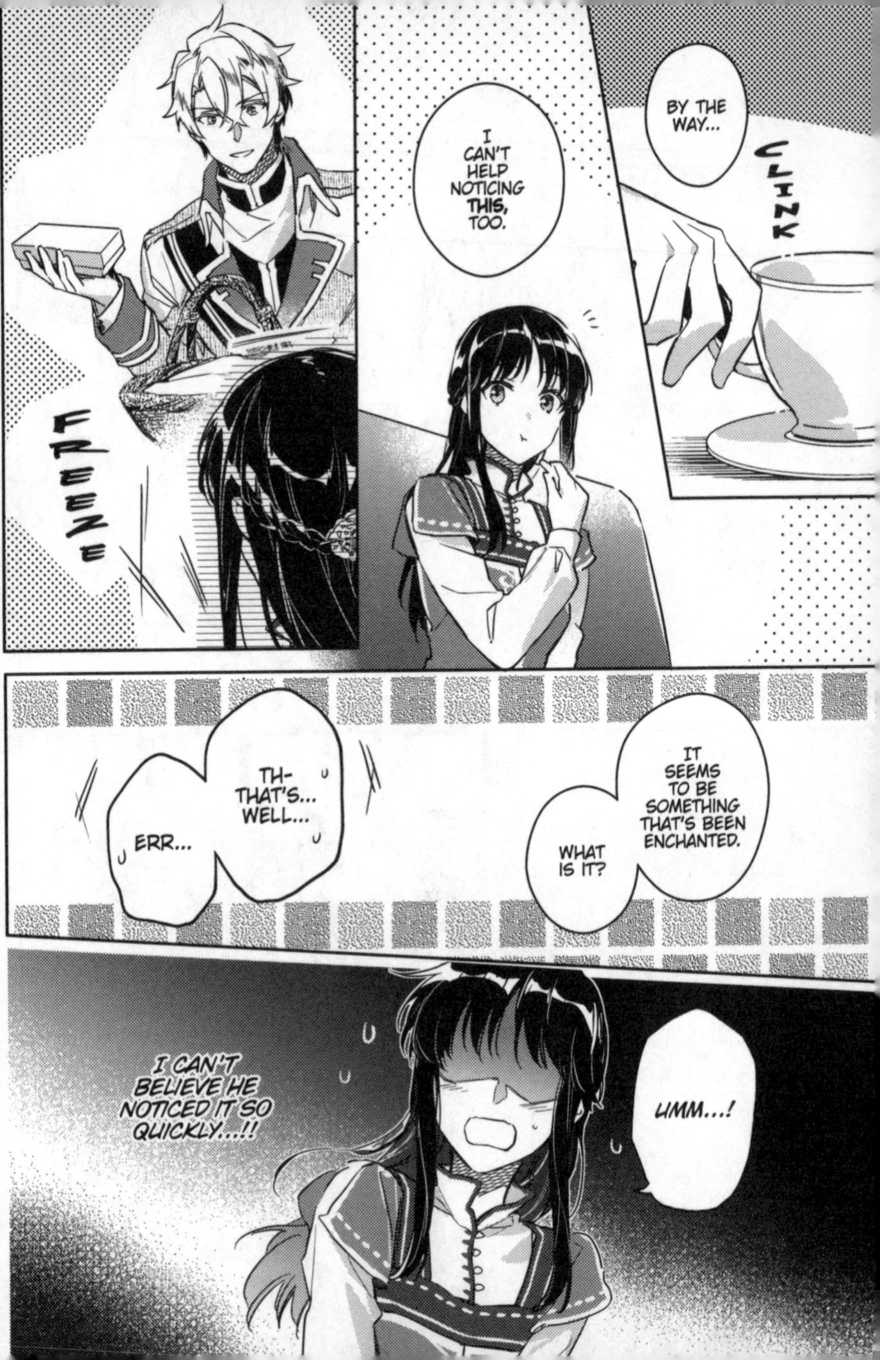
BY THE WAY...
CLINK
I CAN'T HELP NOTICING THIS, TOO.
FREEZE
IT SEEMS TO BE SOMETHING THAT'S BEEN ENCHANTED.
WHAT IS IT?
TH-THAT'S... WELL...
ERR...
UMM...!
I CAN'T BELIEVE HE NOTICED IT SO QUICKLY...!!

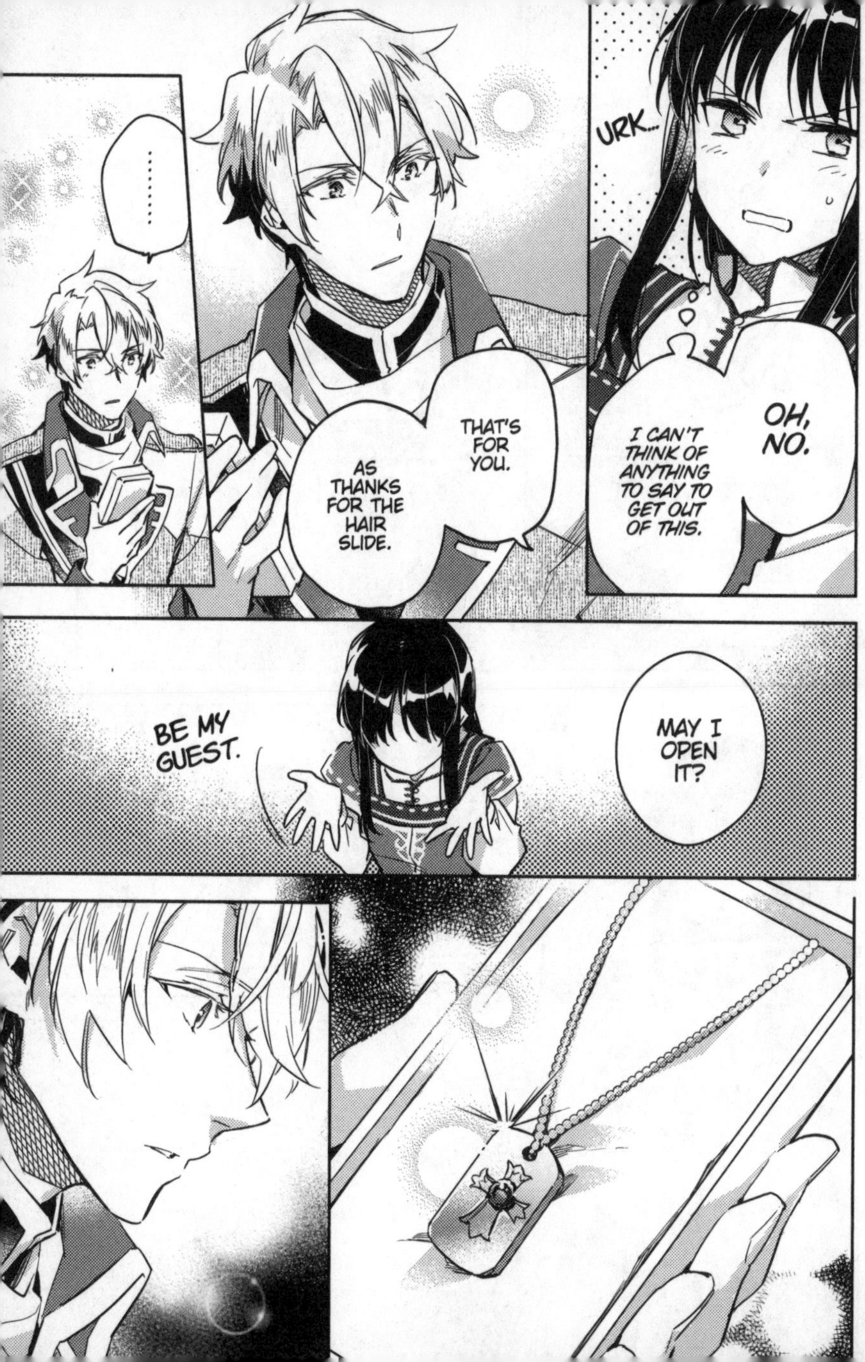
URK...
OH, NO.
I CAN'T THINK OF ANYTHING TO SAY TO GET OUT OF THIS.
THAT'S FOR YOU.
AS THANKS FOR THE HAIR SLIDE.
......
MAY I OPEN IT?
BE MY GUEST.

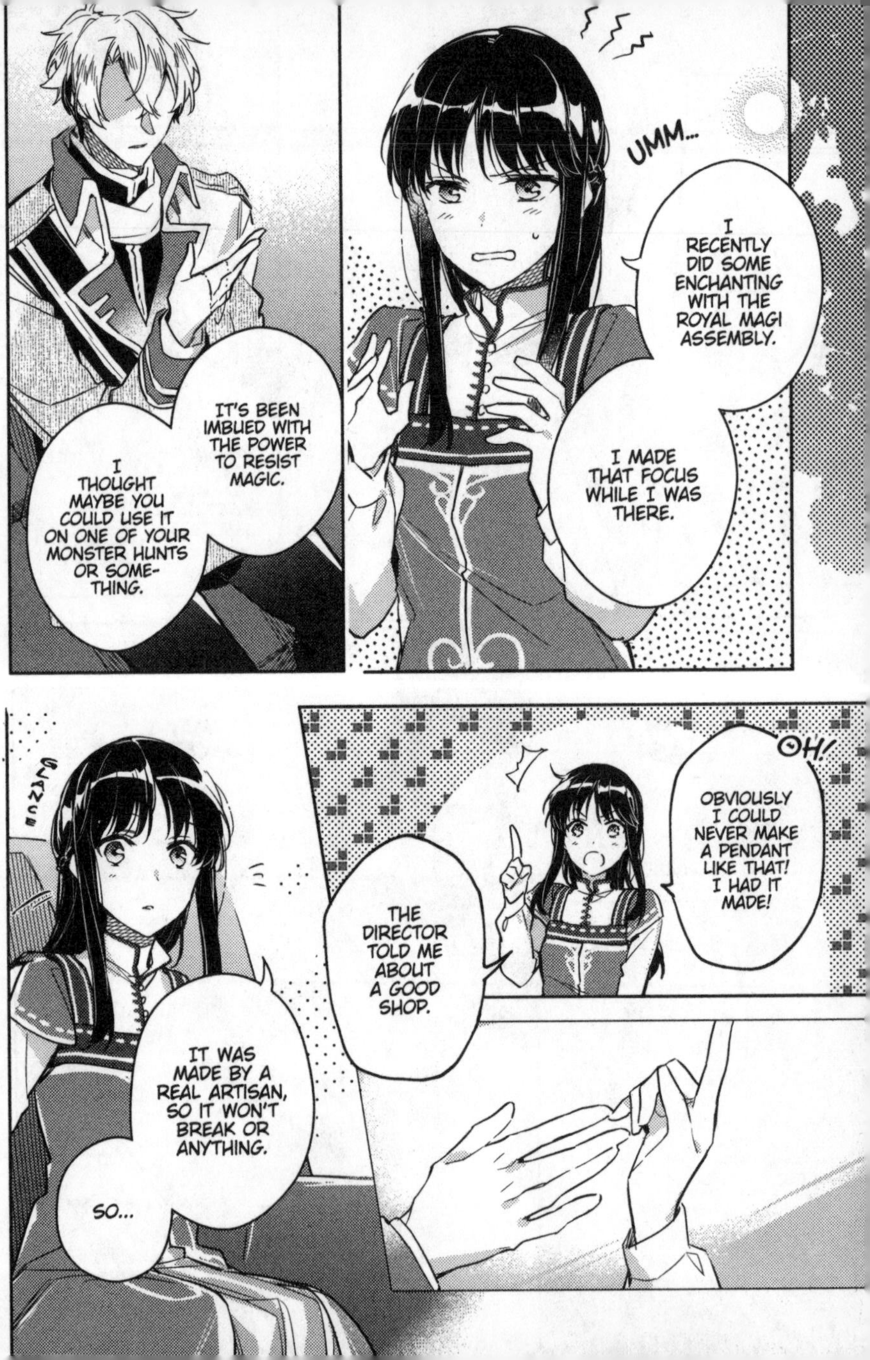
UMM...
I RECENTLY DID SOME ENCHANTING WITH THE ROYAL MAGI ASSEMBLY.
I MADE THAT FOCUS WHILE I WAS THERE.
IT'S BEEN IMBUED WITH THE POWER TO RESIST MAGIC.
I THOUGHT MAYBE YOU COULD USE IT ON ONE OF YOUR MONSTER HUNTS OR SOME-THING.
OH!
OBVIOUSLY I COULD NEVER MAKE A PENDANT LIKE THAT! I HAD IT MADE!
THE DIRECTOR TOLD ME ABOUT A GOOD SHOP.
GLANCE
IT WAS MADE BY A REAL ARTISAN, SO IT WON'T BREAK OR ANYTHING.
SO...

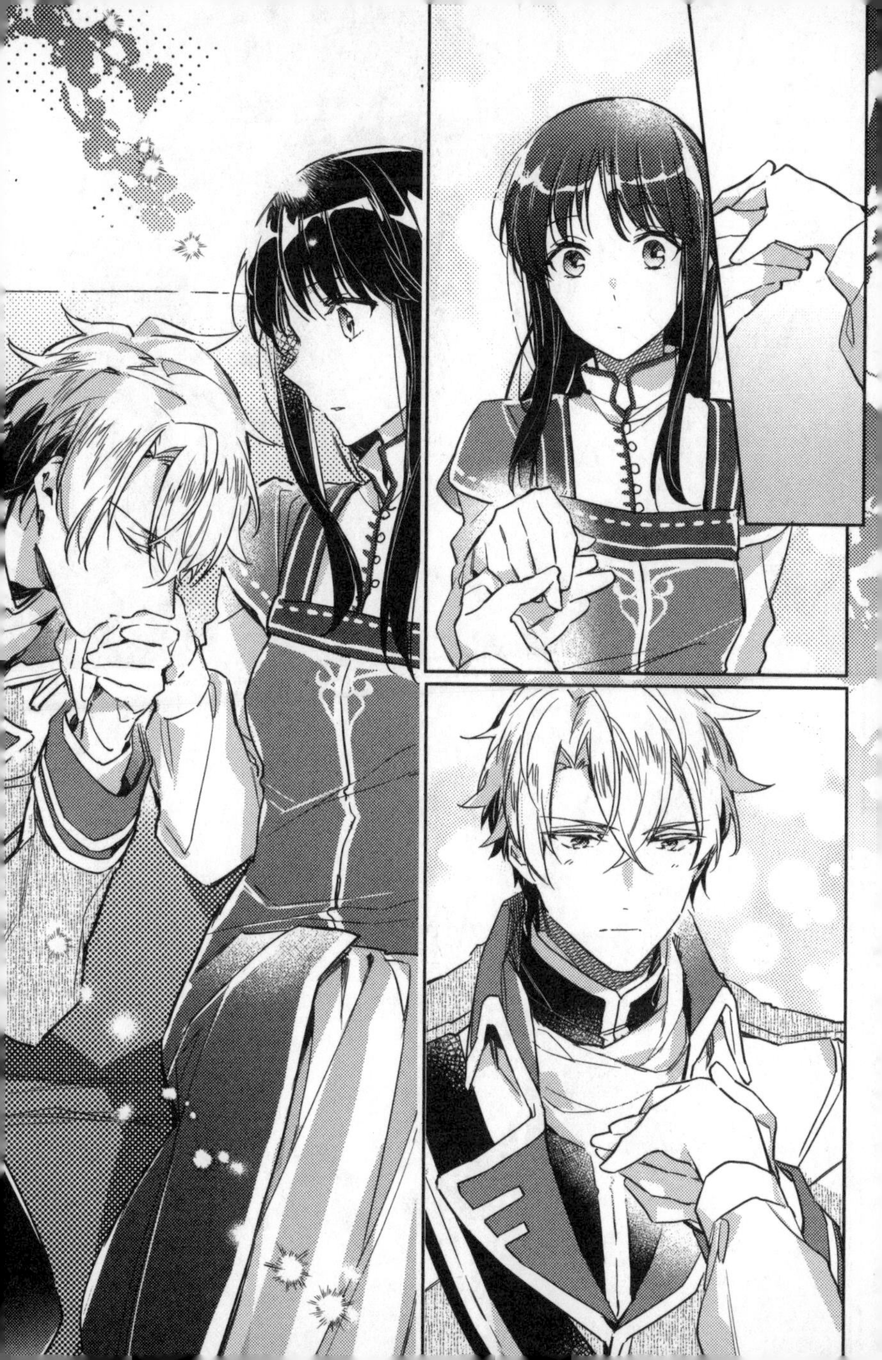

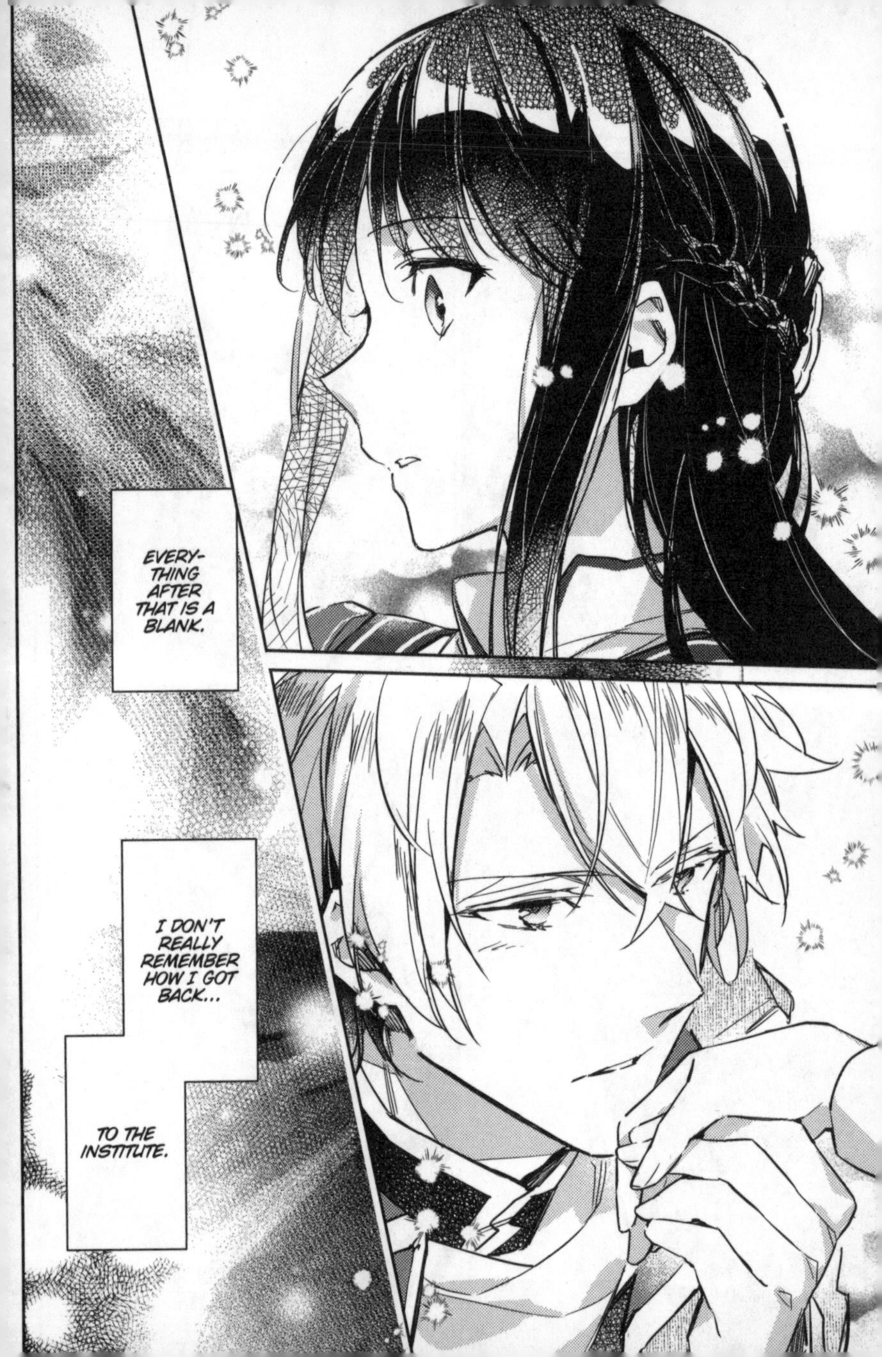
EVERY-THING AFTER THAT IS A BLANK.
I DON'T REALLY REMEMBER HOW I GOT BACK...
TO THE INSTITUTE.

The **Saint's** *
*Magic Power is *
Omnipotent

The **Saint's**
Magic Power is
Omnipotent

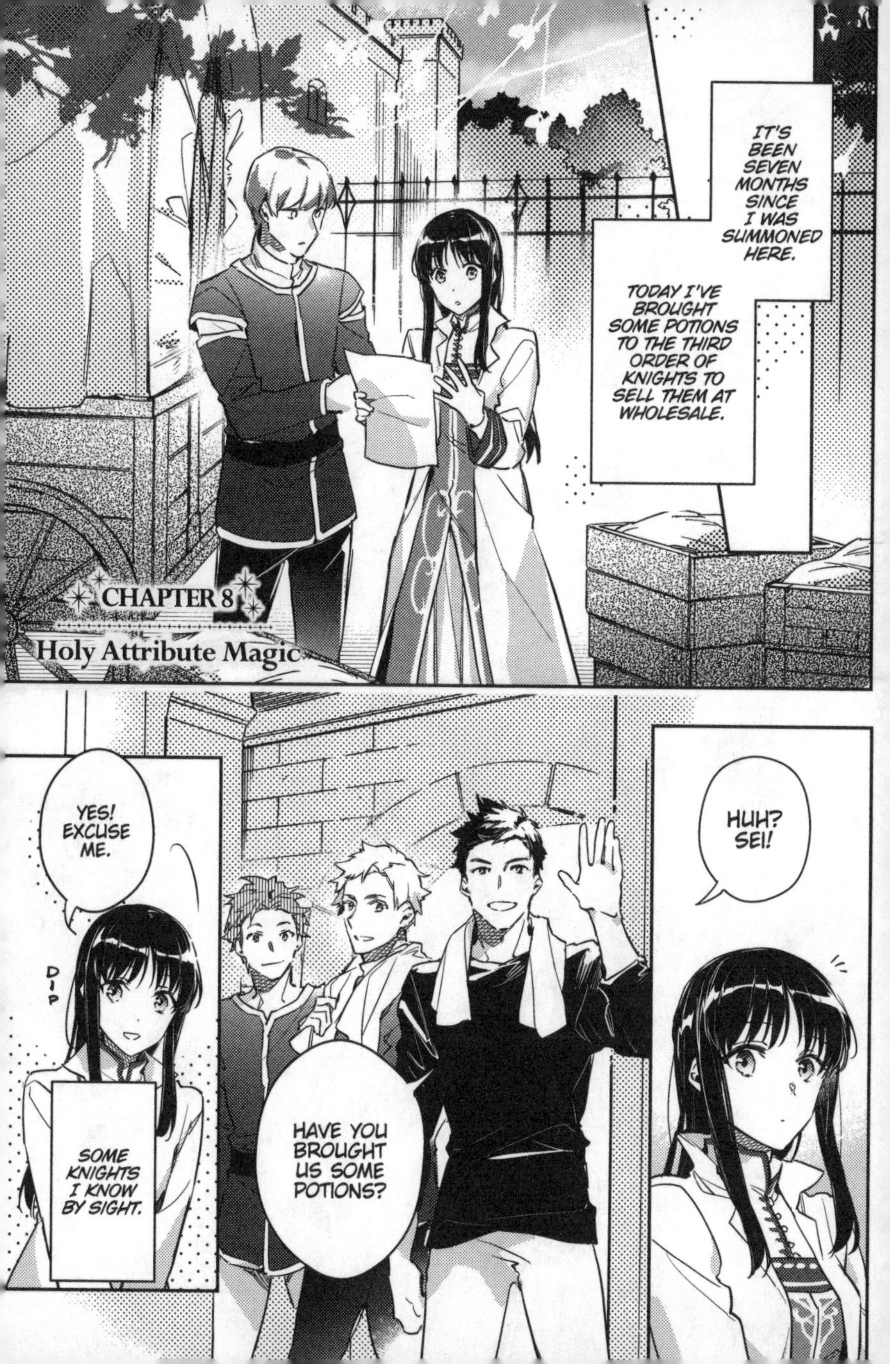
IT'S BEEN SEVEN MONTHS SINCE I WAS SUMMONED HERE.
TODAY I'VE BROUGHT SOME POTIONS TO THE THIRD ORDER OF KNIGHTS TO SELL THEM AT WHOLESALE.
CHAPTER 8
Holy Attribute Magic
HUH? SEI!
HAVE YOU BROUGHT US SOME POTIONS?
YES! EXCUSE ME.
DIP
SOME KNIGHTS I KNOW BY SIGHT.

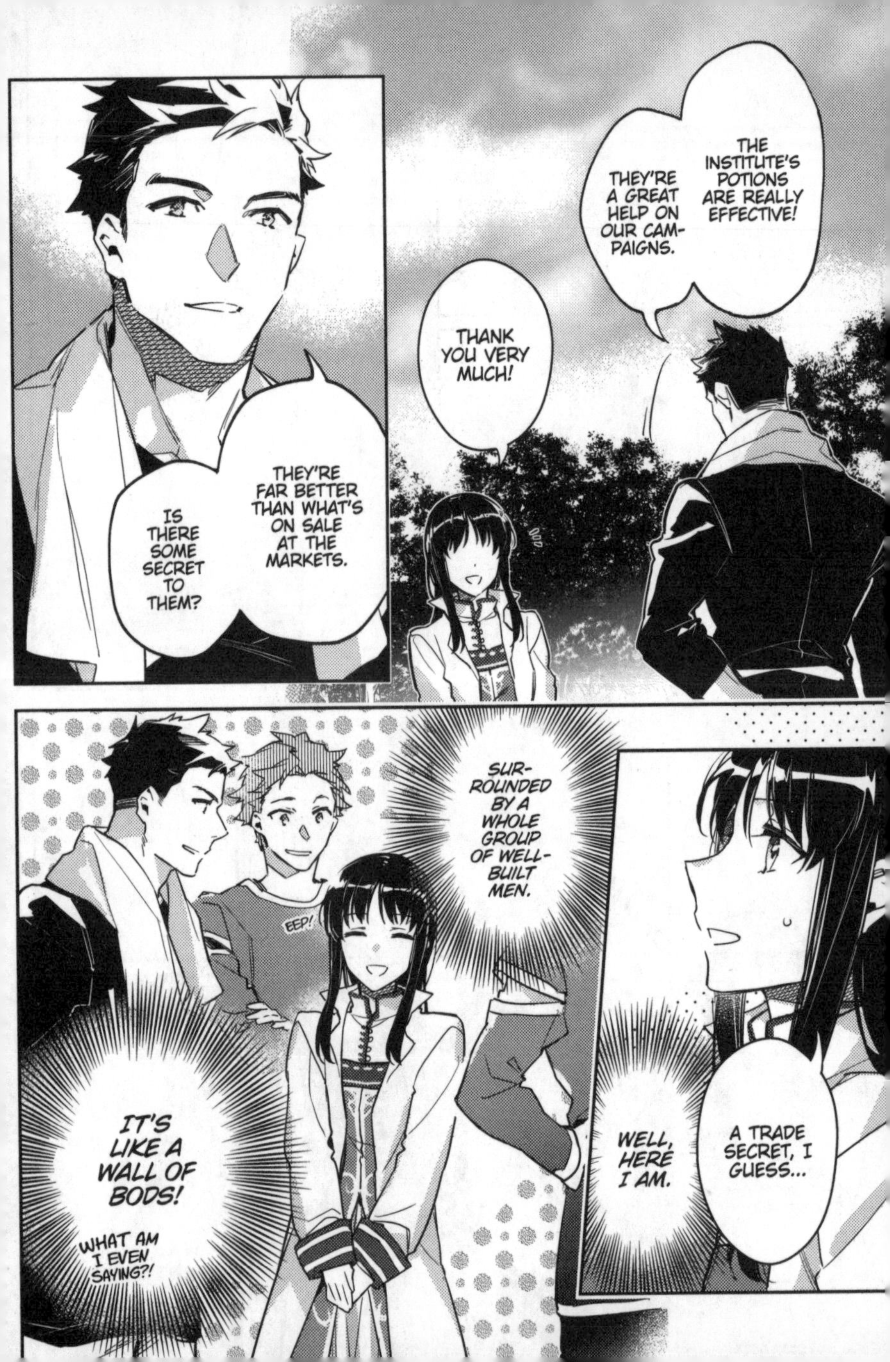
THE INSTITUTE'S POTIONS ARE REALLY EFFECTIVE!
THEY'RE A GREAT HELP ON OUR CAM-PAIGNS.
THANK YOU VERY MUCH!
THEY'RE FAR BETTER THAN WHAT'S ON SALE AT THE MARKETS.
IS THERE SOME SECRET TO THEM?
A TRADE SECRET, I GUESS...
WELL, HERE I AM.
SUR-ROUNDED BY A WHOLE GROUP OF WELL-BUILT MEN.
EEP!
IT'S LIKE A WALL OF BODS!
WHAT AM I EVEN SAYING?!

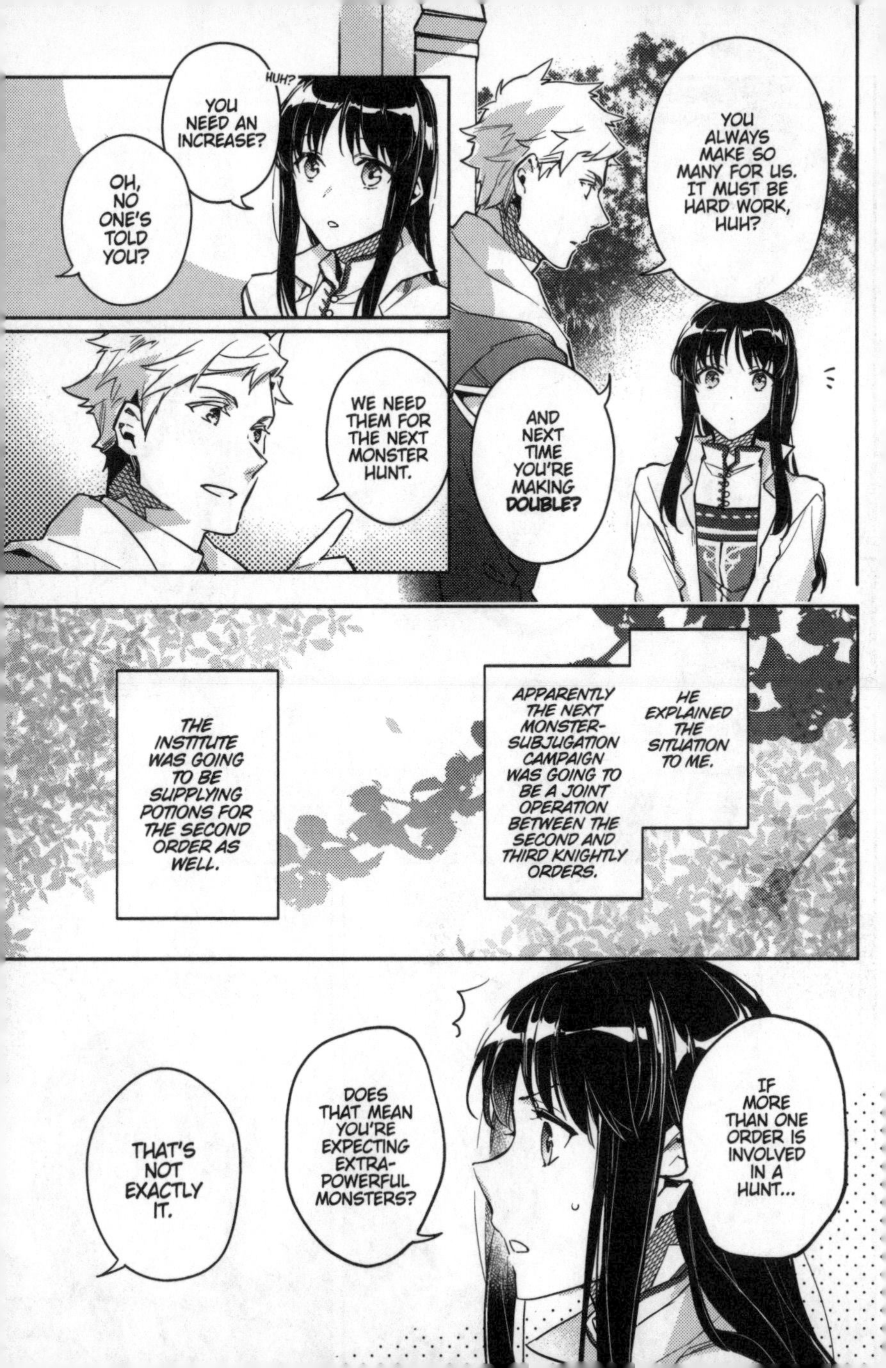
YOU ALWAYS MAKE SO MANY FOR US. IT MUST BE HARD WORK, HUH?
AND NEXT TIME YOU'RE MAKING DOUBLE?
HUH?
YOU NEED AN INCREASE?
OH, NO ONE'S TOLD YOU?
WE NEED THEM FOR THE NEXT MONSTER HUNT.
HE EXPLAINED THE SITUATION TO ME.
APPARENTLY THE NEXT MONSTER-SUBJUGATION CAMPAIGN WAS GOING TO BE A JOINT OPERATION BETWEEN THE SECOND AND THIRD KNIGHTLY ORDERS.
THE INSTITUTE WAS GOING TO BE SUPPLYING POTIONS FOR THE SECOND ORDER AS WELL.
IF MORE THAN ONE ORDER IS INVOLVED IN A HUNT...
DOES THAT MEAN YOU'RE EXPECTING EXTRA-POWERFUL MONSTERS?
THAT'S NOT EXACTLY IT.

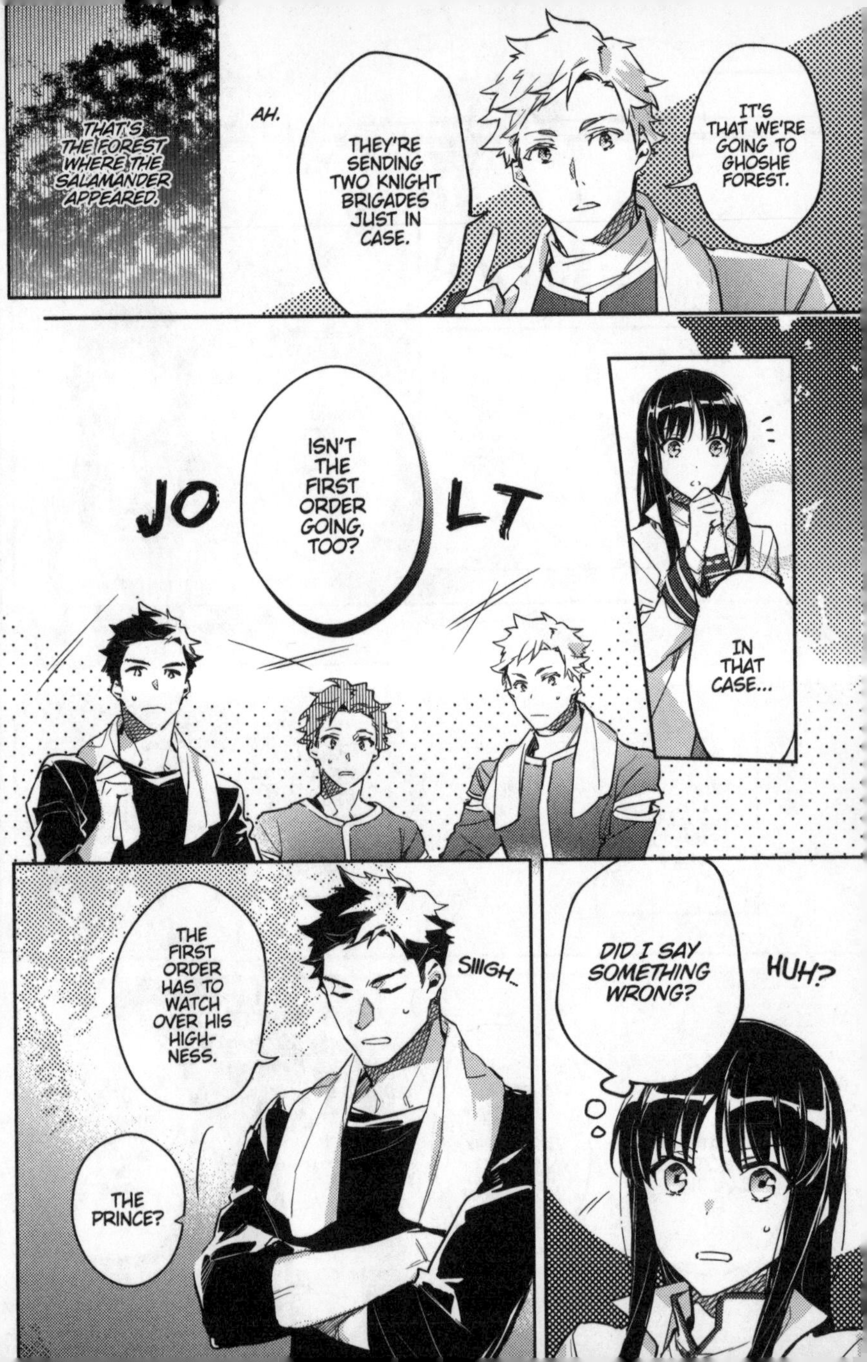
IT'S THAT WE'RE GOING TO GHOSHE FOREST.
THEY'RE SENDING TWO KNIGHT BRIGADES JUST IN CASE.
AH.
THAT'S THE FOREST WHERE THE SALAMANDER APPEARED.
IN THAT CASE...
ISN'T THE FIRST ORDER GOING, TOO?
JOLT
HUH?
DID I SAY SOMETHING WRONG?
SIIIGH...
THE FIRST ORDER HAS TO WATCH OVER HIS HIGH-NESS.
THE PRINCE?

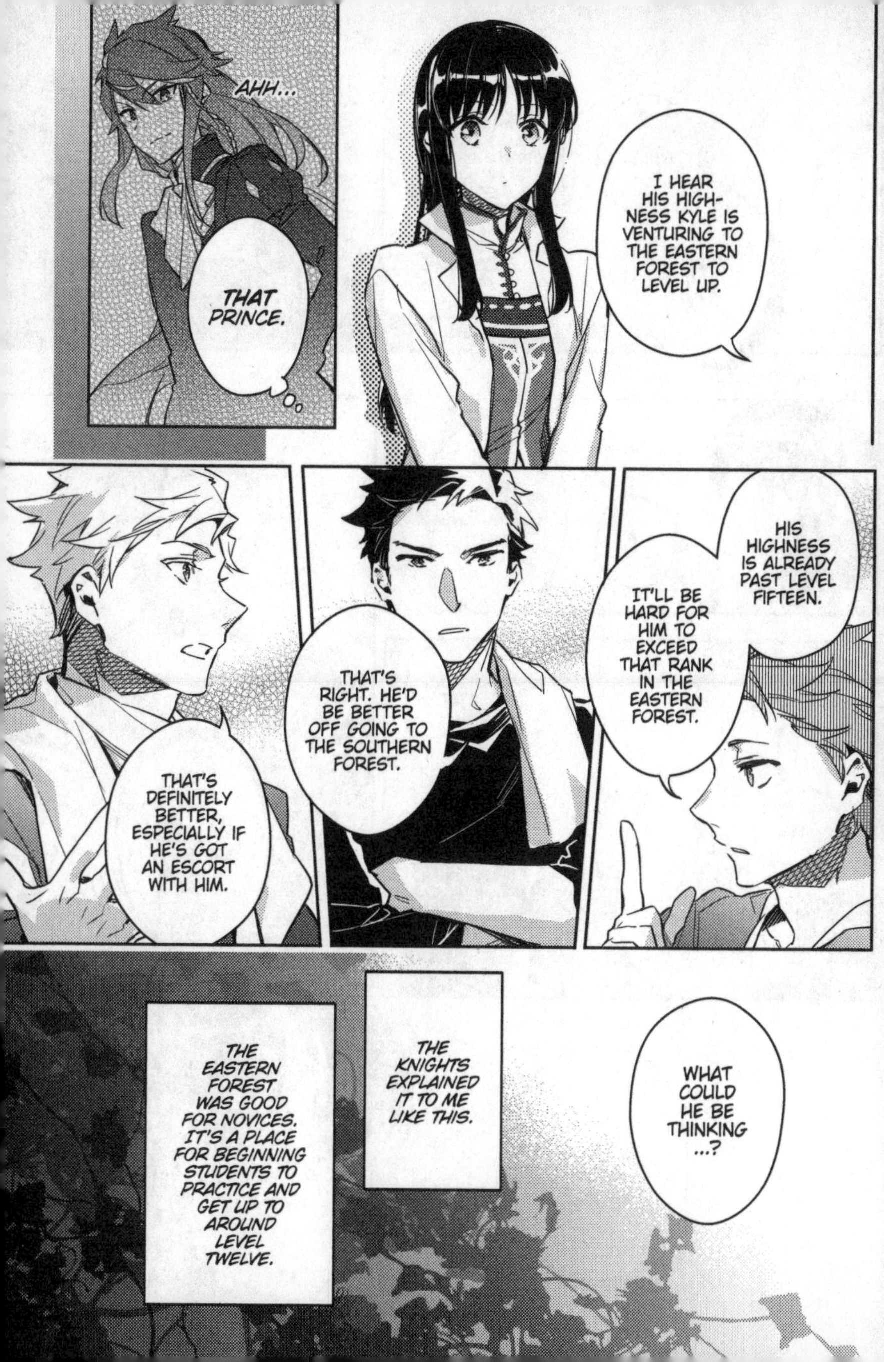
I HEAR HIS HIGHNESS KYLE IS VENTURING TO THE EASTERN FOREST TO LEVEL UP.
AHH...
THAT PRINCE.
HIS HIGHNESS IS ALREADY PAST LEVEL FIFTEEN.
IT'LL BE HARD FOR HIM TO EXCEED THAT RANK IN THE EASTERN FOREST.
THAT'S RIGHT. HE'D BE BETTER OFF GOING TO THE SOUTHERN FOREST.
THAT'S DEFINITELY BETTER, ESPECIALLY IF HE'S GOT AN ESCORT WITH HIM.
WHAT COULD HE BE THINKING ...?
THE KNIGHTS EXPLAINED IT TO ME LIKE THIS.
THE EASTERN FOREST WAS GOOD FOR NOVICES. IT'S A PLACE FOR BEGINNING STUDENTS TO PRACTICE AND GET UP TO AROUND LEVEL TWELVE.

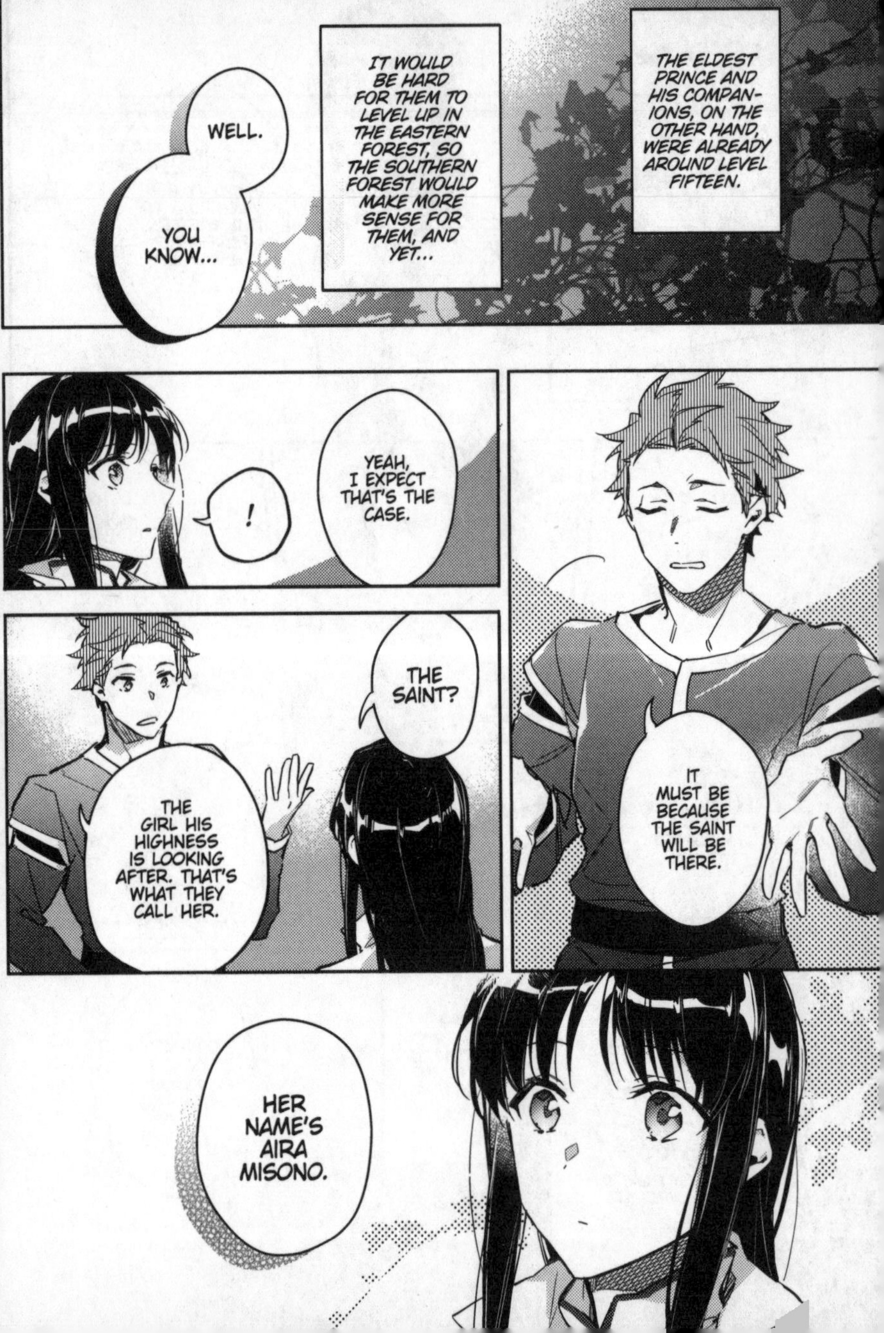

THE ELDEST PRINCE AND HIS COMPANIONS, ON THE OTHER HAND, WERE ALREADY AROUND LEVEL FIFTEEN.
IT WOULD BE HARD FOR THEM TO LEVEL UP IN THE EASTERN FOREST, SO THE SOUTHERN FOREST WOULD MAKE MORE SENSE FOR THEM, AND YET...
WELL.
YOU KNOW...
IT MUST BE BECAUSE THE SAINT WILL BE THERE.
YEAH, I EXPECT THAT'S THE CASE.
!
THE SAINT?
THE GIRL HIS HIGHNESS IS LOOKING AFTER. THAT'S WHAT THEY CALL HER.
HER NAME'S AIRA MISONO.

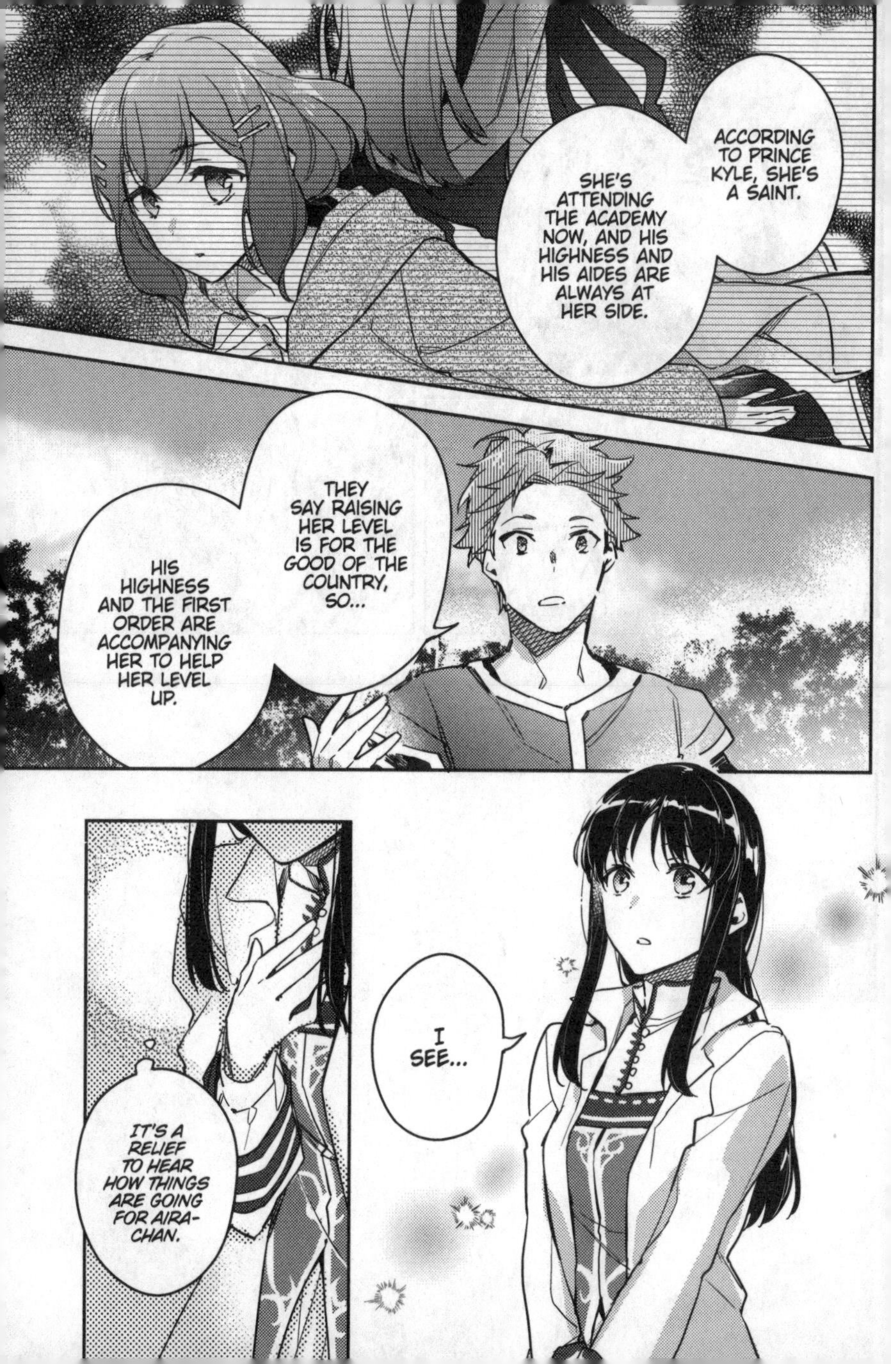
ACCORDING TO PRINCE KYLE, SHE'S A SAINT.
SHE'S ATTENDING THE ACADEMY NOW, AND HIS HIGHNESS AND HIS AIDES ARE ALWAYS AT HER SIDE.
THEY SAY RAISING HER LEVEL IS FOR THE GOOD OF THE COUNTRY, SO...
HIS HIGHNESS AND THE FIRST ORDER ARE ACCOMPANYING HER TO HELP HER LEVEL UP.
I SEE...
IT'S A RELIEF TO HEAR HOW THINGS ARE GOING FOR AIRA-CHAN.

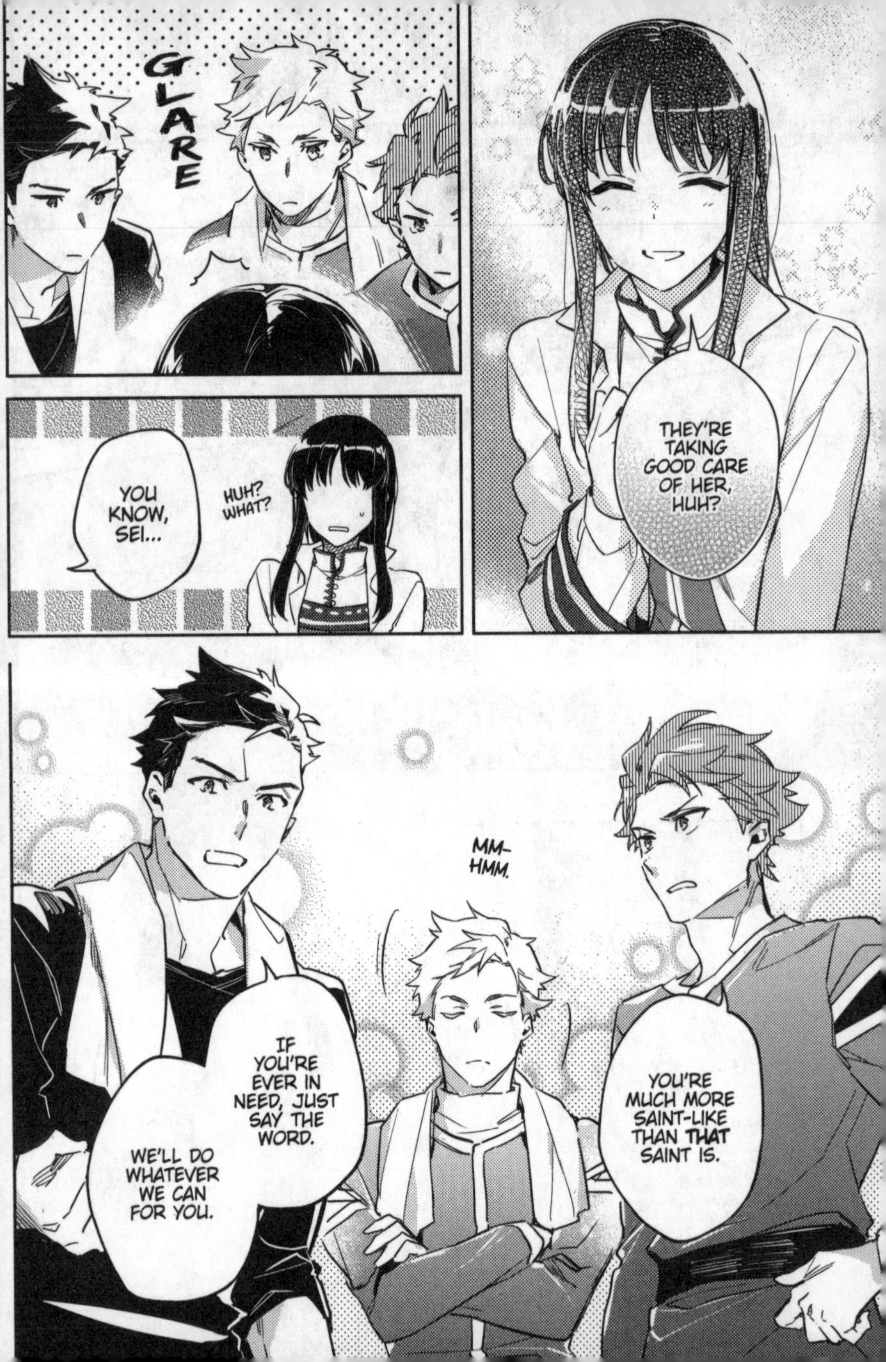
THEY'RE TAKING GOOD CARE OF HER, HUH?
GLARE
YOU KNOW, SEI...
HUH? WHAT?
YOU'RE MUCH MORE SAINT-LIKE THAN THAT SAINT IS.
MM-HMM.
IF YOU'RE EVER IN NEED, JUST SAY THE WORD.
WE'LL DO WHATEVER WE CAN FOR YOU.

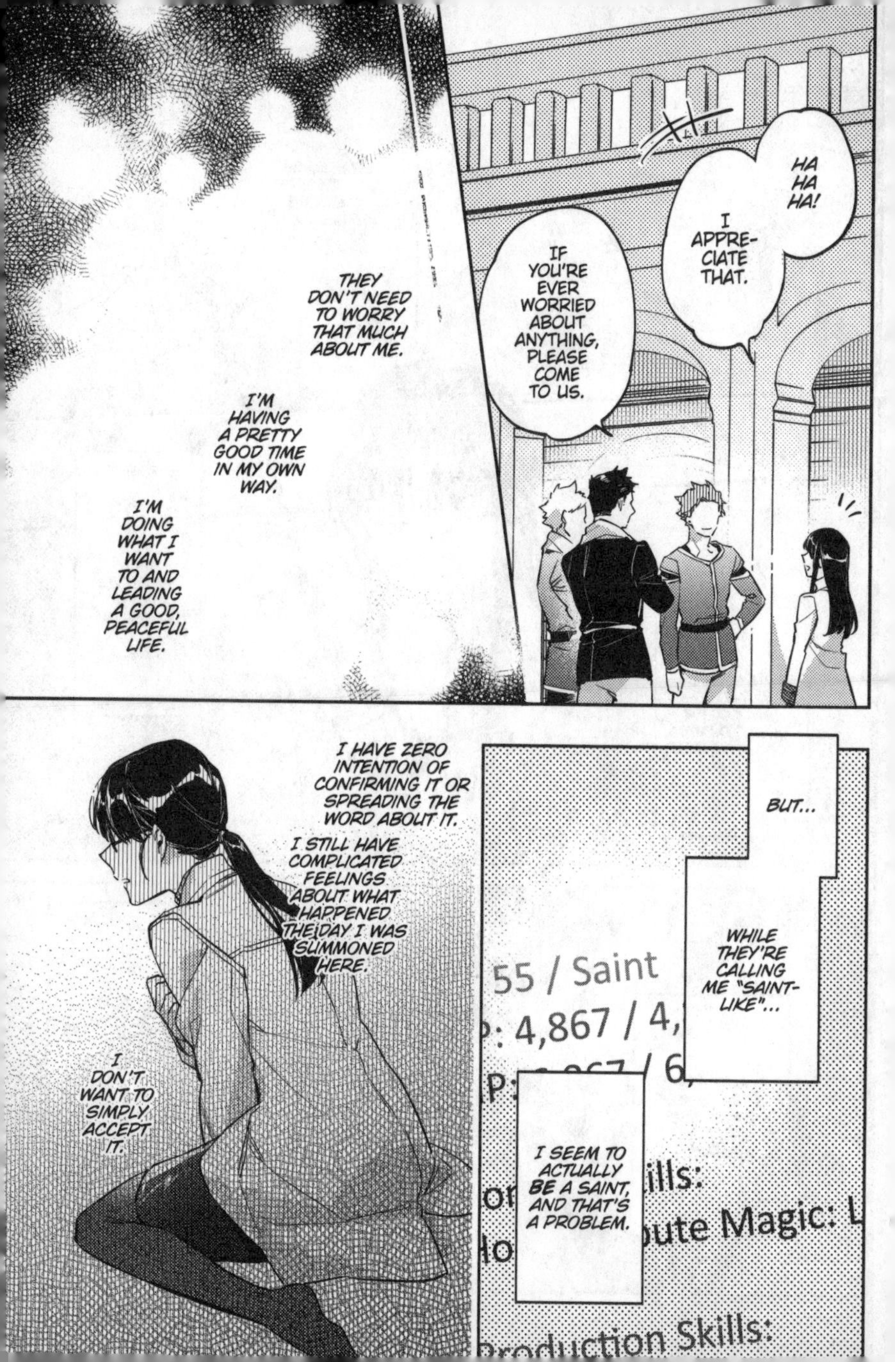
HA HA HA!
I APPRECIATE THAT.
IF YOU'RE EVER WORRIED ABOUT ANYTHING, PLEASE COME TO US.
THEY DON'T NEED TO WORRY THAT MUCH ABOUT ME.
I'M HAVING A PRETTY GOOD TIME IN MY OWN WAY.
I'M DOING WHAT I WANT TO AND LEADING A GOOD, PEACEFUL LIFE.
BUT...
WHILE THEY'RE CALLING ME "SAINT-LIKE"...
55 / Saint
: 4,867 / 4,
I SEEM TO ACTUALLY BE A SAINT, AND THAT'S A PROBLEM.
Production Skills:
I HAVE ZERO INTENTION OF CONFIRMING IT OR SPREADING THE WORD ABOUT IT.
I STILL HAVE COMPLICATED FEELINGS ABOUT WHAT HAPPENED THE DAY I WAS SUMMONED HERE.
I DON'T WANT TO SIMPLY ACCEPT IT.

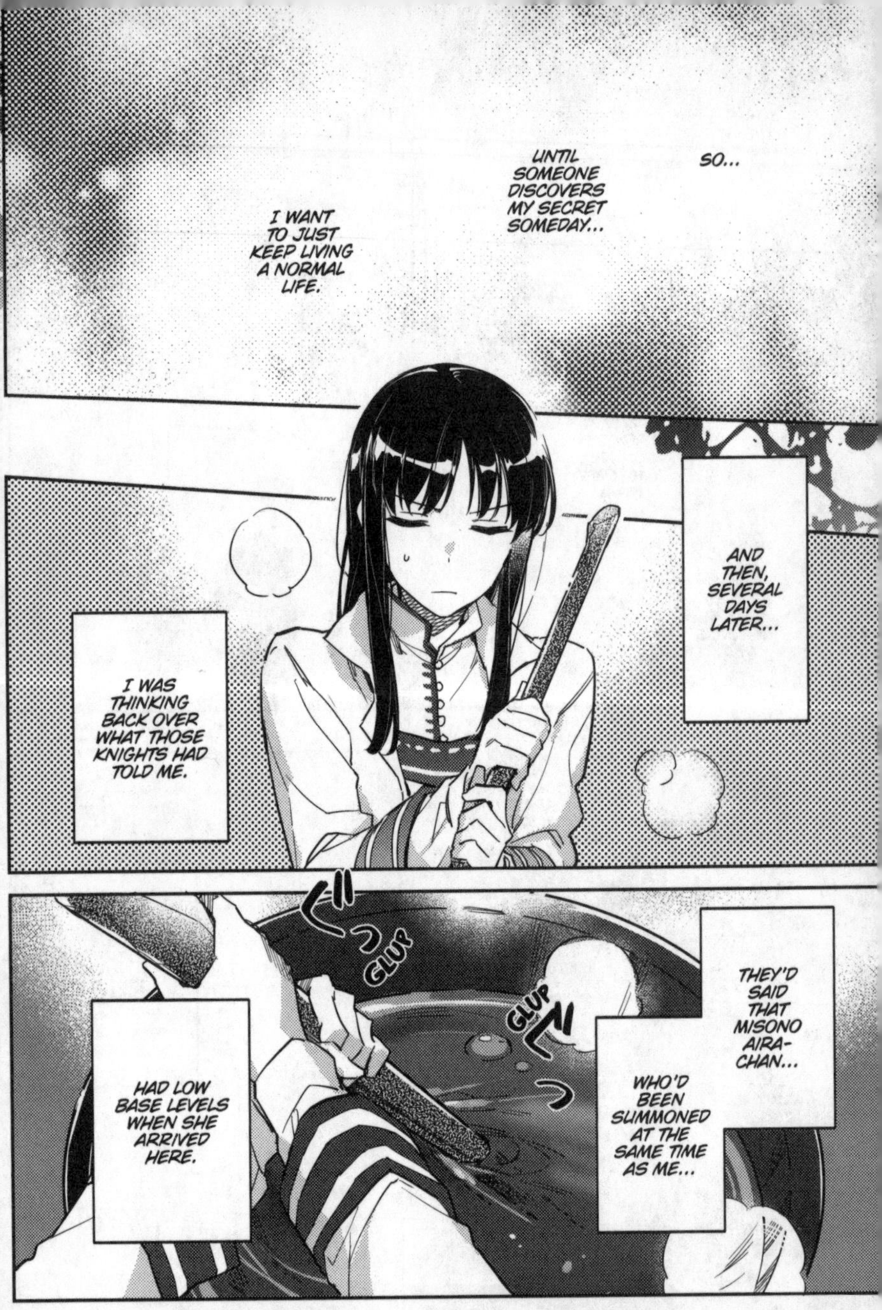
SO...
UNTIL SOMEONE DISCOVERS MY SECRET SOMEDAY...
I WANT TO JUST KEEP LIVING A NORMAL LIFE.
AND THEN, SEVERAL DAYS LATER...
I WAS THINKING BACK OVER WHAT THOSE KNIGHTS HAD TOLD ME.
THEY'D SAID THAT MISONO AIRA-CHAN...
WHO'D BEEN SUMMONED AT THE SAME TIME AS ME...
GLUP
GLUP
HAD LOW BASE LEVELS WHEN SHE ARRIVED HERE.

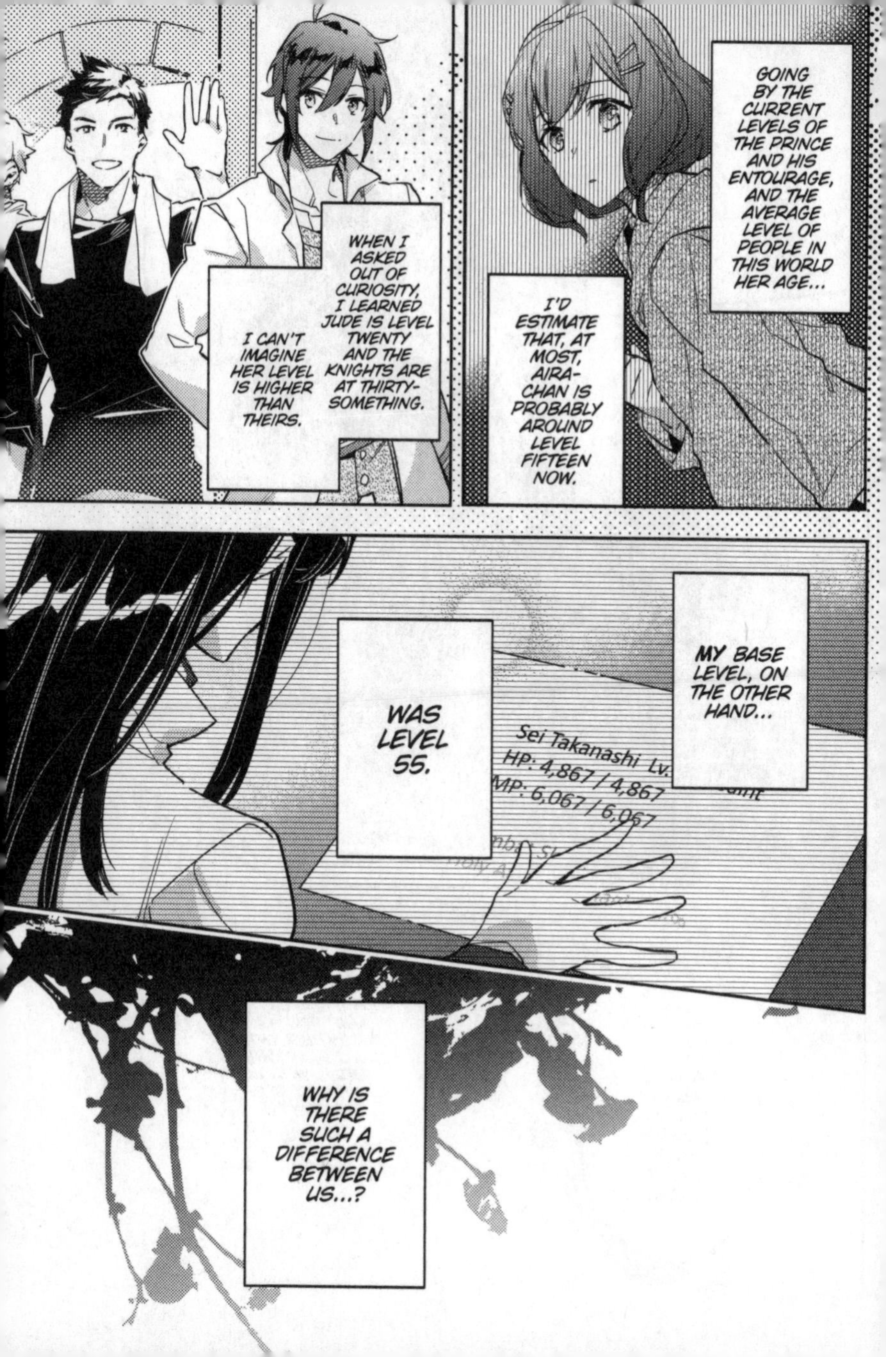
GOING BY THE CURRENT LEVELS OF THE PRINCE AND HIS ENTOURAGE, AND THE AVERAGE LEVEL OF PEOPLE IN THIS WORLD HER AGE...
I'D ESTIMATE THAT, AT MOST, AIRA-CHAN IS PROBABLY AROUND LEVEL FIFTEEN NOW.
WHEN I ASKED OUT OF CURIOSITY, I LEARNED JUDE IS LEVEL TWENTY AND THE KNIGHTS ARE AT THIRTY-SOMETHING.
I CAN'T IMAGINE HER LEVEL IS HIGHER THAN THEIRS.
MY BASE LEVEL, ON THE OTHER HAND...
Sei Takanashi Lv.
HP: 4,867 / 4,867
MP: 6,067 / 6,067
WAS LEVEL 55.
WHY IS THERE SUCH A DIFFERENCE BETWEEN US...?

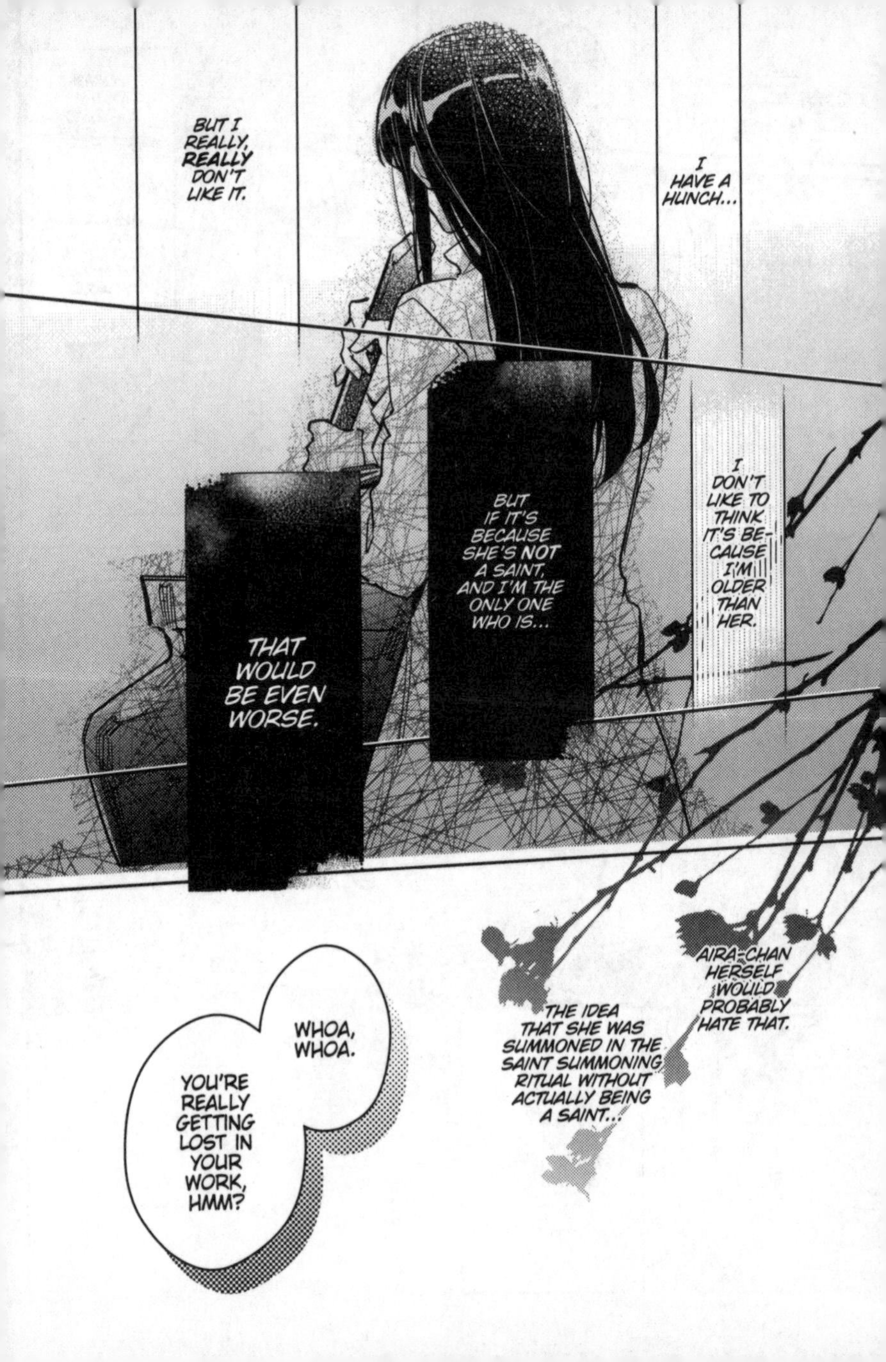
I HAVE A HUNCH...
BUT I REALLY, REALLY DON'T LIKE IT.
I DON'T LIKE TO THINK IT'S BE-CAUSE I'M OLDER THAN HER.
BUT IF IT'S BECAUSE SHE'S NOT A SAINT, AND I'M THE ONLY ONE WHO IS...
THAT WOULD BE EVEN WORSE.
AIRA-CHAN HERSELF WOULD PROBABLY HATE THAT.
THE IDEA THAT SHE WAS SUMMONED IN THE SAINT SUMMONING RITUAL WITHOUT ACTUALLY BEING A SAINT...
WHOA, WHOA.
YOU'RE REALLY GETTING LOST IN YOUR WORK, HMM?

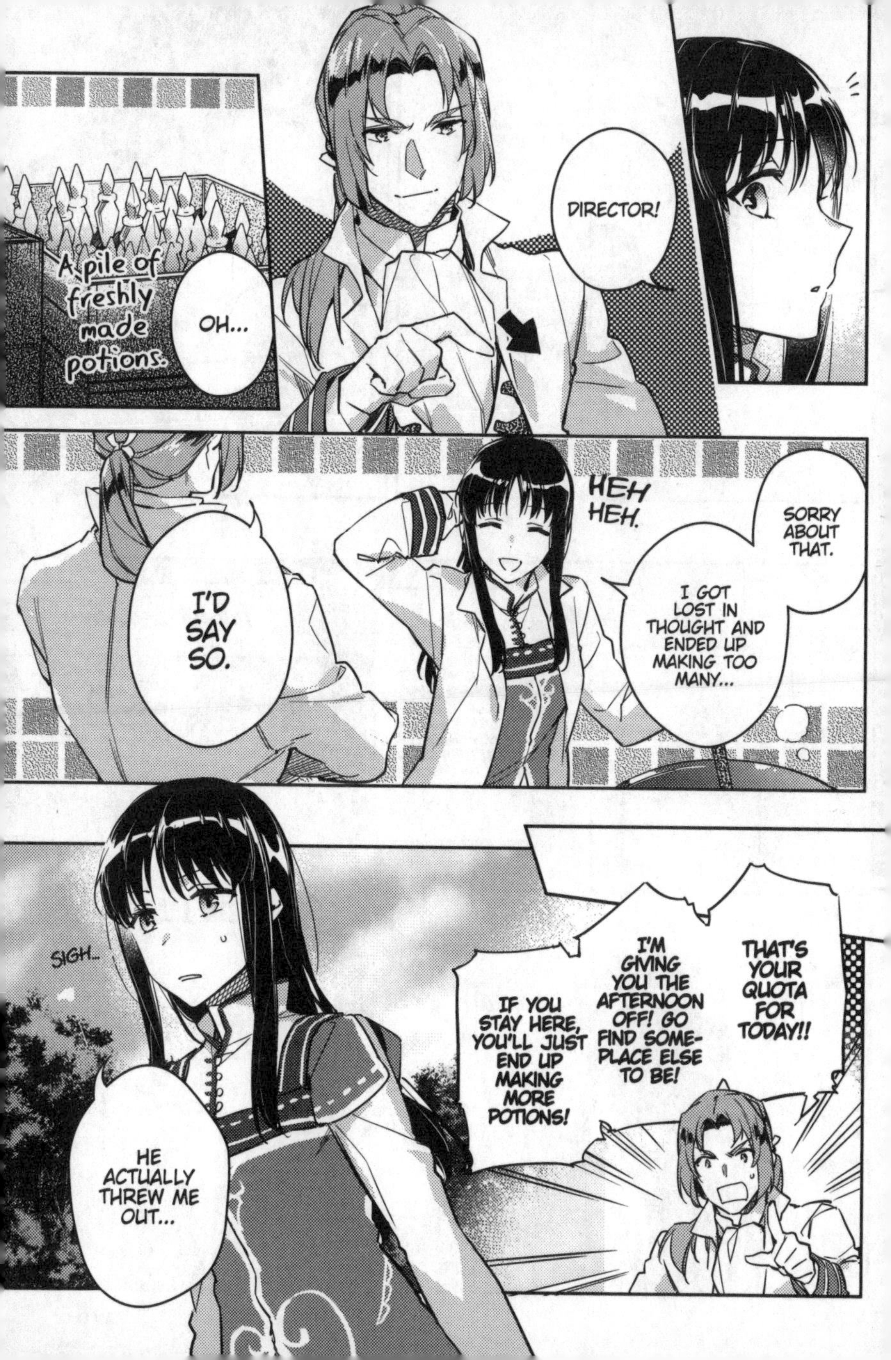
DIRECTOR!
OH...
A pile of freshly made potions.
HEH HEH.
SORRY ABOUT THAT.
I GOT LOST IN THOUGHT AND ENDED UP MAKING TOO MANY...
I'D SAY SO.
THAT'S YOUR QUOTA FOR TODAY!!
I'M GIVING YOU THE AFTERNOON OFF! GO FIND SOME-PLACE ELSE TO BE!
IF YOU STAY HERE, YOU'LL JUST END UP MAKING MORE POTIONS!
SIGH...
HE ACTUALLY THREW ME OUT...

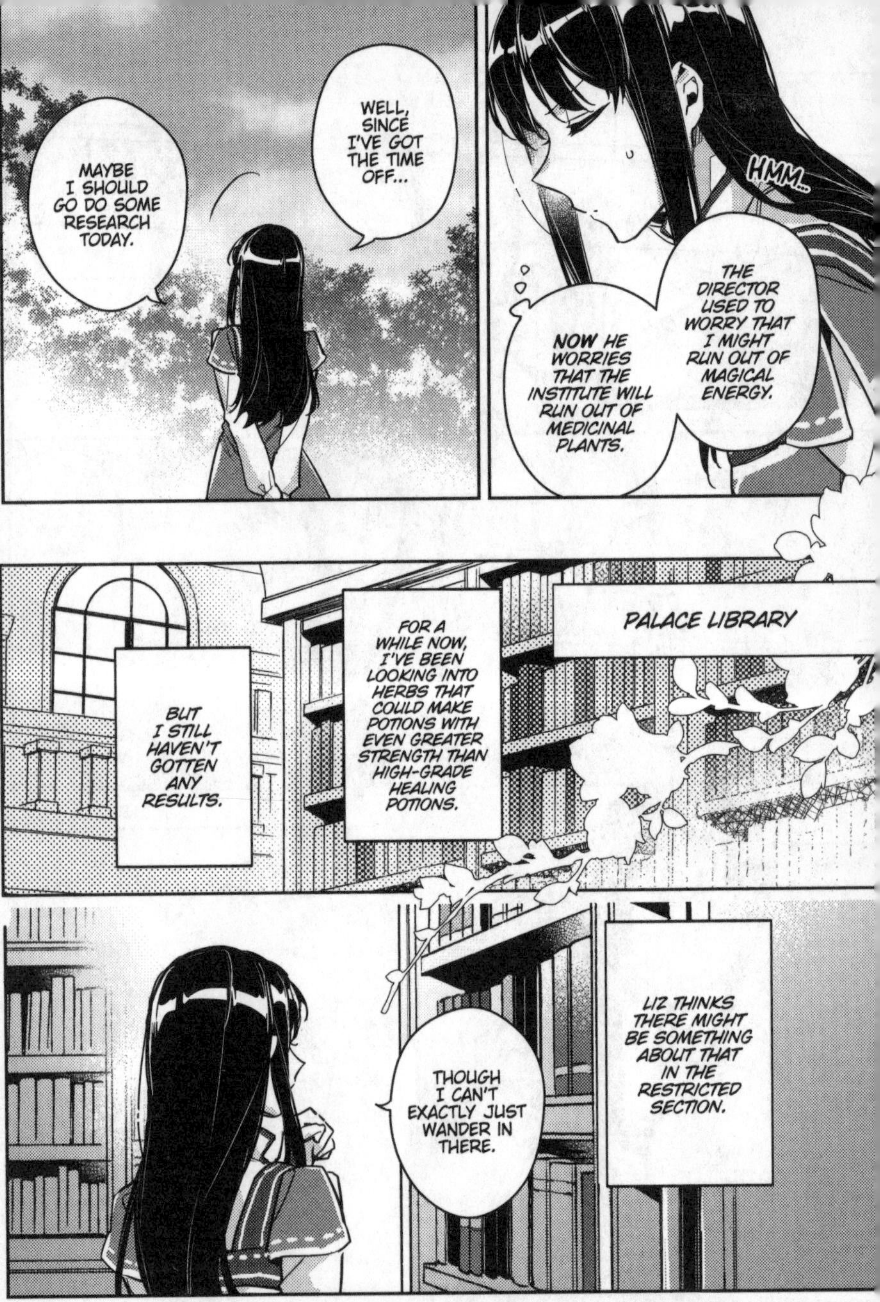
HMM...
THE DIRECTOR USED TO WORRY THAT I MIGHT RUN OUT OF MAGICAL ENERGY.
NOW HE WORRIES THAT THE INSTITUTE WILL RUN OUT OF MEDICINAL PLANTS.
WELL, SINCE I'VE GOT THE TIME OFF...
MAYBE I SHOULD GO DO SOME RESEARCH TODAY.
PALACE LIBRARY
FOR A WHILE NOW, I'VE BEEN LOOKING INTO HERBS THAT COULD MAKE POTIONS WITH EVEN GREATER STRENGTH THAN HIGH-GRADE HEALING POTIONS.
BUT I STILL HAVEN'T GOTTEN ANY RESULTS.
LIZ THINKS THERE MIGHT BE SOMETHING ABOUT THAT IN THE RESTRICTED SECTION.
THOUGH I CAN'T EXACTLY JUST WANDER IN THERE.

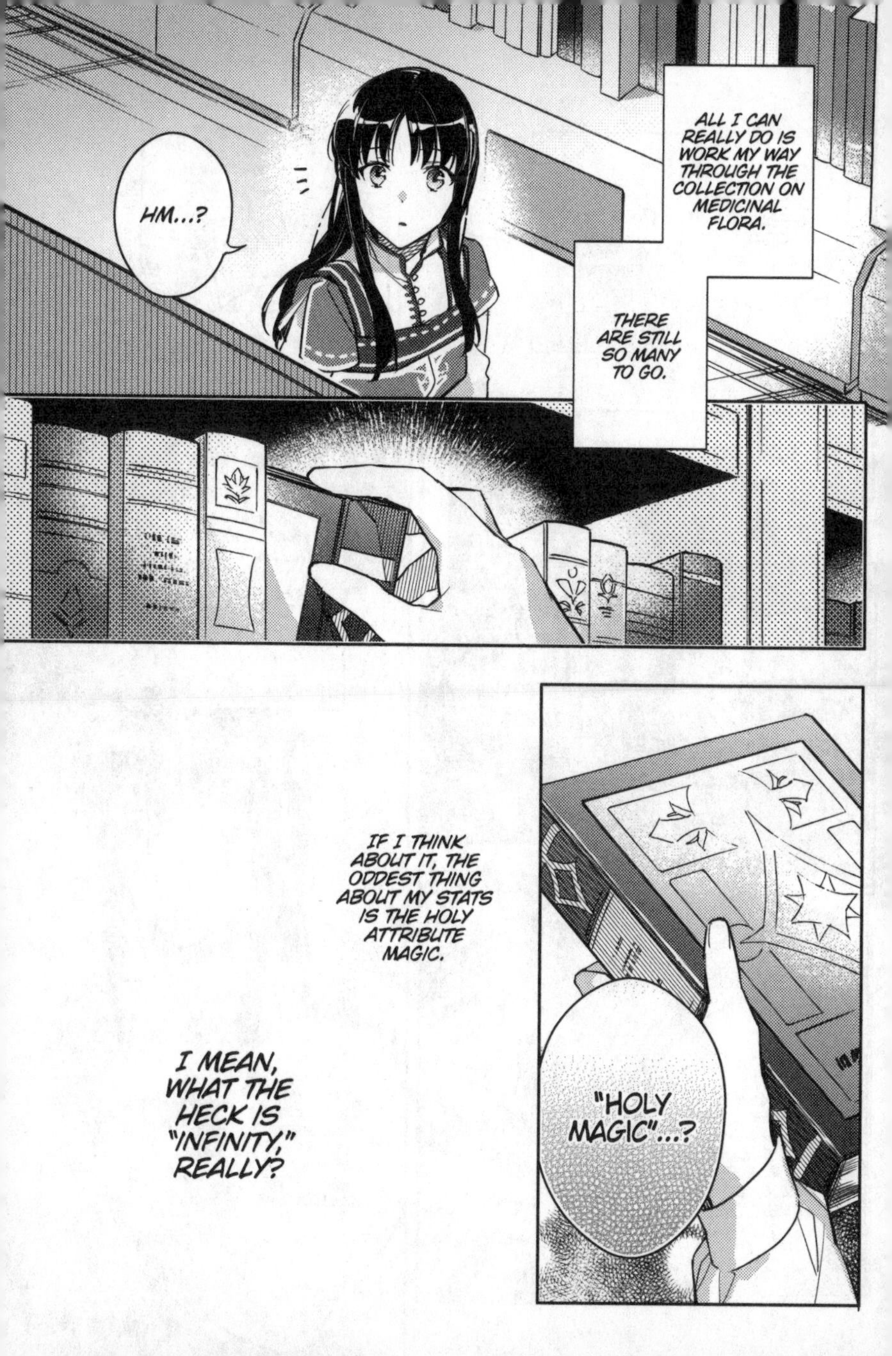
ALL I CAN REALLY DO IS WORK MY WAY THROUGH THE COLLECTION ON MEDICINAL FLORA.
THERE ARE STILL SO MANY TO GO.
HM...?
IF I THINK ABOUT IT, THE ODDEST THING ABOUT MY STATS IS THE HOLY ATTRIBUTE MAGIC.
"HOLY MAGIC"...?
I MEAN, WHAT THE HECK IS "INFINITY," REALLY?

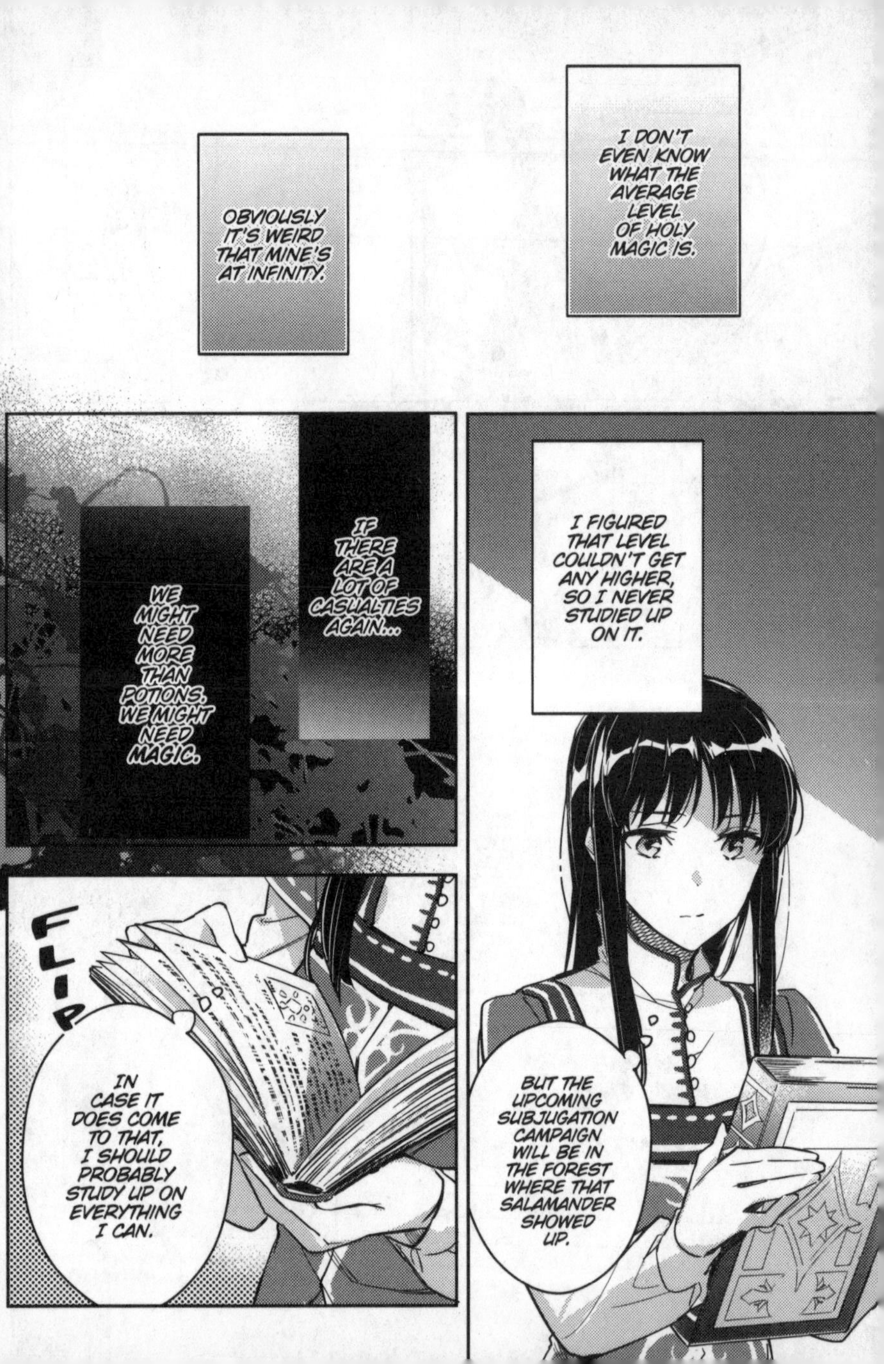
I DON'T EVEN KNOW WHAT THE AVERAGE LEVEL OF HOLY MAGIC IS.
OBVIOUSLY IT'S WEIRD THAT MINE'S AT INFINITY.
I FIGURED THAT LEVEL COULDN'T GET ANY HIGHER, SO I NEVER STUDIED UP ON IT.
BUT THE UPCOMING SUBJUGATION CAMPAIGN WILL BE IN THE FOREST WHERE THAT SALAMANDER SHOWED UP.
IF THERE ARE A LOT OF CASUALTIES AGAIN...
WE MIGHT NEED MORE THAN POTIONS. WE MIGHT NEED MAGIC.
FLIP
IN CASE IT DOES COME TO THAT, I SHOULD PROBABLY STUDY UP ON EVERYTHING I CAN.

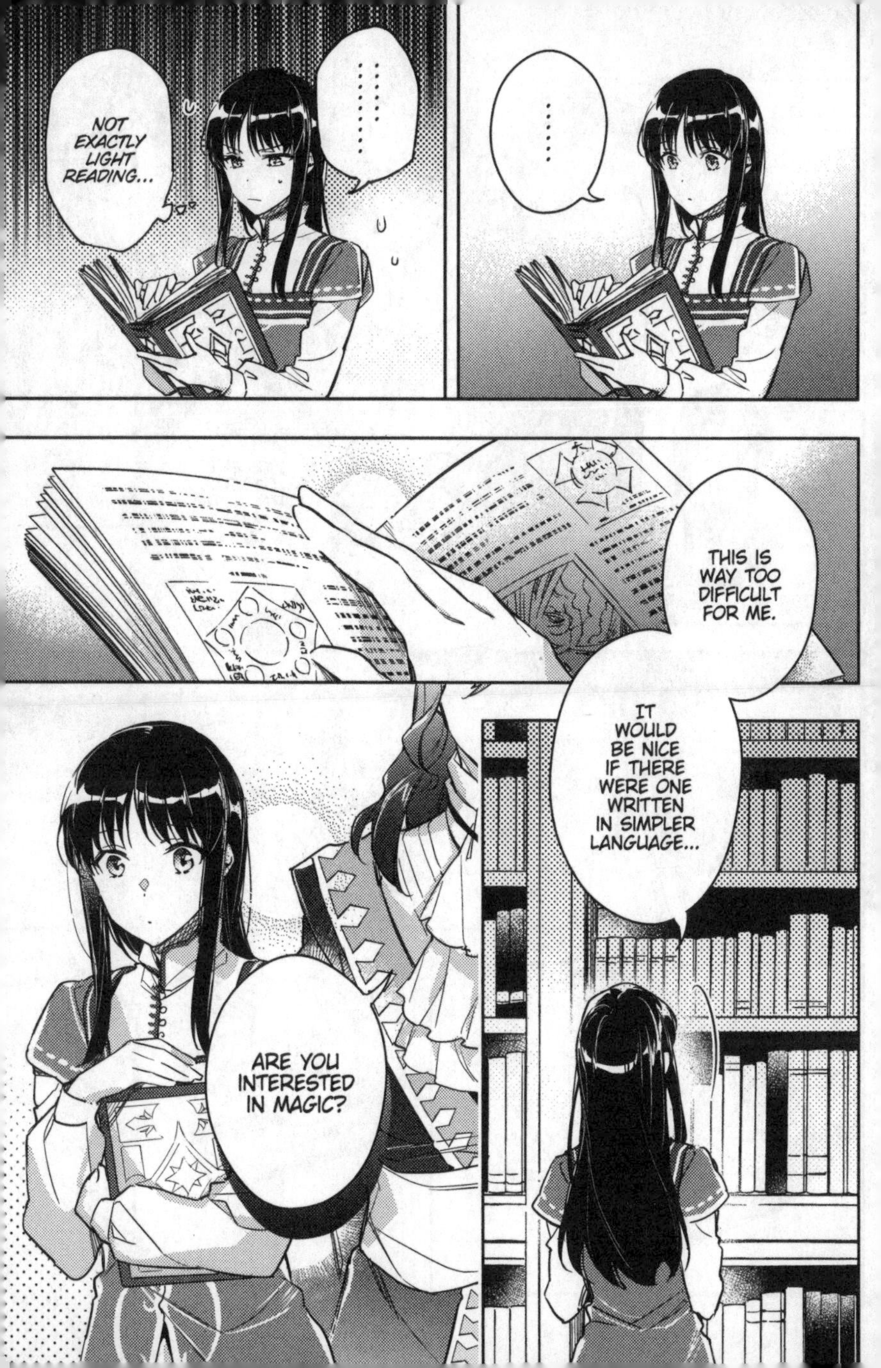
……
……
NOT EXACTLY LIGHT READING…
THIS IS WAY TOO DIFFICULT FOR ME.
IT WOULD BE NICE IF THERE WERE ONE WRITTEN IN SIMPLER LANGUAGE…
ARE YOU INTERESTED IN MAGIC?

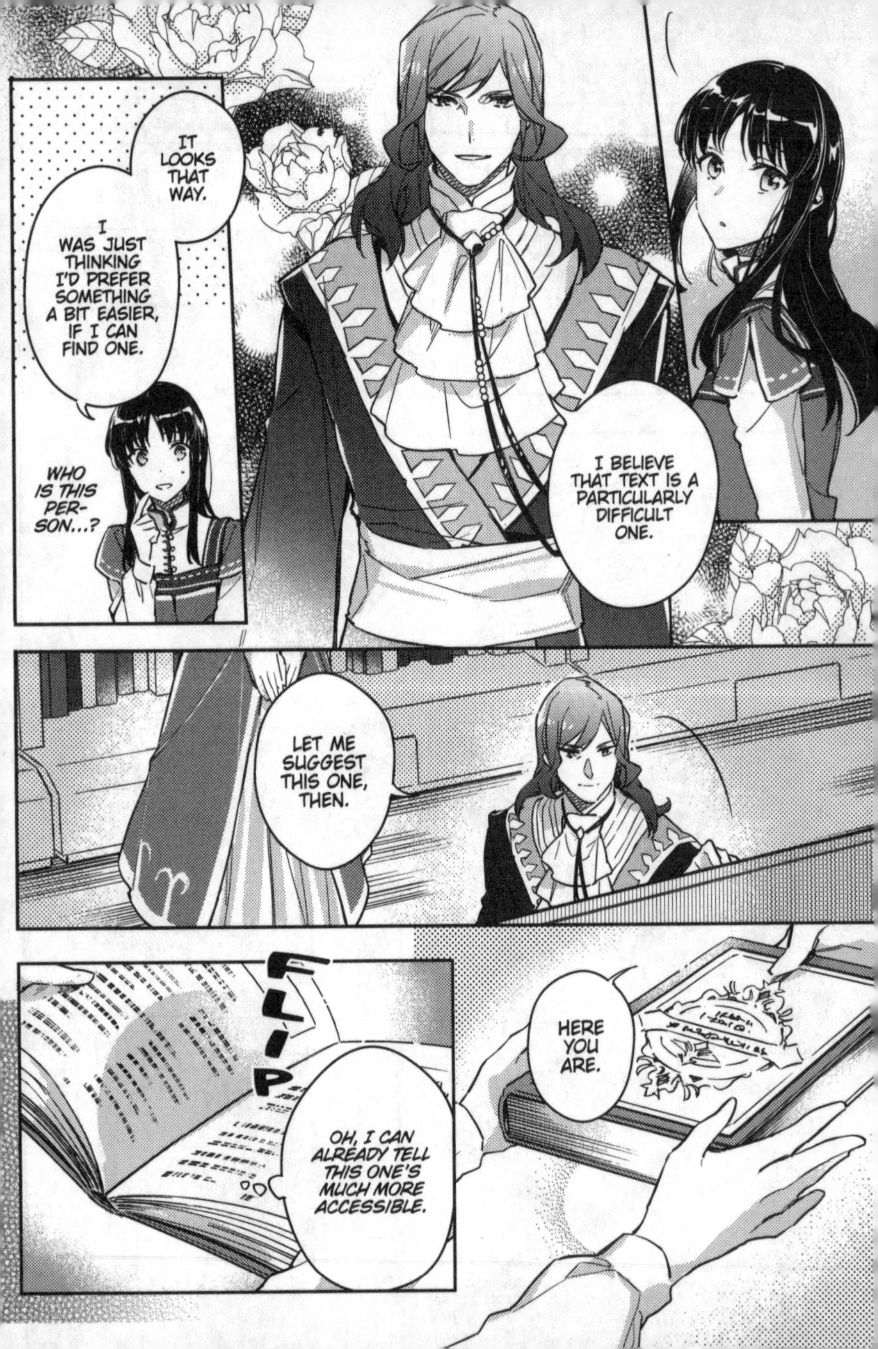
I BELIEVE THAT TEXT IS A PARTICULARLY DIFFICULT ONE.
IT LOOKS THAT WAY.
I WAS JUST THINKING I'D PREFER SOMETHING A BIT EASIER, IF I CAN FIND ONE.
WHO IS THIS PERSON...?
LET ME SUGGEST THIS ONE, THEN.
HERE YOU ARE.
FLIP
OH, I CAN ALREADY TELL THIS ONE'S MUCH MORE ACCESSIBLE.

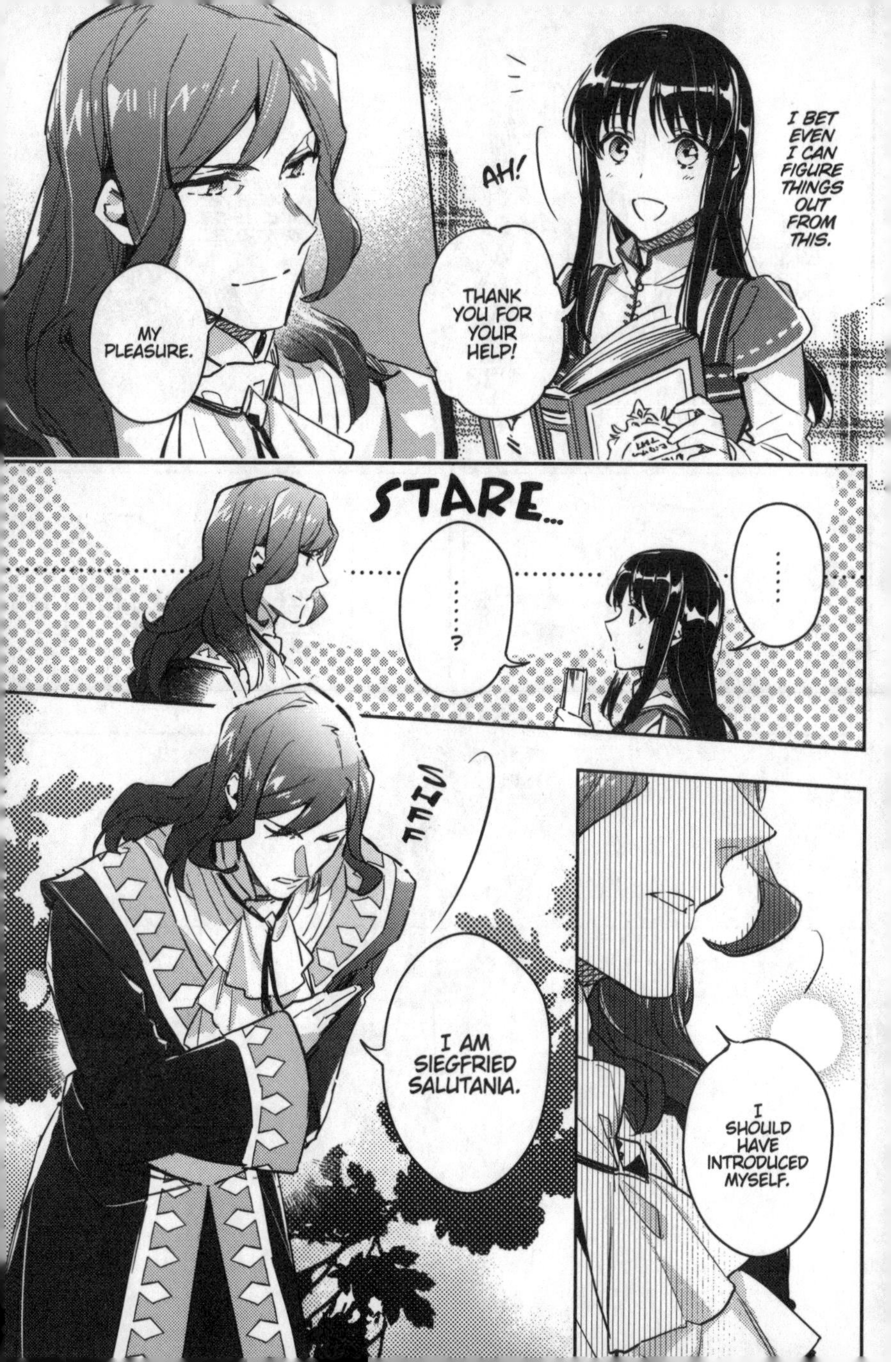
I BET EVEN I CAN FIGURE THINGS OUT FROM THIS.
AH!
THANK YOU FOR YOUR HELP!
MY PLEASURE.
STARE...
......
......?
I SHOULD HAVE INTRODUCED MYSELF.
SHUFF
I AM SIEGFRIED SALUTANIA.

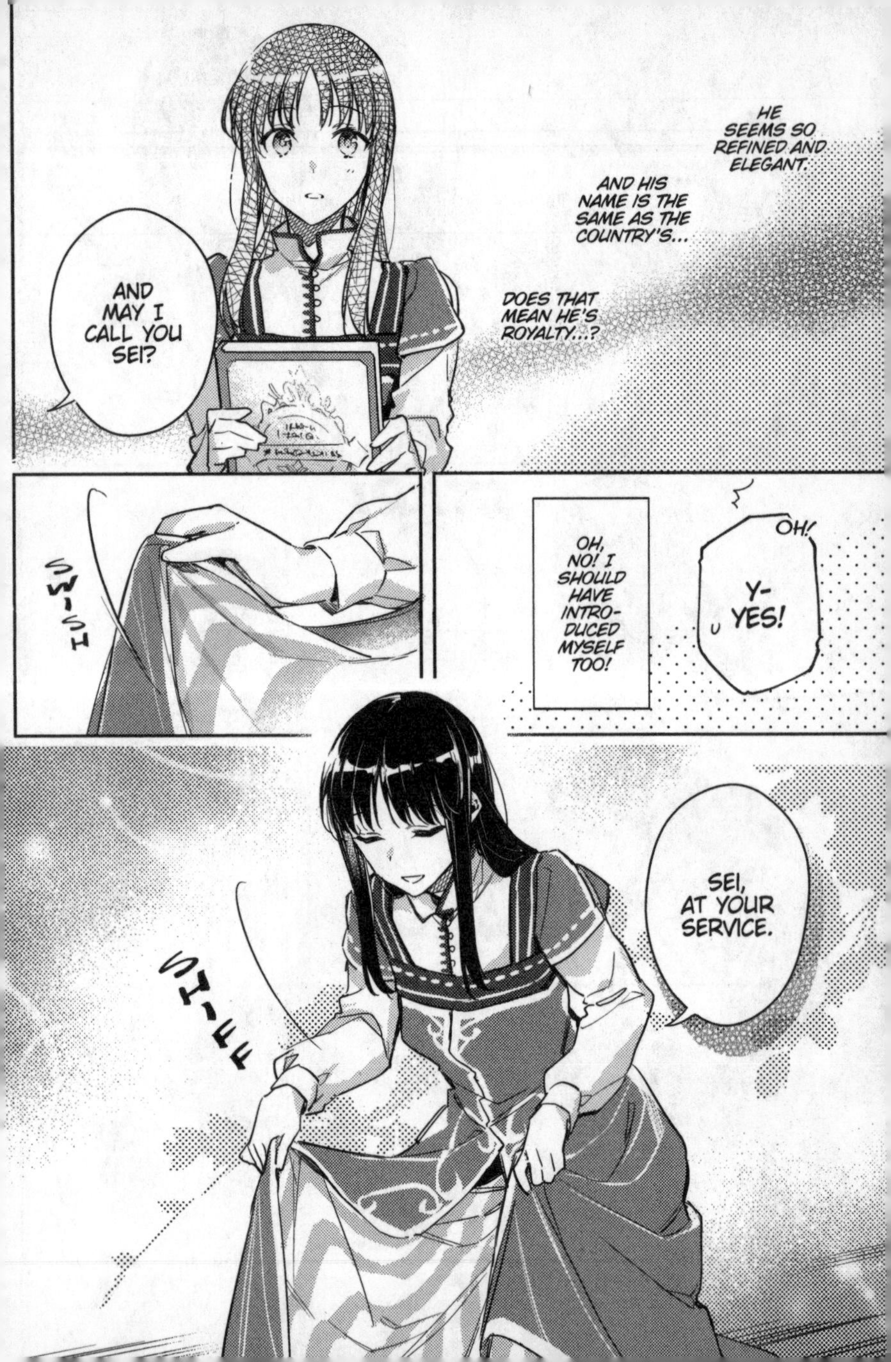
HE SEEMS SO REFINED AND ELEGANT.
AND HIS NAME IS THE SAME AS THE COUNTRY'S...
DOES THAT MEAN HE'S ROYALTY...?
AND MAY I CALL YOU SEI?
OH!
Y-YES!
OH, NO! I SHOULD HAVE INTRO-DUCED MYSELF TOO!
SWISH
SEI, AT YOUR SERVICE.
SHIFF

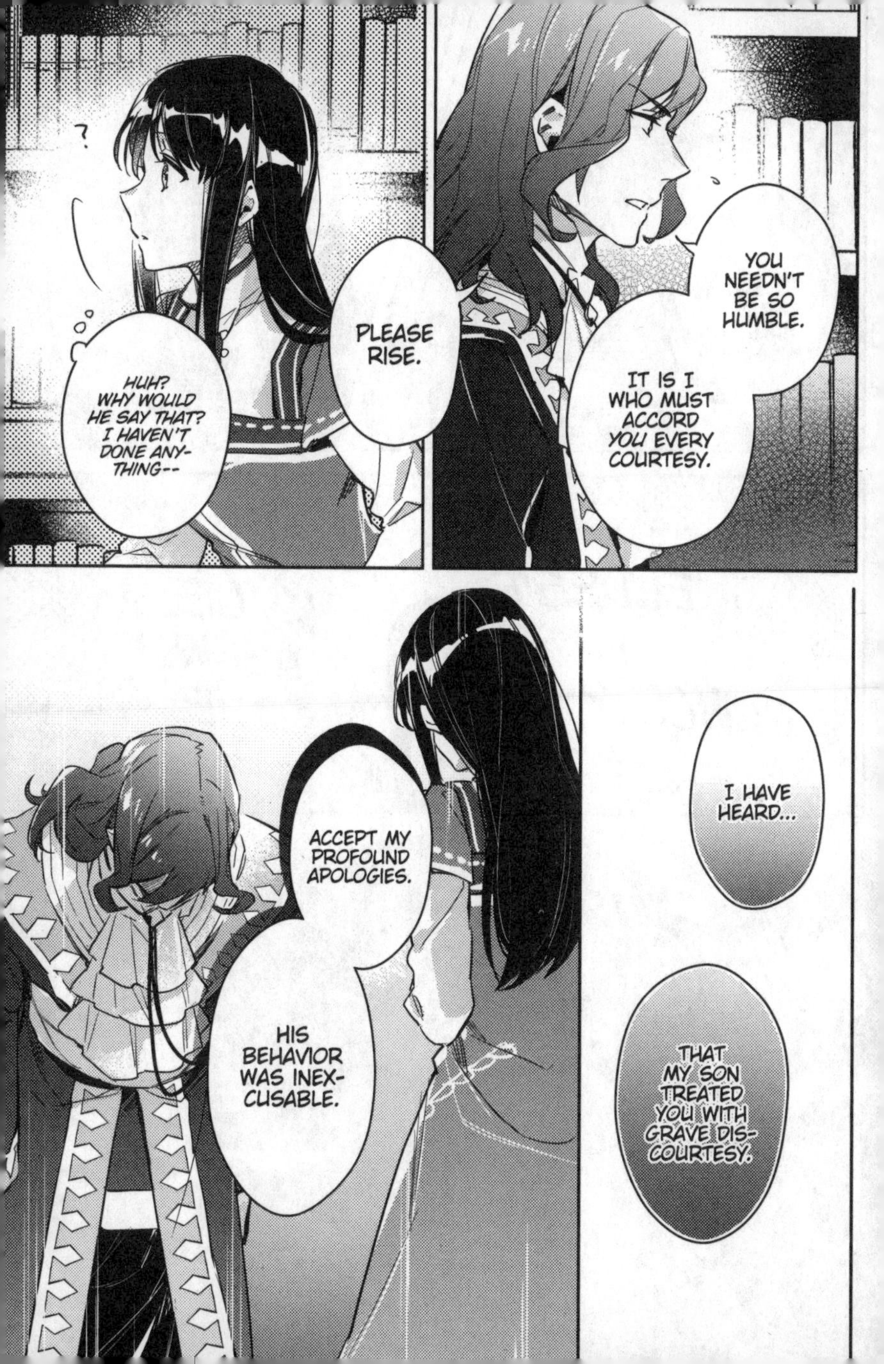
YOU NEEDN'T BE SO HUMBLE.
IT IS I WHO MUST ACCORD *YOU* EVERY COURTESY.
PLEASE RISE.
?
HUH? WHY WOULD HE SAY THAT? I HAVEN'T DONE ANY-THING--
I HAVE HEARD...
THAT MY SON TREATED YOU WITH GRAVE DIS-COURTESY.
ACCEPT MY PROFOUND APOLOGIES.
HIS BEHAVIOR WAS INEX-CUSABLE.

UH... WHAT?

YES.

MY SON, KYLE.

YOUR SON...?

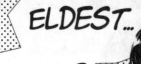

ELDEST...

PRINCE...?

KYLE... AS IN... THE...

THE KING?!

WAIT, DOES THAT MEAN...

THIS MAN IS...

BA-BAAAAM

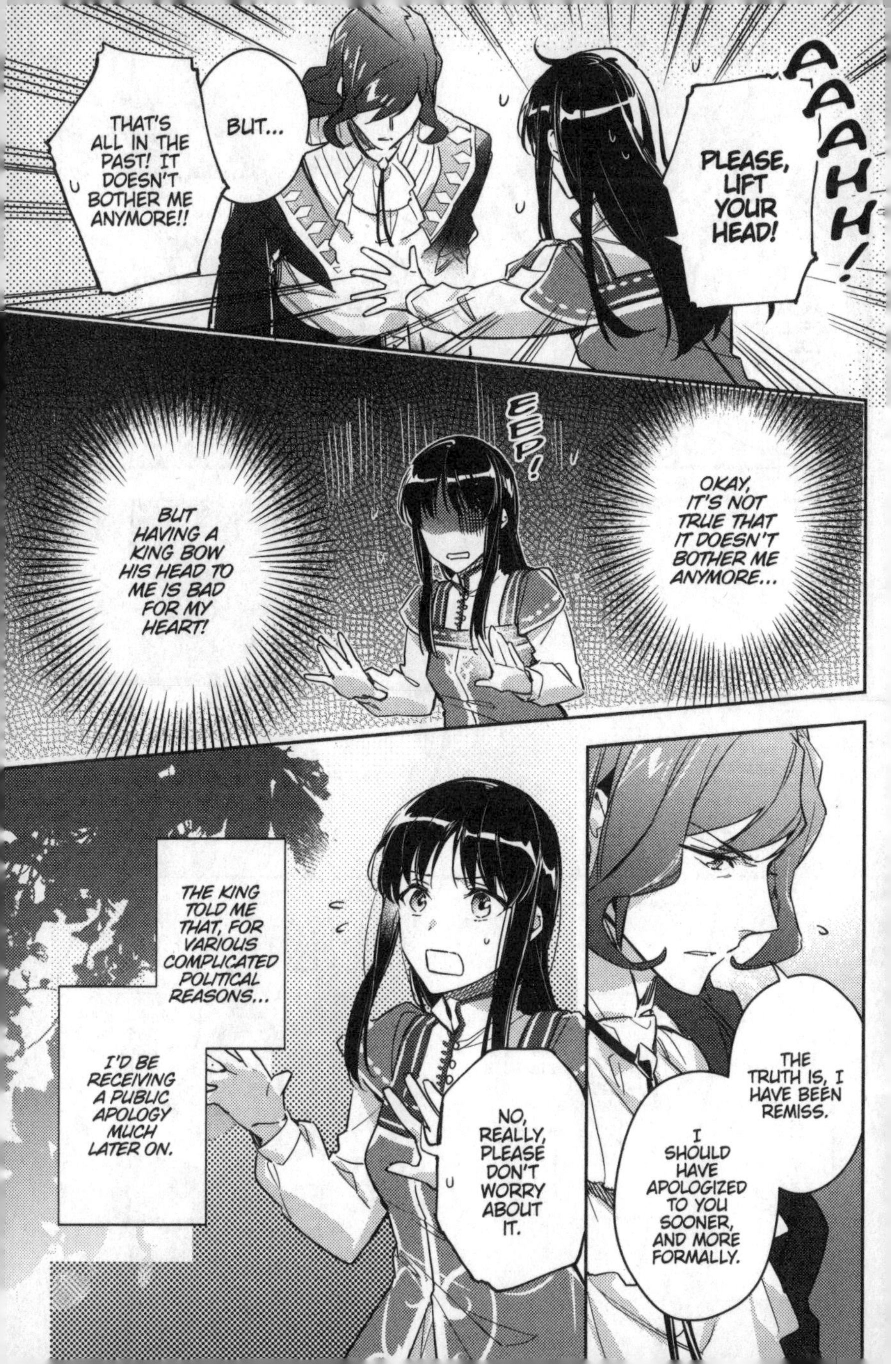
AAAHH!
PLEASE, LIFT YOUR HEAD!
BUT...
THAT'S ALL IN THE PAST! IT DOESN'T BOTHER ME ANYMORE!!
EEP!
OKAY, IT'S NOT TRUE THAT IT DOESN'T BOTHER ME ANYMORE...
BUT HAVING A KING BOW HIS HEAD TO ME IS BAD FOR MY HEART!
THE TRUTH IS, I HAVE BEEN REMISS.
I SHOULD HAVE APOLOGIZED TO YOU SOONER, AND MORE FORMALLY.
NO, REALLY, PLEASE DON'T WORRY ABOUT IT.
THE KING TOLD ME THAT, FOR VARIOUS COMPLICATED POLITICAL REASONS...
I'D BE RECEIVING A PUBLIC APOLOGY MUCH LATER ON.

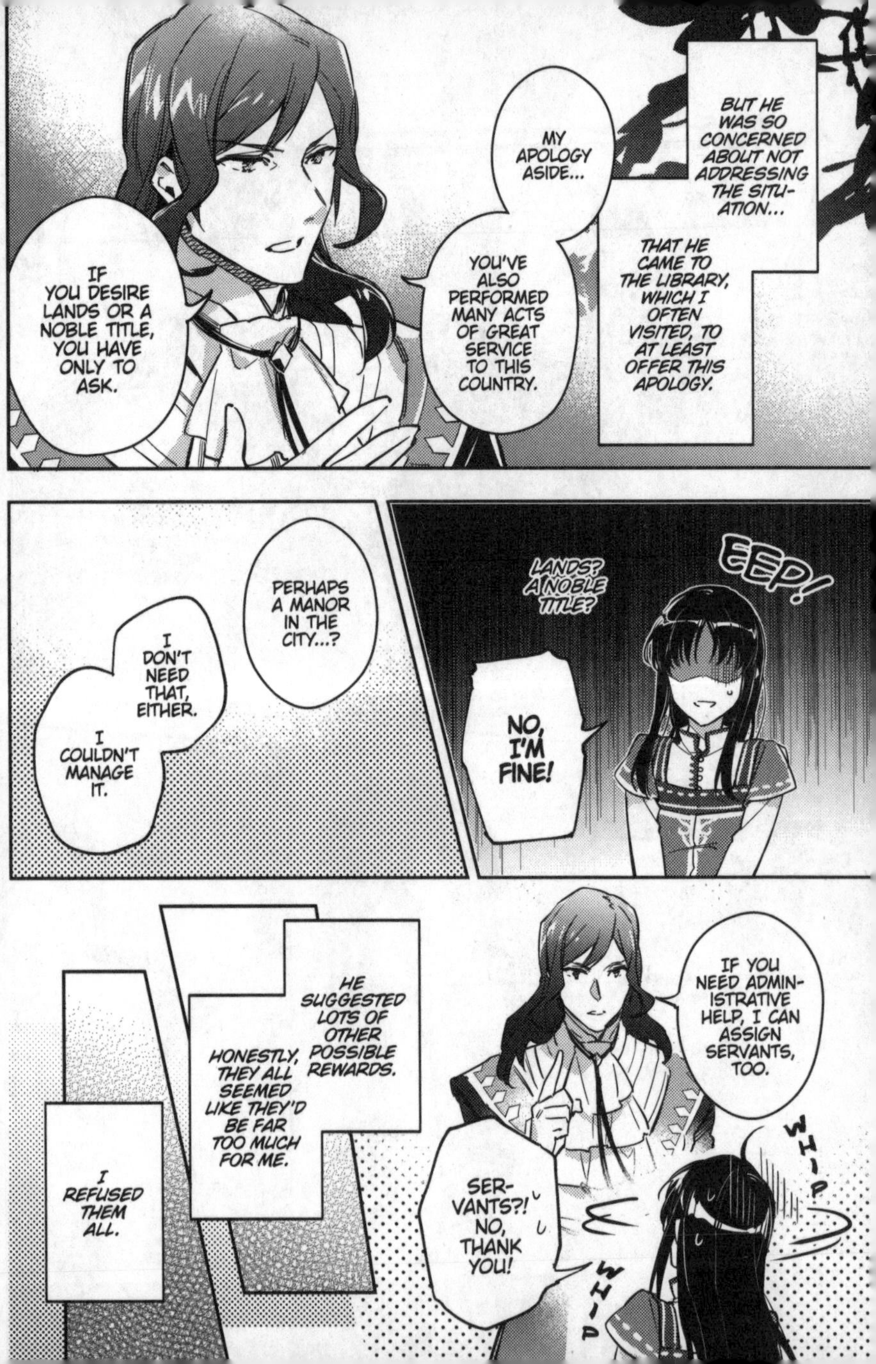

BUT HE WAS SO CONCERNED ABOUT NOT ADDRESSING THE SITUATION...
THAT HE CAME TO THE LIBRARY, WHICH I OFTEN VISITED, TO AT LEAST OFFER THIS APOLOGY.
MY APOLOGY ASIDE...
YOU'VE ALSO PERFORMED MANY ACTS OF GREAT SERVICE TO THIS COUNTRY.
IF YOU DESIRE LANDS OR A NOBLE TITLE, YOU HAVE ONLY TO ASK.
EEP!
LANDS? A NOBLE TITLE?
NO, I'M FINE!
PERHAPS A MANOR IN THE CITY...?
I DON'T NEED THAT, EITHER.
I COULDN'T MANAGE IT.
IF YOU NEED ADMINISTRATIVE HELP, I CAN ASSIGN SERVANTS, TOO.
WHIP
SERVANTS?! NO, THANK YOU!
WHIP
HE SUGGESTED LOTS OF OTHER POSSIBLE REWARDS.
HONESTLY, THEY ALL SEEMED LIKE THEY'D BE FAR TOO MUCH FOR ME.
I REFUSED THEM ALL.

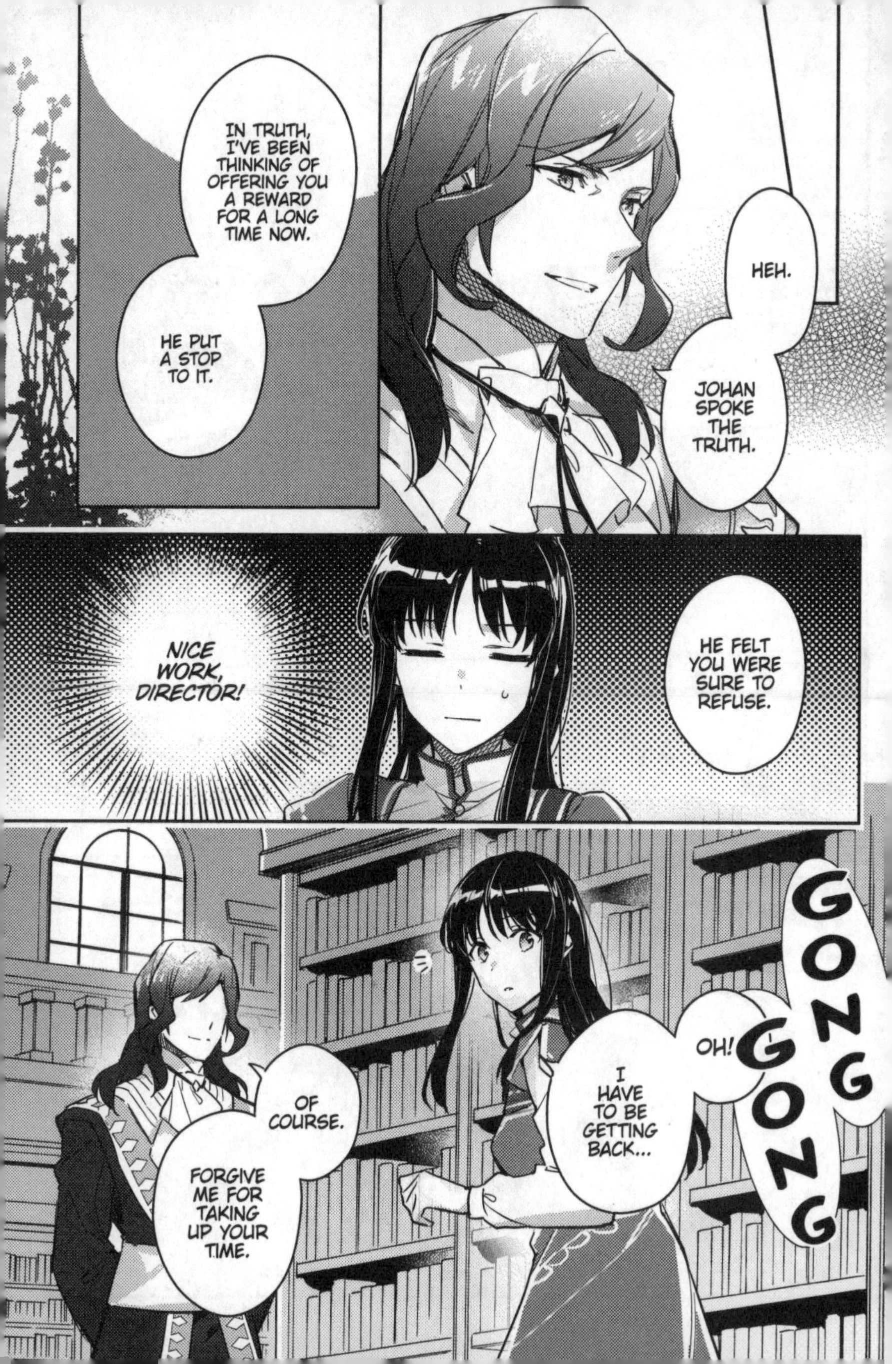
HEH.
JOHAN SPOKE THE TRUTH.
IN TRUTH, I'VE BEEN THINKING OF OFFERING YOU A REWARD FOR A LONG TIME NOW.
HE PUT A STOP TO IT.
HE FELT YOU WERE SURE TO REFUSE.
NICE WORK, DIRECTOR!
GONG GONG
OH!
I HAVE TO BE GETTING BACK...
OF COURSE.
FORGIVE ME FOR TAKING UP YOUR TIME.

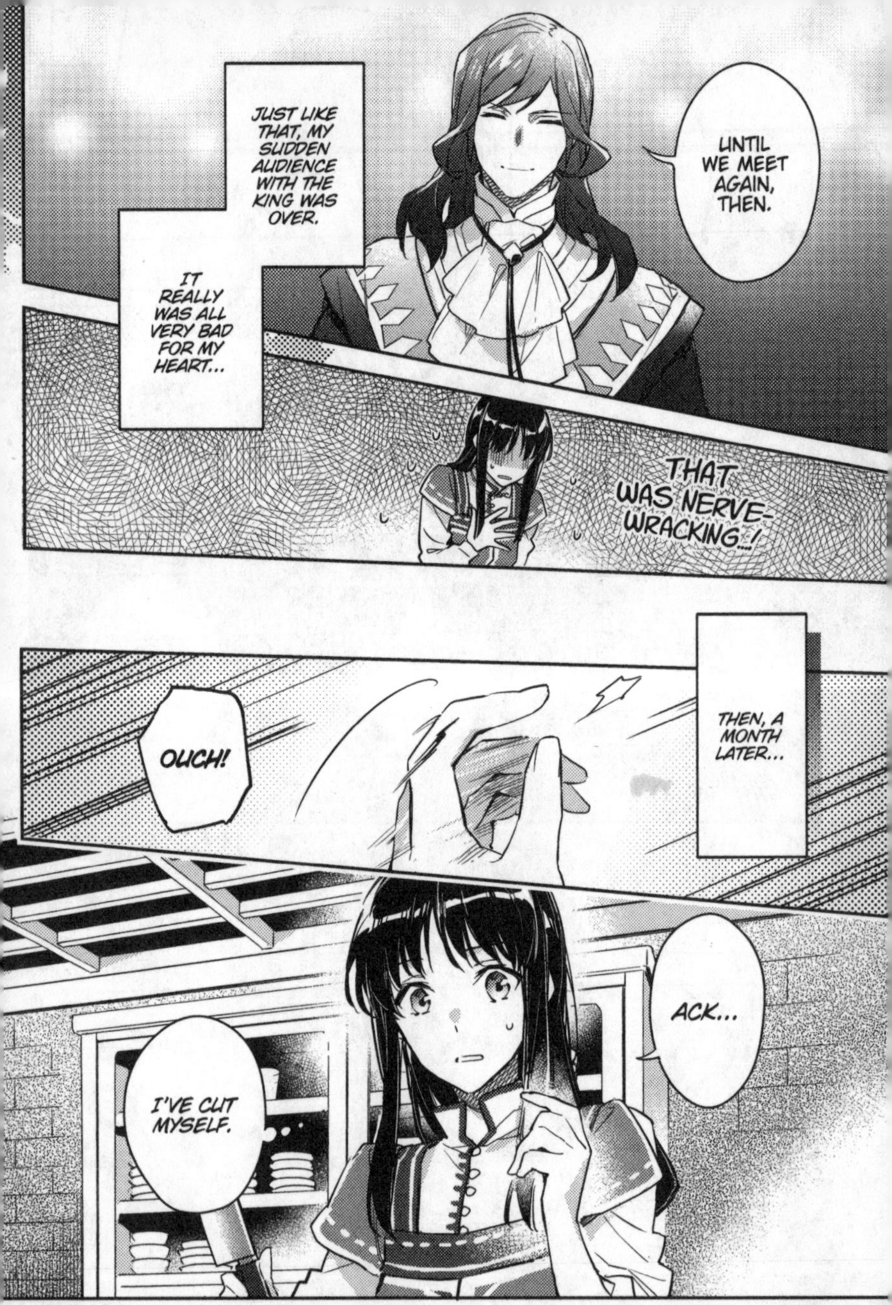
UNTIL WE MEET AGAIN, THEN.
JUST LIKE THAT, MY SUDDEN AUDIENCE WITH THE KING WAS OVER.
IT REALLY WAS ALL VERY BAD FOR MY HEART...
THAT WAS NERVE-WRACKING...!
THEN, A MONTH LATER...
OUCH!
ACK...
I'VE CUT MYSELF.

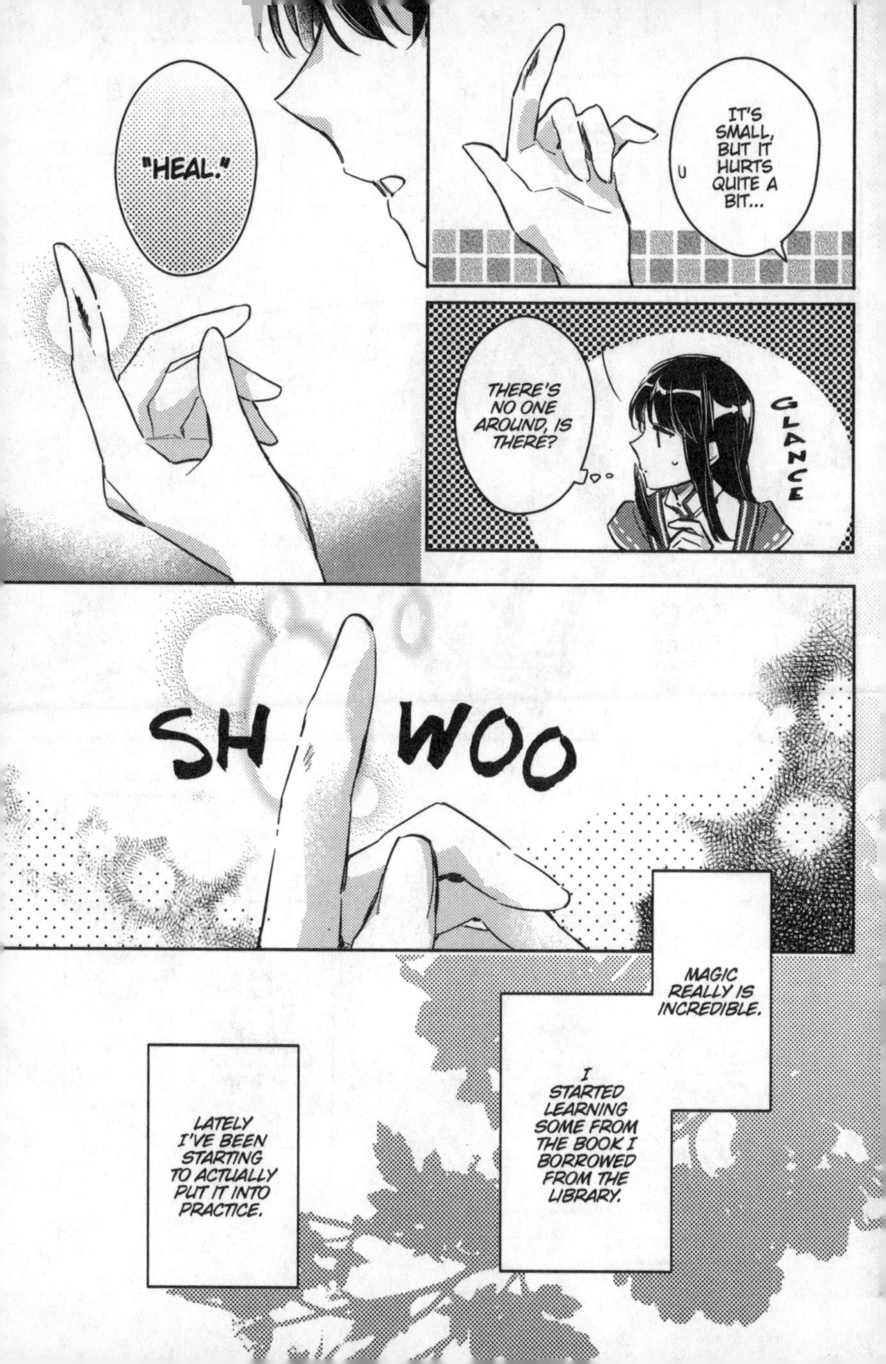
IT'S SMALL, BUT IT HURTS QUITE A BIT...
THERE'S NO ONE AROUND, IS THERE?
GLANCE
"HEAL."
SHWOO
MAGIC REALLY IS INCREDIBLE.
I STARTED LEARNING SOME FROM THE BOOK I BORROWED FROM THE LIBRARY.
LATELY I'VE BEEN STARTING TO ACTUALLY PUT IT INTO PRACTICE.

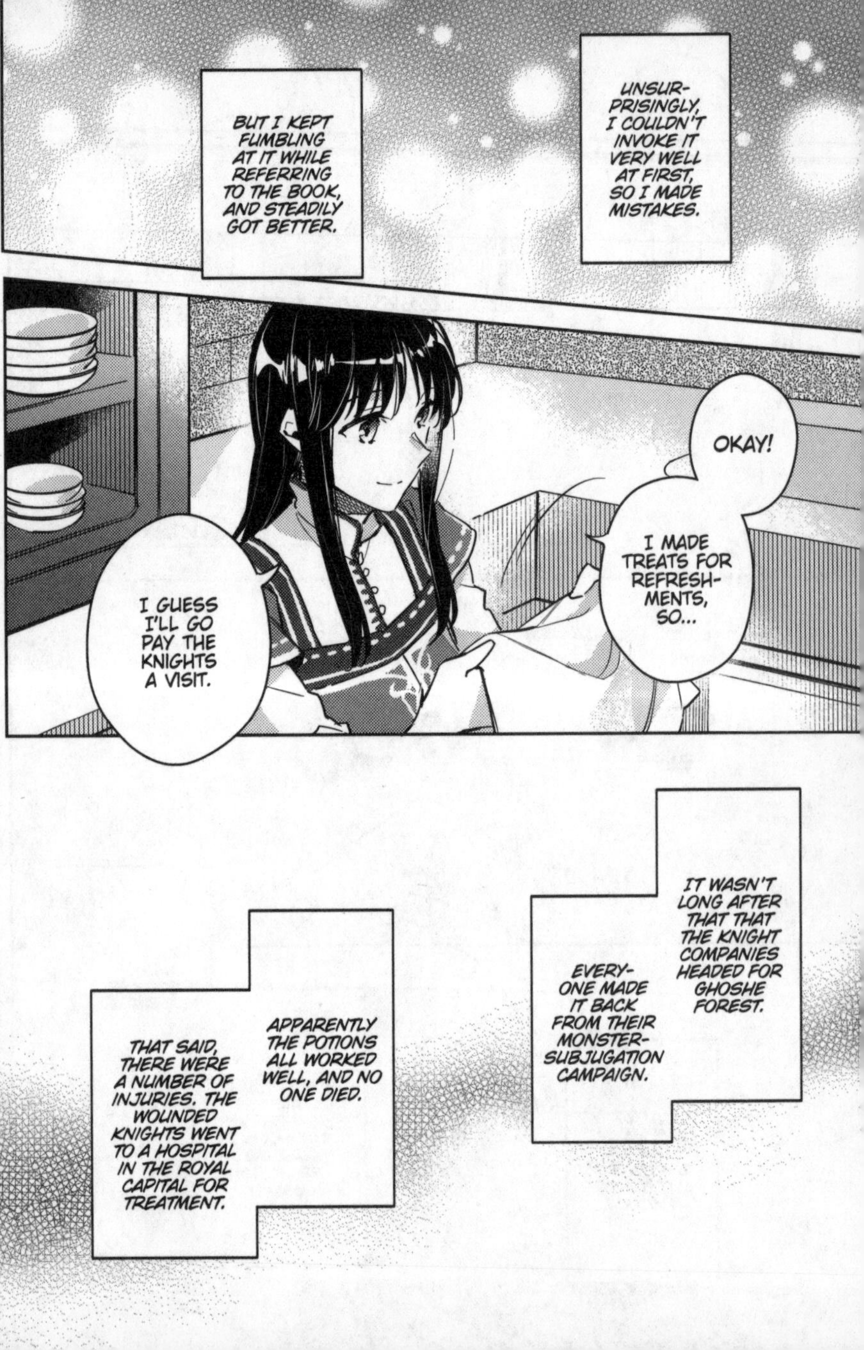
UNSURPRISINGLY, I COULDN'T INVOKE IT VERY WELL AT FIRST, SO I MADE MISTAKES.
BUT I KEPT FUMBLING AT IT WHILE REFERRING TO THE BOOK, AND STEADILY GOT BETTER.
OKAY!
I MADE TREATS FOR REFRESHMENTS, SO...
I GUESS I'LL GO PAY THE KNIGHTS A VISIT.
IT WASN'T LONG AFTER THAT THAT THE KNIGHT COMPANIES HEADED FOR GHOSHE FOREST.
EVERYONE MADE IT BACK FROM THEIR MONSTER-SUBJUGATION CAMPAIGN.
APPARENTLY THE POTIONS ALL WORKED WELL, AND NO ONE DIED.
THAT SAID, THERE WERE A NUMBER OF INJURIES. THE WOUNDED KNIGHTS WENT TO A HOSPITAL IN THE ROYAL CAPITAL FOR TREATMENT.

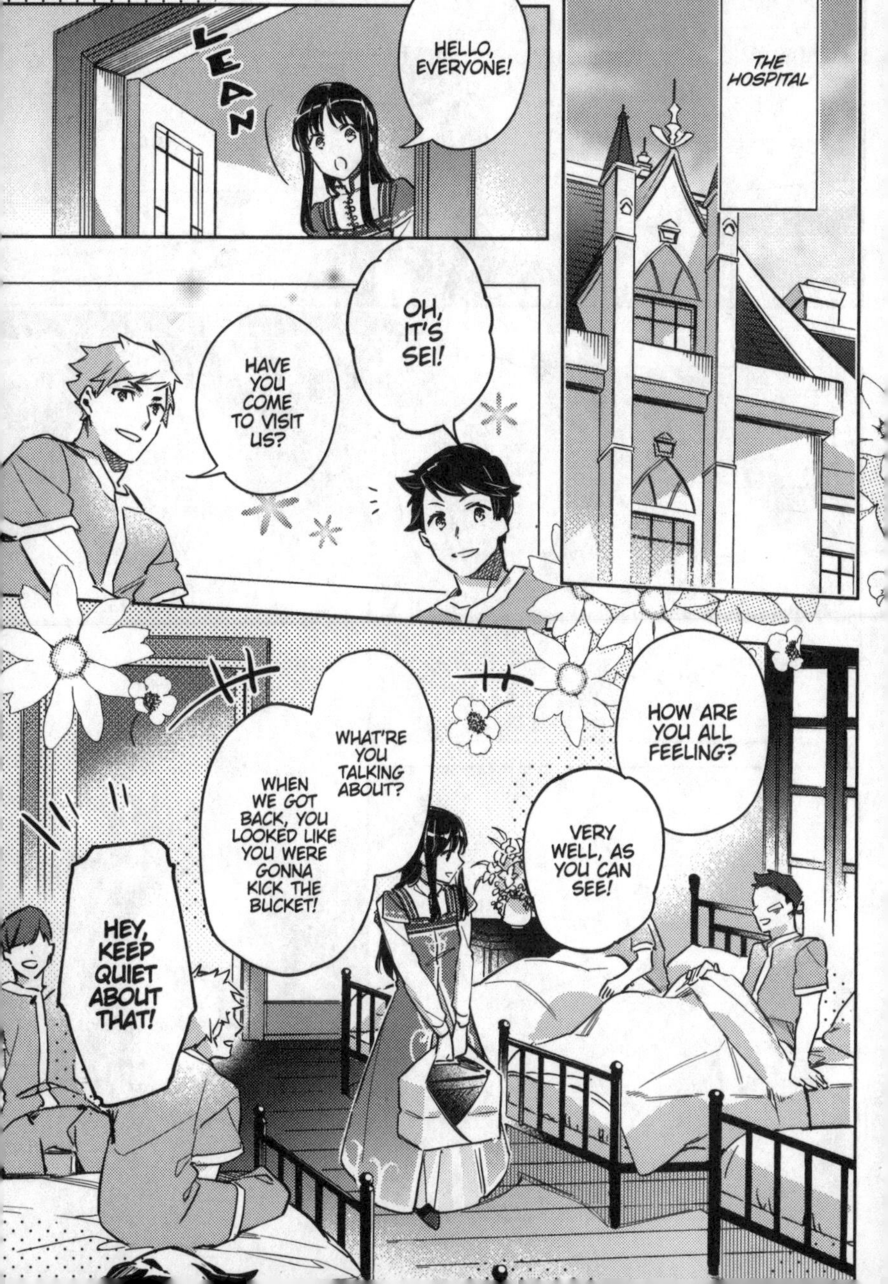
THE HOSPITAL
LEAN
HELLO, EVERYONE!
OH, IT'S SEI!
HAVE YOU COME TO VISIT US?
HOW ARE YOU ALL FEELING?
VERY WELL, AS YOU CAN SEE!
WHAT'RE YOU TALKING ABOUT?
WHEN WE GOT BACK, YOU LOOKED LIKE YOU WERE GONNA KICK THE BUCKET!
HEY, KEEP QUIET ABOUT THAT!

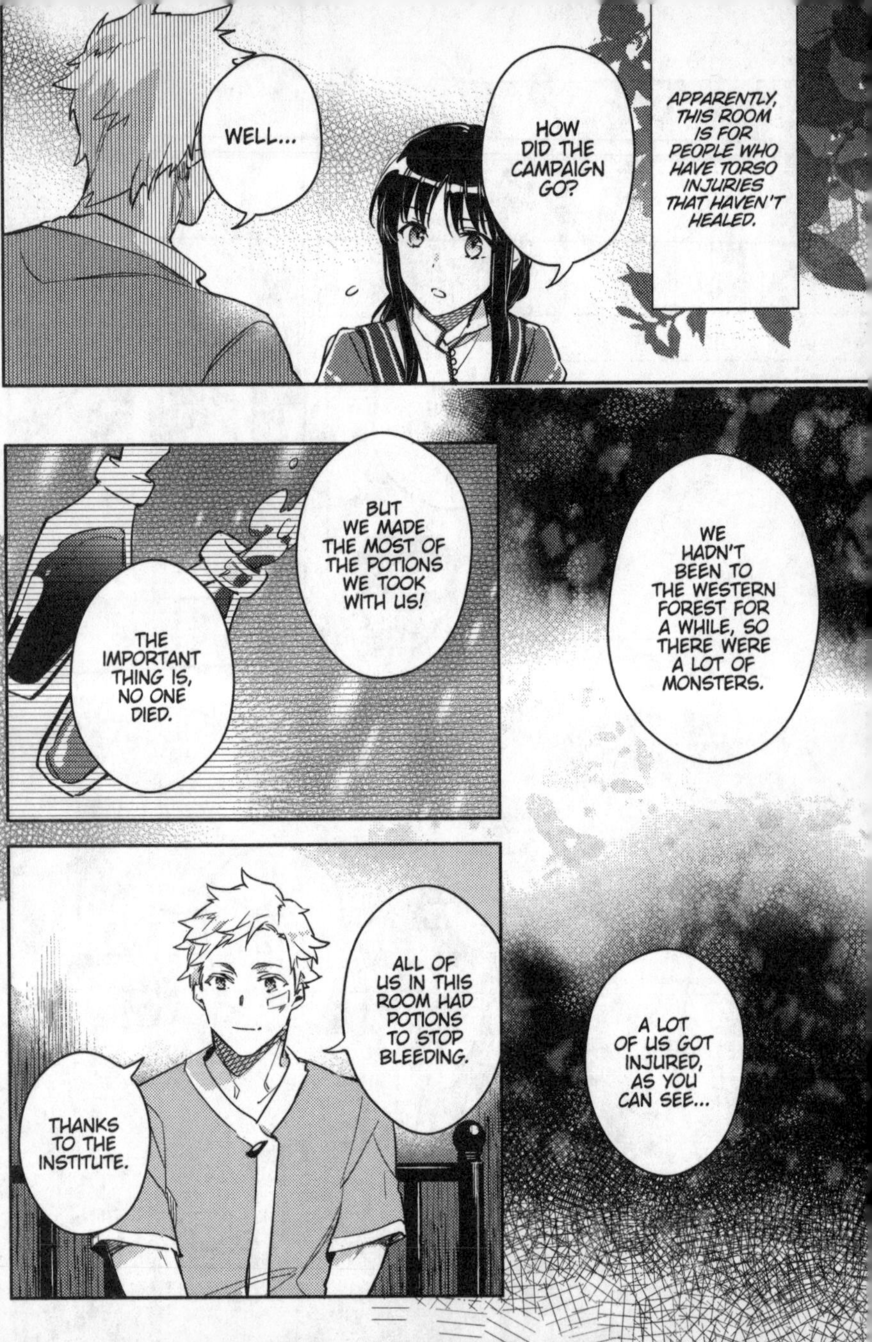
APPARENTLY, THIS ROOM IS FOR PEOPLE WHO HAVE TORSO INJURIES THAT HAVEN'T HEALED.
HOW DID THE CAMPAIGN GO?
WELL...
WE HADN'T BEEN TO THE WESTERN FOREST FOR A WHILE, SO THERE WERE A LOT OF MONSTERS.
A LOT OF US GOT INJURED, AS YOU CAN SEE...
BUT WE MADE THE MOST OF THE POTIONS WE TOOK WITH US!
THE IMPORTANT THING IS, NO ONE DIED.
ALL OF US IN THIS ROOM HAD POTIONS TO STOP BLEEDING.
THANKS TO THE INSTITUTE.

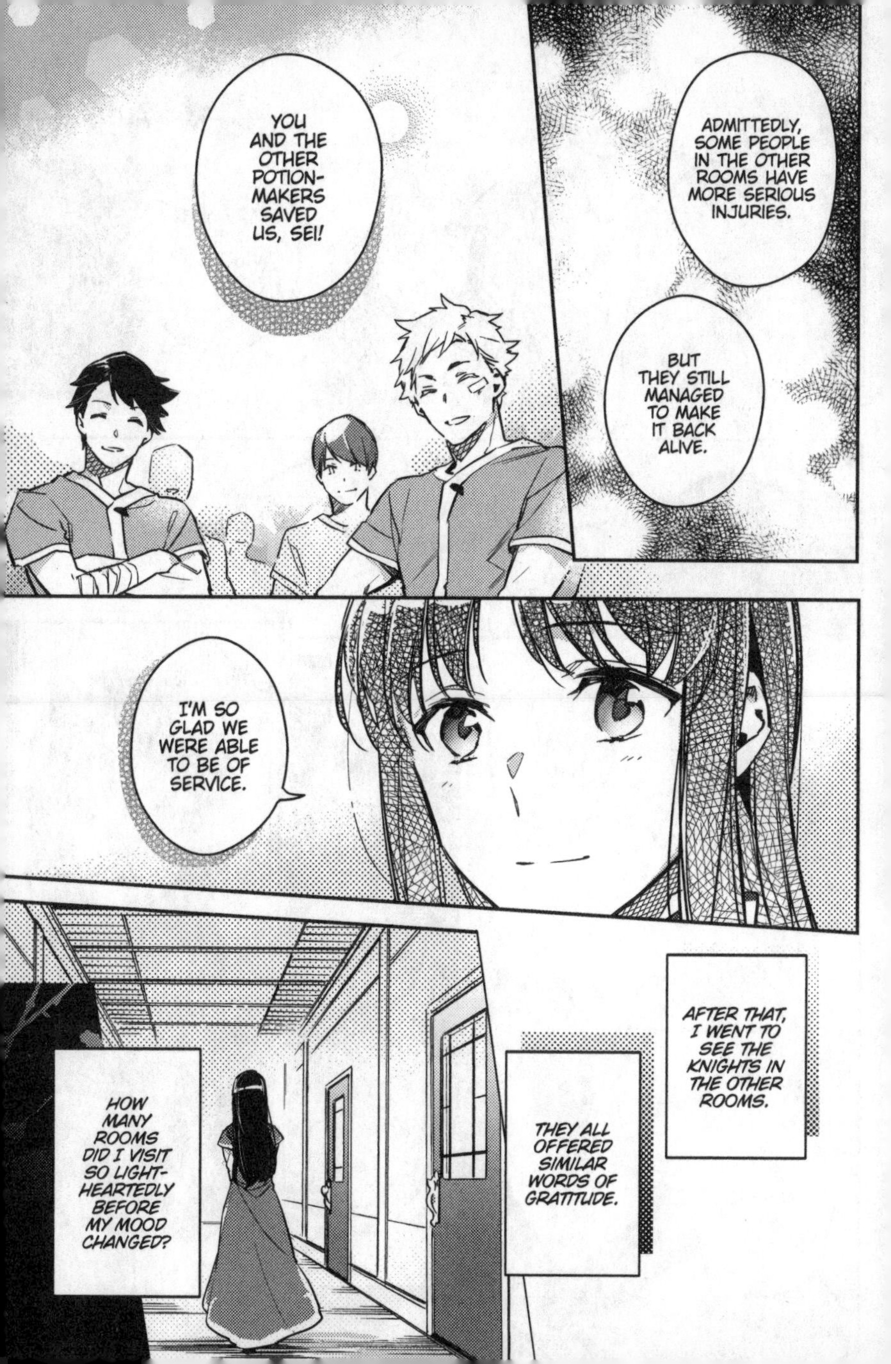
ADMITTEDLY, SOME PEOPLE IN THE OTHER ROOMS HAVE MORE SERIOUS INJURIES.
BUT THEY STILL MANAGED TO MAKE IT BACK ALIVE.
YOU AND THE OTHER POTION-MAKERS SAVED US, SEI!
I'M SO GLAD WE WERE ABLE TO BE OF SERVICE.
AFTER THAT, I WENT TO SEE THE KNIGHTS IN THE OTHER ROOMS.
THEY ALL OFFERED SIMILAR WORDS OF GRATITUDE.
HOW MANY ROOMS DID I VISIT SO LIGHT-HEARTEDLY BEFORE MY MOOD CHANGED?

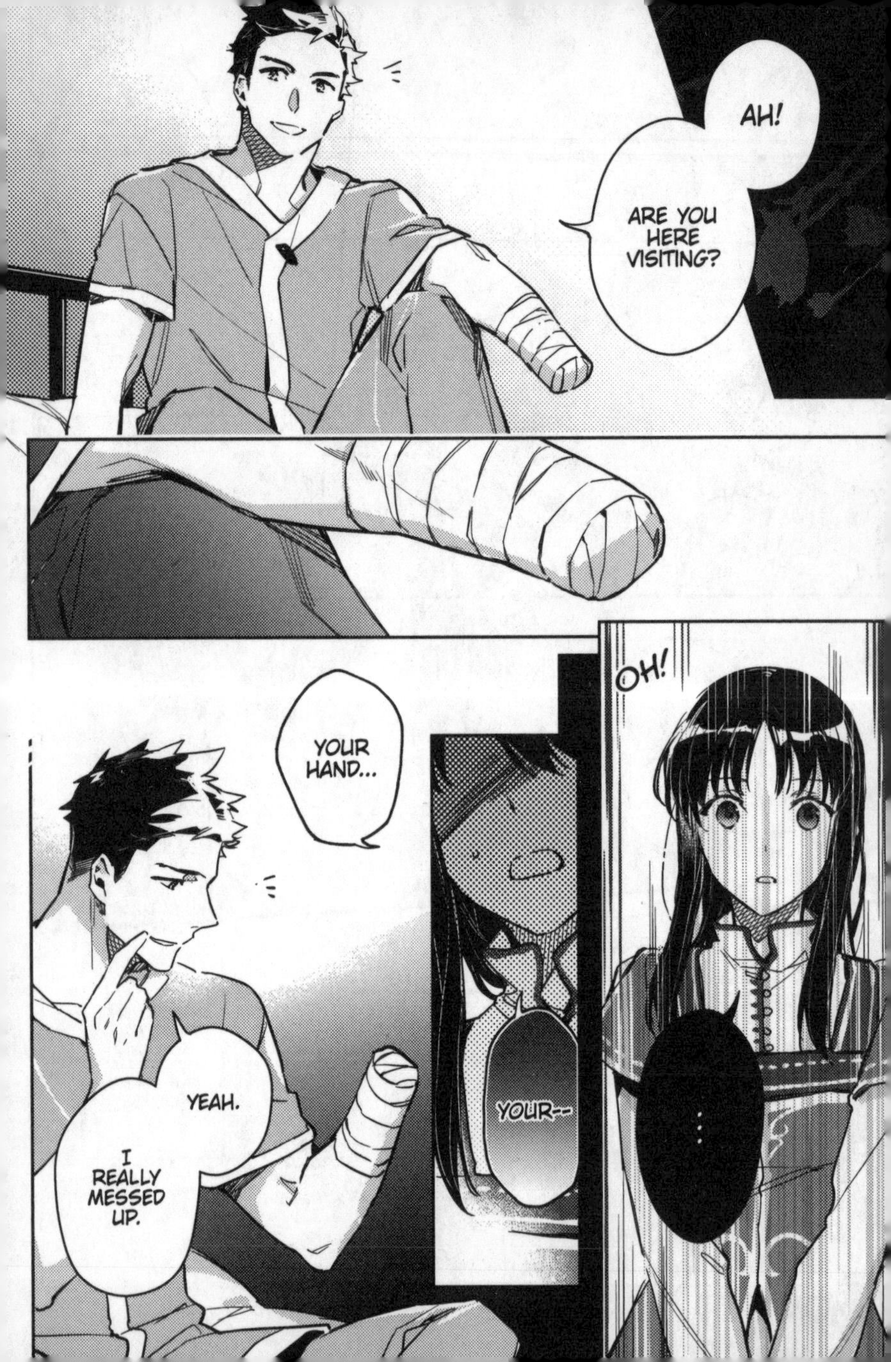
AH!
ARE YOU HERE VISITING?
OH!
YOUR HAND...
YOUR--
...
YEAH.
I REALLY MESSED UP.

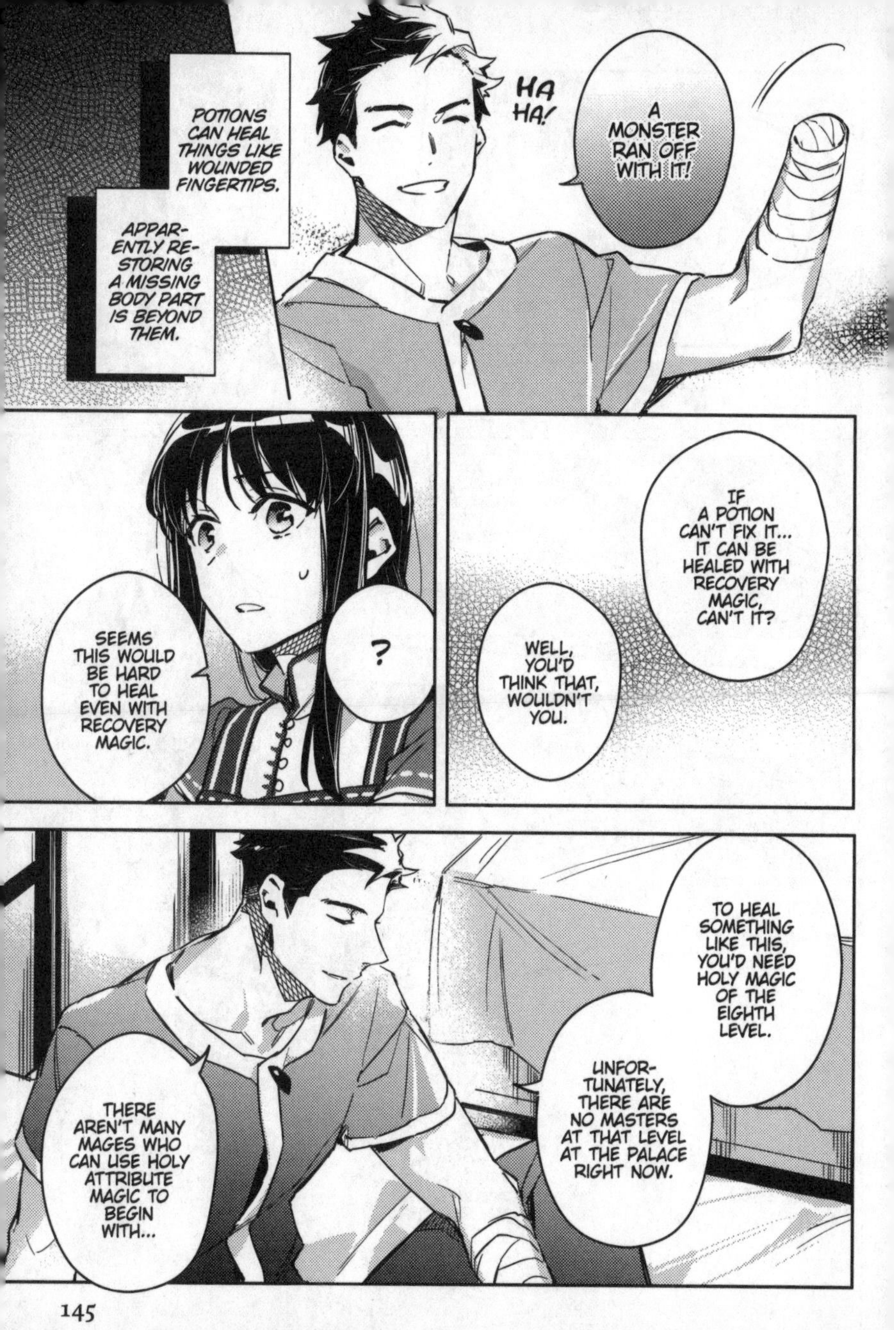
A MONSTER RAN OFF WITH IT!
HA HA!
POTIONS CAN HEAL THINGS LIKE WOUNDED FINGERTIPS.
APPAR-ENTLY RE-STORING A MISSING BODY PART IS BEYOND THEM.
IF A POTION CAN'T FIX IT... IT CAN BE HEALED WITH RECOVERY MAGIC, CAN'T IT?
WELL, YOU'D THINK THAT, WOULDN'T YOU.
?
SEEMS THIS WOULD BE HARD TO HEAL EVEN WITH RECOVERY MAGIC.
TO HEAL SOMETHING LIKE THIS, YOU'D NEED HOLY MAGIC OF THE EIGHTH LEVEL.
UNFOR-TUNATELY, THERE ARE NO MASTERS AT THAT LEVEL AT THE PALACE RIGHT NOW.
THERE AREN'T MANY MAGES WHO CAN USE HOLY ATTRIBUTE MAGIC TO BEGIN WITH...

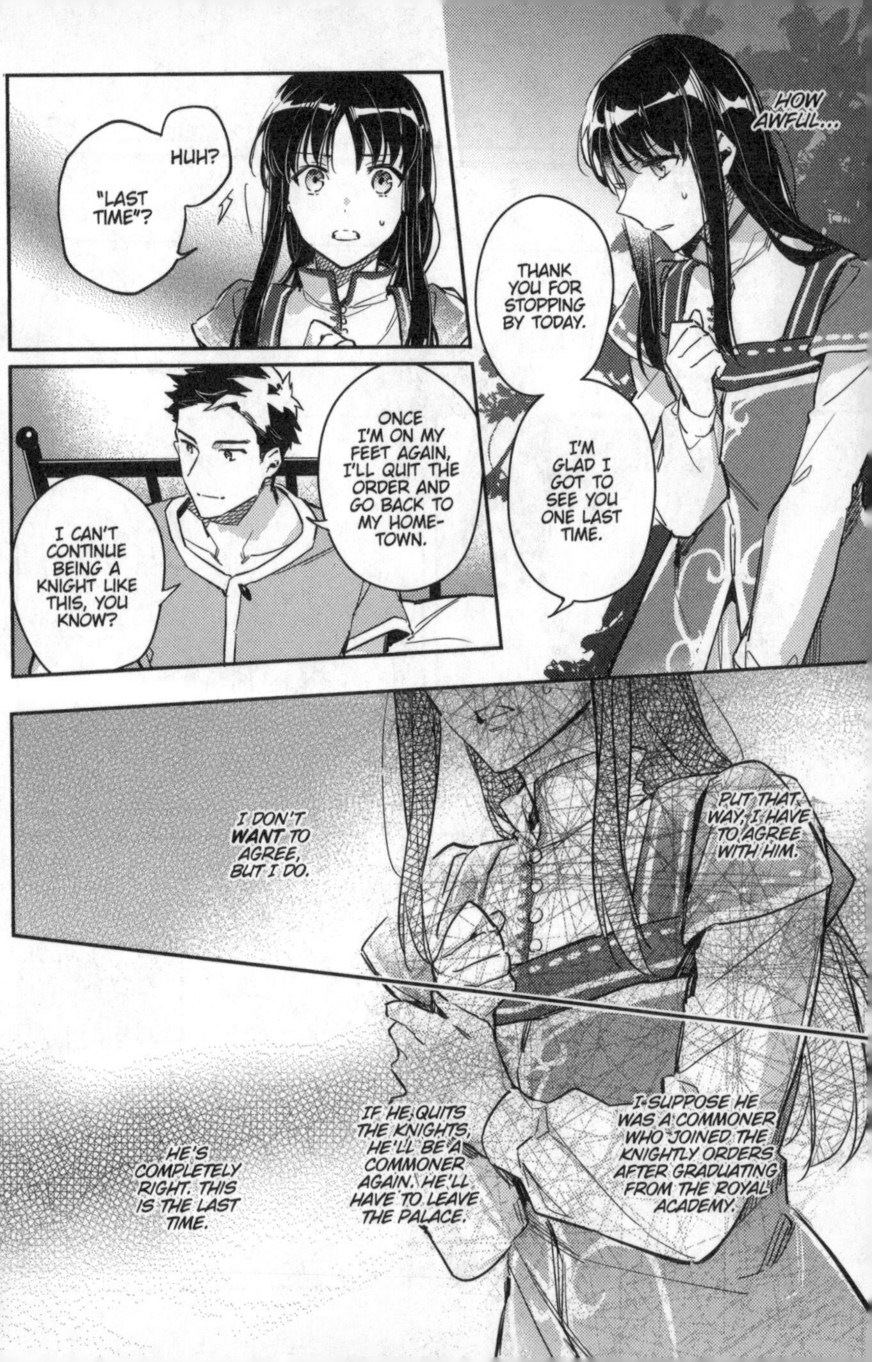
HOW AWFUL...
THANK YOU FOR STOPPING BY TODAY.
I'M GLAD I GOT TO SEE YOU ONE LAST TIME.
HUH?
"LAST TIME"?
ONCE I'M ON MY FEET AGAIN, I'LL QUIT THE ORDER AND GO BACK TO MY HOME-TOWN.
I CAN'T CONTINUE BEING A KNIGHT LIKE THIS, YOU KNOW?
PUT THAT WAY, I HAVE TO AGREE WITH HIM.
I DON'T *WANT* TO AGREE, BUT I DO.
I SUPPOSE HE WAS A COMMONER WHO JOINED THE KNIGHTLY ORDERS AFTER GRADUATING FROM THE ROYAL ACADEMY.
IF HE QUITS THE KNIGHTS, HE'LL BE A COMMONER AGAIN. HE'LL HAVE TO LEAVE THE PALACE.
HE'S COMPLETELY RIGHT. THIS IS THE LAST TIME.

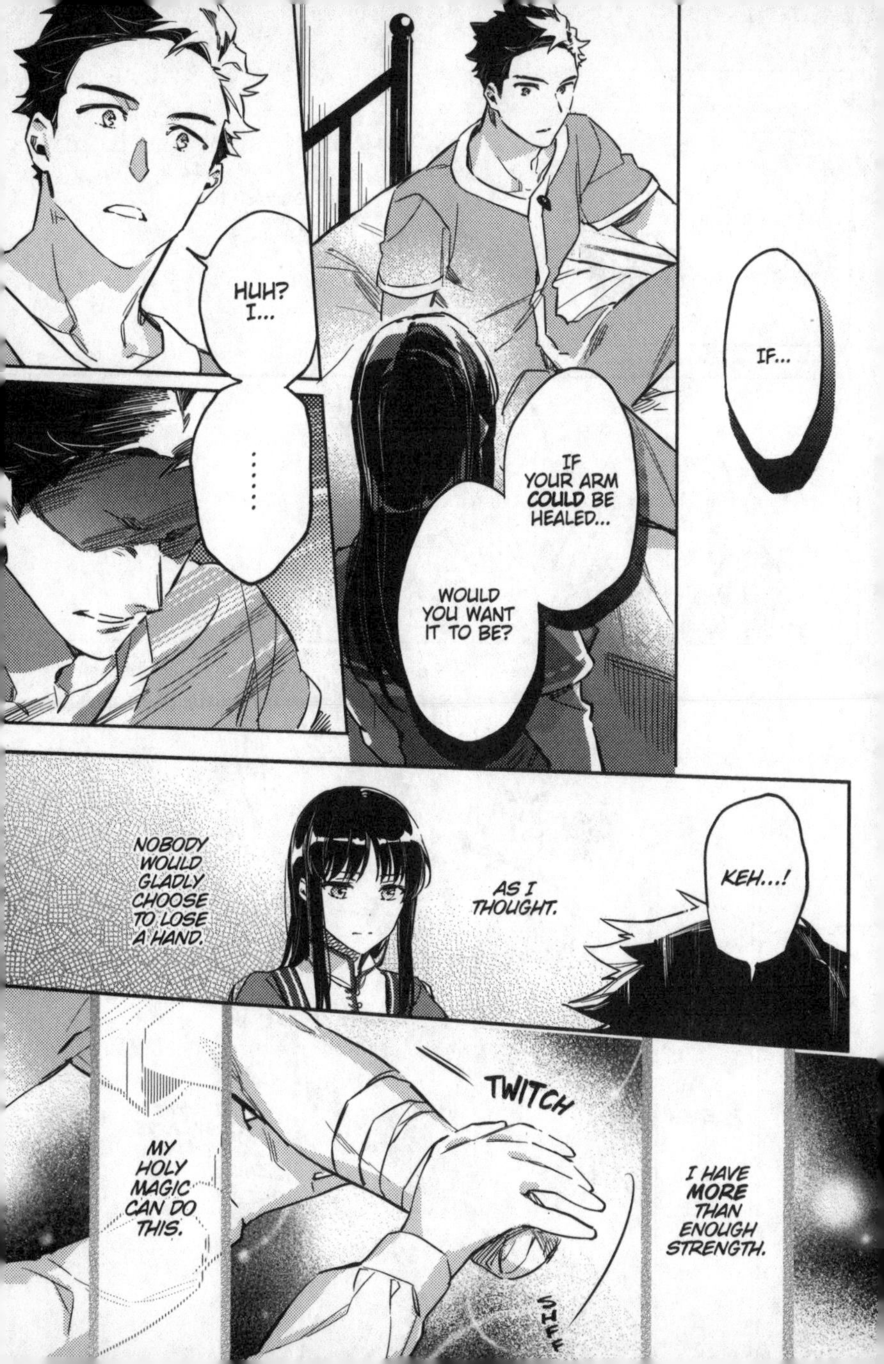
IF...
IF YOUR ARM COULD BE HEALED...
WOULD YOU WANT IT TO BE?
HUH? I...
......
KEH...!
AS I THOUGHT.
NOBODY WOULD GLADLY CHOOSE TO LOSE A HAND.
I HAVE MORE THAN ENOUGH STRENGTH.
TWITCH
SHFF
MY HOLY MAGIC CAN DO THIS.

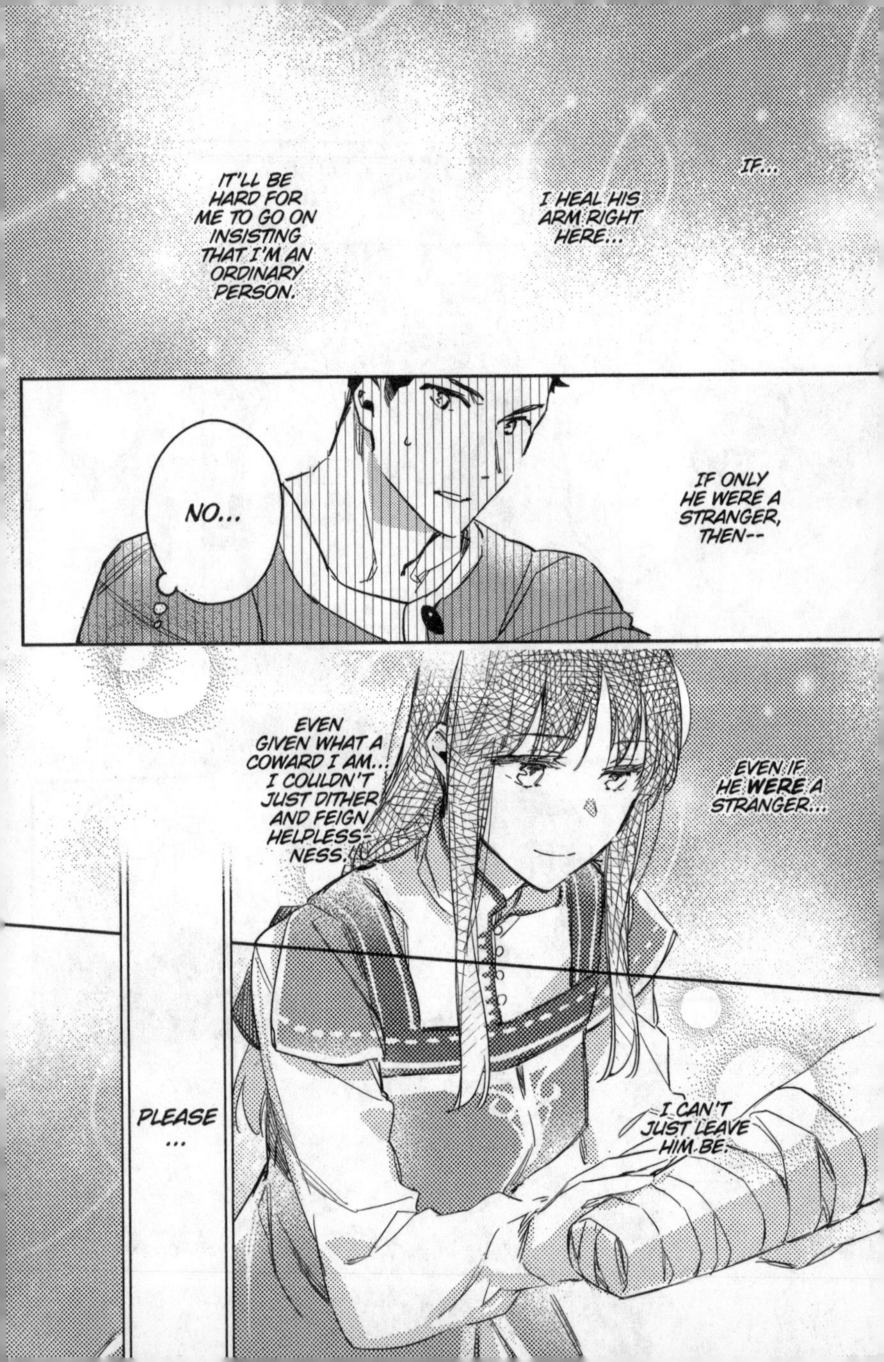
IF...
I HEAL HIS ARM RIGHT HERE...
IT'LL BE HARD FOR ME TO GO ON INSISTING THAT I'M AN ORDINARY PERSON.
IF ONLY HE WERE A STRANGER, THEN--
NO...
EVEN IF HE WERE A STRANGER...
EVEN GIVEN WHAT A COWARD I AM... I COULDN'T JUST DITHER AND FEIGN HELPLESS-NESS.
I CAN'T JUST LEAVE HIM BE.
PLEASE ...

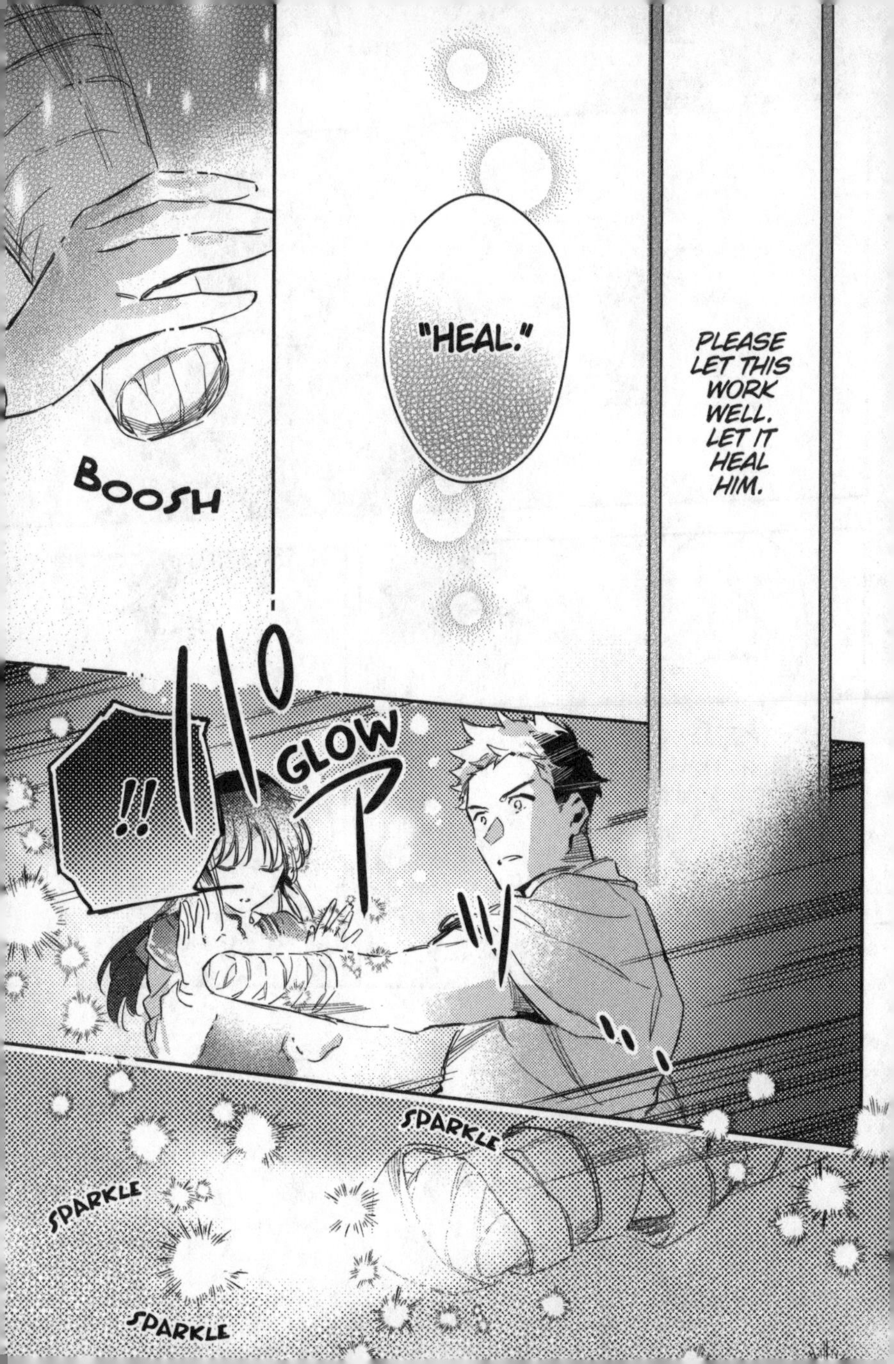
PLEASE LET THIS WORK WELL. LET IT HEAL HIM.
"HEAL."
BOOSH
GLOW
!!
SPARKLE
SPARKLE
SPARKLE

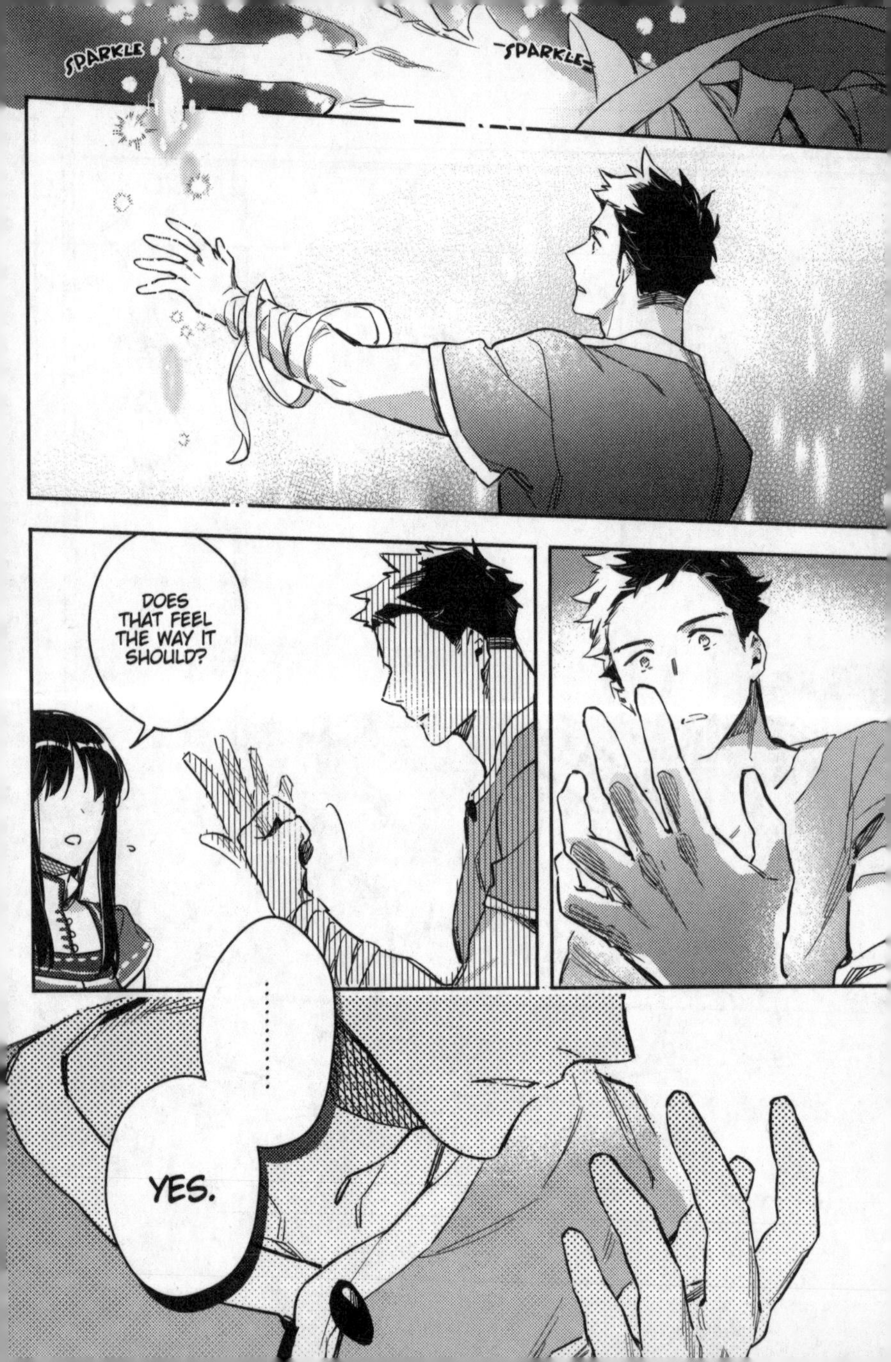
SPARKLE
SPARKLE
DOES THAT FEEL THE WAY IT SHOULD?
......
YES.

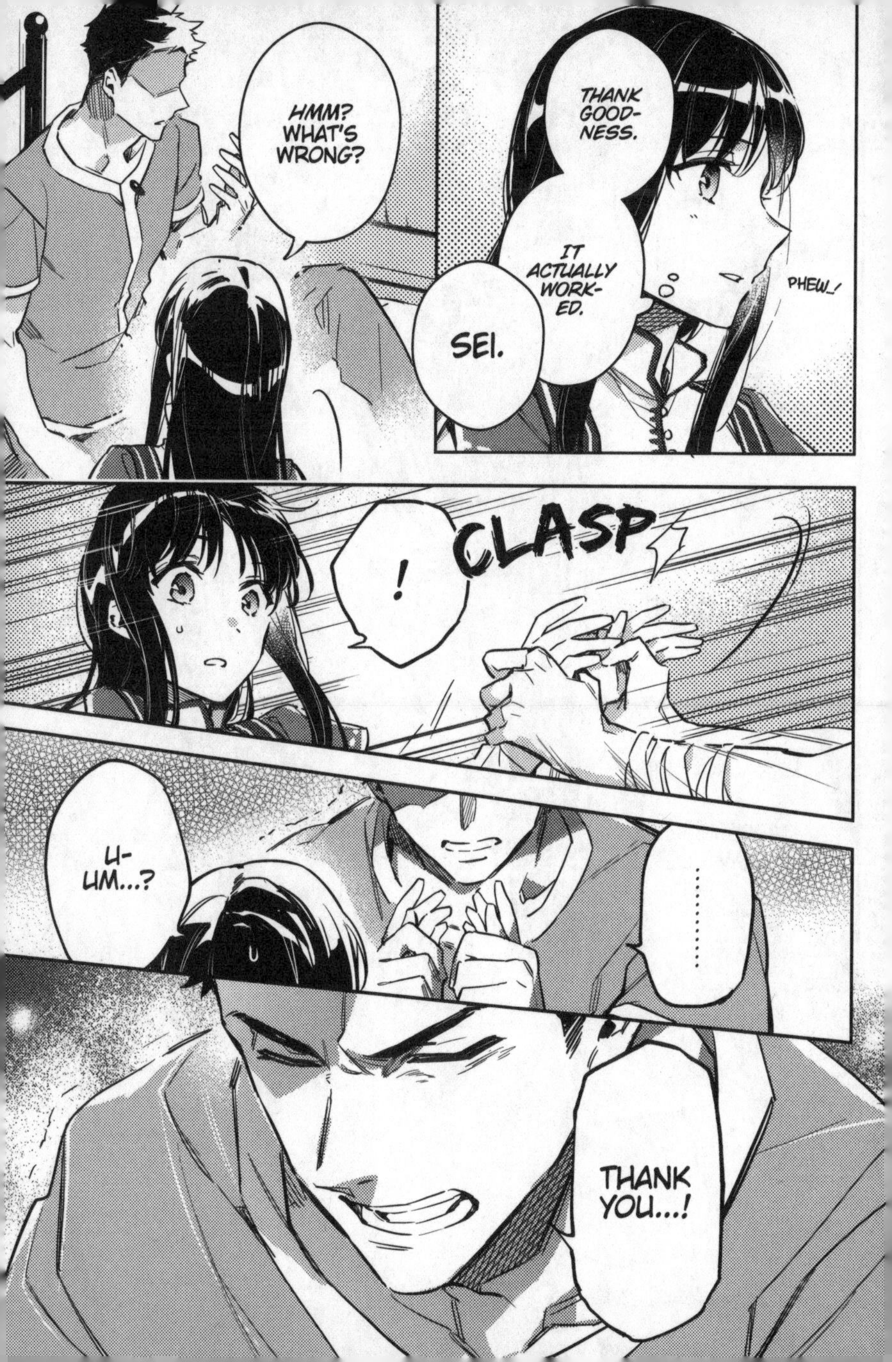
THANK GOODNESS.
IT ACTUALLY WORKED.
PHEW..!
SEI.
HMM? WHAT'S WRONG?
CLASP
!
......
U-UM...?
THANK YOU...!

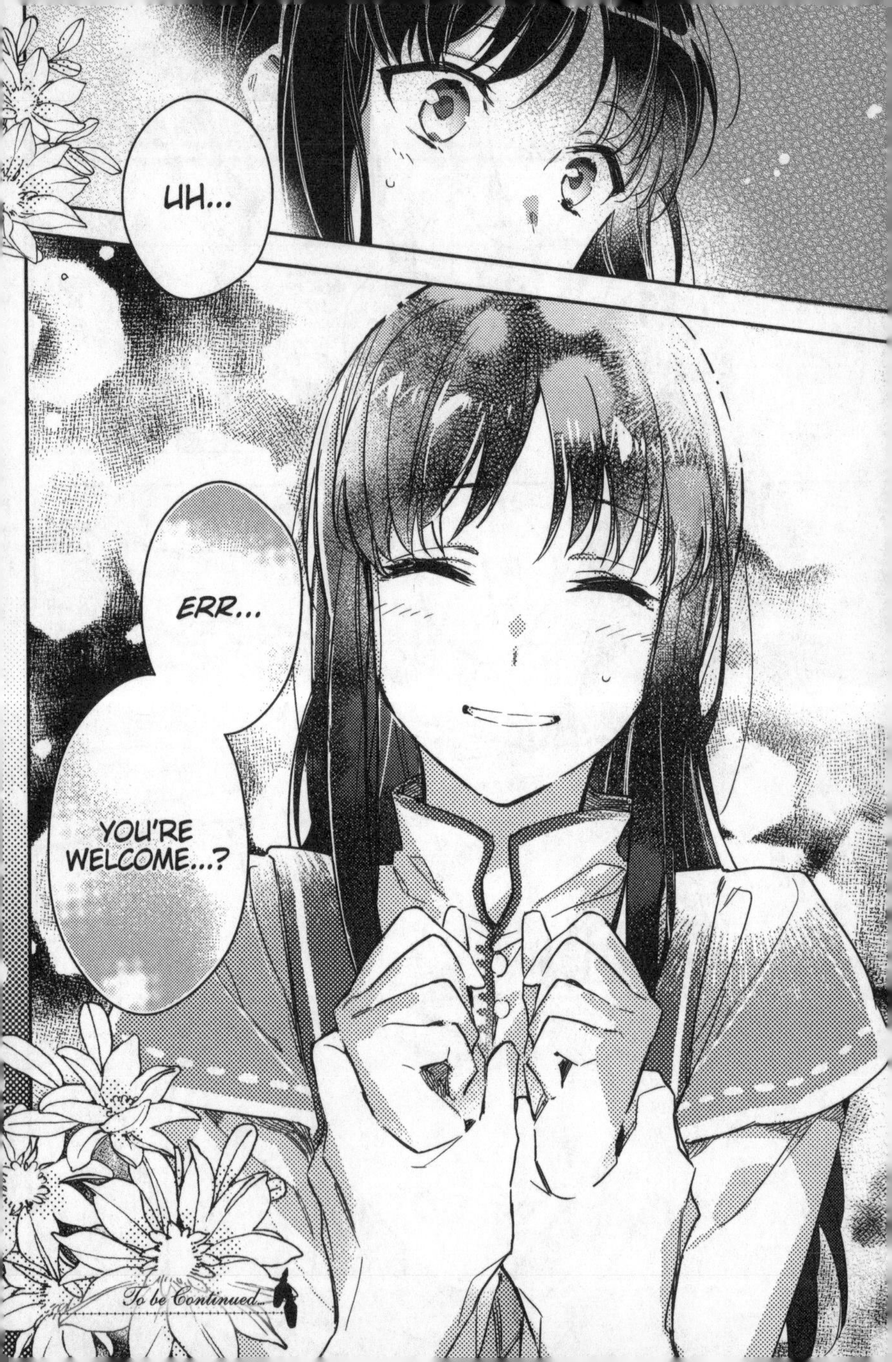
UH...
ERR...
YOU'RE WELCOME...?
To be Continued...

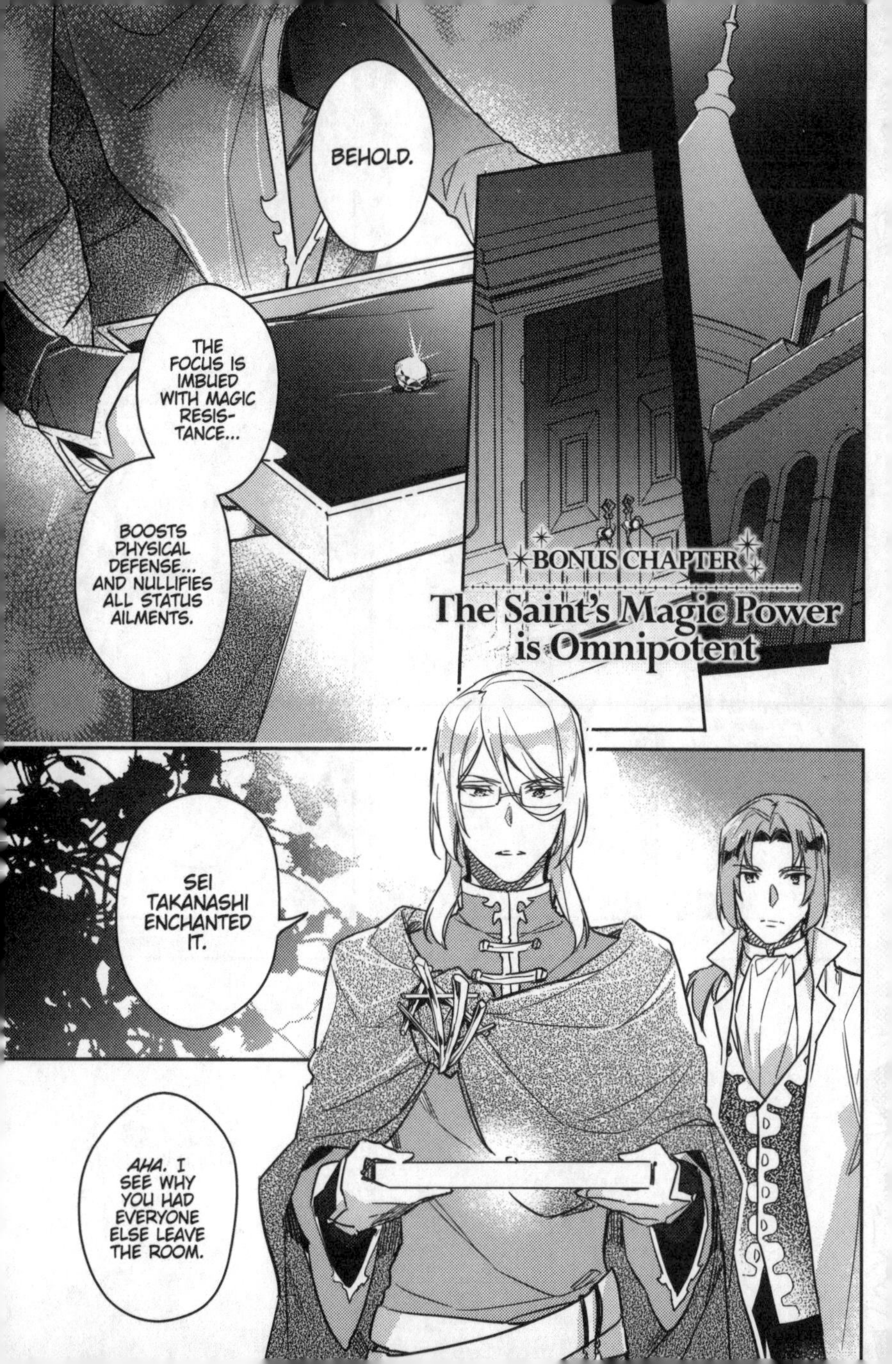
BONUS CHAPTER
The Saint's Magic Power is Omnipotent
BEHOLD.
THE FOCUS IS IMBUED WITH MAGIC RESISTANCE...
BOOSTS PHYSICAL DEFENSE... AND NULLIFIES ALL STATUS AILMENTS.
SEI TAKANASHI ENCHANTED IT.
AHA. I SEE WHY YOU HAD EVERYONE ELSE LEAVE THE ROOM.

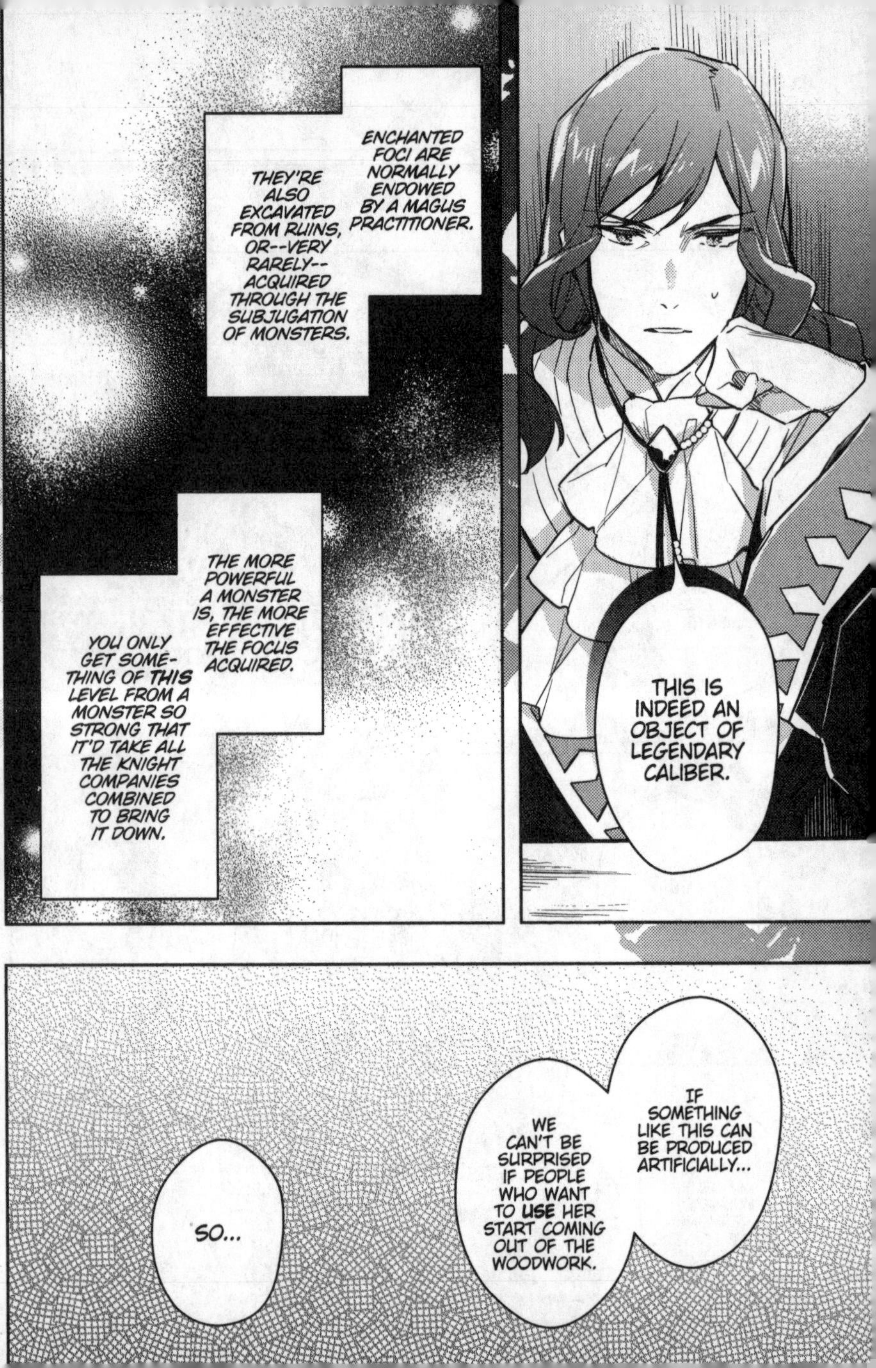
THIS IS INDEED AN OBJECT OF LEGENDARY CALIBER.
ENCHANTED FOCI ARE NORMALLY ENDOWED BY A MAGUS PRACTITIONER.
THEY'RE ALSO EXCAVATED FROM RUINS, OR--VERY RARELY--ACQUIRED THROUGH THE SUBJUGATION OF MONSTERS.
THE MORE POWERFUL A MONSTER IS, THE MORE EFFECTIVE THE FOCUS ACQUIRED.
YOU ONLY GET SOME-THING OF **THIS** LEVEL FROM A MONSTER SO STRONG THAT IT'D TAKE ALL THE KNIGHT COMPANIES COMBINED TO BRING IT DOWN.
IF SOMETHING LIKE THIS CAN BE PRODUCED ARTIFICIALLY...
WE CAN'T BE SURPRISED IF PEOPLE WHO WANT TO **USE** HER START COMING OUT OF THE WOODWORK.
SO...

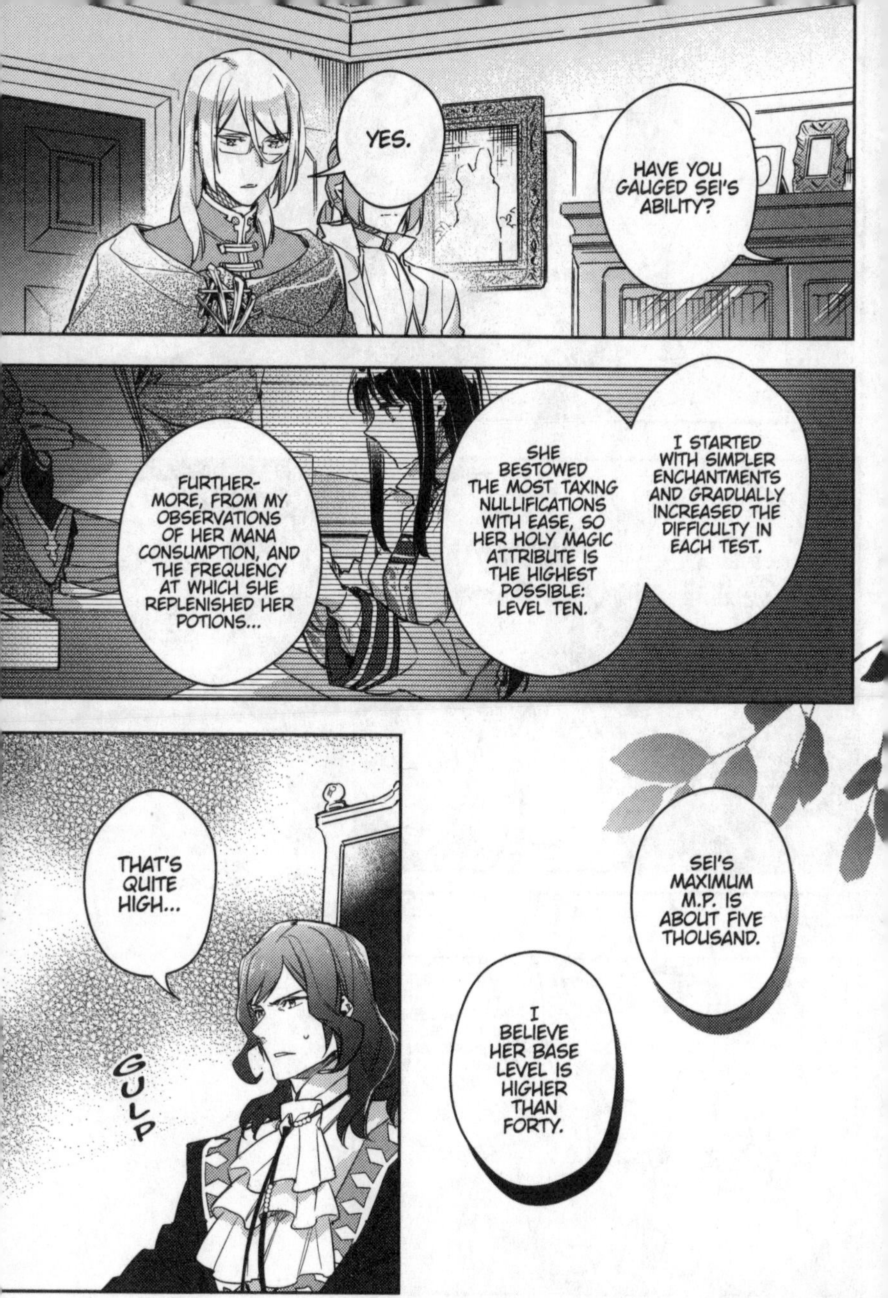
HAVE YOU GAUGED SEI'S ABILITY?
YES.
I STARTED WITH SIMPLER ENCHANTMENTS AND GRADUALLY INCREASED THE DIFFICULTY IN EACH TEST.
SHE BESTOWED THE MOST TAXING NULLIFICATIONS WITH EASE, SO HER HOLY MAGIC ATTRIBUTE IS THE HIGHEST POSSIBLE: LEVEL TEN.
FURTHER-MORE, FROM MY OBSERVATIONS OF HER MANA CONSUMPTION, AND THE FREQUENCY AT WHICH SHE REPLENISHED HER POTIONS...
SEI'S MAXIMUM M.P. IS ABOUT FIVE THOUSAND.
I BELIEVE HER BASE LEVEL IS HIGHER THAN FORTY.
THAT'S QUITE HIGH...
GULP

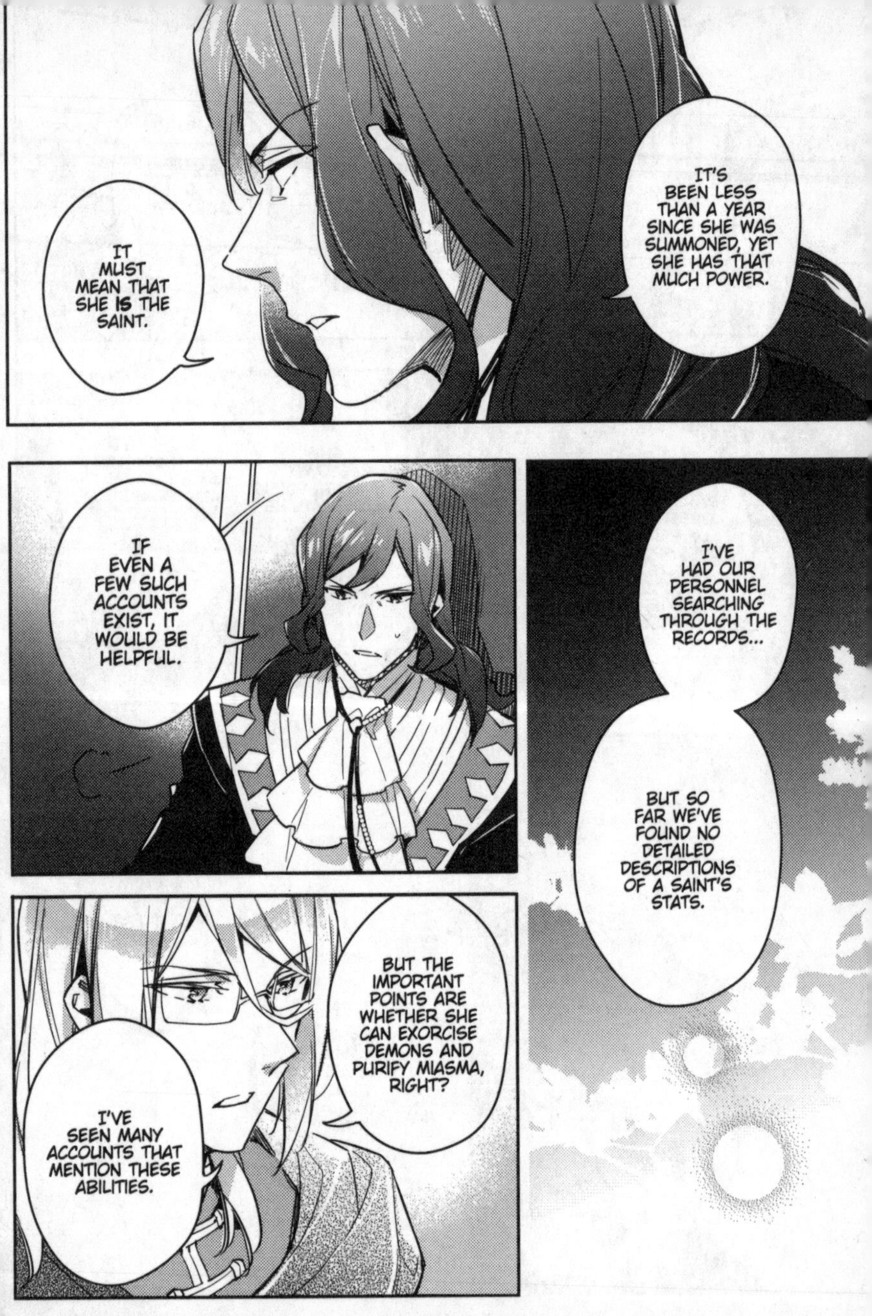
IT'S BEEN LESS THAN A YEAR SINCE SHE WAS SUMMONED, YET SHE HAS THAT MUCH POWER.
IT MUST MEAN THAT SHE **IS** THE SAINT.
I'VE HAD OUR PERSONNEL SEARCHING THROUGH THE RECORDS...
BUT SO FAR WE'VE FOUND NO DETAILED DESCRIPTIONS OF A SAINT'S STATS.
IF EVEN A FEW SUCH ACCOUNTS EXIST, IT WOULD BE HELPFUL.
BUT THE IMPORTANT POINTS ARE WHETHER SHE CAN EXORCISE DEMONS AND PURIFY MIASMA, RIGHT?
I'VE SEEN MANY ACCOUNTS THAT MENTION THESE ABILITIES.

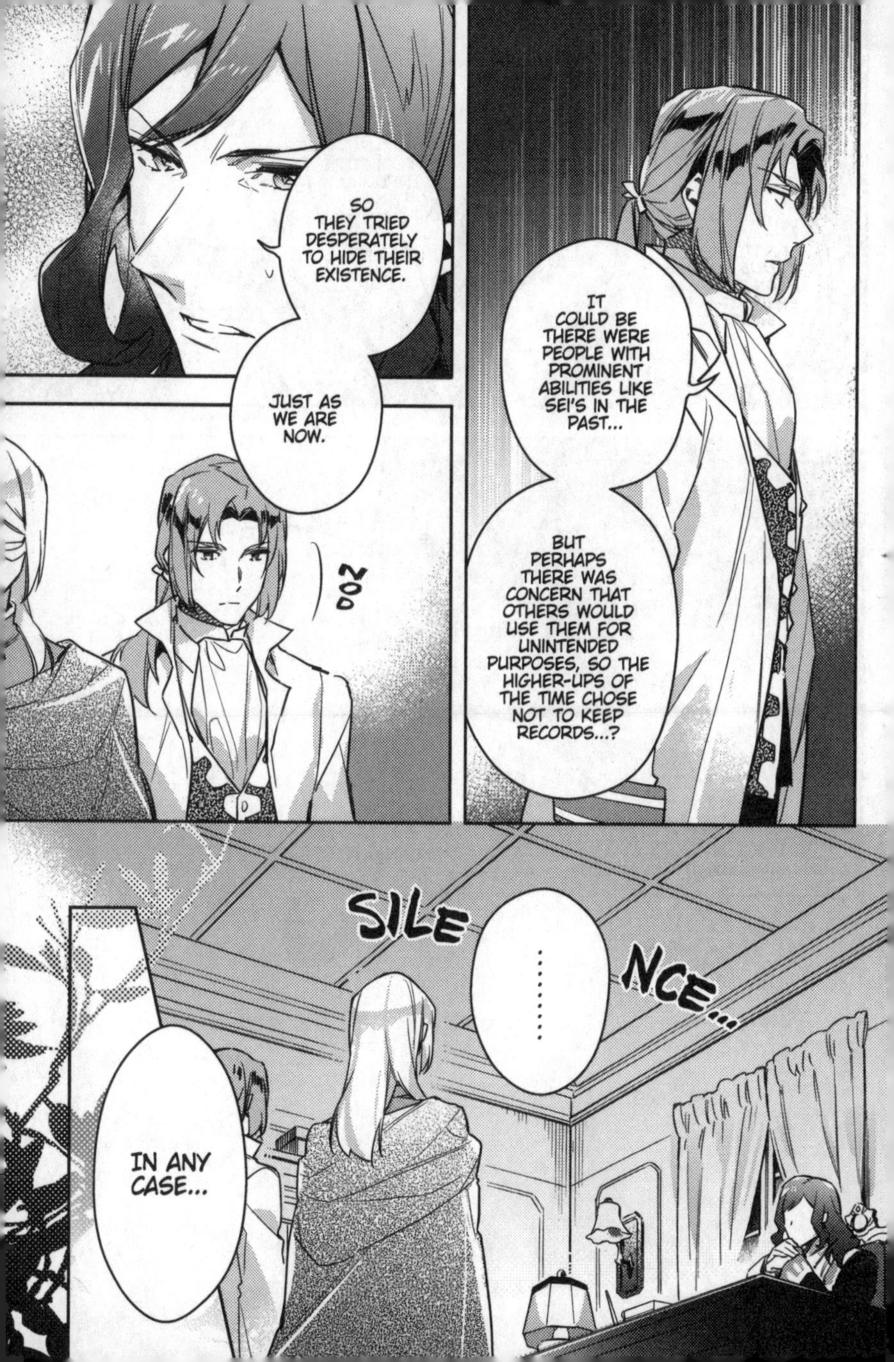
IT COULD BE THERE WERE PEOPLE WITH PROMINENT ABILITIES LIKE SEI'S IN THE PAST...
BUT PERHAPS THERE WAS CONCERN THAT OTHERS WOULD USE THEM FOR UNINTENDED PURPOSES, SO THE HIGHER-UPS OF THE TIME CHOSE NOT TO KEEP RECORDS...?
SO THEY TRIED DESPERATELY TO HIDE THEIR EXISTENCE.
JUST AS WE ARE NOW.
NOD
SILENCE...
....
IN ANY CASE...

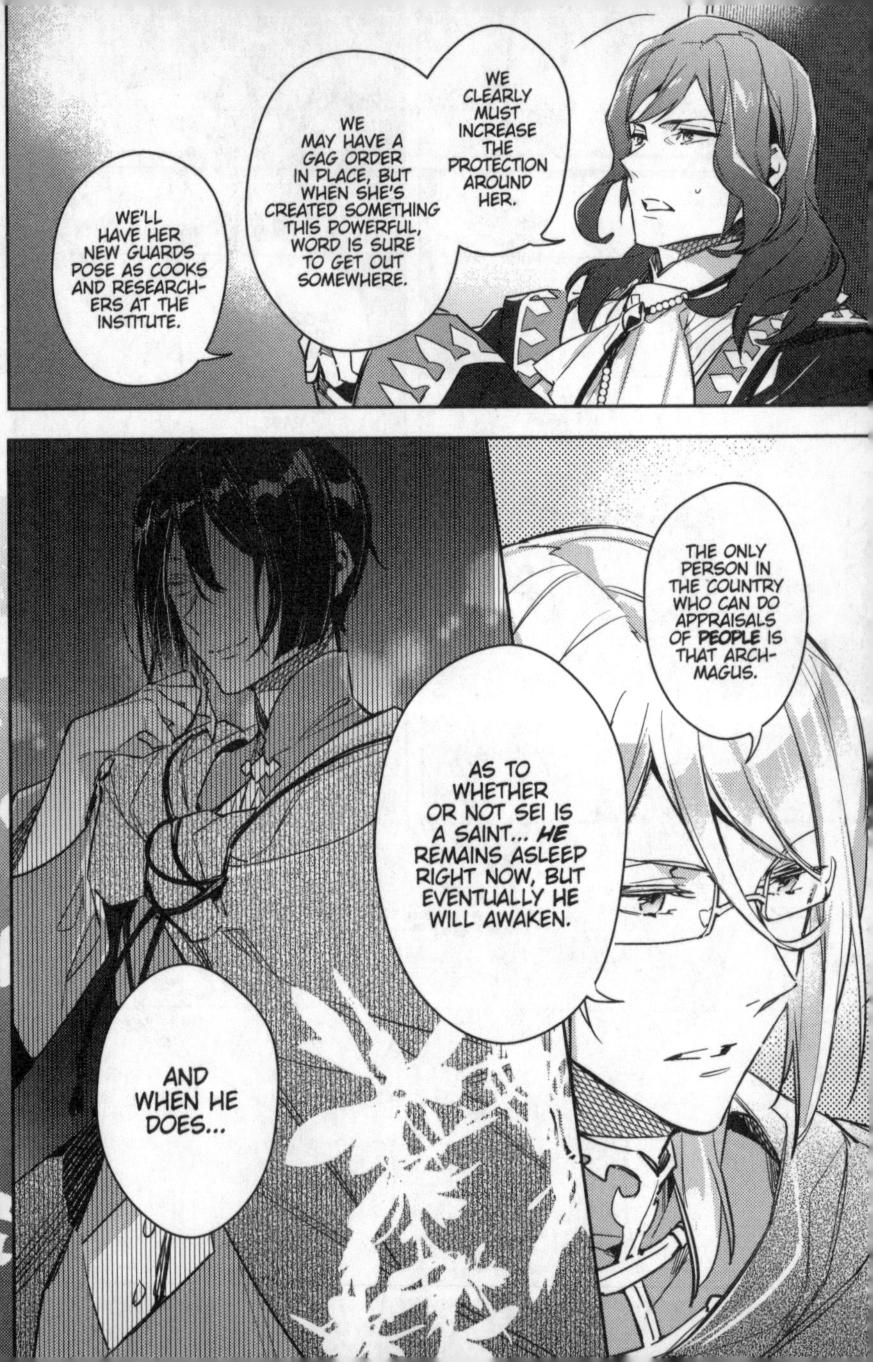
WE CLEARLY MUST INCREASE THE PROTECTION AROUND HER.
WE MAY HAVE A GAG ORDER IN PLACE, BUT WHEN SHE'S CREATED SOMETHING THIS POWERFUL, WORD IS SURE TO GET OUT SOMEWHERE.
WE'LL HAVE HER NEW GUARDS POSE AS COOKS AND RESEARCHERS AT THE INSTITUTE.
THE ONLY PERSON IN THE COUNTRY WHO CAN DO APPRAISALS OF **PEOPLE** IS THAT ARCHMAGUS.
AS TO WHETHER OR NOT SEI IS A SAINT... ***HE*** REMAINS ASLEEP RIGHT NOW, BUT EVENTUALLY HE WILL AWAKEN.
AND WHEN HE DOES...

The **Saint's** *
*Magic Power is *
Omnipotent

The Saint's Magic Power is Omnipotent
Afterword by the Creator

Thank you very much for picking up *The Saint's Magic Power Is Omnipotent* volume 2. I am the original creator, Yuka Tachibana. Thanks to you, we are able to publish this second volume. Sincere thanks to our readers, to Fuji-sensei (who is adapting it as a manga), and to everyone else involved.

Volume 2 records the stroll around town with the commander—a rare romantic interlude. Was it enjoyable? I wrote the original novel as a romance, but Sei-san, the protagonist, does nothing but work and has had extremely little love… Why so little? Sei-san's Romance skill level is low, and work is all she can ever think of to talk about. It's definitely not because the creator was hurt by jealousy or had a fainting fit and couldn't write about it, okay?

Right…
Anyway, sorry. Forgive me.
I'm thinking about putting some romance in a future chapter, so I hope you can forgive me. But honestly, I can hardly raise my head in front of Fuji-sensei, who crafted such a delightfully romantic work from source material that had so little. Fuji-sensei, thank you, as always.

Finally, once again I have to thank everyone who picked up this volume. I think I'll definitely put more romance in the next volume, so I hope you continue to enjoy the world of *The Saint's Magic Power Is Omnipotent*. See you next time.

Yuka Tachibana

Afterword

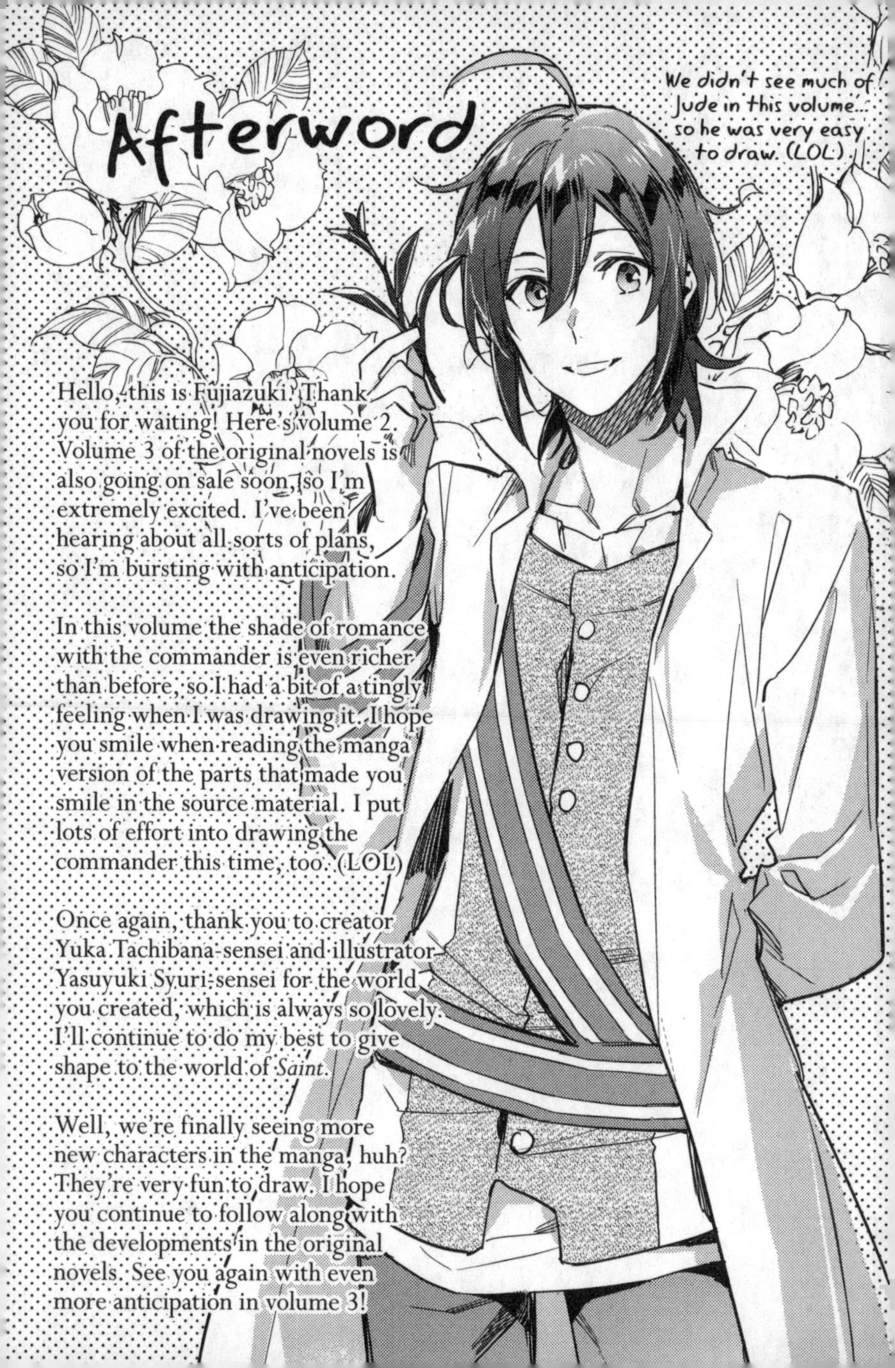
We didn't see much of Jude in this volume... so he was very easy to draw. (LOL)

Hello, this is Fujiazuki. Thank you for waiting! Here's volume 2. Volume 3 of the original novels is also going on sale soon, so I'm extremely excited. I've been hearing about all sorts of plans, so I'm bursting with anticipation.

In this volume the shade of romance with the commander is even richer than before, so I had a bit of a tingly feeling when I was drawing it. I hope you smile when reading the manga version of the parts that made you smile in the source material. I put lots of effort into drawing the commander this time, too. (LOL)

Once again, thank you to creator Yuka Tachibana-sensei and illustrator Yasuyuki Syuri-sensei for the world you created, which is always so lovely. I'll continue to do my best to give shape to the world of *Saint*.

Well, we're finally seeing more new characters in the manga, huh? They're very fun to draw. I hope you continue to follow along with the developments in the original novels. See you again with even more anticipation in volume 3!

The Saint's
Magic Power is
Omnipotent

SEVEN SEAS ENTERTAINMENT PRESENTS

The Saint's Magic Power is Omnipotent

story by **YUKA TACHIBANA**   art by **FUJIAZUKI**   character design by **YASUYUKI SYURI**

TRANSLATION
Kumar Sivasubramanian

ADAPTATION
Ysabet MacFarlane

LETTERING AND RETOUCH
Jennifer Skarupa

COVER DESIGN
Nicky Lim

PROOFREADER
Dawn Davis
Danielle King

EDITOR
J.P. Sullivan

PREPRESS TECHNICIAN
Rhiannon Rasmussen-Silverstein

PRODUCTION MANAGER
Lissa Pattillo

MANAGING EDITOR
Julie Davis

ASSOCIATE PUBLISHER
Adam Arnold

PUBLISHER
Jason DeAngelis

Seven Seas press and purchase enquiries can be sent to Marketing Manager
Lianne Sentar at press@gomanga.com. Information regarding the distribution
and purchase of digital editions is available from Digital Manager CK Russell
at digital@gomanga.com.

Seven Seas and the Seven Seas logo are trademarks of
Seven Seas Entertainment. All rights reserved.

ISBN: 978-1-64505-983-7

Printed in Canada

First Printing: February 2021

10 9 8 7 6 5 4 3 2 1

FOLLOW US ONLINE: www.sevenseasentertainment.com

READING DIRECTIONS

This book reads from *right to left*, Japanese style. If this is your first time reading manga, you start reading from the top right panel on each page and take it from there. If you get lost, just follow the numbered diagram here. It may seem backwards at first, but you'll get the hang of it! Have fun!!

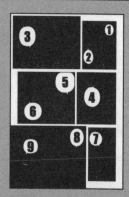